I0682124

The Unraveling of

Raven

Book One: The Unraveled Trilogy

Theresa Sederholt

The Unraveling of Raven
Copyright© 2014 by Theresa Sederholt

All rights reserved. This book or any portion thereof may not be reproduced or used in any manner whatsoever without the express written permission of the publisher except for the use of brief quotations in the book review.

The author acknowledges the copyrighted or trademarked status and trademark owners of the following wordmarks mentions in this work of fiction: Starbucks, Raiders Inc., LaCanda Verde, Trufflepalooza, Bloomingdales, Apple, Droid, Forbes, Dr. Who, Wounded Warrior Project, Battersea Dog and Cat rescue, Jaguar, Die Hard, When Harry Met Sally, Nutella, The W Hotel. The following songs and their performers: Snow Patrol's Chasing Car's and Run. Katy Perry Part of Me, Lady Gaga Do What U Want, The Police Every Breath You Take, One Direction Little Things, Half a Heart, Nickelback I'd Come for You. Ellie Goulding, and Florence + The Machine.

This is a work of fiction. Names, characters, businesses, places, events, and incidents are either the products of the author's imagination or used in a fictitious manner. Any resemblance to actual persons, living or dead, or actual events is purely coincidental.

ISBN: 978-0-9862598-0-7

Cover created by Tracy Beavers: TBeavers@roarmarketinggroup.com
Edited by Jacquelyn Ayres
Formatted by Champagne Formats

Other Books

The Unraveled Trilogy
The Unraveling of Raven
Darkness Into Dawn
Shattered Lies

Uniquely Mine

The Letter: Dear Michael

The Bench

Chapter One

Raven

"RAVEN?" *KNOCK, KNOCK, KNOCK.* "Raven?" *Knock, knock, knock.* "Wake up, Raven! You've overslept for the second time this week!"

This can't be happening. "What the hell, Marco! How could that be?"

He can't be right.

"Your alarm has been going off for the past forty minutes; it's now 6:30 a.m.."

Oh crap! School starts at 7:30 a.m.. "Why the hell didn't you wake me up sooner?" Why didn't I hear the alarm? Damn it all to hell! I jump out of bed, grab a quick shower, do a fast make-up job, and run out the door—smack into Manhattan rush hour traffic.

I'm trying to make some sort of normal look with my long, wavy black hair as I race to catch the train. Thank God I only have three stops to go! I make it to my usual Starbucks with little time to spare. I must look deranged. I'm bouncing from one foot to the other while the girl in the front of the line starts asking about calories in the muffins! *Really, lady?* If it looks or tastes good, spit it out, damn it! Finally my turn and the Barista already knows my order: large redeye with two pumps of sugar-free hazelnut, no cream, and a bottle of water. I don't need anyone's drama today. It's a big day for my second graders and I need to be there now.

I run out of the door, and crash into someone with a chest like a brick wall. My coffee lid pops off and douses both of us. I can feel the weight of his stare as I try to wipe the coffee off of his chest, and I feel like I'm being zapped with a stun gun.

"Oh my God, I'm so sorry."

He growls, "Lady, please, just stop. You're not helping matters any."

As I look up to protest, I'm hit with the deepest blue eyes I have ever seen.

At this point, I'm a flustered mess and all I can do is run away, leaving him with half the damage from the rough start of my morning. *What the hell was that anyway?* I have no time to dwell on it as class starts in five minutes. As I run to class, I toss Mick his bottle of water. "Nice catch, Mick."

I teach second grade at Weinstein Academy, a private school in midtown Manhattan. It just so happens that today is "Bring a Parent To School Day." And not only did I oversleep, douse the most beautiful man and myself with coffee, I now get to meet said parents with a wet shirt. Luckily, Jackie, my best friend and co-worker, has a spare shirt I can borrow. However, with her being smaller on top than me, I now look like a hooch woman!

Jaxson

WHAT THE FUCK WAS that? Or, more to the point, *who the fuck was that?* I'm left standing outside Starbucks with a wet shirt, courtesy of a beautiful woman, and I didn't even get her name! Her delicate fingers, trying to wipe off the coffee, didn't help. I was instantly hard and all I could do was stare at her in disbelief. She had the most beautiful violet eyes. Eyes that felt as though they could look into my soul. Then she ran away! I head inside and ask the Barista if he knows her name. He says he only knows her drink. He then informs me that she comes in every morning for her usual large coffee and a bottle of water for the homeless guy, Mick, across the street.

"She buys him water every morning?"

"Yeah, and when she's not running late, she buys him breakfast."

I order a breakfast sandwich, instead of my usual, and head out across the street. I walk up to the man and hand him the sandwich, "I figured you might be hungry since the girl that usually buys you breakfast was running late."

He looks at me apprehensively. "Thanks, she's a sweetheart."

I need to know more than that. "What do you know about her?"

He gets really quiet, but I wait. "What's it to you?"

I can tell I'm not going to get much past him. "Well, I could stand here and feed you a line of bullshit."

"Yeah, you could, but that doesn't mean I would tell you anything about her."

Well, at least he's honest. "Look, mate, she ran into me this morning, as you can tell by my shirt. I just want to know who she is."

Great, now he's looking me up and down. "By the looks of you, you can afford to buy another shirt so, again, what's it to you, who she is?"

I offer him my hand. "My name is Jax. She is beautiful and I want to know more."

He just looks at me. "Well, Jax, my name is Mick, and yeah, she is beautiful, but more so on the inside. Not very many people will even give me the time of day, let alone buy me breakfast. I'm back from the war and things just aren't right sometimes; she just gets it. She doesn't judge me. What she gives me is more valuable than money—her time. She just gets it. If you want to know more about her, come back tomorrow, she's here every day. That's all you'll get from me, Jax."

He's done talking and I know when not to push my luck. "Okay, Mick. Thanks."

As I head up to my office, I'm even more intrigued. I change my shirt into one of the spares I keep here. Sitting at my desk, overlooking the city, I'm aware that I have all the money I will ever need and yet I'm bored. I own *Raiders Inc.*, a multibillion-dollar company. I raid companies that are in trouble, either because the owners are stupid or greedy. There are only so many companies you can raid before it just gets old. Nothing holds my interest anymore—not work or parties—nothing. At least, not until this morning. I have to find that girl. Her eyes were a beautiful violet color, eyes that looked right into my soul, and her hair was as dark as a raven.

Maybe I should have Max help me find her. Max is my best friend and the head of my security. I hired him away from the Queen, one drunken night, in a seedy, London pub. After the mess with Erica, I usually have Max run a check on anyone I go out with. I don't bring any women out in public, if I can avoid it. The paparazzi are ruthless whenever I step out with anyone. I will have to stalk that Starbucks until I find her.

I'm lost in my thoughts when my new assistant, Duke Jensen, rings to inform me that my sister, Isabella, has arrived. Great, just what I need, more family, reminding me that I'm thirty-three years old and not married. I don't see what the big deal is; I'm happy with my life. Yes, I'm bored, but putting myself out there again just isn't an option that I want to explore.

Bella comes storming into my office, "Jax, Michael got stuck at the airport in Atlanta and can't make it back in time, so you have to cover for him."

I throw my hands up, "Cover for him, Bella. Do you think I don't work for a living?" She has the nerve to think I do nothing!

"Come on, Jax, this is for your nephew. They're having a 'bring your parent to school' day, and Michael is stuck in Atlanta."

I'm not his parent. *What the hell would I do at his school?* "Well, last time I looked, Bella, you're his parent too." Oh boy, she's giving me the evil eye. This is not good—she's almost as bad as Mum.

"Don't be an arse, Jax, no young boy wants to bring his mum to school. Just go to the school and talk a little bit about whatever it is you do all day long. Tell them all the places you go and about all your toys; boys love that shit."

Hmm, let's just see what I can get out of her. "What do I get if I do this for you?" She'll guilt me, I know it.

"Jax, besides the fact that you're doing it for *your* nephew, I will run interference for you next time Mum wants to match you up with one of her friend's daughters."

Well it doesn't take me long to agree to that one, anything to get my mum off my back. "Okay, where and when? But don't forget—you owe me."

I HEAD OVER TO the school and sign in before they escort me to my nephew's classroom. I open the door, walk in, and am hit, square in the face, with those violet eyes. My nephew's teacher is the same beautiful girl that doused me with coffee this morning. I never had a teacher like her. I would have made sure to be held back, if I did. She keeps her eyes fixed on me as she walks towards me.

"Can I help you?" She extends her hand and, upon grasping it, I feel a jolt of electricity from her touch.

"I'm here for the 'Bring a Parent To School Day'. I'm Michael Vizzano's uncle, Jaxson Phillips. His dad is stuck in Atlanta."

She introduces herself as *Miss Raven Anderson*, and directs me to a table, in the back, with other parents. I apparently have to wait until its Michael's turn to introduce me. I don't do *waiting* very well. *Who am I kidding? I never wait for anyone or anything.*

I can't stop staring at her. I can see that's she's changed her shirt. She must have borrowed it because it's much smaller, accentuating her ample chest. Her skin is olive, but her eyes are the deepest violet I have ever seen, they are mesmerizing. Her hair looks *so* silky. How the fuck does my nephew get any work done? She keeps tugging on her ear, and I've no idea why, but it's making me crazy.

As I'm sitting here, thinking of all the ways I can shag her, my cock instantly hardens. Oh no, it's my turn—*fuck!* Michael goes to the front of the room and announces to the class that his Uncle Jax is here with him today. I go up front, doing my best to hide my raging hard-on, and begin to talk a little about the life of a corporate raider in a way, I think, they can best understand. When it's time for questions, of course the first one is, *do you have your own plane?* I don't understand what the big deal is, but when I tell them I do, they get excited. Michael stands up and announces, "My uncle has lots of toys because my mom said he raids companies."

Great! Now the other parents are looking at me like I'm a dick or an evil monster, putting people out of work and taking all their money. I look at the kids and tell them I'm not like that; I help companies that are in trouble. I don't think the parents are buying it. I glance over in Raven's direction. *Oh no, big trouble!* She's tugging on her ear, causing me to lose my train of thought. I need to focus on the kids and their questions instead of my wicked thoughts of what I could be doing . . . with her.

Class is finally over and I hang back to wait for Michael while Raven and I keep staring at each other. Between the constant tugging on her earlobe and the way she has those violets locked onto me, I swear the hair on the back of my neck is standing at attention. I can't take this anymore; it's not like me to be so nervous. I'm just going to lay the "Jax charm" on her. "Raven? Would you like to get a cup of coffee that we can drink rather than wear?"

She's looking at me like a deer in the headlights. "I'm sorry, but I have a couple of hours of work ahead of me, maybe another time, sir."

Sir? How fucking old does she think I am? Before I can say anything, she picks up her stuff and runs out the door. Why the fuck does this girl keep running away from me? Just like that—she's gone and I'm left with a raging hard-on, wondering what the fuck that was all about.

AS JUNIOR AND I head back to my office, I decide to pump him for information. Okay, I know I shouldn't, but I have to find out what he knows. "So, Junior, do you like your teacher?" That's a stupid question, even to my ears; what's not to like?

"She's pretty cool, and funny too." I can't ask him if she has a boyfriend. Okay, maybe there is a way I can. "Does she ever talk about her family?"

He shrugs his shoulders, "I don't know, why?"

Oh shit. Okay, what to say here? "I was just wondering, since all of the kids' parents got up to tell what they do and a little about their families, that's all." I don't think he's buying it but then he starts telling me something that his dog, Vito, did. "Junior, that dog only likes you. He's afraid of your grams, but everyone is terrified of her. By the way, if you tell Grams what I just said, you're in trouble."

He laughs at me. "Don't worry, Uncle Jax, your secret is safe with me. Vito knows when Grams is coming; he hides under my bed!"

I knew that dog was smart. "He's very intelligent, that's why your dad got him for you."

We get back to the office to find Bella waiting for us. "Did everything go okay?"

What the fuck did she think I was going to do? "Of course, what did you think . . . I was going to steal all their possessions and run away? Oh, and why the fuck did you tell Junior that I *raid companies?* Do you know what that made me look like?"

"Jax, what do you do for a living?"

I just stare at her. "I would have explained it a little differently for Junior." I have to watch what I say here, Bella and I can read each other like an open book.

"Hey, we never sugar-coat anything in this family so why start now? And why are you so ruffled?"

I growl, "I'm not ruffled for Christ's sake. I just don't want my nephew thinking I'm a prick."

She's glaring at me. "Oh no, Jax, no, don't you dare!"

Fuck it all, I'm so busted. "Dare what, sis?" The evil eye is back!

"You met his teacher, Miss Raven. I can see it all over your face!"

I can't look at her without laughing. "If you must know, I met her for the first time at Starbucks this morning, so technically, I already know her." She shoots me a look like she's going to strangle me.

"This is why you're good at what you do. You could split hairs with a bald man!"

I need to get her out of here before she sees how interested I am in Junior's teacher. "I have work to do. Glad I could help you today, but don't forget your promise to run interference for me with Mum."

Junior looks up from his homework. "Uncle Jax. Why does Mum have to run interference for you with Grams?" I just laugh, now Bella will have to deal with the questions.

"Junior, I'll let your mum explain it to you on the way home." I hug Junior as I push Bella out the door. "Bye, sis."

Chapter Two

Raven

"MARCO, ARE YOU HOME?" It figures, when I need my crazy-ass roommate the most, he's not around. Why did I say no and run away? *Probably because when he looked at me, I felt it down to my frigging toes—that's why.* I could never get involved with someone like him, he's way too intense. Plus, I would never date one of my student's parents or even his uncle. Besides, love stories are for other people. My life is anything but normal.

I decide to make some tea while I wait for Marco to come home. Finally, he comes through the door, and of course, he is complaining about something. "Marco, can we go out and celebrate the weekend?" He takes one look at me and I can tell he knows something is up.

"Okay, baby girl, what happened? And why are you wearing a shirt that's way too small for your boobs?"

He won't believe this one. "Well, after running late this morning, I was in Starbucks and got my coffee which I ended up not only spilling on myself, but on the most beautiful man I have ever seen. His hair was as dark as coal. It looked so silky and wavy, but his eyes are *so* blue and when our eyes locked, I swear he looked right into my soul."

His eyes light up; Marco loves a juicy story. "Oh, do tell, baby girl."

I curl up on the sofa, "Oh, trust me, Marco, this gets better. Today was 'Bring a Parent To School Day' and one of the kids' fathers couldn't make it, so his uncle came instead. Guess who it was?"

He looks at me with his mouth wide open. "Oh no, Starbucks guy?"

I reach over and lift his chin off the ground. "Yep, Starbucks guy! Apparently, he is some corporate raider, who tried to downplay what he does, so that he didn't seem like a total dick. He asked me to go for coffee that we can 'drink rather than wear'."

Marco curls up next to me. "That was clever. So what did you do?" I don't know why he's asking when he already knows exactly what I did.

"What do you think I did? I freaked out and told him I have too much work to do; maybe another time." Here it comes; he is going to ride my ass for running.

"You ran again. Why, baby girl? You have to let go of the past and test the waters. You need to trust yourself again."

I shake my head, "Not with this guy, he's too much of everything. He's too intense, too beautiful, and way-the-hell out of my league. Oh, who the fuck am I kidding? I don't even have a league."

He takes my hand. "Raven, you are a beautiful girl with a heart of gold, you just need to open it again. Who is this uncle and what's the name of the company he runs?"

I don't know why he cares what company this guy runs. "The only thing I know, is the company is called *Raiders Inc.*, apparently, he owns it. I've never heard of it, but then again, I was too nervous to even think," I admit. Marco looks lost in his thoughts and then, he suddenly throws his hands in the air and orders me to change into something fun. Just like that, the conversation is done.

He informs me that he was able to get reservations in *Locanda Verde* for the *Trufflepalooza*. It is three different courses, each course uses white truffles as the base. The food is very rich and people wait all year for this event. Robert DeNiro owns the restaurant and it is always booked. But Marco has a friend that works there, so he gets us in.

It's a beautiful, fall evening, so I decide to wear a deep violet, sheath dress that matches my eyes with black high-heeled boots. Let's face it, a girl can never be too tall and these boots make my legs look really good. My hair is behaving tonight, so I leave it loose in waves down my back.

We arrive and are seated at a long table with many other diners around us. The music is soft in the background which means we don't have to shout to be heard. The food is like a dream. Three different chefs are showcasing the white truffle. Each course has a different wine to enhance the flavors of the foods that are presented to us. By the time the coffee comes, I'm stuffed and a little tipsy. Marco has made friends with the other diners around us and he is exchanging numbers with a good-looking man across the table. I wish I could be more like Marco. He is so carefree and open; he has everyone at the table laughing and relaxed. I excuse myself as I head to the ladies room, feeling a little tipsy and a bit shaky on my feet. I start to head back to the table, when I turn the corner and come face to face with those deep blue eyes from this morning. *Oh no!* I don't want to get too close or I know what will happen. He puts his hands on my arms and our eyes lock. My nerve endings are on fire. I feel like I'm being zapped again!

"Well, hello again, Miss Raven. I thought you had hours of work, or were you just trying to avoid me?" His voice is deep and smooth, like the most delicious chocolate in the world. He has a slight British accent that I didn't notice before; I was flustered and unable to even think straight.

"Excuse me, if you must know, I'm here with a friend for the Trufflepalooza." As I look into his eyes, there it is—the look that curls my frigging toes. *What the hell is that?* I feel a jolt right between my legs. I'm fixed on those deep blue eyes, onyx silky hair, and only God knows what's under those clothes!

"Can I buy you a drink, Miss Raven?"

I shake my head, "I'm sorry but, like I said, I'm with someone. Maybe another time." I rush back to Marco who, of course, has the whole table in laughter. As I settle back into my chair, Marco leans in to me, placing his arm around my shoulder. "You okay, baby girl? You look flustered, at best."

I lean into him, "I'm fine, just getting a little tired from today."

Jaxson

DAMN! SHE'S RUNNING AGAIN. What the fuck is up with this girl that, every time she sees me, she's running? Well, not this time, sweetheart. I look to see where she went and find her sitting at a window table with a group of people. There is a guy with his arm around the back of her chair—*I don't think so!* As I walk up to her table, I see her tugging that fucking ear again and I want to lick it and drag my teeth over it. Just the thought is making me fucking hard! I step up to her table, reach down, taking her hand in mine, and I kiss the back of her wrist. "Raven, please introduce me to your friend." *Yeah, sweet cheeks, you're not getting rid of me that easy.* She looks at me then back to her friend, but she won't be pulling a runner tonight—that's for sure.

Raven

WHEN I LOOK TO Marco for some help, he is practically drooling. *A lot of good he is.* There is very little that has ever rendered Marco speechless, until now. "Jaxson, this is my roommate, Marco Green."

Maybe he'll think Marco and I are a couple and leave me alone. Yeah, right, I don't think this man would care if the Pope told him to back off. Marco looks very flustered, but then he snaps out of it and invites Jax to join us. I swear I want to pick up my fork and stab Marco with it! Before I realize what is going on, Marco informs me that the table we are at is for singles only, the bill is paid, and he is leaving with one of the guys.

"Don't worry, Marco. I'll make sure she gets home safely." With a wink and a kiss, Marco is gone and I'm left with Mr. Toe Curler! "So, Raven, please tell me all about yourself."

My stomach is in knots. "There's not much to tell, at least, what I would share with a total stranger."

He cocks his head to the side and smirks at me. "Oh, I think you have plenty to tell. Let's start out simple, how long have you been teaching?"

At least it's a subject that's easy for me to talk about. "I have been teaching for three years. I really love it especially when I see the moment they get *it*. That's when I love my job the most." His eyes are locked on mine.

"When do you not love your job?"

My eyes fill instantly with tears, and I fight to hold them back. "I don't like to see the children abused. I will fight for them no matter what," I say quietly. He strokes his chin, and I find it sexy as hell.

"You're in one of the top private schools, in a great neighborhood. You must not see too much abuse."

Why do people think that just because people have money, there is no abuse? "Just because someone has money doesn't mean they're not abused. Abuse comes in many forms, not just physical." Time to turn the tables on this guy. "What about you, Jax? Why do you do what you do?"

Jaxson

SHE COCKS HER HEAD to the side, clearly waiting for me to answer. She starts tugging that ear again. Why does it make my fucking cock hard when she does that? "Contrary to what you may think, I'm not the typical corporate raider."

"Okay, enlighten me. What kind of corporate raider are you?"

Alright, time to grace her with some of the "Jaxson charm" here. "That's just it, I don't just raid companies, break them apart, and sell them off in pieces to the highest bidder. I first look at small companies that are struggling and see if they have a marketable product or idea. From there, I either back them with the funding they need to get over the 'hump' or buy them from the owner who has no clue how to run a business. If it's a viable business, I'll revamp it and get it running. If I can't, then I sell the assets off while trying to place the workers in other companies that I own. Most people that go into business have a great idea but they don't have a solid business plan. I invest in agriculture, technology, and clean energy. People will always have to eat, travel, and use technology."

"You're right. That's not what I was thinking. What made you go into this type of business?" she restructures her question.

I usually play things pretty close to the vest, but for some reason, I find her so easy to talk to. "I grew up very poor and watched my mother work for a big box company that didn't care about its employees. She worked sixty hours a week and then went to work at night, cleaning offices just to keep a roof over our heads and food on the table. I never want to live that way again, and if I can help other families in the process, then I will." I can tell I'm getting to her, she seems to relax and take an interest.

"What about your father, Jax? Is he still alive?"

I scoff, "My father walked out on us when I was five years old and he never looked back. It's always been my mum and my sister; that's all the family I've ever needed." I adjust in my seat. She's tugging that fucking ear! I don't know how long I can last before I lean over and take it between my teeth, slowly grazing down it. Oh fuck, I'm hard—*again!*

"Jax, I notice you have a slight accent. Where are you from?"

I reach up, and pull her hand away from her ear, trying to maintain my concentration. "I was born in Wales. We lived there until I was thirteen, and sometimes my accent is heavier than others." I run circles with my thumb in the palm of her hand.

"When does it get heavier?"

Raven

HE LAUGHS LIGHTLY, "WHEN I have too much drink or when I'm intimate." Then he hits me with that killer smirk. "What about you? Where is your family?"

I tighten up before I bring my eyes back up to his. "It's just Marco and me. My mom died when I was fifteen. After that, I left home and never looked back. Marco has been the only family I have ever needed."

I can see him processing what I'm saying. "What does Marco do for a living?"

I smile, always happy to brag about Marco. "He's a graphic artist and in great demand. He has an eye for details."

"Why did you leave home at such a young age?"

Just at that point, the server comes over to inform us that the restaurant is getting ready to close, which saves me from answering his questions. I can't believe how fast the time went, neither of us realizing the restaurant was empty. As we head out the door, his driver is waiting at the curb. "Jax, I can get myself home; I do it all the time."

"Not tonight, sweetheart, I promised Marco I would see you home safely, and I always keep my promises. Your address, please?"

WE PULL UP TO my building and my stomach starts to turn into knots. Then he does something I never would have expected; he looks over to me, pulls my hand from my ear, and kisses it. He didn't move in for the kill, he didn't even ask to come up. He just kissed my hand, then the inside of my wrist. "Goodnight, I had a wonderful evening, Raven." The driver opens the door and walks me into the building, where the doorman is waiting. And then he leaves.

Jaxson

"MAX, TAKE ME HOME, please." Maxwell has been my driver and best friend for eight years now. I think even *he* was surprised by my actions tonight—I know I was. At least, he has the grace not to call me on it. She makes me feel very different; she peaks my interest and leaves me wanting more. I have never felt that before. Most women throw themselves at me. All they see is money and good looks which, thanks to my mum, I have never been lacking in that department. When Raven looked at me, I felt her passion. That's something I've never experienced before. I want more of her; I need more of her. I decide, in this moment, that I *will have* more of her.

Chapter Three

Raven

I GET UPSTAIRS, UNDRESS, and decide on a cup of tea to settle my nerves. Marco comes flying through the door with the guy from the restaurant. "Sorry, baby girl, I thought you would be out for the night, especially the way Mr. Tall, Dark, and Beautiful was staring at you."

I look at him in confusion. "Well, you're mistaken." I inform him, before focusing my attention on his guest. "Hi, I'm Raven Anderson, Marco's roommate."

"Oh, sorry. Raven, this is Sam. He owns a few hair salons in the village." Marco offers.

I shake his hand. "Nice to meet you. You can have the living room. I have papers to grade. Have fun." *I know he wants all the dirt.*

"Wait, what happened to Jax?" How do I tell him that I'm more confused than ever?

"We talked for hours. He took me home and kissed my hand. That's it, then, he left."

He is gaping at me, "Oh."

I gather my tea and head to my room. "Yeah, *oh.*" I walk away, completely flustered.

SLEEP BARELY CAME FOR me and before I know it, Marco is banging on my door. "You better have a damn good reason for waking me up so early on a Saturday?" I call out. I'm going to smack him.

"Um, Raven. You need to come out here, like now!"

What the hell is his problem? As I open my door, I'm hit with the smell of flowers, coffee, and fresh pastry. I swear the best smell in the world is coffee and pastry together. If it were a perfume, I would wear it. I look at Marco as he watches some strange man set the table for us. The man hands me an envelope, turns, and leaves. Okay, this is very strange.

"I'm busting, baby girl, what does it say?"

I pull out a beautiful hand written note:

> I hope I invaded your dreams like you invaded mine. I look forward to having breakfast with you, but for now, this will have to do.
>
> ~ Jax

Marco looks over at me. "Well, it seems our Jax is very deep, and he has great taste when it comes to breakfast. Let's eat, I'm starved!"

The pastry is like butter melting on my lips, and the coffee is exactly how I like it. We are enjoying the wonderful breakfast when we hear a phone start to ring. It's not Marco's or mine. We look around and find a phone in a box with the flowers. "Hello?" *Oh my God, really?*

"Good morning, Raven. How is your breakfast?"

This man is so over the top. "Jax, the breakfast is wonderful, but why the phone?"

He laughs, "I never got your phone number last night and I wanted to talk to you, it just seemed like a great idea. A phone just for me."

I can't tell if he's serious or snarky. "Do you really think I will carry two phones just so you can have your own phone?" I ask as I take a closer look at the flowers. "These flowers are very unusual, what kind are they?"

"Yes, they are very unusual. They're from Germany and they're called *Abracadabra Roses*—they reminded me of you. They're different from the everyday rose. And to answer your question, yes, I do think you should carry a phone just for me. I'm calling to ask you to accompany me to a charity event this evening. It's being held at Chelsea Pier." He is so confident.

Do I want to continue this? "What type of event is it?"

He sounds very passionate as he tells me about the charity event. "It's part of a children's charity that my company sponsors, and I would be honored if you went with me."

The charity is for children, how could I ever say no? "Okay, what time should I meet you there?"

"Raven, I would never have you meet me there. I will pick you up at eight."

I feel like a teenager again. "Okay, Jax, I'll see you at eight." I hang up and I'm sure I have a stupid look on my face.

"Marco, get your ass dressed, we have a lot to do from now until tonight!"

WE HIT BLOOMINGDALES FIRST, to find something to wear. I need something that will render him speechless. I like to wear plum and I find just the right cocktail dress. The back has a cut-out, covered in plum lace and it has a low-cut front. It has a drop waist and it is very well fitted to my curves. It falls below my knees and has a slit up the back. It's a combination of sexy, yet subtle. I find peep-toe stilettos in black patent leather with a matching bag to complete the ensemble. Next, it's off to the spa for a mani pedi, waxing, and a deep conditioning treatment on my hair. I'm a little nervous. Oh, who the hell am I kidding? I'm scared to death! Marco invites Sam over to help with my hair and makeup. He pulls one side of my hair up and secures it with a beautiful clip. I feel like a teenager going on a first date.

At exactly 8 p.m., my doorman rings to let me know Jax has arrived. Marco opens the door and I am stunned. *He's more beautiful than I remembered!* This is a good thing because if I had remembered, I would have been even more nervous and I probably would not have agreed to go. He's wearing a black tux and a black shirt with a deep violet bow tie—the same color as my eyes. He looks at me and there it is again, my frigging toes are curling and there is a buzzing in my ears.

"Raven, you look amazing, more beautiful than I remembered."

AS WE DRIVE TO Chelsea Pier, I ask him about the charity that he is sponsoring, anything to get my mind off of the buzzing in my ears. "It's to help the families of children with brain tumors."

"Why this charity?"

I see that passion again in his eyes. "My company sponsors many different charities; I believe in giving back to society. Sometimes, it is through a charity and sometimes, it's something random such as, sponsoring a garden in Harlem. If we want change, then we need to do something to bring about that change. Just talking about it does nothing."

I wonder why I never heard of his company. "I agree. However, I've never heard of your company or the charitable works that it sponsors."

He laughs, "Good, I like it like that. I don't need a feather in my cap or recognition on what I do. I do it, expecting nothing, that's what makes it the most rewarding. By the way, I have to warn you the press will be here. They will be hounding me for pictures, which means they will also hound you. I'm sorry."

He looks so sad. "I think I can handle it. How bad could it be? A few pictures doesn't seem like a big deal."

He stares at me and I wish I knew what he was thinking. I wonder why he suddenly looks so lost and sad. "Jax, are you okay?" Before he can answer, we pull up. Holy crap, there are flashes everywhere! I thought this was a small event; there are thousands of people! We get out of the car to head in and are immediately caught up in the frenzy. Flashes are popping in my face as I'm introduced to the *who's who* of New York. By the time we sit down at our table, my face hurts from smiling so much.

"Jax, is this what you go through every time you go somewhere?"

He grimaces. "Unfortunately, yes, but if it means I can get more money for the cause, then I am willing to do it. I usually don't attend these events with anyone, so I'm sure the wolves will be circling soon. Again, I'm sorry."

I try to put him at ease. "Don't worry, I think I can handle them. Let's face it, I handle a classroom filled with second graders every day!" Glancing around, I notice his driver is never really out of sight; he's always within reaching distance of Jax.

Dinner was a typical banquet affair, but instead of dancing, they rolled out gambling tables. "I thought there would be dancing at an event like this."

He smiles. "No. I found, if we offer gambling with all the proceeds going to the charity, more money is donated than just writing a check."

I never really thought of it that way. "How much money can you expect to take in tonight?"

I can see the wheels in his head spinning. "The charity will probably take in three million dollars, after expenses. That will help many families, not just with the initial surgery, but also, with the aftercare. Caring for someone who has had brain surgery takes a lot of time and money. Most of these families are living pay check to pay check." *Wow, this man is nothing like I thought he would be.*

"Let's gamble a little and see if you're my lucky charm, sweetheart."

We walk up to the blackjack table and Jax hands me some chips to play with. "I don't gamble and I don't want to lose your money."

He smirks. "You're not losing my money, you're donating it. Besides, it's easy. Just try to get to twenty-one without going over."

I try a few hands, but it doesn't hold my interest; it seems too much like work. What I do find interesting is the roulette table. There are many different ways to bet, and it's all up to the wheel. Turns out, I'm better at it than I thought. After an hour of gambling, I decide to cash in my winnings. I hand the cashier my chips and she gives me a check for $100,000.00. "Excuse me, but there is some kind of mistake here. This is too much money."

Jax laughs and informs me I was playing with $10,000 dollar chips! I'm glad I didn't know, otherwise, I wouldn't have bet anything. I sign the check and put it in the donation box. I see Jax watching me with a very strange look, but he says nothing.

As we head back to the limo, Jax stops and takes me in his arms, he pulls my chin up, and stares into my eyes. There it is—my toes are doing that curl thing again! "Raven, I had a wonderful evening, and I don't want it to end, will you come home with me?"

"Okay," I whisper. I can't believe I just said okay without a single thought. Even though I'm nervous, I feel so safe with him, which is something I never have experienced before.

WE PULL UP TO a building across from Central Park. As he steps out of the car, he takes my hand and informs me that he lives here. We walk through the lobby and get on his private elevator. We enter the penthouse and I'm struck with the most incredible view of the park. "You live here by yourself?"

He looks at me like I'm nuts. "I have a housekeeper, but other than that, yes, just me."

Taking in everything surrounding me, I'm stunned. "This place is huge! Do you ever get lost in here?"

He strokes his chin and gifts me with that crooked smirk. "Let me give you a quick tour. There is a guest room, office, gym, and then there is a rooftop garden area with a hot tub."

I can't believe he lives here. "Jax, this place is amazing and the views are spectacular. Does your place take up the entire floor?"

He shakes his head. "No, there is another penthouse that mirrors mine. My driver, Max, lives in the other one."

Oh. My. God. His driver lives in a penthouse! "Wait, your driver lives in a penthouse?"

He laughs. "Max is much more than just my driver. He does my security and he's my best friend. He has to be—I trust him with my life and the lives of my family." He smiles at me. "Come, sit down, Raven, I want to know more about you.

"You're so beautiful and not just tonight. When you stumbled into my world, you threw it off kilter." He leans in slowly, his soft lips brushing against mine. The sparks are flying to all my nerve endings and then, I look into his eyes—yep, there's that toe thing again.

He's tender, yet firm; our tongues doing a slow dance. He runs his cheek against mine and the scruff of his beard softly grazes my cheek. "Raven, please tell me you feel that too… that I'm not imagining it."

I hum, "Yes, Jax, just what *it* is, I have no clue."

He slowly puts little flutter kisses up and down my neck, and then, he reaches in and nibbles on my ear lobe. *Oh sweet, Jesus!* His teeth gently pull on my ear. Oh my God, his lips are so soft. He swipes his tongue over my bottom lip and I shiver. He takes my hand and kisses the inside of my wrist. Damn, when he does that, it's like a jolt between my legs. *How could that one spot be so damn sensitive?* This man is way out of my league! He's rich, beautiful, and, I'm sure, a player; he seems used to getting what he wants—when he wants it. I need to stop this before I get to the point of no return. "Jax, I need to go."

His jaw is tight, and he's fisting his hands. He seems shocked I need to leave. "You want to leave now? Is something wrong? Did I offend you?"

I'm trying not to let the tears fall, "It's not you, Jax, I just…I really need to go."

He locks his eyes on mine. "Okay, let me ring Max." As he gets up to leave, I can see the confusion on his face.

Heck, even I'm confused "Jax, I can take a cab, it's no big deal."

Okay, now, he looks pissed off. "Sweetheart, there is no way I would dream of you ever taking a cab home, and if I offended you in any way, I'm truly sorry." He leads me to the elevator.

I can't lose it here. I take a deep breath, "It's not you, Jax," I whisper as we head down the elevator in silence. I really don't know what to say to him. When we get downstairs, Max is waiting for us. We get right into the car and take off.

The ride to my place is long and quiet. I need to stop this now before it goes too far. We pull up and I jump out so fast, it only gives him time to watch me. "I'm sorry, Jax." And with that, I'm gone.

Jaxson

AS WE DRIVE AWAY from Raven's place, Max glances at me in the rearview mirror. "Jax, you okay?"

I stare out the window. "Fuck if I know? This girl keeps running away from me."

"Do you want me to run a check on her?" he asks. Usually, I would have Max run a check, but for some reason, I want to find out about her like a normal guy would.

"No, Max, not just yet. I'm not ready for that." I'm not ready to go home yet, either. "Please drive around the park for a while, mate, I need some time to think. I just don't get why this girl keeps running away from me. I never have this problem." Max glances in the rear view mirror at me again, "Spit it out, Max, I see the fucking bloody looks you're giving. I know you have something to say."

He's laughs. "Well, Jax, you can be a tad intimidating, don't you think?"

If he weren't my best friend, I would probably wipe that smirk off of his face right now. "You know, Max, eight years and you're still cheeky as hell. I'm trying not to bulldoze her, but it's very hard." He laughs at me again. I'm glad my love life, or lack thereof, is amusing to him.

"Jax, you operate at a hundred miles an hour and that can be too much for most people."

I hate when he's right. "That's just it, Max, she's not 'most people', she's different."

He looks at me like he's had some great revelation. "Well, Jax, maybe that is the answer."

What the fuck? Is he Dr. Phil now? "Oh bloody hell, Max! What the fuck are you trying to say?" He doesn't usually give advice on relationships so this should be interesting.

"She is different. So your usual bulldozer approach to life will not work on her. Slow it down, mate, and see how she reacts."

The rest of the ride is in silence. Damn if I know how to slow down.

Raven

WHEN I GET UPSTAIRS, Marco is waiting for me. "How was the ball, princess?" I burst into tears and throw myself on the couch.

"Oh no, baby girl, what happened?"

I let the tears fall. "It's me, I'm such a mess. He was so perfect. We had a wonderful night, then he took me back to his place and I felt like putty in his arms."

Marco pulls me into his arms as I wipe my tears on his shirt. "So, why the tears? Did you panic and run again?" he asks. I nod. I can't even say the words out loud, because then it makes it real. "Honey, give him a chance, just tell him you need to go slow. He's probably never had anyone say no. I mean, look at him. Have you googled him yet?"

I've never googled a date, why would I start now? "No, why would I do that?"

He's growling at me now! *What is it with the men in my life and all their growling?* "In today's world, you almost have to. Do you know anything about him other than what he's told you?" he asks. I shake my head. "Okay, now you're making me worried. You're usually more level- headed than this. Raven, What the fuck is going on in your head?"

Marco grabs the iPad and googles 'Jaxson Phillips.' It doesn't take long. *Holy crap there are thousands of hits!* There are tons of articles about his company; some good and some not so good. A lot of hits are about the different charities he is involved with. But what is most surprising is when I pull up images for him, he's always alone. If he is such a player, why are there no images of him with a girl? Could I have possibly been so wrong about him? Maybe my impression of him was way off base, and he's not a player. Marco clicks on a link—oh my word, it's from tonight . . . and—it's me! *Is that why he kept apologizing?*

Marco looks over to me and then starts reading, "Who is the mystery woman that was seen with New York's most eligible bachelor, Jaxson James Phillips, tonight at Chelsea Pier? Could this mean he's finally off the market?"

"I don't want to know anymore, please shut it down."

He shuts it off. "I think you need to talk to him. He can't read your mind, and the way he was looking at you, I don't think he wants this to end."

I can't listen to this anymore. "I've had enough, I'm going to bed. Do not wake me up early." I head to my room, leaving Marco to himself.

As I get into bed, I replay the night's events. I think about how hard it must be to always have people, watching your every move. Always having to filter what you say would be a big problem for me. It always amazes me how people get so wrapped up in the lives of celebrities. I have a lot to do to manage my own life, let alone wonder what some celebrity is doing or with whom they are doing it. As I try to fall asleep, all I see are the bluest eyes and how sad they looked tonight.

Chapter Four

Raven

IT'S SUNDAY MORNING, I just want to snuggle in bed for a while, but I hear music playing. The music stops and starts again. *Where is that coming from?* I look at the dresser and see the phone that Jax sent, lighting up and I realize the music is coming from there. "Hello?" I can't believe he's calling, especially after last night.

"Good morning, did you sleep well?"

How could he even think that I would sleep well after last night? "Not really, how about you?"

He sighs. "No, I think we need to talk. Can we go for breakfast, Raven?"

This guy just doesn't give up. "Even after I ran, you still want to see me?"

"Yes, I need to understand why you did, and what I can do to stop you from constantly running away from me. You're giving me a complex, sweetheart."

Maybe I'm a challenge for him? "That's a tall order, Jax."

He laughs. "I believe I'm up for the challenge. Can you be ready in an hour? It's a beautiful fall day, and I would like to enjoy it with you."

How could I say no to that? "Okay, Jax."

I HEAD OUTSIDE, AND there's Jax. He's wearing worn jeans, a button down Oxford shirt, with a polo tied around his neck. He has on aviators and is leaning against the most beautiful sports car I have ever seen. He tells me it's a *1957 Jaguar XK-SS;* a replica of Steve McQueen's car. It just takes my breath away. "I hope that look is for me and not just the car."

I can't help but laugh. "I guess you'll never know." I allow him to open the door for me and I get in. Within a minute, he's in the driver's seat and we're off.

We pull up to a little café on the East Side that I have never been to. We enter the quaint café and Jax orders our coffee and pastries. We then grab a table by the window, so we can be alone.

"Raven, I thought we were having a good time last night getting to know each other, but then you ran…again."

He doesn't demand an answer, but I know he is not leaving without one. "Jax, I'm a simple, second grade teacher. I have no worldly experience, and quite honestly, my sexual experience has been very little and very bad. You make me feel things I've never felt before and that scares me." There, I said it as honestly as I could. I'm sure he'll be taking me home now.

"First, sweetheart, let me say, there is nothing simple about you. You don't get to choose what I can or can't handle, only I do. If I didn't want to be with you, then I wouldn't. I feel things with you I've never felt before and I like it; I want more. You said 'your sexual experience is very little and was very bad', is that something you feel you can share with me? I can't fix something if I don't know what it is."

What do I say? "I need time, Jax, I barely know you."

He seems content with my answer. "If time is what you need, then you've got it. I'm not prepared to walk away so don't expect me to," he states. I cock my head, trying to figure him out. His eyes seem to hone in on me tugging my ear (a nervous habit of mine). "Did you expect me to walk away?" he continues.

I laugh, "Quite frankly, Jax, yes. I mean, you can have your pick of anyone."

He smirks again. "Raven, maybe I finally found *my someone*, but how would I know if you keep running?"

I lock eyes with him. "Oh."

"Yeah, *oh*," he whispers.

WE HEAD TO THE car and Jax informs me that we are going apple picking. I've never done that before and I'm excited to try something new, so . . . off we go. It's such a beautiful day. He puts on some music and it's one of my favorite bands, Snow Patrol.

"We seem to have similar taste in music. Jax, I'm going to ask you some questions, for every one that you answer, I will let you ask me a question."

His eyes light up. "So let me get this straight, Raven. I can ask you any question and you'll answer it?"

I laugh, "Nice try, Jax." I'll start with an easy one. "What's your favorite movie?"

He strokes his chin and it's sexy as hell. "Alright, but, Raven, no laughing."

Oh boy, that's going to be hard. "Okay, fess up, Jax, favorite movie?"

He's got a serious look on his face. "If you tell another living soul, I will deny it . . . *When Harry Met Sally*."

"Oh."

He seems surprised. "That's it, just *oh*?"

Not at all what I thought he would say. "Well, it wasn't what I was expecting, that's for sure. Why is that your favorite movie?"

He seems lost in thought. "It's the struggle of friendship and how important it is to a relationship."

Hmm. "I never thought of it that way."

He cocks his head. "What's your favorite movie?"

I know he's going to laugh. "Don't laugh."

"You didn't laugh at mine, sweetheart, why would I laugh at yours?"

Here goes nothing. "Okay, *Die Hard*." He looks over at me and gets hysterical.

"Really, Jax? You promised not to laugh."

"I'm sorry, but clearly you have to see the irony that my favorite is a 'chick flick' and yours is a 'macho dick flick'." Well, when he put it like that, I guess I can see the humor in it.

"Why is *Die Hard* your favorite movie?"

I can't believe this is not everyone's favorite movie. "Well, it's the story of survival, how one man relies on himself to save so many. He is simple, but very brave, and let's face it—the good guy wins."

I think he gets it. "Okay, sweetheart, enough on movies, what's your favorite food?"

This one is easy. "I love pizza, really good pizza, not the kind that comes frozen in a box."

I look over to him and he's thinking. I can tell when he is deep in thought, he strokes his chin. "I would have to say mine is sushi. Not only does it taste wonderful, the presentation is like a piece of art that is made just for me." He pats his chest. Wow, I never thought of it as art but I guess it could be. "iPhone or Droid?"

Another easy one. "I'm an Apple girl, they work great and they keep it simple. You?"

He's like a little boy talking about his toys. "I like Droid phones. They have better apps, but Apple computers, so I guess both."

Jaxson

SHE IS SITTING THERE, seemingly deep in thought, tugging at that fucking ear. I need to keep this conversation going so she doesn't try and pull a runner. But if she keeps doing *that*, I'm going to get crazy hard. "What other types of music do you like?"

She laughs and I love the sound of it. "If you listened to what's on my iPod you would probably be in shock. I like to sing so I have a lot of stuff I can sing along with, but only when no one is around!"

"I would love to hear you sing, and I think you would sound beautiful." I smile.

Raven

NO ONE HAS HEARD me sing except Marco, when he came home early one day. "Ha, I'm tone deaf, so only when I'm home cleaning or driving alone." I bet he has an extensive music collection. "What type of music do you listen to, Jax?"

"I really like many different types; it just depends on my mood and where I am at that moment. My top band is Snow Patrol, most people are aware of their famous songs, 'Chasing Cars' and 'Run' however, I like a lot of their older stuff; it's the lyrics that grab you. They are the ultimate story tellers.

"Okay, Raven, we're here, out you go, sweetheart. We'll take turns climbing up the ladder to pick the apples. Why are you looking at me like I have three heads?"

I freeze. "I'm afraid of heights. No way can I climb up a ladder!"

He's thinking while stroking his chin; it's such a turn on when he does that. "Raven, you can't let fear rule you or fear wins. Why are you afraid?"

I won't even stand on a chair. "What if I fall?"

He takes on a more serious look. "Do you trust me?"

I don't even have to think about that one. "Yes, Jax, totally."

He smiles, "Okay then, up you go."

I grab the ladder, "*Wait!*"

He shakes his head. "No wait, up you go, sweetheart, I've got you. I'll always have your back." He holds the ladder as I slowly climb, maintaining a white-knuckle grip the whole way. "Hold on with one hand and use the other one to pick the apple."

Oh crap, if *he wants me to let go, he is out of his fucking mind!* "Jax, I'm scared." Before the words are completely out of my mouth he's on the ladder behind me. His body blankets mine; he covers my hand with one of his. He takes my other hand and stretches it up to pick an apple.

"I will always have your back, sweetheart," he whispers deep and low in my ear.

After completely filling our bag, we head back to the car. "What are you going to do with all these apples?"

He cocks his head and gives me that look that shoots to my toes. "Oh, Raven, not me. We are going to make an apple pie, of course."

The look on my face must be priceless because he is laughing so hard, he has tears rolling down his cheeks. "Jax, I don't cook and I wouldn't have a clue how to make a pie!"

He tilts his head and hits me with that killer smirk. "Yeah, I kind of figured that by the look of fear on your face. I think it was worse than the look when you found out you had to climb up a ladder. Not to worry, I don't know either, but I did get a book and we can do this together."

I really think he's nuts, but I'm having fun for the first time in a long time so I go along with it. As we get in the car, I notice Max standing by another car. "Isn't that Max?"

He doesn't even bother to look. "Yes, he goes everywhere with me."

He has a bodyguard that lives in a penthouse and follows him everywhere? What am I getting myself into? "Why does he go everywhere with you?"

Jaxson

I DON'T WANT TO scare her into pulling another runner on me. "Max is in charge of security, he is usually with me at all times. When he can't be with me, then he has someone else shadow."

She locks her eyes with mine and there it is—that charge. "Why do you need so much security?"

I pull her hand away from her ear before I lose it completely. "Unfortunately, when someone has money and does what I do for a living, it makes them a target. Max can be a tad overprotective at times, but he keeps us safe."

Raven

WE GET BACK TO his ivory tower in the sky and he gets out a book . . . something about pie baking for dummies. It's not as hard as I thought, and we actually put together something that resembles an apple pie. He puts it in the oven to bake and soon the house begins to smell wonderful. "Would you like a glass of wine?" he asks casually. He seems so sure of himself, so comfortable in his own skin.

"Yes, please."

As he gets the wine, he puts on some music. He tells me that the music is David Garrett, who lives six months in New York and six months in London. And that he plays the violin like it is part of him. He hands me a glass of wine that I never heard of, "Michael's dad and my sister own a vineyard in Italy. This is one of the wines they produce," he explains.

I take a sip and I'm surprised. "Wow, it's very good. I never knew that's what Michael's parents did for a living. Is it hard for them, living here with their business in Italy?"

He just shrugs. "No, they spend the summers in Italy and the school year here; they make it work." He puts his glass down. "Raven, I'm going to jump right in here . . . you said your sexual experiences were very few and very bad, why?" he asks, completely out of the blue. I look up at him and my eyes are filled with tears, Marco is in my head yelling at me to tell him. "I would never judge you, Raven, we all have a past."

I study his face, he's so beautiful and looks so sincere right now, "Jax, that's just it, it's my past."

He pulls my hand away from my ear. "But it's not if it's affecting your future."

The timer rings and I thank all that's holy for the interruption.

THE PIE SMELLS WONDERFUL and looks like something out of a magazine, I take a picture with my phone and Jax laughs.

"Would I be correct in guessing it has something to do with why you left home at such a young age?" Great, we're back on this subject again. He's not going to stop until I tell him.

"Yes, I was fifteen when my mom died from cancer. My dad and I were never close, but after she died, he started drinking very heavily. I guess it was his way of coping. His drinking brought out some nasty things. One night, he came into my room and he tried to rape me. After that, I left."

"Don't stop now, sweetheart. Nothing you can say is going to scare me away."

Okay, wow that is not what I was expecting, so I continue. "I had no one to turn to for help. I have no other family. I found myself volunteering at a shelter and that is where I met Marco. His parents disowned him when he told them he was gay. We took care of each other, never relying on anyone but ourselves. I graduated high school without the school knowing I was homeless. I earned scholarships and worked hard to put myself through college."

He keeps his focus on me, intently listening, "So where does this bad sexual experience come into play?"

I sigh heavily, "I met someone and tried to have a sexual relationship with him but . . . he was only concerned about himself. It was always about his pleasure and his needs. He became physically abusive, and after a night in the ER, Marco convinced me to get a restraining order." There... I put it all out there, and now it's time to make my exit with as much grace and dignity as I can muster up.

As I attempt to leave, he takes my hand, his eyes on mine. "Where do you think you're going?"

"I don't want you to feel like I'm a charity case, and I definitely don't want you to pity me."

He growls. "You know, Raven, I really wish you would stop deciding for me what I can and can't handle. I just said you're not going to scare me away and I meant that. I'm not going anywhere. Not because of charity or pity, I'm with you because I want to be, and for no other reason. Now, I think it's time for pie." Just like that, he's finished. He doesn't dwell on stuff; he deals with it and then puts it away.

"I am very impressed with our pie making ability, and, Jax, I have to say you make the best coffee ever."

He gives me that beautiful smile. "Thank you. My sister, Bella, taught me well, she believes coffee is God's nectar."

He leans in and kisses me quickly and softly. He looks into my eyes, like he's searching for permission. I lean up and kiss him, stroking his velvet tongue. The taste of him mixed with apple pie and coffee is surreal.

He pulls away first, "Stay with me tonight," he whispers.

Part of me wants to stay and part of me wants to run. "I have school tomorrow."

He kisses me softly again, "I promise to get you to class on time."

I shake my head, "I'm not ready to spend the night. I need... time. I'm sorry."

He rests his forehead on mine, "Don't ever be sorry for being honest with me. Let me take you home."

MARCO IS WAITING FOR me as soon as I walk in the door. "Well, baby girl, how was your date?"

"I really like him, but there is so much unknown with him. He is a very private person, considering he's always in the public eye.

Marco furrows his brows, seemingly concerned. "How much have you told him?"

I run over the conversation in my head. "I told him about the ex and the restraining order that is in place, but that's it."

He hugs me. "Maybe it's time to tell him the truth . . . the whole truth?"

I look at him, "I'm going to bed. I have work tomorrow. Love you." I leave him lost in his thoughts as I head to my room for the night.

MY SLEEP IS VERY restless so I decide to get up super early and go for a run. I live in Gramercy Park, one of the only private parks in Manhattan. I like running here. It's two miles with great trails and it's

THERESA SEDERHOLT

safe. I do a total of six miles, then head back home. Running helps clear my head and today it made me realize that I need to steer clear of Jax. He is just too much for me and I know I'm going to get hurt.

I get ready for school and head to Starbucks. Jax is there waiting with my coffee. "Wow, this is nice, can I expect this every day?"

He looks at me with that crooked smirk. "If you want to have breakfast together every day I can arrange it, sweetheart."

"Oh." I have to laugh because he would.

There's that smirk. "Yeah, *oh*."

On that note, I have to leave. I thank him and tell him that I need to run, school starts soon. He hands me a bottle of water and a breakfast sandwich. "What's this for?"

He kisses me softly. "Mick. I know you usually buy him breakfast, and I didn't want him to miss a meal because of me."

Does this guy know everything I do? "How do you know about Mick?"

He smirks, "When you doused me with your coffee, I had to find out who you were, so I asked around and all roads led me to Mick. He's an interesting bloke, that's for sure."

I start to walk. "He just needs someone to listen, that's the least I can do, and give him a meal. I have to run, have a good day, Jax." I look back at him and he's stroking his chin. Hmm . . . I wonder what he's thinking.

Jaxson

AS I HEAD TOWARDS my office, all I can think about is Raven and her constant need to run from me! My mind drifts to every second spent with her, and that fucking tugging on her ear thing; why does that make me instantly hard? Maybe I should have Max run a check on her? As I approach my building, I see Max and he's pacing—that's never a good sign. When I get closer, I can tell he's really pissed off. His hands are flying and he's yelling into the phone. "Max, is there a problem?"

He has fire in his eyes. "You want to know if there is a fucking problem! How about my bloody boss, whom I'm en-trusted to keep safe, wandering off, repetitively, without letting his detail know or giving proper *fucking* notice?!"

I know I have to take Max seriously, but sometimes, he is over the top. "Okay, Max, you need to calm down. I'm not in any danger and I just needed some time to think."

He looks at me like he's going to blow a gasket. "*Think*? You needed to think? Jax, I have guarded the Royal family, I have led Special Forces for the United Kingdom, and have avoided death on many occasions, but you, my friend, will be the one to put me in an early fucking grave! I understand she is frustrating you—fuck, she's even frustrating me, but don't—and I mean, *don't* ever leave your fucking detail again!"

"Okay, just calm down. I need you to look into something for me. There is a homeless man near the Starbucks that Raven checks in on his name is Mick. I want you to find out what his story is and then see what we can do to help him out."

"What's this about, Jax?" he asks with a bit of irritation mixed with the confusion painted on his face.

"Raven buys him breakfast every morning. I spoke to him and he is a war veteran who is most likely suffering from PTSD. It's simple; I want to know what I can do for him."

"Jax, nothing with you is ever simple."

Rather than argue, I decide to head up to my office. I sit behind my desk, looking out at the New York skyline and the only thing I really see are those violet eyes and a beautiful girl tugging on her fucking ear. And I'm instantly hard, *again*! Fuck, I have a meeting in ten minutes. I can't head in there with a raging hard-on. I grab the phone and call my assistant. "Duke, call everyone and change the meeting to my office." At least it's a temporary fix. I will need to come up with something more permanent later, so I'm not walking around with a constant hard-on.

Maxwell

I DON'T KNOW WHAT Jax thinks he can do for this bloke, but I head toward his office with the info he wanted. "Duke? Is Jax in his office?"

He nearly jumps out of his chair. "Yes, Mr. Fleming, he is just finishing up a meeting."

What is this guy's problem? "Okay, I'll wait." I step into the shadows, just watching; it's what I do best. I must make this kid nervous because he always seems so flustered when I'm around. Maybe its new job jitters? Managers are coming out of Jax's office so I head on in.

"I got that information you asked for on Mick." At least this wasn't too much trouble.

"Wow, that was quick."

I laugh, "Yeah, well, most of it is public knowledge, and I wasn't sure how far back you wanted to go since I don't know what the fuck you're looking for."

He strokes his chin, which is a sure sign that Jax's wheels are turning. "Just the basic stuff, for now."

I sit across from him. "Okay, Jax, he is an Air Force veteran who did six tours in Iraq. He was awarded the *Medal of Honor* when his jet was shot down. He saved his crew one-by-one while suffering two broken legs, all while keeping the enemy at bay. He's been diagnosed with PTSD and before you ask, he doesn't get any additional funding. The problem is, funding is low, so it is distributed based on need. He is on the cusp, so he is not seen as a priority. Jax, what are you thinking?"

He paces. "I'm thinking that his situation is wrong. This man fought for his country and this is the way they take care of him?!"

I don't know when Jax finds the time to think about this when so much else is happening around him? "Jax, there are thousands of *Mick's* out there. There is a good organization, *The Wounded Warrior Project*. Let me reach out to them and see what we can do."

He nods, "Okay, but sooner rather than later, mate."

Now comes the hard question, which I'm sure will get my blood boiling. "How are things with Raven?"

He shakes his head. "Just as confusing as ever, Max." He stares out the window, seemingly deep in thought so I decide not to push any further and leave.

Raven

SCHOOL IS UNEVENTFUL WHICH is just fine by me. Jackie and I decide to go out for a few drinks and an early dinner. Jackie is beautiful; her father is Swedish and her mom is Asian. She is very tall and her complexion is light like her dad's, but she has her mom's almond-shape eyes that are almost golden. She is very lean; she runs marathons. And she attracts men like a magnet. We enjoy trying different mom and pop restaurants, so we do this every week.

"Okay, Raven, you have to tell me about Michael's uncle. Don't even think of denying it; I saw the way he was looking at you, so spill." I tell her everything, including my tendencies to keep running from him.

"Are you afraid of him, is that why you keep running?"

I shake my head. "Absolutely not, if anything, I feel very safe with him. I think I keep running because he is so intense and he is everything I'm not."

She rolls her eyes and huffs. "You're kidding, right? I mean, you're beautiful, smart, and I know if you wanted to, you could run circles around him."

I hug her. "I love you, Jackie, but I think you're nuts. With him, I feel very insecure; he's so beautiful and ridiculously rich. I could never be in the same league as some of the people he must run with. What about you? Didn't you have a date last night?"

She throws her hands up in disgust. "Yes, and it was terrible. I mean, one dinner and he thinks I should put out. I know I'm old fashioned in a lot of ways, but I just want someone that does it for me. I want to be someone's end all."

I feel bad for her; she is so sweet but also very smart. Men see her and think she is submissive, which is totally off base. "You're a great girl and you deserve only the best. There is no crime in holding out for it as long as you see it when it's right in front of your eyes. Enough about men. Let's hit some stores, I need retail therapy."

A couple of hours later and I'm back home with at least ten shopping bags! There is nothing better than some good scores, during retail therapy. Marco's not home yet, but the doorman informs me I had a visitor that didn't leave his name. I check my phone and see I have six missed calls, all from Jax. I also have a text message and a voice mail.

I check the text first:

Please answer your phone.

Then, the voicemail:

"I don't understand why you're ignoring me, and why you keep running away. What is it going to take to get you to trust me?"

I trust him, I just don't trust myself. I decide to shut it off and go to sleep. My head hits that pillow and I'm out for the count.

Chapter Five

Raven

MORNING COMES WITH MARCO, banging on my door again. The banging can only mean one thing—I must have slept through the alarm. "How bad is it, Marco?"

"Raven, its 6:30 a.m.!" he yells. *Oh fuck!* This man has me way too preoccupied and now he is making me late again.

"Marco, why does this keep happening to me?" I ask as I jump out of bed and frantically move about my room to get ready.

"Life gets in the way of living, baby girl, you know that." I push him out the door as I race into the shower.

Finally pulling it all together, I hurry out the door to get my morning coffee. Just as I have myself convinced that I should forget about Jax, I run into Starbucks and see him standing there with my coffee. "God, you're wonderful, thank you so much."

His eyes are dark and he's glaring at me. "Are you ever going to answer my calls?"

As I look up at him, I realize, he's really pissed. "I'm sorry, I just need time."

He leans in and kisses me softly on the forehead, "Well, sweetheart, time's up. I'm picking you up after school."

Before I can even answer, he's gone.

I CAN'T FOCUS ON anything today. I thank, all that's holy, Jackie is in my room, helping me. She sends the kids out to recess which gives us a twenty minute break. "Raven, what's going on with you today? You're not yourself."

I know Jackie will understand. "I've been trying to ignore, Jax. I told him I need time, but then I ran into him at Starbucks this morning. He informed me that *time is up* and he's picking me up after school today."

She gives me a big hug. Oh, how I love the fact that I get to work with my best friend. "Go with your gut and get out of your own head; that's half the battle."

The kids all start running back in and before I know it, school is over. I peek out the window of my classroom and see that Jax is waiting at the curb. *God, he's beautiful.* Will I ever get past that? Who am I kidding?—I don't want to. I gather my things and make my way to his car.

"Hi, Jax."

He pulls me up against him and brushes his lips upon mine. *Sweet Jesus, they are soft!* He tastes like vanilla and spice. It's a good thing he is holding me close to him, otherwise I would be in a puddle at his feet right now. He opens the car door, guides me in, and then tosses my stuff in the back.

"Where are we going?" I ask. He's driving like a man on a mission!

"My place. We are going to sit down and talk about why you feel the need to run away from me and ignore my calls."

"Oh."

He pulls my hand away from my ear. "Yeah, *oh.*"

WE REACH THE IVORY tower in the sky, in record time. He says nothing the entire ride, but I can tell he is deep in thought because he is stroking his chin again. We step into the elevator as the doors close and my heart begins to flutter. I'm flushed almost to the point of fainting. He looks over at me, his eyes cutting into my core.

"Lucky for you my mum raised a gentleman, otherwise I would throw you up against that wall and fuck your brains out until you tell me everything. I sense there is more to you and your life that you are not sharing."

I can't believe he just said that! The doors open and my chin is still on the ground. In one quick motion, he turns around, scoops me up, and carries me into the living room. He gently puts me on top of the bar, pours himself a scotch and then smirks at me. "Do you need anything?"

"Water, please," my voice comes out in nothing but a squeak. He hands me my glass, then takes off his jacket, and loosens his tie.

He pulls my hand away from my ear, "Times up, woman. Talk. Why the fuck do you keep running away from me?"

I take a steadying breath. "Jax, this is a hell of a way to have a conversation, don't you think?"

He pulls me towards him, landing his rock hard body up against mine. His long, hard cock is hitting me right at my core, and I whimper. He leans in and starts putting feather light kisses on my lips, my cheeks, down my neck, and up to my ear where he starts to nibble on the lobe… *oh sweet, Jesus, I can't think!* How could I even form a sentence? Let alone talk. "I'll say it again." He puts a smirk on his beautiful face… "Please tell me why you're running…is that better?"

Time for a mental pep talk, Raven. Take a deep breath. "When you're this close to me, I can't think. Hell, I can barely form a complete sentence," I confess.

He throws his hands up. "So, then why the fuck do you run?"

I'm almost embarrassed. I can't even raise my eyes to him. "Because I can very easily lose myself in you. You're too much, too intense. I'm a simple girl, and my sex life was very little and very bad."

He lifts my chin so our eyes meet. "Look. At. Me," he demands. I look into his eyes and there it is, that look that cuts clear into my soul. "Raven, did you ever stop to think that maybe I don't want someone with a vast sexual past. Maybe I don't want someone that is like everyone else, so fake and materialistic. Maybe, just maybe, I'm looking for someone who is sweet and kind, a person who cares about someone other than herself. You can't decide for me what I want and what I can

41

handle. I can do that on my own."

I have a white-knuckle grip on the bar. "There's a lot about me you don't know."

He takes a deep breath, staring into my eyes. "Then you need to let me in, otherwise how will I ever know?"

"Okay," I whisper. Was that my voice? Oh boy, what did I just agree to and why did I agree so quickly? It's okay, this will be fine... don't panic.

He reaches in and softly kisses my lips. "Do you trust me?"

I nod, "Jax, that was never a question. I do." He lifts me off the bar and carries me to his bedroom; it's bigger than my whole apartment. He places me gently on the bed and removes my shoes. He is crouched between my legs, staring up at me with his amazing baby blues. He takes my hand and kisses my wrist. His lips linger there and chills run up my spine.

"I want to discover every inch of you, there will be no rushing and no running. Just you and me, in the here and now." He works his lips up and down my arms, kissing each of my fingertips. My breathing begins to get heavier as his tongue runs up the inside of each finger. He places a kiss in the palm of my hand never once averting his eyes away from mine. He lifts my sweater off and starts kissing my neck. When he reaches my ear he stops, "When you tug on this ear, it makes me crazy. I can't see straight. I just want to nibble it and lick it," he whispers.

Now I understand why he's always pulling my hand from my ear. "Oh," is all I can manage as a response.

"Yeah, *oh*," he barely whispers.

Before I know it, he's working that tongue down my chest. He rubs my nipples through my bra and they become instantly hard. He kisses and nibbles at each one of them, taking his time, driving me insane. Oh my God, he can just hang out here doing this forever and I will be very happy. Just as I finish that thought, he starts working his way down my body. He unbuttons my jeans and slowly pulls them off. "Raven, do you know how beautiful you are?"

I shake my head slowly, he has rendered me speechless. He stands up and removes his shirt and I think I'm going to hyperventilate. He has a frigging *V!* I want to run my tongue up and down his chest, but it seems, he has other plans. He lifts my foot and pulls my ankle to his lips.

He peppers light kisses all the way up my leg, working his way up to the inside of my thigh. When he reaches the top, he stops and picks up the other foot to start the process all over again. He kisses his way up my tummy and in an instant has my bra above my head and my breasts are exposed to him. He begins slowly licking and nibbling my nipples; first one, and then the other. The more turned on he is getting, the heavier his accent is getting which is really hot. In a flash he has my panties off and he is heading south!

"Jax, I never..." but before I can say anymore, he is between my legs, kissing, licking, and nibbling. Lord, I don't know what he is doing, but my whole body is tingling, its magical and all for me. The entire time, his eyes are watching me; becoming darker, hooded, and I can tell we are far from done. He puts one finger inside me and starts to slowly work in and out of my body. On each outward stroke, he gathers my wetness and brings it up to circle my clitoris before repeating the whole tortuous process. My body is quivering and there is a buzzing in my ears. I really think my head is going to explode. My skin is flushed. I am at the peak of what is going to be an epic orgasm when Jax just stops.

"Sorry, baby, you're so wet and tight. I need to be buried deep in you when you come." Jax removes his pants and I get my first look at him totally naked and I think I'm going to pass out. He sees the look of fear on my face. "Don't worry, I'll go very slowly."

He's huge! He puts on a condom; I'm thankful that he has his wits, because I sure don't. I feel him at my opening, but he only works in a little bit before he stops and closes his eyes for a moment. When he opens them, his eyes find mine. "I want to work every inch in very slowly so you feel it all. There is only one chance for a first and I want our first to be spectacular." Propped on his knees, he brings my legs around his waist. He clasps both of my hands in his, above my head. He works himself in and out, stretching me, and going deeper with each move. When he is finally all the way in, he stops. I don't understand why but then I see the look on his face and can tell he is fighting to control the tidal wave that is coming. His eyes are closed and his head is tilted all the way back; his beauty and chiseled face mesmerizes me. He leans down and kisses me. When he starts to move again, it's slowly as if to ensure I feel every inch of him, gliding rhythmically in and out of my body.

He changes our position and tilts me so that he is hitting the tip of my cervix, and then starts to increase the speed of his thrusts. *Oh, God!* I start to whimper as my body begins to climb, I never knew that sex could be this amazing. "Don't come, Raven; hold it. I want us together when we fall."

He can't be serious? "I'm trying, Jax, but I'm losing it!" I cry. He stops. Why is he stopping again?! "Oh, sweet Jesus, and all that is holy, please don't stop!"

He's growling again and it's so fucking hot! "Slow, baby, real slow. I want this to last." He's buried deep within me, rocking up and down, then side to side; he circles right, then left. He leans down, devoting all of his attention to my nipples again. He pulls my nipple between his teeth and I scream as he concentrates on first one, then the other. He pulls out really slow and I think he's going to go back in really slow but all of a sudden, he slams into me! Stars, rockets . . . you name it and I see it. I'm yelling and I don't even feel like it's me!

"Jax, are you there yet?"

"Yes, for the love of God, *yes*!" His voice is low and his accent really heavy. "Raven, look into my eyes *now*!" he yells. Our eyes lock and, for a split second, I see him . . . I mean really see him, and I feel like I can't breathe.

"Oh *fuck*!" we both scream. A heat rushes over my whole body and I can feel him twitching inside of me. My body is trembling. He's looming over me; both of us breathing hard, just trying to get some oxygen into our lungs. He starts kissing me, long and slow, and all I can do is hum. He ditches the condom and continues kissing my lips so softly. I curl into him and finally find a calm within me that I never had before.

His eyes are darker and so intense. "You're beautiful, sweetheart."

He starts kissing his way down my chest and my body is buzzing. He runs his tongue around my belly button really slowly as he nibbles his way down my body and parts my legs. His tongue is soft, yet firm. And all too quickly, he has me worked into a ball of nerves. "You want to come again, sweetheart?"

I nod, "Oh God, yes." He stops again. Now I'm fucking growling!

"Hold on, baby, I want more, too. I'll always want more with you."

He puts on another condom and, this time, he gets us both there a little quicker. We roll into another orgasm together and I'm totally spent. I just lie here sprawled across Jax. He pulls the comforter over us,

"Sleep now, my beautiful girl," he whispers.

I drift off, dreaming of the beautiful man whose arms I'm wrapped up in.

I'M WARM . . . ALMOST TOO warm. My eyes flutter open and I realize where I am. My head is on Jax's chest and my arm and leg are wrapped around him. I try to undo myself without waking him, but apparently, he's already awake and I notice him staring at me.

"Um, hi."

He graces me with a crooked smile and his blues are twinkling. "Um, hi yourself, sweetheart."

I jump up, "What time is it?"

He doesn't move. "It's early yet, no worries. Just let me enjoy this for a little bit." He pulls me back down so I'm on top of him; his morning erection wedged between us, hitting me in just the right spot.

"Jax, I need to get back to my place and get ready for work."

He sighs, "I know, but I need you more… cut me a little slack here. I just woke up from a wonderful evening with the most beautiful girl curled up next to me. Right now my cock needs to be buried in her." His hand slides down my body. I should be offended by some of the things he says, when we're intimate, but with the hint of the British accent, it has the opposite effect. His dirty talk makes me totally wet and ready for him. He leans over and grabs a condom from the bedside table, slipping it on quickly. He lifts me up and then impales me on to his cock. "Take the lead, baby, I know you can; just let loose and feel me buried, balls deep inside you."

I start to move slowly up and down, clenching my core muscles as I go. I knew Pilates classes would pay off. He holds my hips and I lean back, allowing him to go even deeper. He leans up as I arch my chest and he flicks my nipples with his tongue. First, the right, then the left, and back again. That's all it takes, I'm at the top of the cliff, ready to fall. "Are you ready, baby?" he asks as he pulls me back towards him.

"I'm there," I whimper.

"Open your eyes and look at me!"

Oh God, there it is! "*Now!*" We fall off the cliff; it's an amazing feeling. I crash into him and just hold on, waiting for the quivering to stop. There is something so deep and intimate at the way he demands my eyes on his when we come together.

"Jax, why do you demand my eyes?"

His eyes find mine again and it's so intense. "When you're at the top of the cliff and ready to fall, it's at that point there, in a split second, that I can see all the way into your soul. And I know you're real and all mine. Now, let's shower before you have to go." He carries me into a huge bathroom and places me on the vanity while he gets everything ready for our shower. He has the most amazing shower! It has four heads, hitting us from every direction, and at the top is a huge round disk that water falls from; like a giant cloud in the sky.

He begins to worship every inch of my body while paying special attention to my nipples, then he drops to his knees. *Sweet Jesus!* He lifts my leg and places my foot on his shoulder, burying his face, he starts kissing, licking, nibbling . . . one finger in, then two. His thumb swipes over me and that's all she wrote—I'm done. I pull his hair, riding the wave. I feel his finger start moving my moisture from front to back, and I panic. "Jax, I've never had anal sex. I don't know if I can."

He doesn't stop. "Relax, baby, not today... just a little fun." Working his finger in the back, his tongue plays up front while his other hand reaches up to play with my nipples. I scream, my knees buckle, he has me totally spent. He looks up at me, his eyes twinkling, "I could watch you come undone all day; it's such a beautiful sight."

I feel like I'm floating on a cloud, I only pray that I don't come crashing back to earth, anytime soon.

JAX GETS ME BACK to my place in record time; Manhattan traffic seems to be very afraid of his driving. He waits for me to change and get my stuff for work. I know Marco wants to ask a million questions but since Jax is here, he has to control himself.

"Baby girl don't forget we have a class tonight. Are we meeting there or will you come back here first?"

That's my reminder to grab my gym bag, "We'll meet there."

"What kind of class do you have?" Jax inquires.

I smile at him because I know what he's going to be thinking. "Marco and I do Pilates classes twice a week." I explain. He raises one eyebrow and I try not to laugh. I know I'm going to give my instructor an extra thank you tonight.

I'VE NEVER SEEN ANYONE handle New York traffic like Jax does, it's like they are moving out of the way for him. We pull up to my school, and he helps gather all my stuff for me. We get out of the car and Jax turns me to face him. "When can I see you again?"

I don't want to be one of those weak girls, waiting on his every whim. "I'm not sure, let's see what our schedules look like."

He grabs me and pulls my hand from my ear. "I told you what that does to me," he says, before he gives me a very deep and sensual kiss. "Telling me *you're not sure*, is not a good answer. While you're looking at your schedule, just think of what is waiting for you," he says with a painstakingly beautiful smile. He gets back in the car and takes off.

I get all my stuff settled in my classroom—still flustered. I jump when the phone in the room rings. When I answer it, it's Sheryl from the office, informing there is a delivery for me that I need to come and pick up. I thank her, hang up and head to the office. I get to the office and there is a coffee just the way I like it and a box with a huge piece of the apple pie in it, and a note:

> *Raven,*
> *You didn't have breakfast and I wanted you to be thinking about me, and all I will do to you when I see you again.*
> *Your Jax xo*

Sheryl starts to laugh. "What are you laughing about?" I can tell she is happy for me.

"Honey, in the three years you've worked here, I've never seen you look so happy."

All I can say is, "Oh." but I know I have a ridiculous smile. I go back to my room, enjoying my breakfast. He signed it *Your Jax* . . . could he really be mine? I need to stop this daydreaming before it gets me into trouble.

MY DAY FLIES BY, which is good because I can barely concentrate on the work. When I get to the gym, Marco is already warming up.

"Okay, girl, I want all the dirt, I can't believe you didn't call me and let me know you were spending the night with him. Didn't you think I would worry?"

Shit, I forgot. "Oh." I think he's pissed off.

"Yeah, well, that seems to be your answer for everything lately."

First he wants me to go for it, and now he's getting mad? "I'm sorry. You're right, I should have told you, but it just happened so fast."

He laughs, "Well, I hope not!" he says with a knowing smirk.

"Very funny, wiseass. The sex was mind blowing and . . . I enjoyed it! I can't believe it."

He hugs me. "I tried to tell you that but you never listen to me, baby girl."

My feelings are all over the place. "Well, he wants more. Just what that means, I have no idea. I don't want to rush this and screw it all up. For the first time, in too long, I am actually happy and comfortable—and that scares the hell out of me!"

We start our warm up. "Just take it at a pace that works for you and if he really cares, he will understand. How much did you tell him about your past anyway?"

Tears instantly fill my eyes and I fight to hold them back. "I told him almost everything; I didn't give him too many details about my ex. He doesn't need to know that he beat me, to within an inch of my life. I don't want pity."

He wipes away a tear, "You know if someone digs, they will find the police reports?"

"If it comes up, I'll deal with it, but for now, I just want to experience normal." *Who am I kidding? I don't think normal is in my dictionary.*

"Raven, have you told him about the adoption yet?" He changes the subject slightly. I glance at Marco and I can tell something is bugging him, but I'm guessing he's not ready to share.

"No, maybe in time, but for now, I want to keep it simple," I reply. He shakes his head. He's obviously disappointed in my answer, but he doesn't keep pushing. I start to ask what's bothering him but class starts, so I drop it.

CLASS WAS BRUTAL BUT good. It was just what I needed to give my mind a break for a few hours.

"Want to grab a pizza? Or do you have plans with Jax?" Marco sounds like he is almost pleading.

"Pizza sounds great. I'll meet you out front."

When I step outside, Marco is yelling at someone. It looks like he is getting ready to slam him to the ground, but I distract him. "What the hell is going on?" The guy rushes off but not before getting a picture of me.

"Baby girl, that guy was a reporter and he is looking for a story about the girl that Jaxson Phillips is 'nailing.'"

What the fuck? "You're kidding, right?"

He's shaking his head as we start making our way down the street, "Afraid not, dear, the hounds have been released and they are circling for blood."

On the way, we stop and pick up a bottle of red wine and Ray's pizza—my kind of comfort food. We are a block away from home when Jax's phone rings. "Hello? I can't believe you have me carrying a second phone, why?"

He laughs, "Why not, sweetheart? I like knowing it's just for me. I don't share, Raven. *Ever*."

I need to tell him what happened and I don't think he is going to be happy. "Jax, listen, a reporter was waiting outside the gym for me tonight, asking questions. Marco handled it, but the guy took my picture." Oh no, he's really quiet.

"I'm so sorry, they must have figured out who you were from Saturday night. Is Marco with you now?"

I sigh, "Yes, we're walking home now."

"*Walking*? You're walking home?" he yells, "Put Marco on the phone *now*!"

Wow, he sounds pissed. "Marco, Jax wants to talk to you." I hand him my spare phone and Marco cocks his head, giving me a curious look when he takes the phone.

"Hey, Jax, what's up?" Marco holds the phone away from his ear.

"Marco, what exactly did the reporter say?" Jax asks loud enough for me to hear. Marco tells him what the reporter said. "Okay, I'll handle the press, but why are you walking home instead of taking a cab?"

Marco looks at me for help but I put my hands up and just keep walking. "Jax, we do this every week and Raven is safe with me. Can I say the same thing about you?"

Why does Marco have to poke a burning fire? "Don't be an arse, Marco. I would never, knowingly put her in danger."

I can tell neither one is happy. "Hold on, Jax, I'll give you back to Raven." Marco hands me the phone back.

"When can I see you?" Just like that, he is done with that part of the conversation and moving on to the next.

"Saturday, if that works for you." He doesn't say anything and I look at the phone thinking maybe the call dropped, but then I hear him take a deep breath.

"I'm not waiting a whole week. How about Wednesday?"

Before I can even give him an answer he declares, "Wednesday. Dinner. I'll pick you up at seven."

I squeak out, "Okay." And with that, he hangs up! Truth is, I didn't want to wait till the weekend but I didn't want to seem like I was needy and desperate. I don't know who I think I'm kidding, when it comes to Jax—*I am needy and desperate.*

"So, I take it you're seeing him again? Even though you're going to be in the spotlight."

I want to see him; he is working his way under my skin. "I'll have to tell him the rest of the story. I feel like I don't have a choice, and it has to be sooner rather than later. Do you have a problem with Jax? You seem upset tonight."

He shakes his head. "I just worry about you, baby girl, that's all." By the time we reach home, both of us are lost in our own thoughts; our appetites are gone and we just head off to bed.

I TRY TO SLEEP, but I keep seeing those beautiful eyes and then they are being pulled away from me. I end up tossing and turning all night, finally giving up now, at 3:30 a.m., I start grading papers, instead. Morning comes, and I'm dragging ass. I head to my favorite Starbucks and Jax is sitting in the corner, smiling at me with his twinkling baby blues and I'm done. Good thing they already know my order, because the man renders me speechless. He gets up and pulls my chair out for me. "Good morning, sweetheart."

I wave to Max. I'm getting used to having him always around. "Morning, Jax, can I expect to see you here every morning?"

He smirks. "Well, I am typically at this exact spot every morning but I usually come here a little later. Now that I know you come here every day, around this time, to answer your question, yes."

I have to laugh at him. "Well, I would love to sit with you all day but I have to get to work. Have a great day."

I get up to leave and he walks me to the door, he pulls me into his arms and he brushes his lips over mine. "I will, now that I have seen you." He gives me a toe-curling kiss before sending me off to work. God, he is so sweet and beautiful. My stomach knots, waiting for the other shoe to drop, but hoping it doesn't.

I see Mick on my way to school and give him his breakfast. "Raven, can I walk with you for a little bit?"

I can tell something is bothering him. "Of course, Mick, everything okay?"

He's apprehensive. "Your friend, Jax, brings me breakfast when you can't. He asked me about you."

I have to laugh, "Did he? He's a good guy, Mick. How are the nightmares, any better?"

He shrugs, "Some days are better than others, what about you?"

I squeeze his hand. "Some days better than others for me too, Mick."

The bell rings and I hug Mick before running into school. I get settled in my room when Jackie comes in, looking a little flustered. "Hey, girl, is there a problem?" Her eyes are wide which is unusual; not much rattles Jackie.

"I'm not sure. I had playground detail this morning and I just felt like I was being watched. I know it's crazy, given the quality of security we have here, but I just felt like something was off."

Wow, not what I was expecting. "Did you let the front office know?"

She shakes her head. "Do you think I should? I mean, nothing happened, it was just a feeling."

I give her a reassuring hug. "I would just give them a heads up." The bell rings and starts off our day.

"Okay, but the kids are all coming in now. I'll talk to them at lunch time."

Jaxson

I JUST GET SETTLED in my office, when Duke rings to tell me that Michael Sr. is on his way.

Michael Sr. comes barreling into the door, "Hey, Jax, thanks for covering for me at school last week."

"I was more than happy to, mate." I grin.

"Oh, don't tell me you met Miss Raven?"

I laugh, "Yep, and we have been seeing each other outside of school. I took her to the charity event Saturday night."

He smiles, shaking his head at me. Suddenly, he lets out a big sigh and gets a somber look on his face, "Well, we have bigger problems. There is a reason I was not here, Jax, I only told Bella I was stuck in Atlanta."

"What the fuck is going on, Michael?" I already don't like the sound of this and I don't even know what *this* is.

He heads over to the bar and grabs a bottle of water. "A threat came through."

All right, not a big shock, that's for sure. "We get them all the time, what makes this one different?"

He takes a steadying breath. "They sent this." He gives me photos and they are of Junior and Bella at school. The next one is my mum and Junior at school.

"They came with a note. I gave a copy to the FBI and Interpol."

I'm trying to keep it together. "What did the note say?"

"*We can get to them at any time.*"

What the Fuck?! "Did you notify the school?"

He starts pacing. "Yeah, and I put an extra guard at the school."

The school already has good security, Max made sure of that. "What did the FBI and Interpol say?" Not that I expect them to do anything.

"They are looking into it, but I'm not holding my breath. Usually, when something like this happens, they don't do anything until something actually happens."

I'm just staring at the photos. "Did you tell Bella and Mum?"

He looks at me like I should know the answer. "No, I was waiting to tell you first, it's just… something is off."

I take a deep breath. "What do you mean by '*off*'?"

"Well, you're the high profile guy, not me!" he yells. "I'm a wine-maker who runs a successful winery in Italy. I have no enemies, so why target my son and my wife?"

I pick up the phone and call Max. He needs to be informed about what is going on since he handles security for my whole family. I barely get off the phone with, Max, before he's running through the door. After turning everything over to Max, I remember something Raven mentioned. Max and Michael are studying the note and the pictures.

"You know, guys, Saturday night I took Raven to the charity function at Chelsea Pier and there were a lot of paparazzi. Then the other night, Raven said one of them showed up at the gym but her roommate, Marco, handled it. I'm just wondering if any of this could be connected."

Michael huffs, "You draw attention no matter where you go, so I would think anyone with you would get some attention, as well."

Max starts his usual pacing. "I would still like to talk to Raven and Marco, just to be on the safe side."

I pick up the phone to call the school. "Okay, I will give her a heads up that you're coming."

Max takes a deep breath and I know what's coming. "I also want to pull a background report on Raven and Marco, just as a precaution. I know you told me to wait but I think your waiting time is up."

"All right, Max, I know you're going to do what you have to do. Keep me posted."

Chapter Six

Raven

JACKIE COMES BACK AFTER lunch recess with a message from the front office for me. "Did you tell them about this morning?" I ask.

She seems calmer. "Yes. They said that Michael's father ordered some private security, and that's probably what was going on. What's the message about?"

I open it, "Apparently, Jax's security detail has some questions for me and he just wanted to give me a heads up. I need to let Marco know, too. I went on a date with him to a charity function Saturday night. The press had a field day with it. One of them followed Marco and me to the gym last night."

I know she understands about this kind of high profile stuff—she grew up with it. "Wow, that sucks. I know what it's like living in a fish bowl."

I fold the note up and give her my attention again. "I know, I can't begin to understand what that must feel like. Always having to watch everything I say and do, especially since my brain to mouth filter is on the fritz half the time!"

THE DAY IS FINALLY over and I find Max waiting outside for me. "Miss Raven, I will give you a ride home and we can talk along the way, if that's okay with you?"

I smile at him, "Sure, Max, but you can just call me Raven." I inform him as he opens the car door for me to get in.

He laughs at me. "I'm a gentleman and old habits die hard, Miss Raven." He closes the door after me and within a minute, he's made his way around to get into the driver's seat. "The man that approached you outside the gym, what did he look like?" he begins his inquisition as we pull away from the curb.

I have to think, it all happened so fast. "He was average, everything about him was average: height, weight, and looks. "

"Okay, how old do you think he was?"

I close my eyes to try and picture the guy, "He was maybe in his thirties."

As I glance at Max in the rear-view mirror, I can see such intensity in his eyes. He's focusing on every detail. "What exactly did he say to you?"

I see real concern on his face and I wonder what this is really about. "He didn't, he was having words with Marco when I stepped outside the gym. He saw me, snapped my picture, and then left without another word."

Before I know it we arrive at my apartment, and head upstairs. We find Marco isn't home yet. "Marco should be home soon, if you want to wait for him."

Max just nods. "You have a nice home."

I look around and smile. "Thank you. Would you like a cup of tea?"

He busies himself, looking at all my window and door locks, seemingly inspecting the security quality. "Sure," he replies.

I fix tea and then start to pull out my work. "Would you mind if I grade papers while you wait? A teacher's work is never really done."

He laughs, "That's no problem, Miss Raven. Would you like some help grading them?"

I will take help anytime when it comes to grading papers. "That would be great."

As we sit there, I study Max; I find him very interesting. He has a very heavy, British accent, where Jax's accent is only heavy when he's drinking or having sex. Max is shorter of the two, he keeps his hair short, and he always seems to have a five o'clock shadow with hints of grey in it.

"How long have you worked for Jax?"

He is very focused on the papers but glances up at me. "I've been employed by Jax for eight years."

I know Jax is thirty-three. "How old are you?" He gives me his attention again and I realize he has very light, pale-blue eyes.

He laughs, "Probably older than you think." And with that, the conversation was over.

After about an hour, all the papers are done and Marco comes strolling in. "Oh, hey, baby girl, didn't know you had company."

"Marco, this is Max, he does security for Jax and he has some questions for you about the reporter the other night." I inform him after introducing.

As they shake hands, I can see each one, eyeing the other up, not saying anything.

"Hi, Marco, I need to know what he said to you?"

Marco takes a deep breath. "He asked if I knew Raven and I asked what it was to him, he said *'I can get to them at any time.'* Then Raven stepped out, he snapped her picture, and ran away."

Max is pacing, he seems to do that a lot. "Did you notice if he had any identifying marks, such as: tattoos, scars, or maybe an accent?"

Marco shakes his head. "No, nothing. He was just creepy... should we be worried?"

"Jax takes security very seriously, I'm sure he will talk to Miss Raven about this later," he replies, walking back over to us. He shakes Marco's hand, turns, and wishes us a good evening before heading out the door.

Marco greets me with a giant smile. "Well, that was interesting to come home to, and . . . what a hunk of a security guy."

I roll my eyes, "I swear you have sex on the brain all the frigging time!"

He cocks an eyebrow at me. "Hey, the guy is very built, very good-looking... kind of Daniel Craig like, and he has a frigging accent! Of course I have sex on the brain!"

Marco is right, Max could very easily pass for Daniel Craig, maybe it's the whole security and James Bond thing. "Marco, all I did was go on a date. Now I'm being hounded by the press and have extra security at my school!"

"So Jax put extra security at the school?" He glances up from flipping through the mail on the table.

I gather up all my papers, "Yeah, just a couple of dates and now this!"

"Yeah, dates, with the most eligible bachelor in the world, who is also on Forbes billionaire list for the *4th year* in a row, I might add. You don't get like that and not make some enemies along the way, you know."

I glance at my watch, "Marco, if we leave now, we can still make it to our kickboxing class."

"Okay, but then we are going for drinks," he demands. I nod in agreement and we grab our gear, then head out.

CLASS WAS BRUTAL TONIGHT but I really needed to get out some frustration and the bag is the best place for that. After we shower and change at the gym, we find a little Cuban bar that has wonderful tapas and are seated in a nice quiet booth, toward the back.

"So how do you feel about Jax?" Marco asks.

I have to laugh. "Well, just start off with a bang, why don't you? I really like him, Marco, a lot, but I feel like I'm out of my league with him. He's just so much, that's really the only way I can explain him and it scares me. I know I'm going to get hurt, I'm going to fall hard—*oh fuck*, who am I kidding? I've already fallen hard and I don't want it to end."

He rubs my hand. "Baby girl, you need to trust yourself; you're a good person who has a lot to offer someone, so don't sell yourself short."

"You have to say that because you're my best friend."

He hugs me. "No, I'm saying that because it's the truth."

I study his face and I know what he's going to say, but I have to ask.

"You think I should tell him about the adoption . . . why?"

He takes a sip of his wine and waits before he answers my question. Almost like he is I processing his thoughts. "Raven, he needs to know. And if he is a keeper, you'll know . . . when he doesn't run."

"Maybe I'm the one who needs to be running, with all the threats and the spotlight."

He shakes his head. "No, baby girl, maybe it's finally time you *stop* running." We head back to the apartment in silence. I don't know, maybe I can be the more that Jax is looking for. We get upstairs and I head into my room to get ready for bed. As I brush my teeth I glance at my tiny shower. I would love to be in that shower in Jax's Ivory Tower. That shower was kick ass and so was the man I was in it with. I'm exhausted and head straight to bed.

I STROLL UP TO Starbucks and there he is, just like clockwork. "You don't have to meet me here every morning."

He brushes my lips with his then leans in and grates his teeth along my earlobe. "You're right—I don't have to, but I want to and I only do what I want, not what anyone else thinks I should."

"Oh," I whisper.

He grazes his teeth up my jaw to my ear, "Yeah, *oh*." He gives me a slow, sensual kiss, and then he's done. And just like that, I'm speechless. "Don't forget our date tonight, sweetheart." Forget the date? I'm still trying to pick my scrambled brains up off the ground!

"I won't forget, and thanks for the coffee and for Mick's breakfast. He may not say it but he appreciates it." He gives me that crooked smirk and then he's off with Max, not too far behind him.

I cross the street and give Mick his breakfast. "Thank you, Raven."

"Mick, walk with me to school." As we walk I ask him, "What can I do to help you move forward?" I know he is a good guy who has been to hell and back. He deserves a hand, and it's the least I can do. He's quiet, and I know this is hard for him. "Mick, let's sit for a bit, I'm early." We sit on the bench outside the school.

Mick's eyes wander, seemingly taking the surroundings in. "Raven, why is there more security at the school?"

Wow, nothing gets by him. "There have been some threats to Michael, and Jax wants to make sure he is safe," I answer.

After a few minutes of silence, "You, just being here and listening to me, are all the help I can handle right now. I will keep an eye on the school grounds, too—just to make sure."

I hug him. "Mick, you're a wonderful guy and someday, you'll realize it. I have to go in, the bell is going to ring. Have a great day." I look back over my shoulder and see that he stays put on the bench, watching the grounds and the kids running into the building.

When I get inside, I find two dozen of the Abracadabra Roses; they are so unusual and I can't help but stare at them. I pull out the card:

*You render me speechless.
Looking at you takes my breath
away.*

Your Jax xo

Well, I could say the same about him, too, that's for sure. I bring them to the classroom and the smell fills the room.

"Wow, Raven, they are so beautiful; very different." Jackie gapes at them.

I smile. "I know. Oh, Jackie, I'm really falling hard for this guy."

She smiles at me while smelling the roses. "Just approach the relationship with an open mind and an open heart." What did I ever do to have such great friends? Jackie, Marco, and even Mick are always worrying about me.

"You're such a great friend, Jackie." I hug her quickly before turning my attention to my students walking in.

THE DAY WENT BY smoothly and I rush to finish my after-class work. I decide to surprise Jax at Raiders, Inc. As I head to his building, I realize I know so little about this man. I walk in and ask the guard, "What floor is Jaxson Phillips' office?"

"Is he expecting you?"

I look up at him. "No, it was going to be a surprise."

He raises one eyebrow, looking at me like I'm a nut—who knows how many other women have tried getting into his office? "Mr. Phillips does not do surprises." I give him my ID and he rings Max. "Sir, I have a Miss Raven Anderson here, she says she is trying to surprise Mr. Phillips. Yes, of course, sir." I don't know what Max tells him but he immediately gives me a visitor pass and escorts me to the bank of elevators.

"What floor, sir?"

He holds the door for me. "I've been instructed to escort you up, Miss Anderson, top floor." When we get to the top, I thank him. He nods and the elevator doors close behind him.

I look around, taking in my surroundings and notice everything is glass. Everywhere I look, there is a view to die for; how does this man get any work done? There is a bevy of beautiful women at the reception area and they are all staring at me. I think this was a bad idea. I feel very inadequate, in comparison to them. Just as I decide to bail, a man walks up to me and introduces himself as Duke Jenson, Jax's assistant. "Hello, Miss Anderson, Mr. Fleming has instructed me to escort you to Mr. Phillips' office." He has a familiarity about him, but then I see Jax and I lose all reason.

"Hey, sweetheart, this is a nice surprise. What brings you here?"

I look at this man and I'm amazed; he is so beautiful. "I finished work early and I thought I would surprise you. It looks like you're busy."

He opens his arms for me. "I am never too busy for my beautiful girl." He pulls me close to him and I give him one of those toe-curling kisses that he always gives me. I'm sure all eyes are on us now.

"Wow, what did I do to deserve that?"

I stare into those deep, blue eyes and I could just melt right here. "Well, honestly, you rendered me speechless this morning with a wonderful cup of coffee and a kiss that blew me away. Then I get to school and there are two dozen of those beautiful roses, waiting for me. I thought I would brighten your day like you do mine."

We walk into his office and I'm blown away, I still don't know how he can get anything done with that view! I turn back around towards the door and lock it. He watches me, totally speechless. "Jax, tell your assistant to hold all your calls."

He walks to his desk and pushes a button on his phone, "Duke, I do not want to be disturbed for the next hour."

I pull him into one of the club chairs and he stares at me, intently. "I have decided I want to have my way with you. Please sit back and let me have a little fun."

He has the most beautiful smile on his face and his baby blues are twinkling. I flash him an eager and sultry smile. I get down on my knees, between his legs and keep my eyes locked on his. I brush my hand up his cock to undo his belt and he sucks in a breath. *He's really hard.* I find my prize and slowly work the head of his velvet cock. He has a white-knuckle grip on the chair—*oh, yeah, I've got him.* I run my fingertips up and down his *V.* He closes his eyes and tries to steady his breath. "Eyes on me, Jax."

His eye's lock onto mine; violet to blues. I want him to watch so he will always remember this moment. Slowly I dip my head down, licking the tip of his beautiful cock and never taking my eyes from his. My hair is loose and draped over to one side. His lips part and his tongue starts to slowly stroke them while I swirl my tongue around his massive cock head. I lick the vein all the way to the base and back up again. He just watches me, not saying anything. His breathing speeds up. I swirl around the top again, then I put my lips around his cock and go all the way down. I relax my gag reflex to take him even further and that's when he lets out a strangled moan. *Oh yeah, he's coming undone.* He has both hands wrapped around my head. I'm sure he's trying not to pound into me but once my hand finds the underside of his sac, he loses all control. His grip tightens as I go deeper. When I reach the head of his cock, I bare my teeth. Just like that he comes endlessly and I swallow every drop. He finally pulls me off of him and drags me up onto his lap. Even after what I have just done, he kisses me.

"You're so beautiful. This was a great way to release stress." He runs his thumbs up and down both my cheeks.

"Well, I know there is so much going on and you're worried about

Michael, so I just wanted to lighten your day."

He looks at me, smiling like a Cheshire cat. "I think I can get the rest of my work done now, or I can call it a day and take you home. I could make love to you day and night but it still wouldn't be enough." He gifts me with his beautiful smile.

"I would love that, but I have to run now. I have a class at the gym."

He gives me a look like a wounded puppy. "What class?"

I'm going to see him tonight so I can't give in, even though I want to.

"I go to the gym two days a week for Pilates and two days a week for kick boxing. One day a week I try different things. This week its Krav Maga."

He leans in and kisses me softly. "Okay, I'll bring Epson salts tonight," he laughs. We both fix our attire before he walks me to the elevators. All eyes are on us, but he's only looking at me.

JAX IS AT MY place at exactly seven, that's good, because I'm starving. "I brought all the stuff to cook in tonight."

I panic, "That's nice, except I don't cook, so I have no pots, pans, or anything."

He laughs hysterically at me. I'm so glad that I'm his source of amusement. "Yeah, I figured that, so I came prepared." He wasn't joking. Max walks in, just then, with half of Bloomingdales' kitchen department! He gives me the Epson salts and shoos me to the tub for a much needed soak. Wow, I really needed this—every part of my body feels bruised. I put some music on, close my eyes, and relax. I recently put some new music on my iPod, everything from Ellie Goulding to Florence + The Machine. I close my eyes and sing along. After a nice long soak, I put on my robe and head to the living room. He pours me a glass of wine, and I sit back and watch the man work. "Sweetheart, I must tell you, I love your singing!"

Oh crap! I must have been singing loud enough for him to hear! "You weren't supposed to be listening, and stop smirking at me. A real gentleman would never smirk at a woman's singing."

He comes around the counter and pulls me into his arms. He pulls my ponytail back so I'm looking into his eyes; violet to blues. "Sweetheart, I could listen to your singing all day long." He reaches down and gently kisses my lips, nibbling and swiping his tongue across them. He searches my eyes and I want him right now! He lifts me up and I wrap my legs around his waist. He's hard as stone and I can't help but whimper. Just as he's about to lift me onto the counter, Marco comes flying through the door and I swear his chin hits the ground. I can't help but laugh at him. Jax lifts me into the chair and whispers, "We'll finish this later, sweetheart."

"Don't worry, Marco. I'm making enough for you to eat, too."

Marco grabs a glass of wine and sits next to me. "Have you guys thought about what you're going to say to Michael?"

Jax puts his wine glass down and cocks his head. "What do you mean, mate?"

He eyes us both. "You're dating his teacher, which is every boy's fantasy. You need to tell him something."

I look at them both, "I never thought about it."

"Babe, it's every guy's wet dream to have a teacher, that looks like you and then—"

"—Enough!" I silence him before he can continue. I can't have that visual stuck in my head!" They both have that faraway look. *Oh, my God, what the hell are they thinking?*

"Don't worry, Raven, I'll talk to my sister and see how she wants to handle it."

We all begin to eat and the food is fantastic: chicken franchisee, roasted new potatoes, and a salad. Marco grins at Jax and declares his new found love for him. It probably has to do with the cooking.

"Marco, were you born in New York?"

He shakes his head. "No, I was born and raised in Washington, D.C. What about you, I hear a slight accent."

Jax smiles. "I was born in Wales and lived there until I was thirteen. Which is when we moved to New York. Where were you born, Raven?" Jax asks me before taking another sip of wine.

Oh shit, I'm not ready for this conversation. I glance at Marco, hoping he can help me. "Raven and I grew up together in D.C.," he pipes up. *Okay.* I let out the breath I was holding. If Jax noticed my panic, I'm not sure. A nice espresso and pastry for desert, and I'm officially stuffed.

Marco excuses himself, leaving us alone. We get up from the table, not worrying about the dishes, and head into the living room to snuggle up on the couch. No stress; just us.

"Why did your family move to the States?" I ask as his thumb traces circles on my arm.

"There were more opportunities here, and the people didn't judge my mum for being a single parent."

I know I should tell him and this would be a good time, but I'm not ready.

"What made you and Marco decide on New York instead of D.C.?"

I've rehearsed this answer so many times that after a while, I started to believe it myself. "We both liked the East Coast and city life. It just seemed logical that New York should be home for us. After college, I applied for a job here, and Marco followed. Jackie came about three months later. Jackie and I were roommates in college."

Jax's phone rings and he excuses himself to get it. He looks at me as he's speaking to someone. "Okay, I'm on my way."

"I had a wonderful time, but I have to go. I'm sorry. Something came up. Can we get together Friday?"

I shake my head, "I can on Saturday. Friday night, Jackie and I are going out." I don't always want to be available, but who am I kidding? I am. He starts stroking his chin, a sure sign he's deep in thought.

"If that's my only option, then okay." He leans in and gently kisses my lips, slow and softly. I moan and he's all over me, our tongues doing a sexual dance, his hands are roaming my body. We pull apart and I want more, so much more. "I'll leave you with that. Since, you're busy on Friday, we'll have to continue this on Saturday." Just like that, he's out the door.

J axson

"MAX, WE NEED TO get to my sister's house right away. Michael called, he got another threat that he says we need to see," I order before

I'm barely in the car.

"Jax, when the hell did this happen?" he asks, speeding off as soon as he starts the engine up.

"Just now, I think."

Michael is already outside when we pull up to his house. "This must be serious if you're outside, waiting for me."

The look on his face is not good. "Look, Jax, first, I had to tell your sister since she got the envelope before I could intercept it."

Michael hands it to me. Inside is a picture of Raven taken outside her gym with a note that says, *"No one is out of my reach, ever."*

Max grabs the envelope, reading it before he shifts his eyes to Michael. "How was this delivered to Bella?"

Michael opens the door, "I'll let you ask her yourself, come in."

Bella is sitting in the living room, staring into space. Max puts the envelope down in front of her, "Bella, how was this delivered?" he asks.

Her eyes snap back into focus and she stares at the picture. "Max, I never heard anything, but Vito was barking. I went out to see why, and it was at the front door. I never saw anything. Why wasn't I told about the other threats? Why was I not aware that my brother is dating my son's teacher? Why does everyone feel it's okay to keep me in the fucking dark?!"

My sister is really pissed off and I'm not sure if it's at me, Michael, or both of us. "Bella, where is Junior?"

Michael steps up, "He's fine, Jax. He's upstairs watching *Doctor Who.*"

Bella turns to me. "Jax, what about Mum and Raven? Are they aware?"

I shake my head, "No, we weren't sure if the threats were real, and it all happened very quickly."

She glares at me, "Why did you take Raven to the charity function on Saturday? It's so high profile. You never do that."

No matter what I do, I'm always fucked. "I didn't find out about the threats until Tuesday. I try to keep my personal life private, but with all the latest acquisitions, it seems the public wants to know my every move. Bella, if I go out, you yell at me. If I don't, you yell at me!"

Max grabs my arm. "Jax, did you know Raven was adopted?"

Well, that floored me. "No, but apparently you do. What else do you know?"

"Not much. Her adoption records are marked as classified, which is really strange. She did have an abusive boyfriend. He beat her pretty badly before she was able to get a restraining order against him."

I feel like I'm in a bloody pinball game that just keeps tilting. "Jax, I take it by the look on your face that you didn't know any of this?"

I take a steadying breath. "She mentioned an ex, but not to that extent. Tonight, at dinner, we talked about where we were born and grew up. I told her we were originally from Wales. Marco said he was from D.C. When I asked Raven, Marco said they grew up together. However, Raven told me that she met Marco while volunteering at a shelter. She said his parents threw him out when he told them he was gay. She told me her mum died when she was fifteen and she left home right after that."

I didn't think I needed to share with everyone why she left home—after all, it was her story to tell. "Max, do you think Raven could be the target in all of this, or is it me? Now that they have seen us in public together, does she have a target on her back?"

Max starts pacing. "My first thought would be that she is just collateral damage in this. However, the adoption thing is making my hair stand on end." I know when he paces, he's processing information, but right now, it's fucking driving me nuts. I thank God when he stops.

"Do you think we need to bring her in on what's happening? I'm sure if I ask her directly, she would tell me, at least, I'd like to think so."

"What do you know about her roommate Marco?" Michael furrows his brows at me.

"I ran a background check on him at the same time I ran one on Raven and he's clean. Very protective of Raven, though. However, he just showed up one day."

First, I find out my girl is adopted and it's classified, and now, I find out her roommate just showed up one day! What the fuck?! Michael and Bella are both staring at me, probably waiting for me to lose it. I get up and grab Max's arm. "What do you mean, he *just* showed up one day?"

"Look, Jax, I don't like this anymore than you do. It's seems like they didn't meet until she left home. He's older than she is, so they didn't go to school together or even grow up in the same neighborhood. He just suddenly appeared in her life one day."

Max finally stops pacing. "Jax, I think for now, we should put extra security on everyone, and we need to find out from Raven about the adoption. I just feel like it's a missing piece of the puzzle."

I need answers and I need to keep everyone safe. "All right, but I want to talk to her about it myself—alone."

Bella grabs my arm, "Jax, are you going to call and tell Mum what's going on?"

The last thing I want to deal with right now is my mum. "Not just yet, Bella, I'm not even sure myself what the fuck is going on!"

Chapter Seven

Jaxson

I GET TO THE office early after trying to catch Raven at Starbucks. She never showed up there this morning but after racing to her school, I discovered she went in early. At least—for now—she's safe. "Everything okay, sir?" Duke asks, pulling me out of my thoughts.

"You're early today." I snap. I'm pissed, but I don't want to take it out on my employees.

"Yes, I just have some paperwork to catch up on. Can you get my sister on the line, please?"

"She's already in your office, waiting for you."

Wow, I wonder if she is going to rip into me, yet again. I head into my office and prepare myself to deal with Bella. "Hey, you're here early."

She gets up and hugs me, "Cut the bullshit, Jax, you really like her a lot, don't you?"

Bella and I can read each other like an open book, so I can't bullshit her.

"Why wouldn't she tell me something so simple, like being adopted? Does she think I would think less of her?"

"No, Jax, I really don't think so. Anyone who knows you would know you're not that kind of person. That's why I think there is much more to the story than we know. Did you go talk to her this morning?"

I sit in one of the chairs, remembering Raven on her knees, and fuck, I'm hard again! "I tried to catch her for coffee but she was already in school."

Bella looks at her watch. "I was so preoccupied last night, I almost forgot parent teacher conferences are today and tomorrow."

Well, at least I know Raven's not running away from me for a change. "What time is your meeting with her?"

She gets up and heads toward the door. "In an hour, so I have to go. I know, don't say anything, but you better get to the bottom of this and quick, oh and call Mum, please."

I don't want to make that call but Bella leaves me no choice. She is right, Mum needs to hear it from *me* about what is going on. The problem is that, I have *no* idea what the fuck is going on! Bella gives me a final wave before heading out. I take a deep breath as I pick up the phone and dial Mum, knowing I'm going to get an earful. I'm surprised she hasn't just shown up here and taken me to task for putting extra guards on her without telling her. She must be pissed. She answers on the first ring, and usually, I can't even get her to answer the fucking phone!

"Hey, Mum, how are you?" I take a deep breath, and wait for the storm—my mother.

"Don't you give me that *how are you* stuff, I already know that something is not right. If you were here, I'd box your ears, lad."

I can never get anything past this woman. "Mum, you need to calm down. I put extra security on everyone because there've been some pictures and notes that I'm concerned about."

Wow, she's growling? This is a first. "Jaxson James Phillips, when did all of this happen and why am I just finding out now?"

When she uses my middle name, I know I'm in deep shit. "Now, Mum, remember your high blood pressure."

Probably not a good idea to mention that. "Don't even think of going there, son. There's no need for you to remind me about my blood pressure. Just tell me everything, from the beginning. Maybe if you'd done that already, we wouldn't have to worry about my pressure."

My mum and I are very close. I don't have a problem telling her everything I know about Raven or about the different pictures and threats. She's been very quiet since I've finished. "Mum, are you there?"

"Yes, son, I'm just surprised. First, that you have kept me in the dark about the threats—you usually tell me everything. And second, that you have finally met someone that holds your interest for more than five minutes and this is how I find out about her. Really? I understand your need to protect us; you've always felt like it was your duty to keep us safe. But you need to keep Isabella and me informed about what's going on. We're not helpless women."

I know they are capable of taking care of themselves, but it's not easy for me to give up that kind of control. I've watched over them my whole life. "I know, but it's just hard for me. I want to keep everyone safe. And after getting burned by Erica, I never thought I would be vulnerable again. I'm at such a loss with Raven. She makes me crazy mad and then crazy happy. She runs from me, *a lot*, and I don't understand why." Maybe she can shed some light on this, because I sure can't.

"I raised you and Isabella to be direct and honest. Have you asked her, point blank, why she runs?"

I laugh, "Of course, and she said I'm intense and too much. Mum, I don't think I'm like that."

Now it's my mum who's laughing. "Son, life is not rainbows, fields of flowers, and butterflies. Its compromise, and unfortunately, you're not very good at that. I think it is time I met my grandson's teacher."

Oh, crap. "Mum, can you just try and go easy on her? She has already pulled a runner more times then I like to admit to." I know that no matter how much I protest, she'll just do whatever she feels she should. We hang up, and I know, for sure now, that I'm so screwed.

Raven

MY NEXT PARENT IS Mrs. Vizzano, Michael Jr's mom. She is as beautiful as her brother. This is going to be awkward. "Hi, Mrs. Vizzano, please, have a seat."

"Please, call me Bella. I have to ask, have you figured out what you're going to tell Michael Jr about you and Jax?"

This family is amazing. Everyone is so open and direct with each other. "Well, I can see that you and Jax are very much alike; you both jump right in," I laugh.

"I'm not one to beat around the bush, and neither is Jax."

I'm embarrassed that I'm involved with a student's relative, but I have to deal with this. "I have never dated someone related to one of my students, so I'm at a loss. Do you have any suggestions?" I'm hoping she has some ideas.

"I spoke to my husband about it and he started saying something about every boy's wet dream. I just cut him off," she giggles.

"Yeah, Jax and my roommate, Marco, started in on that and I cut them off, too. Guess it's a guy thing. Bella, I will do whatever you think is best for, Michael."

"I think we should just tell him you and Jax are friends and leave it at that. Sometimes if you make more about it, then it becomes a problem," she suggests.

I like her; she doesn't pull any punches. "Okay, I agree with you. As far as school, Michael is doing great. He struggles a little with math, but my co-teacher, Jackie, has been working with a small group of boys on mental math. It seems to be helping." I show her some of Michael's papers.

"If you think he needs a tutor, let me know."

I love it when parents take an active role in their children's education. So many just think the work is done when the school bell rings. "He is a very sweet boy and pleasure to have in class. He's very respectful of others and tender hearted."

She smiles. "Thank you, his dad is away a lot so sometimes Jax has to step in to help. We are a very close-knit family."

I wonder how much influence Jax has had with Michael. "Well, it shows. He's a great little boy."

After Bella leaves, I only have one more conference and then I am done for the day.

I PACK UP AND head home. As I round the corner to my building, I see Jax leaning against the car. Damn, he's beautiful. I can't help myself; I just stop and take him in. He's wearing a fitted, charcoal-grey suit with a dark, violet shirt and a frigging bow tie!

"Hey," I reach up to kiss him, taking note of his stolid expression. "Are you okay?"

"We need to talk. Is Marco home?" His eyes burn through me.

I shake my head, "No, he won't be home for, at least, two hours. Come on up."

As we head upstairs, I can tell he's upset. We are barely in the door, and he spins me around. "Why are you hiding the fact that you're adopted?"

I almost laugh, thinking, yeah, he is just like Bella, but then it hits me—*he knows.* "How do you know? I never mentioned it." He probably had Max run a check on me!

"This showed up last night." He shows me the picture that was taken outside the gym, with a threat. "I had to have Max run a check on you. You need to understand, I am high profile and with that, comes a whole lot of shit. Why are your records sealed and marked classified? Raven, what are you hiding?"

Clearly, he is really pissed off. But I think I should be the one who's pissed off. He can't just invade my privacy like that. "Jax, please leave."

He glares at me. "What? You're just going to throw me out—without an explanation? You need to know that I put security on you and Marco, as well as my whole family. You're going to have to tell me *what the fuck* is going on!"

I understand that he is worried and upset, but this is private. "Jax, this is a very private matter for me and the only one who knows all the details is Marco. I don't know if telling you is the right thing to do. It may put you in more danger."

He searches my eyes for the answers, I think. "Just tell me. We will deal with it together. I have a lot of resources at my disposal." He doesn't move, and I realize he's not leaving until he knows everything. Maybe Marco is right. Maybe it's time to share this with him. If he is a keeper, he won't run for the hills.

"Okay, Jax. I was born in California. My mother was a heart surgeon and my father was an FBI agent. I was seven-years-old when I was kidnapped."

Jaxson

I FREEZE AT THE word *kidnapped*. I'm feeling dumbfounded, not believing what I'm hearing. I step closer towards her, still in disbelief. "Oh, sweetheart, please don't stop now, not when you're on a roll."

She sits down and takes a deep breath. "At first, the FBI thought I was kidnapped because of something that my father might have been working on, but as it turned out, it had to do with my mother. She was a top heart surgeon, who had just perfected some new technique, that could possibly save the life of a very bad person. That person was the head of a Chicago Mafia crime family. I was being held so that my mother would perform the surgery."

Raven

I LOOK UP AT Jax and he raises an eyebrow at me, so, I continue. "In the process of all this, my father and his partner, Joseph Adessi, were able to rescue me. During the rescue, my father was shot. He lingered for two weeks in ICU before he died. My mother performed the surgery but the man didn't make it. My mother felt she sent my father to his death, and she killed herself. I was left in the care of Joseph. He brought me to Washington D.C. to live with him. Joseph didn't feel like I was safe, and after speaking with the director of the FBI, they agreed that I was young enough to be adopted and have a total name change. I was a very scared seven-year-old. I stopped talking and turned inward, trusting no one. I was entered into the Witness Protection Program and sent to live in a private boarding school in England. Eventually, a very nice family adopted me. They put me into therapy, and I was able to put the past behind me and move forward. That was, until, my adopted mother died from breast cancer. Well, then you know the rest. Oh, and while we're at full disclosure, my father and mother had a lot of insurance, which Joseph invested for me, so I'm a very wealthy woman.

His face turns to stone. "So when you and Marco were supposedly living on the streets, you really weren't?"

I shake my head, "No. I used some of the money for a small apartment that Marco and I lived in until I went to college. Now if you're done, can you please leave?"

His eyes cut me to the core. "Oh no, sweetheart, I'm not going anywhere, and we are far from done here. How did you meet Marco? He is older than you, so I know it wasn't in high school."

I take some steady breaths. "I told you, I met Marco when I was volunteering at a shelter. I would go help out one day a week. It made me feel like I had some sort of family. He was also a volunteer there and we just clicked."

His eyes search mine. "Max ran a check on Marco and he has no past until he showed up with you one day."

Marco and I never talked about any of his past, we only look forward. "I told you, I met him at the shelter. Prior to that, I don't know what he was doing. I just know he was always there for me."

He takes my hand. "What's your real name?"

Another deep breath and I'll be done. "My real name is Cara Josephina Giaconna. I have not said that out loud in twenty years." I get up and head toward the door. "Now, I think you should leave."

He's not budging. "I told you, sweetheart, I'm not going anywhere. I still have questions. Why do you think I should leave? Why didn't you tell me any of this sooner? How much does the school know about your past?"

I turn to him, "I want you to leave because my brain is on overload right now. I didn't tell you sooner because I really didn't know you, and I didn't think I would see you again after the first time I ran. The school knows nothing. My past is buried very deeply. I did nothing wrong but be born to parents who wanted to help right the wrongs in the world. I've suffered enough, now will you leave?"

He follows me to the door, takes a hold of my hand, but he's not moving. "Raven, I told you, you don't get to decide what I can and can't handle. I'm capable of that all on my own. How do you know there isn't a money trail?"

Another question. I just want this to be over. "Because Joseph made sure that nothing could ever be linked back to me."

He runs his hands through his hair, and strokes his chin. His wheels are definitely turning! "How do you know that Joseph can be trusted?"

I put my hand on his shoulder and look into his eyes. "Well, I have to trust someone, and my father trusted him with my life. He's now the Director of the FBI."

"That doesn't mean he can be trusted. Does he know what your adopted father tried to do to you? What about your ex-boyfriend beating you up, does he know about that?"

I shake my head. "No, I didn't turn to him. I felt he did enough and I needed to stand on my own two feet."

He paces and starts at his chin again. "There have been threats to my mum, sister, nephew, and now, you. Do you think this has to do with your past?"

I throw my hands up, "Jax, I honestly don't know. I don't think so. I mean, after all this time, why now? What has changed?"

I watch him fist his hands. His jaw begins to tick. I can tell he's losing any calm he had. "Raven, being in the spotlight with me could be what has changed. If I would have known, I would have never put you in that position, but I guess it's too late for that now!"

He reaches for the doorknob and I know he's pissed off, but then he turns to me. "I need time to process all this and then figure out our next step. In the meantime, I've put guards on everyone; I'm not taking any chances." He pulls me close to him and I just melt; he smells wonderfully of vanilla and spice.

"I'm not running for the hills, so you're just going to have to get use to me being here, and you're not running. either. Done! I need open, honest communication—at all times. If you're scared, tell me, but *no more fucking running!*"

Just as he leans in to kiss me, the door flies open and Marco comes barrelling in. "Why do you have one of your people following me?"

Marco looks as if he's ready to bust a gut. "Calm down, have a seat, and let me fill you in. Marco, I told Jax everything."

He is looking back and forth from Jax to me like a Ping-Pong ball. "Oh."

"I received another threat. It was attached to the picture of Raven, outside the gym, the other night. I'm not taking any chances, so I added extra security, until we can get to the bottom of this."

Marco's eyes grow wide. Maybe he's shocked, that I told Jax everything. "Do you think it has anything to do with Raven's parents?"

Jax shrugs. "I honestly don't know. I've made my share of enemies in my business. Nothing would surprise me, but I'm not about to take any chances." He pulls me close.

Marco gets up. "I'll give you both some space."

Jax shakes his head, "It's okay, Marco, I need to get going. I want to talk to Max and see if he's found out anything new." He leans down and gives me a long, soft kiss. "I will see you for coffee, in the morning." It was not a request, it was an order. He leans in and rubs his nose up the side of my neck, kissing along it with little flutters. He takes my hand and kisses my wrist, and I feel a jolt right down to my toes. I'm lost. He turns and leaves me a jumbled mess.

Marco gets up, pulls out the brandy, and pours us each a drink. He hands me a glass, "This is just fucked up on so many levels," he spits, looking as if he's about ready to blow a gasket.

"Raven can you say something? Because right now, I want to scream!"

Like I don't? I want to bury my head in the sand! "Don't you think I want to scream, too? But what good would it do? I can't change what has happened. If I could, I would go back twenty years to that awful day. Maybe I just need to walk away while my heart is still intact and before someone gets hurt."

He snorts at me, "That's bullshit. If you want this man, then fight for him. If you want a safe and happy life, then fight for it, but don't fucking sit there and do nothing."

I hate it when he's right. I'm just tired, really tired of all the bullshit. "Marco, do you think Jax and I have a chance at making this work?"

He hugs me. "Baby girl, if you want him bad enough, then yes. The ball is in your court."

I give him a hug. "I love you, but I'm just too tired right now—both mentally and physically—to deal with another thing." I cross my arms, rubbing them up and down. "Listen, I'm going to bed; I've got a lot to think about."

"That you do, baby girl." He puts his glass in the sink then wraps his arms around me for a hug. "Hopefully, you'll have everything figured out in the morning. Goodnight." And with that, he kisses the top of my head and sends me off.

AS MUCH AS SLEEP was hard coming last night, my exhausted body finally took over only to be greeted by morning too quickly. I head out the door to meet Jax at Starbucks. I'm happy to see him waiting with my coffee. Every time I see him, I am rendered speechless. He is just so beautiful, yet he doesn't flash it. He's wearing a black suit, black shirt, and a deep violet bow tie. I can't help but stare. My eyes keep traveling up and down his muscular body. He spots me and then gifts me with that crooked smile and his twinkling blue eyes; I'm done.

He walks up to me, "Are you enjoying the view?"

I reach up and adjust his tie. "Well, you already know the answer to that question. I have to say, I'm really surprised you wear bowties."

He hands me my coffee and smiles. "Well, if it's good for the *Doctor*, then who am I to argue?"

I have no clue what he's talking about. "Sorry, Jax, you lost me. What doctor?"

He actually has a look of disbelief on his face. "Raven, please don't tell me you've never heard of *Doctor Who*? Because this could be a big problem for us."

"Sorry, Jax, I've never heard of *Doctor Who*."

He's really very shocked. "Okay, Raven, I'm going to have to educate you. We need to have a *Doctor Who* marathon."

It must be some sort of television show, but I hardly watch any television. "Whatever you say, Jax. On another note, have you learned anything new since last night?"

His grip tightens on me at the mention of the threats. "Max has been in touch with Joseph. Apparently, when Max started looking into your past it sent a red flag for Joseph. Add to that, Michael contacting the FBI and Interpol when the first threats came in, and I can assure you, Joseph is very aware of the situation now." He sighs. "I'm going to sit down with the local FBI field agents and run through my business to see if something shakes loose. In the meantime, just be smart and don't take any chances." He leans in for a kiss, and I can't help but feel sad—my past might be responsible for all his trouble. "I'll pick you up this afternoon, after school."

I don't want him to worry about me. "Jax, you don't have to pick me up. I'll be fine. Just focus on getting to the bottom of this."

Oh holy hell, he's growling again! "Just, please, do what I tell you without any running away. I couldn't handle it if something happened to you, so just humor me, okay?"

I kiss him softly, "Okay, whatever."

The smirk is back. "Thank you."

MAX SHOWS UP TO take me to school. "Max, do you think I need protecting, or is Jax just over reacting?" I inquire as we stroll down the street. I see the stress on this man, and it worries me.

"Miss Raven, it can't hurt to be careful," he offers. This can't possibly be because of my parents. That was twenty years ago.

I decide to ask him anyway, "Do you think this is happening because of my parents?"

He's, seemingly, lost in his thoughts. "I honestly don't know, but what I do know is, Jax won't stop until he has all the answers."

As we walk together, I decide to try to pump him for some information about Jax. "How did you and Jax meet?"

He just smiles at me—which is not something I'm used to seeing from this man. "That, Miss Raven, is a tale for another day." Just like that, he's done.

JAX GETS STUCK AT work so he sends Max to pick me up. I let him know that Jackie and I are going shopping and then for drinks. Before we do this, I have to lose Max. It's ridiculous that he is following me around the city.

I call Jax and get his assistant, Duke. "Sorry, Miss Anderson, but he's in a meeting. Can I give him a message?" *He never puts me through to Jax.*

"Just tell him I'll meet him later at home." Before I can say any more, he thanks me and hangs up.

Losing Max is not as easy as I thought, but the sales lady lets us slip, out back, after we changed into our new outfits for clubbing. Jackie grabs my arm gently, "Why are we doing this?"

"Really, Jackie, I just want to go out for a few drinks and have fun. I don't need or want a bodyguard following me around town. Jax might be high profile, but I'm just a second grade teacher. Besides, I told Jax we were going out, and sending his bodyguard with us is like having a babysitter!"

"Raven, I wouldn't mind him following me," she admits.

I give her a once-over. Yep, there it is; *the look.* I can't believe I didn't notice this before. "Oh really, you like Max?"

She's blushing! "Well he's rugged, extremely handsome, and very *James Bond* looking, so what's not to like?"

I have to laugh. Everyone thinks Max is Bond. "Marco thinks he looks like Daniel Craig."

She gasps, "Oh, please tell me Marco's not after him, I would just die."

I can't believe she's really interested in him. "No, I don't think Max is gay, but I can ask Jax."

"*No*, I would die of embarrassment," she squeals, putting her hand to her chest.

I can't help but laugh. "Come on, girl, let's have fun."

We head down to the Village and find a really cute club with some of the most interesting people. I can just sit and watch people all night long, especially in the Village. Oh, the sights! I'm such a lightweight drinker, but Jackie has me drinking something called a *Bushwhacker.* It is heaven: Kahlua, rum, coconut milk, and ice, blended together, in a frozen cup. The entire inside of the cup is drizzled with chocolate syrup. The syrup is drizzled on top, as well, for the final touch. I'm officially a goner; I'm finally relaxed. It's been a long and stressful week.

The DJ starts playing fun dance music. I take my long hair out of its clip and hit the dance floor to Lady Gaga singing, "Do What U Want". He goes right in to Katy Perry's "Part of Me", and some random guy starts dancing with us. Before I realize what's happening, I feel hands on my hips and Jackie's face looks like she just got a jolt from a stun gun.

I'm not turning around—I know exactly who I'll find. *Damn it, how the fuck did he find us?* The DJ puts on The Police's" Every Breath You Take". I can't help but laugh—the frigging stalker song—how appropriate. I turn around and there it is . . . that toe-curling look. Jax pulls me close and sings in my ear. It's raspy and such a turn-on. He leans down to kiss me, "You're drunk."

I get lost in those blues, "Maybe, a little bit." He gives me that crooked smile and I melt. We are swaying to the music and I can feel his rock hard cock, hitting my core. Sweet Jesus, what this man does to me.

I look over to Jackie and Max is holding her up. Oh, she likes him. Interesting.

"Sweetheart, why did you ditch Max?" I know he's trying not to bulldoze me.

"I just wanted to go out with Jackie and have fun. Life with you is so much more." He looks confused. Maybe he just doesn't get it. Nothing is simple anymore.

"I'm confused. What do you mean, *so much more?"*

I don't want to hurt him. He's looking at me with such tenderness. "It's intense. You're intense. I'm only twenty-seven, and life has had more downs than ups. And you're so beautiful. Do you know that?" I can't believe I just said that.

"You're drunk, I'm taking you home."

He nods to Max and just like that, we're leaving. Apparently, Jackie's not allowed to stay, either. When we get outside, Max doesn't say anything. Jax has a word with Max and before I know it, Max is taking Jackie home. She looks very happy about it.

"Jax, I'm going back to my place tonight." Not that I want to, but I can't possibly let him win all the time.

"Do you really think you're going to win this argument?"

I throw my hands on my hips. "I'll have you know, I took a Krav Maga class and I take kickboxing classes too, remember?" I have no idea why he is laughing so hard that I can defend myself. Well, I can sort of defend myself. He reaches for me. I make an attempt to swat him away but he is on me in a second—and he has me in the fireman carry. "Jax, everyone can see my panties!"

He's still laughing at me. "Only I can, and I know what's under them."

I try to wiggle free and he smacks my butt. "Keep it up and I'll do it again."

Now I'm growling like he does! "You wouldn't." Who am I kidding? He would in a heartbeat and I know it.

"Oh, do you want to try me?" He places me in his car, runs around to get in on the driver's side, starts it up and drives like a crazy man (which is hard to do in Manhattan). Before I know it, we're in his ivory tower in the sky. I'm too tired and too drunk to argue anymore. I drift off to sleep, smelling vanilla and spice.

Chapter Eight

Maxwell

I SWEAR THIS WOMAN frustrates me. I don't know how Jax is dealing with her. I'm used to order and routine. I have to be like that for the safety of my charges. I can't believe that Raven and Jackie ditched me! What the bloody hell were they thinking?

Thank God Jax is a crazy fucker and installed a tracker app on the phone he gave Raven. I thought Jax was going to rip my head off when I called to tell him what they did. I hack into the phone and find out where they ditched me. I call Jax and we both arrive at the club within minutes of each other and head in. Both girls are pissed and barely able to stand. Some random guy is on the dance floor with them, until Jax and I step in—this guy seems to know that he needs to slink back to wherever the fuck he came from.

I'm trying to guide Jackie off the floor but she's not having any of it. I decide to pull her into my arms and just sway to the music. Fuck, she smells fantastic, and I'm instantly hard! Finally, the music starts to change and Jax gives me the nod. Just like that,we are out the door.

"Jax is going to take Miss Raven home. I will be escorting you." I didn't give her much of a choice. As I put her in the car, I can't help but notice how long and lean her legs are—beautiful. We pull up to her flat. The first thing I notice is that security in the building is really good. At least that's something positive.

"Thank you, Max, for making sure I got home okay." I take her hand and guide her past the doorman.

"Excuse me, Miss Jackie, apparently you don't understand. I'm your security until I can make other arrangements."

She looks at me all wide eyed. "You mean you're coming upstairs?"

I nod, "Yes, I can assure you, I will be the perfect gentlemen."

She looks surprised. "Why?"

I guide her into the elevator. "Why will I be a perfect gentleman?" I'm playing with her, but I couldn't help having a little fun.

"No, Max, why are you coming upstairs?"

As the doors close, I look at her. *She really is beautiful.* "We will talk upstairs."

"But…" she starts to protest.

I swiftly pull her towards me, "No buts and no choice. Done. Especially after the stunt you and Miss Raven pulled earlier."

She opens the door and disarms the alarm. "Please wait here while I do a quick sweep of the flat." I know I'm over cautious, but I have my reasons.

"Don't you think you're being ridiculous?"

I glare at her. "Humor me. After all, it's the least you can do after ditching me earlier."

She has the nerve to smirk at me! "Whatever, Max, just make it quick."

After I give the "all clear," she comes in and locks up. I'm impressed she has an alarm and actually uses it—so many people don't.

"I'm going to change, make yourself at home."

I walk around the flat, taking in all the windows and making sure they're secure—just a habit. When I turn around, she's standing in the kitchen, wearing flimsy shorts and a short little top. *Oh bloody hell, I'm fucked!*

"Tea?"

She must think I'm an idiot. I can't take my eyes off of her legs! "Excuse me?"

I'm sure she knows what she is doing and just smiles. "I said, would you like a cup of tea?"

I'm trying to keep my eyes off of her legs or it could be game over. "Yes, please."

I sit down and she starts to question me. I'm having a hard time concentrating.

"Max, are you okay?"

I grit my teeth. "Yes, sorry, I just have a lot on my dish right now."

She smirks. "Plate."

I keep reminding myself to focus. "Excuse me?"

She cocks her head to the side, and her beautiful blonde hair cascades around her face.

"You have a lot on your plate. Sometimes the words are the same but different meanings."

I nod. "Plate . . . got it."

As she passes me my tea, she's back to questioning me. "Can you please fill me in on why I am in need of security?"

I try to play everything close to the vest. I'm not ready to tell her anything. "Well, it seems Miss Raven has some security issues that could be a problem, so better safe than sorry."

Her tongue rolls over her lips; fuck it all to hell I'm as hard as stone! "Well, Max, here's the thing, I am an educated woman and I know when someone is trying to bullshit me. You're in way deep here. Let's start again, except this time with the truth."

"Well, Miss Jackie, I don't know how much I'm at liberty to tell you, I don't want to put you in any danger."

She sips her tea and stares at me. "Max, did you do a background check on me?"

I shake my head. "Honestly, no. I didn't see any reason to. I'm not a bad guy. I'm just trying to keep everyone safe."

She puts her tea down, "My mother is from Japan and my father is from Switzerland. My father helped negotiate relations between Switzerland and Japan. He is a prominent businessman. I am very used to security and threats. I live in New York because it allows me some anonymity. As you can tell, I'm in a very secure building. However, if you feel I might need some additional protection, I won't question you on it."

She has rendered me speechless. She gets up, goes to the closet, and comes back with a pillow and a blanket. "The couch is pretty comfortable. If you need anything else, let me know." She turns and goes into her room, closing the door behind her. I can't imagine I will get much sleep tonight. I'm left with a raging hard-on and a cold cup of tea!

Jackie

I CAN'T BELIEVE SOME gorgeous man is asleep in my living room. If my parents knew, they would freak out. Shit, I'm freaking out. What the fuck did Raven get into that she needs this level of security? I try to get some sleep, but all I can think about is Max on my couch. I decide to read for a while. As I finally drift off to sleep, I realize, I don't even know his full name!

AS THE DAY DAWNS, I get out of bed and throw on my running gear before heading out to the kitchen. "Where are you going?" Max asks when he glances over at me from the coffee maker.

I need to work off frustration, and I'm training, but he doesn't need to know everything. "I like to start my day with a run, usually alone."

His jaw ticks. I can tell he's trying to control his temper. "Well, Miss Jackie, if you insist on running, then running it is, but we need to stop by my place to pick up my gear."

This is ridiculous. "Really, Max, you don't have to come with me." He glares at me, and I realize . . . it's fruitless to argue. "Okay, Max, let's go."

When we get to his place, I look around in shock. "You live here?"

He smiles and seems proud of where he lives. "Yes, there are two flats on the floor—I have one and Jax has the other. It makes it quite convenient since I head up Jax's detail."

The place is beautiful, but sadly, it doesn't look like a home. "Do you entertain much?" I ask him and see such sadness pass over his face that I just want to give him a hug.

"The only people that have ever been in here are Jax, his family, and now, you." He averts his eyes from me after the last bit. "I'll be right back," he adds then walks down the hall to his room, I bet.

He changes quickly and re-joins me. I am finally getting an up close and personal look at him. I realize he is very well built; his muscles are very well defined. He is so handsome. I have no clue how old he is but I know he is older than Jax.

"How far do you usually run? I like long distance running, so I hope that won't be a problem for you."

Maxwell

DOES SHE THINK I'M too old to keep up with her? "Not at all, Miss Jackie, whatever you decide, I promise not to hold you back."

As we enter the park, she does a few quick stretches, which I'm sure are for my benefit. Oh fuck, she's stretching out those legs. *When the fuck did I become a leg-man?*

"Any time you're ready, Miss Jackie."

Jackie

OH REALLY, WELL HE should know that I usually run marathons, and I've been in training for the NYC marathon, next weekend. We start to run and I keep the pace light. I don't want to kill the guy, especially since I don't know how old he is. He seems to be keeping up, maintaining a steady pace right behind me. When we finally finish, I stop on the grass and do my usual stretching so my muscles recover quickly. I glance over at Max and notice he's wincing. "Max, are you okay?"

He grimaces. "I'll be fine, just a sore muscle." Some men can be so stubborn.

"Max, in all fairness, I've been training for the New York City Marathon. Maybe this was too much for a man your age." I can't help but giggle. "Lie flat on the grass and let me help you."

He puts his hand up. "Don't worry, Miss Jackie, I'll be fine." I just want to smack him. He is so bull-headed!

"I can't have my bodyguard hobbling around all day. Sit now, mister."

Maxwell

I DO AS SHE says and sit on the grass. Watching her, I can't believe she's real. She takes off my trainers and massages my foot. Oh my God, I can't do this; I'm getting hard! She moves her hands up my calf to my thigh, pushing her whole body into the massage. I've got to stop this now! "Okay, thank you, Miss Jackie, I think I'm good now." I think she's doing this on purpose. I quickly put my trainers on. I take her hand and we head back across to my flat. I need a shower and I have to check in with Jax.

Jackie

"I'LL JUST JUMP IN for a quick shower. You can make yourself at home."

I walk along floor to ceiling windows, taking in the beautiful views. I grab a bottle of water and begin to wonder around the rest of his home. Everything is very neat, nothing out of place. He must like scotch, he has a very well stocked bar. As I go in search of the restroom, I pass by a home office. I head further down the hall, past an open door. When I glance over I can see his silhouette in the mirror. He has a towel wrapped around his waist, and his body is wet from his shower. Sweet Jesus, he's got the most beautiful body I have ever seen. I can't take my eyes off of him. Just when he begins to remove his towel, he catches me ogling. I'm sure I've just turned a million shades of red. I'm about to turn around and give him his privacy, but he gives me a huge smile, turns his back to me, and drops his towel. *Holy fuck, what the…* He has the most beautifully sculptured ass I have ever seen! I'm still stunned when he enters the room. He walks up to me, leans in, and puts his hand at the base of my neck. He pulls me close, reaches in, and gently kisses me. The whole time, his eyes are open, searching mine, almost like he's asking for permission but knows the answer.

"I have wanted to do that since last night," he growls. "Jax left me a message that they will not be available till tomorrow. Do you want to go back to your place to shower?"

I'm still flustered. "Um sure."

I PRACTICALLY RUN INTO the shower when we arrive at my place. I don't know what is going on with me. He is older than I am but I have no idea how old—shit! I don't even know his full name! I put on leggings and a sweatshirt and head out to the living room. "Wow, where did the breakfast come from?"

He's busy dishing it all up for us. "I made a few calls. Sit before it gets cold."

He keeps his eyes on me as we eat in silence. "Miss Jackie, what's the matter? You seem upset about something. Was it the kiss? Did I offend you?"

Crap, I'm blushing again; I can feel the heat rising to my cheeks. "I wasn't offended, just surprised. You slept in my apartment, I saw you naked, you kissed me, and I don't even know your full name."

He puts his coffee down. "Maxwell Fleming."

"Excuse me?"

He takes my hand. "My name is Maxwell Fleming."

I take a deep breath. "Okay. Maxwell Fleming, can I ask you some questions?"

He nods. "You can, and I will answer them as best and as honestly as I can."

I have so many. Where should I start? "How old are you? Where were you born? How did you meet Jax? And are you an only child?"

He laughs, "Whoa, one at a time, babe. I'm thirty-eight years old. I was born in Scotland, but went to live with my grams in London when my mum died. I have no siblings that I'm aware of. I don't remember much about my biological father, so I can't really know for sure. I met Jax eight years ago, in a bar, in London. I'm not married, and I don't do relationships. Now what about you?"

Everything he said, and yet what sticks is his comment on relationships. *So what are we doing here?*

"I'm twenty-five. I finished my degree at the age of twenty-two and

I got my teaching job right out of college. I graduated from high school when I was sixteen. Raven is my closest friend. We were roommates in college and we've been teaching together for three years. I've never had a long-term relationship and I've yet to meet anyone that would make me want to have one. I'm very close to my parents. I have a brother who is older than I am, he lives in Japan. I speak Japanese, French, Italian, German, Romansch, and English. I like running, but you know that already. I will be running the NYC marathon next week. I have been skiing since before I could walk. I don't eat meat, but I do eat fish. I love very strong coffee, and I can't live without chocolate."

He looks at me. "Wow, no meat?"

I laugh. "After all that, and all you can say is, '*Wow, no meat?* '"

He hits me with a killer smile. "What would you like to do for the rest of the day?"

Just like that, he's done. I hope Raven is having better luck getting through to Jax than I am with Mr. Maxwell Fleming . . .

Chapter Nine

Raven

I'M HAVING THE MOST wonderful dream. The air is filled with vanilla spice and I feel warm kisses all over my body. There is soft music playing and I feel like I'm floating on a cloud. I wake up in a haze, slowly opening my eyes only to be hit with the sparkling blues I've come to love. *Oh my God, did I just think the "L" word? Fuck . . .*

"Good morning, my defiant one, how are you feeling?"

I need to focus. "My brain feels like someone is playing ping pong. Why didn't you take me back to my place?"

"I didn't want you to be alone just in case you felt sick or you felt the need to pull a runner," snarky Jax replies. Oh, he's pissed. I start to get up to leave but he grabs me and throws me onto the bed, straddling me. "You're not going anywhere, sweetheart, so just forget it."

He's crazy. "Jax, you can't keep me here!"

He growls. "Wanna bet? I think it's time for a little chat about your defiance in having security!" With that, he takes both my hands and holds them above my head and slowly kisses them. Leaning his chest right over my face, I get a blast of vanilla and spice. I lean up and lick his nipples; first one, then the other. *Two can play at this game.* Oh, he tastes so wonderful.

"Why did you sneak away from Max last night?"

I'm trying to focus on him, but he's not making it easy. "I just wanted to go out with Jackie and have fun."

He locks his eyes onto mine, and what I see scares me—he's really worried. "Well, you do realize that, if *you're* the target, then you just put a big bullseye on Jackie's back?"

My heart drops, "No, I didn't think about that because I don't think this is about me. None of this started until I met you!"

He kisses me, trying to calm my fear for Jackie, I think. "Well, either way, I can't be sure, so I've also put a guard on Jackie. Max is with her now, and he will keep her safe. Now, back to what I was doing." With that, he is back, kissing my arms and neck.

He works his way down my body. My brain is buzzing. I'm not sure if it's from him or those bushwhacker drinks. Before I know it, he has me spread open and he's nibbling, sucking, and licking me front to back. *I think I'm going to pass out.* He flips me over and starts massaging me at the top of my head, then my neck, and down my back. He follows his path with kisses. It's so soft and peaceful. I feel him everywhere. He lifts my hips and slams into me. "Oh my God!" I scream.

He leans over me and growls, "No, sweetheart, that would be me, not God. Now you're not going to ditch your security detail, are you?" He pulls back, waiting for my answer but before I can give him one, he slams in again! He pulls back out of me slowly. "Let's talk security. Are you going to ditch them?"

I know I shouldn't get him riled up, but I can't help myself. "Why do I need to have a monitor?"

He smacks my ass and slams into me again. "Sorry, wrong answer, sweetheart."

If he does that one more time, I'm going to come and he knows it. He pulls out, bends down, and kisses my ass—slow, deliberate kisses. "Now are you going to ditch your security detail again?"

He licks right up my spine. Oh, sweet Jesus, now back down again, his finger following the path of his tongue and just like that, anal play is back. He works his finger into me really slowly. Oh God, it's going to hurt. I tense up.

"I would never hurt you Raven, you're so wet for me," he tries to reassure me probably picking up on my body language. He pulls out and starts working himself into my rear. All I feel is pressure and my panic, rising. I never thought I would want to try this.

"Jax, it's going to hurt," I finally voice my fear.

He trails kisses up and down my spine. "Sweetheart, I would never hurt you, I promise. You're so wet. I'll go slow, just relax and breathe. Do you trust me?"

"Yes," I don't hesitate. I know he wouldn't hurt me.

He pushes forward very slowly. "Push back and let me in," he says soothingly. As I push back, he pushes forward. There's a lot of pressure. "I'm almost in, baby, little bit more." He pushes a little more until he's all the way in. It's such a full feeling. "Oh God, Raven, you're so fucking tight, you feel so warm and tight around my cock. He stops and I know he is trying to control himself. I feel him squeezing the base of his cock to stop his impending orgasm. He hooks his arms under mine and pulls me into a sitting position on his lap. With one hand, he reaches around my body and goes back and forth from one nipple to the other. His free hand goes right to work on my clitoris. He starts to move, slowly at first, but then he starts to really pick up speed. The feeling is amazing. I never thought it could feel this unbelievable.

"Jax, I'm there, are you?"

He nibbles on my ear, "Come for me, baby," and with that, we both let go—screaming our release. We both collapse and he drapes over me. He pulls out and flips me over. He ditches the condom before setting his eyes back on me. He seems worried and stressed. I feel really bad, like I brought this on. "Are you going to ditch your security detail again?"

I search his eyes. "Jax, why is this so important to you?"

His gaze becomes intense. "I need to know your safe. I can't think and I can't work while I'm worried about you. Having security takes away a little bit of the worry."

I fight the tears back, I don't want to hurt him. "Okay, if it's that important to you, I won't ditch my detail."

He gifts me with that crooked smile and twinkling blues. "You have made me so happy." He nuzzles into my neck, stroking his fingers up and down my arm.

"Jax, how can you possibly be able to go again?"

He laughs, "Sweetheart, it's you. This is what you do to me. My cock always wants to be buried in you. It's a happy place for him." He slowly works his cock in and out. He pulls out again, but then he slams into me and my mind loses all reason. This man has moves that render me speechless. He presses his lips to all different parts of my body—parts that I never knew could be so sensitive. "You're quivering, baby. I love it when you quiver. I can feel you clenching my cock. It's beautiful. You're beautiful."

Oh God he's doing that swivel with his hips while he's buried so fucking deep! My hands fist his hair, "Jax! Oh! My! God!" I scream to all that's holy.

He laughs, "That would be me again, sweetheart. Oh fuck, Raven, I'm there. Please do that clench thing again!"

We both scream our release, barely catching our breath. I'm speechless, exhausted, and totally satisfied. "You are so beautiful, please don't run away." It's barely a whisper but I hear him. I wrap myself around him and drift off to sleep.

AFTER THE PROMISED *DOCTOR Who* marathon, we've been spending the entire weekend in bed, which is fine by me. He brings a tray in with coffee and pastry—*heaven!* "I need to ask you something. Are you on birth control?"

After almost choking on my coffee, I look at him and find him stroking his chin. "Why are you asking me now? You've been using condoms, so what's the problem?"

"I want nothing between us. I want you—one hundred percent. And I hate those cock blockers. I had my yearly physical, and I have a clean bill of health. I can give you a copy."

I made my ex wear a condom all the time, which was what fueled the beating he gave me. I trust Jax. "I've been on the pill for years to keep me regulated. I have a clean bill, also. We have to be tested at the beginning of every school year, and since I have not had sex in almost two years…"

He is on me, kissing me, doing a dance with his tongue that makes me instantly wet for him. He locks his eyes on mine, "Are we good?" he asks. I nod, but he doesn't continue. "I need to hear the words, baby."

"Yes, Jax, we're good. I trust you," I whisper.

The words barely leave my mouth and keeping his blues to my

violets, he slowly enters me. The feeling is unreal. He is so hard and pulsing. When he is all the way in, he stops and closes his eyes. "Do you feel that? We can never be closer than we are, right at this minute. We are one body, one heart, and one soul."

I melt at the words. He says so much during sex, but my mind becomes a jumbled mess. He opens his eyes and starts to move real slowly. The feeling is unbelievable. When it comes to sex with this man, I am so out of my league. "Jax, I can't hold it much longer, please tell me you're close." I'm trying to hold on, but it's so hard.

"Go, sweetheart, I'm right behind you."

And with that, I fall, locking my eyes back onto his, holding onto him as if my life depended upon it—it probably does. He lets out a yell and floods me with his warmth. He stills, but his cock is still throbbing.

"I don't think I will ever get enough of you. You're like a book that I never want to put down." I'm not sure if I was meant to hear his words.

I'm curled up in Jax's arms as he runs his fingers up and down my spine. "Jax, this has been a great weekend."

He stops, "Why do I hear a "but" coming?"

I really don't want him to worry, but I have to think about my kids, too. "Well, tomorrow when I go to school, do you think the security can stay outside? I'm in a high security school and I don't think anyone would try anything. I really don't want the kids to be afraid that there are guards in the room. I know most of them are probably used to it, but still… Besides, can you picture Max in one of those little chairs in the back of the room?"

He laughs at the thought, "Okay, but no ditching Max. I need to know that you and Junior are safe." He traces circles on my arm. That was easier than I thought it was going to be.

"What would you like to do today?" he asks.

I need to get a run in. "Well, it's nice out, do you want to go for a run?" I can't believe we are having this conversation and he is still buried so deep within me.

"Whatever you want to do is fine with me."

WE HEAD DOWN TO Central Park and it's beautiful outside. Even though it's fall, it's still a little warm. We do the entire park. It's long, but it feels good to just run with no thoughts and no purpose.

"I really didn't think you were into running, but you're good." He smiles.

I have always loved running. "Thanks. I got into college on a track scholarship and I just kept it up. I try to run two times a week. It really depends on what workout classes I have planned. I never miss Pilates."

He gives me that smirk. "Well, you know I'm happy about that. Tell me about Pilates, I've never taken a class."

"It's all based on a technique developed by Joe Pilates. I like using a machine called *The Reformer*. The key is, the core muscles are always engaged. Picture Yoga with resistance."

He is stroking his chin, deep in thought. "I will have to put one of those machines in the gym so you can teach me."

I'm sure that's not the only reason he wants one!

WE HEAD OFF TO that wonderful shower. I swear, I really can't get enough of it. Jax washes my body like he's studying every inch, and then he washes my hair. The feeling of having my head massaged under that massive showerhead is unreal.

Jax steps in front of me and begins slowly kissing me. "You're so beautiful, sweetheart. I want to hold you forever." He lifts me up. "Wrap your legs around my waist and hold on tight." He rears back and slams into me, but then he stops.

"Why are you stopping?" His eyes are closed and his head is tilted all the way back. "Are you okay?"

He hums, "Yeah. Do you feel that? Just hold on tight and don't move." He looks down at me, and we lock eyes. He swipes his tongue across my lips, but he's still not moving. "Do you feel how deep I am? I don't have to move—I'm pulsing inside you, and you're clenching my cock." He throws his head back again, "Oh, Raven, fuck! What you do to me!" he yells, coming apart within me, and the thought that I have that much power, sends me over the edge to my own release. We slide down the wall, neither one of us saying a word. We finish cleaning up, when we start to come back to life. Both of us silent, lost in our own thoughts.

WE HEAD BACK TO my place for my stuff. Marco is there and he doesn't seem happy. "Hey, what's up? You look upset."

He's really pissed off, slamming stuff, and glaring at Jax. "Well, you could say that. My roommate doesn't come home for almost two days, doesn't return my calls or text messages, and I couldn't *fucking* find her!"

I didn't think he would be this upset. "Oh."

He steps towards me. "So help me, baby girl. If you say *oh* one more time, I just might throw you over my knee and..."

Jax jumps up. "Hold on, Marco." Jax is standing toe-to-toe with Marco.

"No, Jax, *you* hold on. Do you know how worried I was? There has been so much shit going on between guards and stalkers, and then she disappears without a trace. Put yourself in my shoes."

I step between them both. "I'm sorry, Marco. I shut my phone off, I will leave you Jax's number too so you can call him. I will also try to be more considerate." I touch his arm. He seems to calm down. Jax and I decide to hang around for a while and catch up.

"ARE YOU STAYING HERE tonight?" Marco questions, giving his bones a stretch.

"No, I'm staying at Jax's ivory tower in the sky."

Okay, crap! My brain-to-mouth filter is not working today. I watch as Jax takes on a perturbed expression and Marco laughs out loud. And with that, we head back to Jax's. When we get in the elevator, he comes towards me real slow, like a predator. "Ivory tower, eh?"

He grabs my hand, bringing it up to his lips and kisses my wrist.

Damn! Why does that get to me? He pulls my hand away from my ear with a growl—I don't even realize I do it. When the doors open, he guides me inside, still kissing me. He turns on the fireplace and then slowly starts to undress me. Before he can have his way, I'm on my knees, working his cock out of his jeans. He's hard, and I slip my lips around the head. He's like silk on my tongue, leaving a trail of his arousal behind. "Take it deep, sweetheart. All the way." He holds my head, pushing himself in deeper. If I thought I was in control, boy, was I mistaken. He is totally in control now. I work my way around his sac, flutter kisses, and lick all the way around and back up again. I'm back on his cock, and he holds the base to stop from coming. He starts moving again and I bare my teeth slightly, causing him to lose it. He slams all the way to the back of my throat, screaming and coming in a hot flood, and I swallow it all. He pulls out and he's still hard!

He lies down in front of the fire. My eyes glide down every inch of his magnificent body, "Jesus, you are so beautiful."

"Sweetheart, you have on way too many clothes." He tugs on my shirt. I slowly start to remove my clothes and he gives me that crooked smile and opens his arms. "Come here," he beckons. I crawl onto his lap and wrap my legs around his waist. "Ride me, sweetheart, make me come inside you."

That's it, I'm done! I impale myself on his hard cock. He plays with my nipples. I know I'm not going to last much longer, but then he stops and flips me over! He starts slamming me from behind, pulling me back against him.

"Why is it an ivory tower?" *Now he wants to talk about this?* He smacks my ass. "Tell me why?" I can't think, let alone answer him. "Tell me," he growls, and he smacks my ass again; right then left. It's not hard, just enough to buzz. If I die right now, this is a hell of a way to go. "Tell me, Raven," he demands, pulls out, and waits. He starts rubbing his cock up and down my ass, spreading my cheeks, and begins to push himself into my ass.

I know what's coming and I want it. I grit my teeth, "You're up in this glass tower all alone, like something out of a fairy tale." I'm panting like a crazy woman. "It's like your hiding from the real world!"

He smacks my ass again. "Push out for me and I'll give you what I know your craving!"

I push out and he breaks through that barrier. The fullness is overwhelming. This is so new for me, yet I crave the intensity. I can feel my skin flush as he pushes even deeper. I'm there, and I can't hold it any longer. We are both screaming and coming. It's so powerful, and then we collapse and I can hardly move a muscle. We lie in front of the fire, in silence, trying to steady our breath. He gets up and gets a blanket from the couch. He covers us, and pulls me close to him.

"Raven, I'm not hiding in an ivory tower. I'm just a private person. The press is always hounding me. If I were just a blue-collar worker, they wouldn't care. It's only because I have money that they think they need to know everything about my life."

I don't see the logic in hiding. "Maybe if you show them you could care less, they might not bother with you. They all want what they can't have; you make it a big deal, so it's a big deal to them."

He runs his fingers up and down my spine. "Normally, I would agree with you. However, because I'm a billionaire, that puts everyone around me at risk. I'm not prepared to go through that, again."

My eyes fly up to his. "Jax, what do you mean by, *again*?"

His fingers stop. "Sweetheart, what are you talking about?"

I lift my face to focus on his expression. "Jax, you just said, 'you're not prepared to go through that again'. Go through *what*, again?" I push further. "Jax, your hiding stuff from me, makes me want to run."

He pulls me close to him, holding me really tight. "Okay, when I first started in this business, I realized I was good at it . . . really good. I can somehow anticipate the next move. I was dating someone and I believed her, when she said she loved me. What she loved was my money and the power that came with it. I started taking some business risks that could have destroyed everything I had built, if it wasn't done just right.

"During this time, the press was all over her and me because we were together. As it turns out, she was not in love with me. She was a corporate spy out to destroy me. I found out what she was up to and got her blackballed from the business she loved so much. Max and I got the press to agree to bury the story and all pictures of her and me together. I offered them an exclusive interview with access to *a day in the life of a corporate raider*.

"So, while you think I'm hiding in my ivory tower, I'm actually protecting the little bit of privacy I have left. People think that having money will give them freedom, but it's just the opposite. My money has put me in chains and the people around me at risk—a risk I'm not willing to take."

"Did you love her?" I whisper.

He pauses for a moment. "I thought I did. What I learned was, saying *I love you* is easy, but showing someone you love them is what matters. Those words are sometimes just words thrown out way too much. Raven, I'm not prepared to walk away from you, I need to keep you safe. If something happened to you, because of me, I couldn't take it."

I see so much in his eyes—so much pain and worry. I rest my head back down and snuggle into his chest. He resumes stroking my hair and my back with his fingers. He needs me and, at this moment, I let him have what he needs.

MORNING COMES TOO SOON and of course, Jax wants to drive me to school. "Make sure you don't lose Max, and keep your phone, so I can call you, please."

Now that I understand his fear, I will humor him. "No worries, Jax. I have two phones and Max. You have a great day. I'll call you on my break." I lean in and he gives me that toe-curling kiss. With that, he's gone.

FINDING IT HARD TO concentrate on anything but Jax all day, I'm about to call him, since it's break time. However, I stop when I hear a woman call my name. I turn to look at her and I know, in that instant, I am looking at Jax's mom. She has the same intense eyes, penetrating me. "Hi, I'm Raven, and you must be Mrs. Phillips?" She takes my hand and asks me to sit on a bench in the playground with her. "Are you here to see Michael?"

"No, dear. I'm actually here to meet with you. Please, call me An."

Why would she want to see me? "Oh."

Her smile is warm and inviting. "I understand, from my boy, that you and he are getting involved."

Okay, wow, I was not expecting that, but then again, this whole family just comes right out and says whatever they want. "Um, well, we have been seeing each other."

She picks up my hand. "My dear, sometimes in life, you have to just trust yourself and take that leap of faith. Fear should never define who we are. As Albert Einstein said, 'A person starts to live when they live outside themselves.'"

She takes my hand and she stands up. "I'll leave that thought with you and let you get back to work." Just like that, she's gone, and I'm left wondering, what the fuck that was all about.

I call Jax, as promised, but Duke tells me he's in a meeting. It's very strange that Duke never puts me through to Jax when I call. I'll talk to him about it tonight.

I'M TAKING JACKIE'S TURN as playground monitor today while she works one-on-one with a student. I actually enjoy being out here with the kids. Seeing them run and laugh without a care in the world, gives me faith. The bell rings, pulling me out of my thoughts. I get all the kids lined up and we start heading back in.

Within seconds, all hell breaks loose! Two men with guns come charging towards us. I'm looking for Max. I see him, trying to fight them to get to us, but they hit him with something and knock him out.

Then I see Mick running to help, but they hit him with their guns! I'm trying to push the kids through the door when they grab Michael out of the line. He is kicking and screaming as they are dragging him towards a van.

I reach him just as they are going to hit him, stepping in front of him. They hit me in the face and I'm dazed just long enough for them to grab Michael and me, shoving us into the back of the van. They toss my cell, but not both of them. Guns are pointed at us; Michael is crying. I try to put him behind me, protecting him from the kidnappers, but they duct tape our hands and feet and threaten to gag Michael to get him to shut up.

"Why are you doing this?"

He points his gun at my head. "Shut up or we'll gag you, too."

They all have on ski masks, preventing us from seeing their faces. But I recognize one of the voices as the one, from the other night, outside the gym. The ride is long, and there are no windows in the van. The sounds of the city seem to dissipate. I can feel thumping, almost like we are driving over a bridge. I think we're in New Jersey. I can hear a bay door go up. They open the doors and pull us out. We are in a warehouse; they were able to pull the van inside and out of sight.

"Michael, we need to work together and stay focused. Can you be really brave for me, please?"

He stops crying and looks at me. "Okay."

I need to be calm and focused. "We are going to sit back to back, and I'm going to try to untie you."

After a little bit, I'm able to untie him, and then he gets to work on me. "Michael, when they come in, we need to let them believe that we are still tied up."

He's trying so hard not to cry. "Miss Raven, I'm scared. What do they want?"

I see his fear, I need to help him. "I'm sure we'll find out, soon enough."

I try to use the spare phone to call Jax, but there is no signal. I leave it on.

Why is this happening to me again? I feel like I'm a little girl for a second, transported back in time. I need to keep it together for Michael. I know what he is feeling, and the fear is real. I can't let the fear win—not this time. Michael needs me, and I'm not that little girl anymore.

Jaxson

BELLA AND MICHAEL COME storming into my office. Bella is shaking and has a tear-stained face, and Michael looks grim.

"Jax, I just got this." She hands me a picture of Michael Jr. and Raven, being tossed into a van.

"Have they called yet?"

Michael looks at me. "Where the fuck was Max?" Just then, Max walks into my office, and he is visibly shaken. They beat him pretty good by the looks of his face.

Before I can tear into him, "They shot me with a tranquilizer, so they were able to grab them both. Raven tried to pull Michael away from them, so they grabbed her, too. There were, at least, four of them. Mick was outside the school, and he tried to stop them, too. Jax . . . they beat him pretty bad. They've taken him to the ER," he informs me.

Time seems to stand still before mayhem and madness erupts and then so much starts happening. My office door swings open and a very large man bounds in, announcing that he is Joseph Adessi, Director of the FBI.

He walks up to me. "So, you must be Jaxson James Phillips. "I've kept her safe for twenty years and it took you only two weeks to fuck it all up."

The scene unfolding before me is like something out of a Hollywood blockbuster. One of Joseph's men brings Marco in here. He looks pale and scared.

"Marco, I've been paying you all these years to keep her safe. First, it was the ex-boyfriend. We handled that, but didn't you learn anything from it?"

I jump up. "Marco works for you?"

Marco doesn't know whom to answer first, until Joseph bellows, "Marco, pay attention here! What the fuck happened? How could you let him anywhere near our girl?"

Marco looks scared—*he should be.* "I had no idea who he was until after the charity function, and by then, the photos were already out there."

Joseph gets in his face, "It's your fucking job to know who everyone is that she comes into contact with!" he yells.

Max steps in between the two of them. "I think it's time you filled in all the blanks, if we stand a chance of getting them both back alive."

Bella loses it. She tries to punch me before she hauls off and slaps Joseph across the face. Everyone freezes. Joseph turns to her, "Ma'am,

I'm going to let that go because you're distraught over your child. Raise your hands to me again and you'll find yourself very alone, in a cold cell, for assaulting a federal agent." he warns. Michael grabs Bella before she hits him again. She starts a painful, wailing cry.

Joseph tells everyone but Michael, Bella, Max, and Marco to leave the room. "I have no choice but to tell you everything about my Cara. That's right. Her name is Cara Josephina Giaconna. She is my goddaughter and my namesake. Cara's father, Antonio, was a very proud man. He was embarrassed by his family heritage and chose to join the Academy, turning his back on his Chicago Mafia crime family. He moved his wife to Los Angeles. That's where Cara was born."

"Antonio's wife, Gabriella, was a skilled heart surgeon. She was a rising star. She had the tiniest hands and the biggest heart. Gabriella was also doing cutting-edge research. She developed a new method to repair a part of the heart. Before her discovery, the patients could only wait for a transplant, but there was no guarantee that they would get one or that it would work. With this innovative method, she could give them a chance to extend their lives.

"When Cara was seven years old, she was kidnapped. At first, Antonio and I thought it had to do with some high-profile cases we were working on, but then Gabriella was kidnapped, as well. She was told that if she wanted her child returned safely, she had to perform the surgery she pioneered, on a very dangerous criminal. Of course, Gabriella agreed. In the process, Antonio and I were able to rescue Cara, but Antonio was shot. He hung on for two weeks, in the ICU. During that time, he made me Cara's godfather. He entrusted his family to me. He asked me to try to save Gabriella and protect them, at all cost. Gabriella performed the surgery, but the patient died—he was just too far gone, the years of the life he led, finally caught up to him. The patient's son held Gabriella a prisoner for two months. He beat and raped her. I was able to rescue her, but the damage was done. Gabriella was pregnant." He brings his gaze down to the floor, shaking his head before bringing his eyes back up with their sorrowful expression. "She didn't want the child, but her oath was to first, do no harm. She gave Cara to me and asked me to please raise her as my own. I didn't know what to do with her. I got her the therapy, she so desperately needed, to help her deal with the trauma. In the meantime, Gabriella gave birth to a healthy boy, but she couldn't look at him. Everyday she saw that boy, she was reminded of what she went through. She reached her breaking point and Gabriella hung herself. I thank God that I found her before Cara got home. I sent Cara to a private boarding school in England. I put the boy up for adoption, which went through, successfully, to a family in the Midwest."

There is more to this story than the version that Raven told me. "So why change Cara's name and put Marco on her?"

For the first time, I see fear register on Joseph's face. "The man who raped Gabriella was Antonio's brother, Vincent, and the patient was Antonio's father. They are the largest Mafia family in the Chicago area."

All I can do is stare at Joseph. It's as if he is talking another language. "Why target her now, if she even is the target? Joseph, by Max's account of what happened, it sounds like Michael Jr. was the target and Raven tried to stop the abduction, so they took her, too."

Marco stands up. "That would be something Raven would do, always trying to right the wrongs of the world."

"Damn it!" I yell at Max, "Do you remember anything else from the abduction?"

He begins to pace and I know, he's running over it again in his head. "They threw her phone out the back of the van."

"Oh shit, she has a second phone!" I jump up. Every head turns towards me. "I gave her a second phone that was only for me. She kept giving me a hard time about carrying two phones, but she promised she would. If they don't find the phone, we can locate her from the tracking app I put on it," I say, feeling hopeful. They all stare wide-eyed at me like I have issues. . "I know, I'm a little over the top, but I guess, right about now, everyone here is a little happy about that."

Joseph has me write the number down and he gives it to his assistant.

Max turns to Joseph, "Do you know where the half-brother is?"

Joseph's face turns pale. "When he was adopted, everything about the boy was turned over to the local office in Lansing, Michigan. I never saw him again. They are sending over everything they have on him. We didn't view him as a threat, and everything has been quiet, until two weeks ago, when Jax stepped into the picture."

Duke rings me. "I told you, no interruptions." He informs me that I have a delivery. *What the fuck?* I go out to his desk. "What's so important that you had to call me out here?"

He hands me an envelope. "I was opening the interoffice mail and this was in it."

I grab it from him. "Oh shit." I head back in my office and hand it to Joseph.

"Who took delivery of this?" he asks.

Michael jumps up. "Who cares? What do they want in exchange for my son?" "It was in interoffice mail which means; it could have been dropped off at any time, and handled by many different people. Max, we can pull security footage to see who has come in and out of the building."

Michael steps up. "What is it?" He looks and turns pale. It's a picture of Michael Jr. and Raven with a sticky attached:

"We have the boy and the teacher. The price just doubled, we will contact you soon."

The first thing Joseph does is put a tap on all my phones, as well as Michael and Bella's. We pull security footage from right after the abduction so Max can go through all of it. There is someone dropping off the envelope, but the person always keeps his head away from the cameras, so there's no way to tell if it's a man or a woman.

"Bella, where is Mum?" I ask her, suddenly feeling panicked. She stares through me like she's not really hearing me. *"Bella, where the fuck is Mum?"*

"I don't know," she whispers.

I ring my mum. She is not answering her phone. *Fuck.* "Max, call the detail that is on my mum and find out where the fuck she is and why she is not answering her phone!"

Bella rocks back and forth. She keeps repeating, "Jax, please get my baby back safe."

Max calls mum's detail. "The detail said your mum hasn't left the house since she got back from the school."

"Then, why the fuck isn't she answering the phone?! Why was she at the school?"

Max orders them to enter the house. "Jax, your mum is fine. She was in the shower. She is a little shaken up."

"Have her brought here. I don't want her alone right now. And find out if she saw anything when she went to the school today." I walk up to the bar in my office and pour myself three fingers of scotch before I have to deal with my mother.

"Joseph, how much do you think they're going to ask for?"

He shakes his head. "It's a lot more complicated."

"What the fuck do you mean; it's a lot more complicated? Isn't this about money? Wasn't Raven collateral damage?"

Joseph glares at me. "Well, let's see. First, they grab a billionaire's nephew. And at this point, I have to assume they know who Raven really is. Vincent, her uncle, is an animal and has made many enemies. The rival families will also come into play."

I pick up the phone and Joseph grabs it. "What the fuck do you think you're doing?"

I yank the phone away. "I am calling my banker and my broker to make sure I have enough liquid capital to pay whatever they ask for, if that's okay with you!"

He growls, "Okay, but don't do anything or talk to anyone without going through me first, Understood?"

Like I would really trust this guy. "Yes, understood," I humor him before ringing up the necessary people. When I finish getting things lined up, just in case, I decide to step outside of my office for a breather.

Duke is getting ready to leave for the day. "Sir, I'm leaving if that's okay, unless you need me to stay?"

I shoo him away. "It's fine, Duke. I'll see you in the morning."

Max steps out of my office. "What do you need that you don't want anyone to know?"

This is why Max is my best friend. "What did Mick say?"

I know he doesn't want to tell me something. "Just that Raven was trying to stop them from taking Junior, Raven stepped in front of him. They hit her in the face before they tossed both of them into the van. They beat Mick pretty good, but he did get a partial on the plate and a description of the van. Jax you've got to keep it together."

He knows how hard this is for me. "Yeah, for now."

Chapter Ten

Raven

WHEN THEY COME BACK, still concealed under ski masks, they take a picture of Michael and me. "We know you worked off the duct tape—you saved us the trouble," one of them says. Without another word, they turn and leave.

"Michael, look at me, please." I cradle his face in my palms. "When I was a little girl, about your age, I was kidnapped."

His eyes grow large. "What did you do, Miss Raven?"

I have to keep things positive for him. "Well, I was alone, so I had to trust myself and try to stay calm. I did what they asked, and eventually, my dad and uncle rescued me."

He smiles. "Do you think we will get rescued?"

I give myself a mental pep talk before I answer him. "I know that your dad and your Uncle Jax will move heaven and earth to find us." I don't doubt that they are trying; I just hope they find us in time, but I won't tell Michael that. I get up and start to explore our surroundings. There is a door to a bathroom with a toilet and sink. There are no windows. It is cold and when night comes it will get colder.

"Michael, we can get water from the bathroom sink. At least we can stay hydrated. Remember when we did the experiment with the flower in science? We colored the water, which made the flower change color"

He laughs. "Yeah, that was a cool trick."

Kids always think things they don't understand are tricks. "That wasn't a trick. It was to show you how everything the flower needed, it got from the water. We might not have any food right now, but we have water. That is what we need to survive."

He gets a huge smile on his face and I know he gets it. "Miss Raven, can I ask you something?"

"Of course."

He furrows his brows. "Do you ever do anything other than teach? I mean, you're always thinking about teaching stuff. Don't you just want to play video games or something?"

I burst out laughing, "Oh, Michael, thank you, I needed that."

He just shakes his head, smiling at me. "Miss Raven, are you going to marry Uncle Jax?"

I'm in total shock. "What would make you think that?"

He shuffles his feet. I can tell he's unsure of what to say. "My mom and dad were talking, and Mom said *'the handwriting is on the wall'* and then she was yelling at my dad... something about a dream. What did she mean by that? I would get into trouble if I wrote on the wall."

I really don't want to go into this with him but I need to be honest with him. "Okay, Michael, first, you shouldn't be listening to your parents when they're talking to each other and not to you. That's called eavesdropping. Secondly, I barely know your uncle; we're just friends."

I think it's time for a subject change, and quick. "Michael, do you have any pets?"

His face lights up. "Yeah, I have the coolest dog. His name is Vito. And he is a very big German shepherd. You would like him. He is very strong. Do you have any pets, Miss Raven?"

My mind goes back instantly to Winston. "Not now. I did when I was your age. I had a dog, too. His name was Winston, and anyone that came to my house would take one look at him and wait outside." I smile as I am telling him the story of the first time a boy tried to get close to me, "Winston walked up to the front door and that boy ran for the hills. He was a 235pound, chocolate-brown Newfoundland. When I walked him, people would cross the street. They thought he was a bear."

He pulls a kid's *Doctor Who* wallet out of his back pocket, opens it up, and shows me a picture of his dog. "This is Vito. When we get out of here, will you show me a picture of Winston?"

I hug him and give him the reassurance he needs that we will get out of here. "Sure. Why don't you go to the bathroom and wash up."

When Michael comes back in the room, he's back to his reticent behavior. I need to keep him distracted. "So, Michael, is your favorite television show, *Doctor Who?*"

His face takes on a serious expression again. "Miss Raven, it's okay if you're scared. I will protect you."

He is so precious, I just want to cry. "Thank you, Michael. We both need to stay strong together. So, back to television shows."

Sometimes, when I look at his face, I see the same facial expressions that Jax makes. "Well, isn't *Doctor Who* everyone's favorite television show?"

I start to laugh so hard I cry, which causes Michael to laugh along with me. Suddenly, one of the kidnappers comes in and videotapes us.

"Michael, do you watch *Doctor Who* with your Uncle Jax?"

He hits me with a huge smile. "Oh, all the time, Miss Raven. We wear bowties, eat PB and J's, and drink chocolate egg creams while we watch the show."

My heart is in my throat. This boy loves his uncle so much. "So, Michael, you could be a young *Doctor Who*."

There's that smile again. "Well, I guess when you put it like that, I could be!"

I pull him close to me, hopefully giving him the assurance he needs that we will be fine.

"Michael, now I know we will be fine because the *Doctor* is in the house."

Jaxson

MY MUM WALKS INTO the office, pale and crying. She runs right into my arms. Jesus, I can't take seeing her like this.

She pulls back a little, "Jaxson James Phillips, you get my grandson and future daughter-in-law back safe, right now!"

All heads turn to me. My mum has rendered me speechless. "Mum, what makes you think Raven will be your daughter-in-law? And what were you doing at the school today?"

Oh no, she's giving that look that will stop me in my tracks. "Well, if I waited for you or your sister to introduce me to Michael's teacher, I would still be waiting. I met the girl and I like her. She's genuine. You can always tell when someone is tender-hearted, and, my boy, she is. Now, do what you have to, but get my family back!"

Mum turns to Joseph, who is just staring at her, speechless. "Do you have a problem, sir?"

Joseph puts his glass down and walks up to my mum. "No, ma'am, I just wasn't expecting a ball of fire to come barrelling through the door."

Mum puts her hand out to Joseph, "I'm Anwen Phillips, and you are?"

He extends his hand. "I'm Joseph Adessi, Director of The FBI. Your name is very different; Welsh, if I'm not mistaken. I believe it means *very beautiful*."

Oh really, please tell me he's not hitting on my mum now! I'm about to say something but leave it to my mum to step up. "Mr. Director of the FBI, your knowledge of Welsh names is very impressive, however, that is not going to get my family back. So cut the crap and do your job," she bites. Joseph is speechless, and I'm pretty sure I have a stupid grin on my face.

My phone beeps. There is a short video of Raven and Michael, but there is no sound. I can see Michael laughing at something Raven is telling him. Leave it to my girl to find something to make him laugh at the worst possible time. Another text comes right after informing me that instructions will follow.

Joseph calls his tech guy in and gives him my phone. "There's a video on here. See if you can trace it through the cell towers. How are we doing with tracing the second phone?"

The tech informs us that the phone is indeed on, and they're trying to narrow down the location. All we can do now, is wait. Waiting is something I've never been good at.

Max decides he is going to Jackie's flat to see if there might be something she saw at the playground.

Maxwell

I PULL UP TO Jackie's building and I notice the doorman is helping another resident, so I wait.

"Please ring Miss Jackie Gerhard and let her know Maxwell Fleming is here."

The doorman informs me she's been expecting me, and I should go right up. When I get upstairs, I knock and the door fly's open. "Miss Jackie, are you crazy? You didn't even ask who was at the door!"

She looks so scared, and it rips me up inside to see it. "Oh, Max, you're the only one the doorman was instructed to let up."

I know I'm growling but I just can't help it. "I don't care. I have enough on my dish—I mean plate—right now!" I step inside and close the door. I turn around and she jumps into my arms. *Oh Fuck.*

"I'm sorry. Please, I'm scared. My best friend and the sweetest little boy were kidnapped right in front of me today." She's trembling and I pull her tighter to me.

"First, thank you for helping me today when they knocked me out. They used some sort of tranquilizer on me."

She runs her quivering fingers across my lips. "You should have let the paramedics look at you. They beat you up pretty good."

I shake my head. I need to keep it together, and right now—I just want to feel her touch all over. "I needed to get to Jax. Can you tell me what you saw prior to the kidnapping?" I hear the vulnerability in my voice, but I don't care to shake it. Holding her like this, feeling her breath in my face; it's giving me an achiness and a sense of urgency I haven't felt in a long time.

Her eyes instantly fill with tears. "Well, it was supposed to be me, not Raven."

She starts to rock back and forth, crying.

"Please explain. I'm confused. What do you mean; it was supposed to be you?" We sit on the couch and she takes a few calming breathes.

"We have a set schedule and this week was my turn to monitor the playground. I had a new student that I needed to do an assessment on, so Raven took my place. Oh Max, this is all my fault."

I pull her into my arms. "Hush, you don't know that. Did you notice anything this week that seemed odd or out of place?"

She looks up at me. "I did have a feeling like I was being watched, and I told Raven. She had me talk to the office about it but they said it was added security from Michael's dad."

I hold her tighter, not wanting to let her go. "Do you remember ever seeing the van before today?"

She shakes her head, "No, but I don't notice that kind of stuff. I'm too busy watching the children." She averts her eyes for a moment but brings them back. "They beat Mick up when he was trying to help. Do you know how he is?"

Gazing into her eyes, I see she genuinely cares about Mick. "He'll be okay. He was taken to the ER." I glide my hands up and down her arms to comfort her. "I'm sorry, Miss Jackie, but I need to get back to Raiders. I'm putting a guard on you, though. Do *not* ditch him. I'll call you later and update you. Lock the door and set the alarm, okay?" I pull her in for one final hug before getting up to head out. She follows me to the door and before I can walk out, she wraps me into another urgent hug, crushing me to her. I pull away and give her an encouraging nod. "I'll call, I promise." I reassure, and then leave.

I call Tony on my way back to Raiders. "Hey, Tony, how's the phone tracing coming along?"

"I should have it sooner, rather than later," he grumbles. I know he is working as fast as he can. "What did Jackie say?" I need to bounce this off of Tony before I let Jax know. Tony is my sounding board; he helps keep my thoughts clear.

"She said they have a set schedule and she was supposed to be on the playground, not Raven. That makes me think that Raven was never a target, but something has changed. Something is off and I can't put my finger on it."

He's quiet for a bit. "Do you think Jackie was the original target?" he finally asks.

I know where Tony is going with this. "I don't think she was, but I can't rule it out, either. Her father is a powerful man, but I know nothing about the brother. Maybe we need to pull a check on them." I rub the back of my neck to release some of the tension. "Just keep it between us right now." I wait for his agreement. "Any luck with the partial plate number?"

"The plate was reported stolen last week. This seems very well planned. If they knew who Raven was, then why do it this week when Jackie was on playground duty? Did they know about Jackie's dad? Maybe she and Michael where the original targets?" he rambles off his questions, barely a hint of breath taken between them. Even Tony is coming unhinged by all of this.

Fuck, this is so cocked up. "Just get that trace done. I'm almost to the office." And with that, I end the call.

Chapter Eleven

Duke

FUCK. FUCK. FUCK. WHAT the hell did I get myself into? She told me he would just pay up, and then we could go to one of the islands and never look back. I try calling her but she's not answering the fucking phone. This was supposed to be my one shot to get out of that hellhole in Michigan—permanently.

I can't go back home, but this is way more than I bargained for. *Why the hell does she not answer the phone?* Freezing my ass off, I decide to grab a coffee. Just as I step inside the coffee house, my phone rings. It's her—*finally!* "Where the fuck have you been?" She doesn't answer me right away. I actually look to see if she is still on the line.

"Relax, everything is going better than planned," she says, nonchalantly. *She's got to be kidding me.*

"Are you fucking nuts? They took the boy and the teacher. Why both?" I want to tell her to just fuck off and leave me out of this, but I'm in too deep now.

"Look, the boy was planned. I know Jax will pay up and pay big for his only nephew's safe return. The best part is, we now have a bonus—his girlfriend."

I get my coffee and sit down. "What makes you think he'll pay to get her back, too? He's only been with her for two weeks, and besides, she wasn't supposed to be out there this week. That's why we did it now." She's not answering me. "Hello, are you still there?"

"Where are you right now?" I close my eyes and tell her the location of the coffee house.

"Just wait there. I'm on my way. There is a lot you need to know." The phone goes dead; all I can do is wait. In the meantime, I try to calm down . Finally, she comes breezing through the door. Her long blonde hair and beautiful body renders me speechless. She sits next to me, stroking my arm. "Are you calm now? Can we talk?"

"Erica, you said this would be easy, this is anything but."

"Have you figured out who she is yet?"

"What are you fucking talking about, she is the teacher," I snap.

She laughs an almost sinister laugh. "Duke, guess again. She's not just the teacher. She is your half-sister."

I stare at her in total shock. "Erica, how long have you known?"

She leans in near my ear, "I found out two weeks ago," she whispers.

What the—is she fucking kidding me? "You've known for two weeks, and you're just telling me this now? How did you find out?"

She seems so proud of herself. "I have a friend at the Bureau, and when Jax hooked up with *the teacher*, red flags went up. He gave me a copy of her file."

Realization hits me. "Erica, is that why you pushed me to get the job as Jax's assistant?"

She's smiling like she's already won at this game of chess. "Duke, this works for both of us, don't you see? I get my revenge on Jax, and you get your revenge on a half-sister who took away your claim to any of your mother's money and your birth right within your Chicago Mafia family—".

"—Wait! What the *fuck* are you talking about?" I cut her off, unable to process the words that just flew out of her mouth. "Mafia family? Birthright? I don't know what you're talking about!"

"Duke, your adoption was arranged by the FBI. Your father is, Vincent Giaconna. He is the head of Chicago's largest crime family. That is your birthright Duke, that's what was taken from you.

"You have lived in near poverty when you didn't have to; never knowing your true family. As for me, because of Jax, I have been permanently banned from top businesses all over the world, and disowned by my family. It's time they both pay, and pay dearly." She hands me a file. "This is everything I could get on your sister."

"What's the next step? I mean, have you told anyone else who she really is?"

There's that sinister look again. "Not yet, but that doesn't mean that I don't have a plan in place to protect myself." I get her threat loud and clear. I'm seeing a side of Erica I didn't know existed. She gets up to leave, and then leans into my ear, "Just go to work tomorrow like you know nothing and I will be in touch." With that, she's gone, leaving me with the file.

I open it. It is filled with pictures of Raven and everything detailing what happened to our mother, including pictures of my father and grandfather. Reading everything, I realize I'm in way over my head here. It's not about a kidnapping anymore. It's about saving my own neck. This can of worms has been opened and there is no turning back. It's time to make a phone call and meet dear, old Dad.

Jaxson

MICHAEL TAKES BELLA AND Mum home, in case they try to contact him there. I decide to stay in my office. I can't go back to my house. Everything smells like her, and when I close my eyes, I see her everywhere. I don't understand how could she have become so embedded into my life, so quickly?

The sun is starting to rise and I go into the break room to get some coffee. On my way back, I notice another interoffice envelope on Duke's desk. It's addressed to me. I really don't think much about it, since I am running a major corporation—life goes on. I open it and watch a note fall out. *Oh fuck!*

I run into my office, "Joseph, they've made contact!" I yell.

Joseph jumps up. "Wait, don't touch it!" He opens the letter using gloves so he might be able to get some prints.

"What does it say?"

Joseph stares at the note, his eyes going left to right as he reads. "They are giving you the boy back for a transfer of fifty million to an off shore account."

"But what about Raven?"

Joseph is pale and visibly shaken. "They say that 'the teacher goes to the highest bidder.' They are contacting all the major crime families and letting them bid on her. They'll allow you to enter the bidding, too."

I look at Joseph in total disbelief. I pick up the phone to call Michael and Bella, letting them what is going on before I call my banker and arrange the transfer.

Joseph is sitting here, blank look on his face, obviously in shock. He finally looks at me. "I understand you're going to pay the fifty million for your nephew, but what are you going to do about Cara?"

As I pour myself a scotch, I turn to Joseph, "I will do whatever I have to. I need her back safe with me. But something is bothering you, I can tell. What is it?"

Fear washes over Joseph's face. "Jax, this is a bad can of worms that is being opened, and it might not be that easy to get her back."

I never thought it would be easy, but I would never tell him that. "Why? I have enough money to outbid everyone, and I will."

He nods and shuffles a finger at me and my canteen of scotch. I pour him a glass. "Jax, it's not that easy." He takes a quick sip as soon as I hand it to him. "These families are ruthless. They didn't get to where they are today by playing by the rules."

"Neither did I." I raise both my eyebrows before taking another swig. Before I know it, my whole family is back in my office, including Junior's dog, Vito. Apparently, Vito has not stopped crying since Junior's been gone.

Duke comes in to offer everyone some coffee and food, but Vito starts freaking out. Duke puts everything down on the table and backs out of the room. Vito is trying to get out the door, his fur standing up. Michael tries to calm him down, but he's not moving.

Max starts pacing and *I know* that's not a good sign. I pull him aside, "Max, what's the problem?"

He shakes his head. "I don't know, Jax, I just feel like something is off. I spoke to Jackie. She was supposed to be on that playground, not Raven. They switched at the last minute. They have a set schedule, which apparently, someone knew about." He resumes his pacing and intermittent shaking of his head.

I'm about to question him further when Max's right-hand man, Tony, comes barrelling into the office. "I've got them. I've narrowed it down to a one mile radius of warehouses in Trenton, New Jersey."

Michael and I jump up to go, but Joseph yanks my arm, pulling me back. "Where do you guys think you're going?"

Michael grabs Joseph. "My son is in there; where do you think?"

"Did you think I would leave it up to you to find them?" Max barks, gaining Joseph's attention. " You're welcome to come with us, Joseph, but stay out of my fucking way!"

THE AREA IS DESERTED. No cars. Nothing. Max has a heat sensor that can detect body heat. Focusing on a row of abandoned buildings, the screen suddenly lights up with two body figures. One looks to be the size of a child, and the other could possibly be a woman. This gives me hope. Joseph grabs his radio, alerting his team and the paramedics which building we are at. The strange part is, there are no other figures. Before we can question it, Max is storming into the building. Michael, Joseph, and I are right behind him. All the rooms are empty until we get to a small room in the basement. That's when we find them huddled together. *They're not moving.*

Max yells, "They're alive, just drugged! Get the paramedics in here now!"

So much is happening so fast: yelling, pushing, and men holding us back. They set up IV's, put them on gurneys, and they're out the door in record speed with Michael and I running behind them.

When we arrive at the hospital, I have them put Raven and Junior in the same room. The doctor examines them both carefully and says they'll be fine—little dehydrated, but the IV will fix that. All we can do is wait until they wake up. The room fills up with family. The nurse starts to protest but Joseph just gives her a death glare that even makes me shiver.

Raven starts to stir. She is whimpering, "Daddy, don't die, please don't die."

My heart goes to my throat and I glance at Joseph. He's got tears running down his cheeks. I realize this is reliving a nightmare for him, losing his best friend and partner. I want to say something to him, but what could I possibly say?

I look over to Junior, and his eyes flutter open. He sees everyone and smiles, but then he springs up in bed, "Miss Raven, where is Miss Raven?" he yells.

We move so he can see her sleeping in the bed over from him. "Daddy, is Miss Raven okay?"

He strokes Junior's face. "Yes, son, she's just sleeping, same as you were."

Just then, Raven's eyes open and she yells for Michael. Quickly, it seems to register with her where she is, and Junior calls to her that he's okay. This seems to calm them both. Raven spots Joseph. Her eyes fill with tears, as do his. Their silence, I think, speaking volumes for both of them.

Finally, Joseph picks up Raven's hand. "My beautiful, Raven."

"Joseph, it's been so long. I'm sorry . . . so very sorry," her voice, soft.

"Shush, I will hear none of that *sorry* nonsense. None of this is your fault, not the first time and not now!"

Raven turns to me, and I get hit with those beautiful eyes. Violet to blues. "Hey, no more tears, sweetheart."

Before anymore can be said, Joseph starts asking questions and then Marco steps up doing what he usually does—lots of fussing. It hits me, just then, that Raven doesn't know that Marco works for Joseph.

Just as that realization hits me, Joseph grabs my arm. "Step outside with me, Jax, now."

We step into the hall, and before he can say anything, "This is the part where you're going to ask me to keep my mouth shut about Marco." I beat him to the punch. He raises his eyebrow as if he is surprised. "Joseph, I didn't get to where I am today by being a fucking idiot. I'm a leader, not a follower, and I'll decide what I want her to know. For now, your secret is safe, but I can't make any promises. Now, I'm going back to my girl."

Michael is not letting anyone question Junior right now. He is taking him home, which sounds good to me.

"Raven, the doctor gave the all clear, so I'm taking you home now."

Before I can say anything more, she starts laughing and so does Junior.

All eyes turn to the two of them, but they just keep laughing. Bella looks at Junior. "What exactly went on with the two of you?"

"Uncle Jax, which doctor gave the all clear?" Junior tries on a curious tone but starts chuckling again.

Bella turns to Raven, "Please, don't tell me my brother got you into *Doctor Who*, as well?"

Raven and Junior are too busy laughing to even answer. I'm glad they found a way to get through this together.

I DECIDE TO TAKE Raven to the Ivory Tower tonight. "You know, Jax, you don't have to carry me I can walk."

I cradle her in my arms even tighter. "I know you don't need to be carried, but right now, I need this."

She lifts her head, "Oh."

"Yeah, *oh*," I whisper. I head right to the bathroom so we can have a shower. I want to check every inch of her beautiful body.

"Jax, I have a confession to make." I put her on the vanity and look into her eyes. I'm nervous about what she might want to confess.

"I had a dream the other night about your shower and I have to say, I think I had an orgasm in my sleep, dreaming about it."

Okay, well, not quite the confession I was thinking. "Raven, I would like to think that it was the man in the shower with you who gave you the orgasm and not the shower!" I start to undress her and she is smiling at me—pulling at that fucking ear. I pull her hand away from her ear and start kissing her wrist. I feel the jolt go right through her. *Oh yeah, gotcha, sweetheart.* We step into the shower. I want to kiss every inch of her beautiful body and she lets me. I kiss her cheek where a bruise has formed, and my blood starts to boil.

"Jax, it doesn't hurt much. I'll be okay."

"It slays me to think someone hit you, sweetheart." *She is so strong.*

"I'm okay." She kisses me so tenderly and I just want to be inside her. Right now though, it's not about what I want. It's all about her and my girl needs comfort, so I do just that. I put her into bed and head to the kitchen to prepare something for us to eat. My housekeeper was in today and left macaroni and cheese—now that's comfort food. I head to the bedroom with a tray of food and wine, but when I enter, I find Raven asleep in the throes of a nightmare.

"Please don't die, Daddy, Pleeeeeease!" My heart is in my throat. I take her in my arms and rock her. Finally, she wakes and starts crying. "Jax, I'm sorry, so very sorry."

I hold her tighter. "Raven, if you keep saying you're sorry, I'm going to lose it. You have nothing to be sorry for, you're so strong and so brave. You put Junior's life ahead of your own. I'm in awe of you."

She tilts her head back to look into my eyes and I know she gets it. Little by little she is knocking down my walls. "You need to eat. My housekeeper made mac and cheese."

She sits up, takes a sip of wine, and a few bites. "Jax, I was so scared, not just for me, but for Michael. He's the same age I was when I was kidnapped, all those years ago."

I need to keep her talking so she can try and get past this. "I know you were being brave for him. They sent a video. You were both laughing. It surprised us all. Why were you laughing?"

She gifts me with the most beautiful smile. "I had to distract him, he was getting very quiet. We talked about the things that he loved: his dog, Vito, and *Doctor Who*. You know he loves that show almost as much as you do, but, Jax, I think what he loves more is the bond the two of you have over it."

I don't know when it happened or even how, all I know is, I'm in way too deep to turn back now. I have fallen in love with this woman very hard. There's no going back and I don't want to.

"I'm glad that I have that connection with Junior. Family is very important to me. I cherish and respect it. I know how fragile it is, I've seen it disappear overnight. I think that's part of why I'm a little overbearing. Enough with all this talk; you need to eat."

Just like that, the conversation was done.

MORNING COMES AND I'M having the best dream. My cock is hard and warm, wet kisses are caressing it up and down like soft light flutters and it's the most amazing feeling. I slowly open my eyes and see Raven between my legs, slowly licking my cock up and down. Oh fuck, I died and went to *cock heaven,* if there is such a thing.

She locks her violets on my blues and takes me deep; really deep. My conscience thinks I shouldn't be doing this, she just got home from the hospital, but my cock has other plans. I'm about to stop her when she bares her teeth. I grab her head. I've lost all control. I'm screaming, slamming into the back of her throat, and start coming hard. The tidal wave finally slows down. I try to pull her towards me, but she shakes her head. She pleads, "No, Jax. I need this, please." She crawls up my chest, kisses me, and impales herself on my very firm cock.

"Sweet Jesus. It's okay, sweetheart, take charge." I understand right now she needs that, it was something that was taken away from her and she's reclaiming it. She takes my hands, leans in and licks and nibbles each of my nipples, back and forth, just like I do to her. She's riding me hard and I know I'm not going to last. I tilt up to meet her, and my cock hits the tip of her cervix. She starts bucking and screaming. "Eyes on me, baby, now!" *Fuck me!* Our eyes lock, and we crash together. I pull the comforter back over us and hold her tight, letting us drift back to sleep.

We wake and it's about an hour later. I'm still buried balls deep. I start to stroke her back, and she hums, "Thank you, Jax."

"Sweetheart, why on earth are you thanking me? As I remember, you gave me quite the fab morning!"

She giggles, and it's such a beautiful sound. "Yeah, I can feel you're ready to go again. Are you even human?"

Hmm. "Oh, believe me, I'm human. It's just the affect you have on me." I tilt my hips up, down, and around again.

"Jax, you have such a beautiful body. How often do you workout?"

"I do some sort of exercise six days a week, including weights. I eat healthy, so I'm able to have little indulgences without the guilt."

She slowly runs her tongue around my lips. "Six days a week is a lot. I've never seen you workout."

I can't help but laugh at her. "Sweetheart, you've been giving me my daily cardio!"

She smiles at me as she's working herself up and down, and I know

I'm not going to last long. We lock eyes, and I know she's there. Then she does it! She does that fucking clench thing and I swear she needs to patent it. I explode so hard, I swear by all that's holy, the tip of my cock is going to burst!

"Jax, are you okay?"

I can't put two words together and she wants to know if I'm okay? "Sweetheart, when you do that clench thing, I swear—let's just say you need to patent it." I sigh "Cock heaven," I add in a whisper.

"We need to get ready. We're supposed to meet with Joseph this afternoon to answer questions."

She's not moving, and I can sense her apprehension. "Jax, I just want to put this all behind me and move on. Do we have to go?"

I feel sorry, but we don't have a choice. I know this is not over, and there's stuff she isn't even aware of yet. "Yes, we have to go, Raven. We can't just move on because there are more questions than answers. I'm not willing to take a chance that this might happen again. We were very lucky this time. I won't give them another chance. Done. In the shower you go, and I'll be in shortly."

Raven heads to the shower and I call Max. "Max, have you found out anything yet?" I know he's working non-stop on this, but he knows, when it comes to information—I want everything yesterday.

"Not just yet. However, there are a few things that are really bothering me."

Knowing Max, he's probably pacing. "Yeah, I could tell yesterday in my office. What's going on?"

He's distracted by something. "I'm not sure yet. I want to check a few more things. I'll meet with you before you see Joseph."

I hang up and head into the shower. *My girl is so beautiful.* She renders me speechless. I realize, yeah, she is my girl and there is no going back—*ever!* I just need to convince her of this. I stand in the doorway, watching her. She has her back to the door, her head tilted back, and water cascading everywhere. Fuck it, I'm hard again! Stepping into the shower, I trail kisses down her back, slowly turning her, dipping my fingers in and out, nibbling, and licking. She starts to quiver. She yells my name; a benediction from her beautiful mouth. I work my way up her gorgeous body, worshiping every inch of her and lift her up. "Wrap your legs around my waist." My beautiful girl doesn't hesitate as I lower her slowly onto my cock.

She throws her head back. "Ohhhhhhh."

I sigh, "Yeah, baby, *ohhhhhh.*"

She knows I need this slow right now, and she lets me. Up and down then, a swivel of the hips. First to the right and then to the left. She leans in and nibbles on my lower lip. "Jax, I can't hold it much longer."

I pull her in tighter. "Show me your soul, baby."

Her violets lock onto my blues and we're gone. I slide down the shower wall and just sit with my girl in my lap, my cock throbbing in cock heaven. "Jax, we need to get going."

"Hmm..."

"Is that all you're going to say? Hmm...?"

I can't even open my eyes, let alone move. "Sweetheart, my cock is enjoying being in cock heaven. I can't deny him this pleasure, don't you agree?"

She laughs at me. "I can't believe you call your cock *him,* and what the hell is cock heaven?"

All I can do is smile. "It's the happy place. Not everyone finds it— it's reserved for the special ones, a soul mate."

She gets up and offers me a hand. "Jax, once again you have rendered me speechless."

Raven

AS WE FINISH GETTING ready, I look over at him. He still has that crooked smirk and faraway look on his face. I realize, yep, I love him. Done.

Chapter Twelve

Jaxson

A S WE HEAD TO my office, Raven calls her school, reassuring them that she is fine and will be back to school on Monday. *Not if I have anything to say about it, but that argument is for later.* Right now, we have to meet Max and then Joseph.

We walk in, and Duke is at his desk. He informs me that Max is already in my office. He stares at Raven. The little fucker better keep his eyes off her or I'll cut his prick off and kick him to the curb. Duke gets back to work when he notices *me* watching him. Satisfied, I lead Raven into the office. Max jumps up when we get inside. "Miss Raven, please except my apologies. I'm so sorry."

Raven puts her hand up. "Max, it was not your fault. They knocked you out with something. I saw you trying to fight them off to get to us."

He shakes his head. "Still, Miss Raven, I'm sorry." She hugs him.

"How is Mick? He was trying to help us." My girl has such compassion.

He sits her down. "They are releasing him today from the hospital. What do you think we can do to help his situation without offending him?"

She looks so lost in her own thoughts. "I need to see him, Jax. I need to let him see that I'm okay. I hope this didn't escalate his nightmares."

I can only imagine what this has triggered off for this man.

"Sweetheart, I will do whatever you feel is necessary to help him."

She smiles. "Thank you, both of you. What Mick needs most is to not be judged by anyone. People look right past him and they don't take the time to just listen. He's a proud man and very strong. He's just needs time to heal and someone to listen to him."

I sit in one of the club chairs and I smile at Raven. She returns with one more mischievous, confirming she knows I'm remembering that afternoon, in this very chair. My cock springs to life.

Trying to give my thoughts a different direction, I turn to Max, "Okay, mate, what's bothering you? What else have you found out?"

He looks at Raven. "First, Miss Raven, what did the kidnappers say?"

She takes a steadying breath. "They knew that Michael and I got out of the duct tape, and they said it saved them the trouble. The voice was the same as the man that was outside the gym. Their faces were covered the whole time. They came into the room one time, when Michael and I were laughing. They videotaped us, and walked out without a word."

"Jax, here's what's bothering me. First, Miss Raven wasn't supposed to be on playground duty that day. Second, when we got to the warehouse, there was no one there, almost like they knew we found out where they were and didn't have time to move them. Third, the interoffice envelopes are bugging me. We saw the first one being delivered, but not the second one. Fourth, they knew everything about Miss Raven's past, stuff that was classified. How were they going to sell her to the highest bidder? By the ransom they demanded when they asked for Michael, they knew you would pay. So, why not just offer you Miss Raven, too. It would be easier that way. This is about something more. I can tell you now; this is a puzzle that we don't have all the pieces to."

My eyes shoot back and forth between Max and Raven. I still hadn't told her about her being offered up for auction. She is white and shaking. I jump up and grab her. *Fuck.*

"I'm sorry, baby. I didn't get a chance to tell you everything. Fuck!"

"Jax, is there anything else you haven't told me?"

I run my hand through my hair and rub the back of my neck as I glance over at Max. He gives me a knowing nod, gets up and steps out of the room, allowing us some privacy. "Sit."

"This must be bad, Jax ,if you're telling me to sit."

Fuck, I could snap Joseph in half right now. "I didn't want to be the one to tell you this. It should be Joseph, but you need to know everything." I proceed to tell her everything Joseph told me about her, the half-brother, and finally, about Marco. She's shaking and very pale. I scoop her up and wrap my arms around her, holding her tight. I'm worried; she's being so quiet. "Baby, you're safe now. I promise you, no one will get to you."

There is a commotion outside my door. Joseph barrels through it while Max tries to hold him back. "Max, if you don't fucking let me go, so help me, I'll shoot your fucking Scottish ass and kick you over the pond!"

Raven jumps up and runs to Joseph. She reaches back and smacks him so hard across the face that even Max and I wince. I want to stop her, but I realize that she needs to have closure. She closes my office door and leans against it, not saying anything. She walks back up to Joseph, "Why?"

He has the decency to look ashamed. "Cara, sit, I'll answer your questions."

I see fire in her eyes. "My name is Raven, and I never want to hear that other name again."

He has the grace to look embarrassed. "Okay, what do you want to know?" She starts to pace instead of sitting like Joseph suggested. "Why didn't you tell me I have a half-brother?" She stops and glares at him.

"Raven, I honestly felt it was for the best. He was a product of your father's evil brother; a brutal, vicious and jealous man." He pulls a handerkerchief out from his back pocket and wipes his brow before sitting.

She steps in front of him, leaning into the chair with her arms on each side, trapping him. "He was also part of my mother; a beautiful, kind, and tender hearted woman. Don't you think I should have had the right to know that there is someone out there? That I *actually* have a family member somewhere? Do you know how hard it was, after my adoptive mom died? Did you know my adopted father tried to rape me?! Is that why you put Marco into my life? After all this time, I thought he was my best friend—a brother—only to find out he is your *fucking* employee!" I see her fighting the tears and I want to take her in my arms, but she needs this more.

"Raven, I promised your father that I would protect you, no matter what. Hate me if you have to, but I would do it all over again. Antonio was not just my partner—he was my best friend, and he saved my life!"

"What do you mean; my father saved your life?" She asks through her tears.

"Raven, that day we rescued you, your father pushed me out of the way, and took a bullet that was meant for me."

I reach her just as she's about to hit the floor. "Fuck, Joseph, anything else you want to do to fuck up her life even more?" I snap. Max gets a cold towel for her head and she starts to come around. "I'm not letting you out of my arms, so don't even ask, sweetheart."

She nods, "That's fine. I don't want you to."

Max looks over his shoulder at Joseph. "Jax and I will keep Miss Raven safe. You need to find out who your leak is—and fast."

Max turns back to me, "Jax, that's the other thing I wanted to talk to you about. There has to be a leak somewhere. First, the Lansing office conveniently lost all traces of the kid. Then, the second interoffice memo was already here, yet the tapes don't show anyone delivering it; not like the first one. I told you . . . *something* is off. I need to have you stick to Miss Raven until we get to the bottom of all this."

Raven gets up. "Jax, I need to go back to my place and get some stuff. And I need to see Marco."

I don't want to bulldoze her, so I do my best to remain calm. "Sweetheart, everything you need, I can have brought to the Tower. We can deal with Marco, later."

"Jax, I know you just want to protect me, but I need to do this and I need to do it alone."

"Sweetheart, I'll take you to talk to Marco. However, I plan on being there the entire time. Deal with it!" I know I'm yelling, but this woman drives me fucking crazy. She takes in a deep breath, gives me a curt smile, and nods her head in agreement. *Good.*

Just like that, we're out the door. As we were leaving, I hear Joseph and Max arguing, but we're not sticking around to find out why. "Duke, I'll be out of the office for the rest of the day. If you need anything, I'm on my cell." We ride the elevator to the parking garage in silence. Maybe it will give us *both* a chance to calm down. "We'll stop by the hospital to see Mick before we go to your place, okay?"

She hits me with that smile. "Thank you. I know you're trying to protect me."

I pull her into my arms. "Stop thanking me. I would move heaven and earth to keep you safe and happy. I just wish you would let me." I kiss the top of her head and breathe her hair in.

"Do you think Mick would be open to working with Max in security? I could have Max put him downstairs as security for the building. Maybe if he has a job, it would be something for him to hold onto—a lifeline. I'll have Max talk to him about it." I ramble on without letting her get a word in edgewise. She doesn't really attempt, either.

I wish I knew what she was thinking right now.

WE GET TO THE hospital just as Mick is being discharged. He lets Raven give him a hug, which, I'm guessing, is such progress for him. "Mick, thank you for trying to help us. I'm so sorry they hurt you." She pulls away and gives him another once-over. As I watch their interaction, I realize how much Raven means to this man. It's a friendship she forged on kindness and respect.

"Raven, I'm sorry I didn't get to the school sooner to stop them."

She sits next to him rubbing his arm, offering him comfort. "Why were you at the school?"

He drops his gaze to the floor, seemingly uncomfortable with my question. "The other day, when we walked to the school, I noticed the van. It felt off to me. So, I thought I would keep a closer eye on you. Like I said, I'm just sorry I didn't get there sooner."

I extend my hand to Mick. "I'm grateful that you tried to help my girl and my nephew. I would like to help you, and before you say anything, please listen to me." I hold my other hand up to emphasize. We could use a man with your proven courage. You stepped up to the plate to help, when nothing was expected of you. A lesser man would have turned away. Just promise me you'll think about it." I reach into my back pocket, pull out my business card wallet, and retrieve one for him. "Here is my card; when you're ready, call Max or me. And again, thank you."

"Thank you." Mick extends his hand out for another shake. With that, we say our goodbyes and leave him to finish anything that needs finishing with his discharge.

Raven

WE HEAD BACK TO Jax's car in silence. This man has rendered me speechless. He is willing to take a chance on a man that most people walk past every day without a second glance. It's all the little things that make up a person. He might not show it, but he is tender hearted, and at this moment, I realize how deeply I love this man.

Jaxson

"I NEED TO CALL Max and let him know what Mick said about the van."

She takes my hand. "I wonder how long they were watching before they made their move. I was not supposed to be on playground duty, I took Jackie's place."

"Yeah, she told Max. She was distraught; she thought maybe it was supposed to be her. Max has been keeping a close eye on her." I reassure her.

"How long have you been friends with Jackie?" I decide to change the subject a little bit.

She smiles at the mention of Jackie and their friendship. "We were roommates in college. She is my best friend, and her family treats me like I'm their daughter. I could never ask for a better friend." Her grip on my hand tightens when I ask her why Jackie doesn't like Marco. "I'm not sure. I just know they don't get along, at all. I wanted the three of us to live together, but once they got to know each other, I knew that would never happen. Jackie looks sweet—almost submissive, but she is very intelligent and always observant. I think it has to do with the way she grew up. Most of her formative years were spent at her family's compound in Switzerland. She always had at least one, sometimes two, security guards."

"I'm sure growing up with such tight security made her more cautious when meeting new people," he states. "I better let Max know right away; what Mick said."

While he calls Max to tell him what Mick said, I think I'll check in on Jackie. "Hey, Jackie, I'm checking in."

She squeals, "Oh my God, Raven, I'm sorry. It was supposed to be me!"

I take a deep breath. "Calm down, we don't know any such thing. I'm just glad everyone is okay." *She really is like a sister to me.*

"Raven, can we get together tomorrow? I need a girl talk."

"Only if you bring the chocolate!"

She laughs. "I knew I loved you for a reason. It's a date!"

WE GET TO MY place in record time, which I notice, is the usual for Jax. I'm not even sure Marco will be home.

"Raven, do you know if Marco is even home?" Jax asks as if he's just read my mind.

Part of me hopes that Marco is home and part of me hopes he's not. I don't know if I'm ready to face him and his betrayal, just yet.

"Sometimes he works from home, but I'm not sure where he is today." We get upstairs to find the place empty. "Jax, I'm just going to pack an overnight bag. It shouldn't take me too long." I put my purse down on the counter and notice some of my magazines came in. I grab them and a pad out of the junk drawer before heading down to my room. I decide to leave a note for Marco, letting him know that I'm staying with Jax and also informing him that I've spoken to Joseph. *"We need to talk,"* is what I finish the letter off with. I walk out of my bedroom and Jax is leaning against the counter. Dang it, he is so beautiful. Before I leave, I have to dig out a picture I promised Michael, so I quickly go back in. I see Jax coming into my room out of my peripheral vision and he watches me dig through a shoebox.

"What are you looking for?" He comes over to see what I'm doing.

"I promised Michael I would show him a picture of my dog."

Jax is looking at the pictures in my shoebox. He finds a picture of my real mom and dad. "You look like a combination of both parents."

I'm about to comment but then I see it. "I found it! Look, this was my dog, Winston."

"Raven, that is not a dog, it's a grizzly bear!" he says wide-eyed.

I laugh, "He was a very protective Newfoundland, and he scared away many of my dates. That's probably why I never had a boyfriend in school."

Jax is stroking my arm, making me feel safe with his constant touch. Part of me wants to close the door and walk away from here, never looking back. The other part of me is determined to live my life without fear. He pulls me into his arms, and I need him. "Raven, you don't ever have to come back here or see Marco if you don't want to. I can handle it all for you." He understands my fear without having to tell him.

"This is my home and I love it. I'm not ready to let it go, and as far as Marco is concerned, I don't know what I'm going to do. I would like to see Michael today. Do you think that's possible?"

Jax smiles, then he calls Bella, informing her we're on our way. I have to laugh, he just does whatever he wants, whenever he wants, and watch out if you're in his path . . . *my bulldozer.*

*J*axson

WE PULL UP TO Bella's and Vito comes out to greet us. Raven kneels down, petting him and he loves it; licking and nuzzling her. I find this amazing since that beast only likes Junior. Junior comes running up to Raven as soon as we get in the door. I'm guessing he's excited to introduce her to his dog.

"Michael, he is just as sweet and strong as you described him."

We head into the living room where Bella, Michael, and my mum are waiting, but it's Junior I'm worried about. He's clinging to Raven, not wanting to let go. She kneels down so she's face to face with him. "Hey, buddy, you okay?"

He seems embarrassed, looking down at his feet. "Yeah, I was really worried about you. Mom said you're going to be fine. Will you still be my teacher?"

She smiles at him. "Miss Jackie will take over for a couple of days while I sort everything out, but then I'll be back. No worrying, okay?" She palms his face. This seems to pacify him, but I can tell something is not right with Raven. "I stopped at my place and found that picture I promised you." She retrieves it from her purse. "This was Winston."

He gasps. "Wow, Miss Raven, he really was huge and he does look like a bear."

My mum comes up to Raven and embraces her, and the tension in the room seems to ease.

"Hey, Junior, why don't you take Vito out back?" I suggest.

He laughs, "Uncle Jax, if you want me out of the room, you could just ask."

"When did you become such a wisearse?" I growl. Raven is giggling.

"Um, sweetheart, what's so amusing?"

"Well, it seems to me that Michael Jr. has inherited the Phillip's gene for directness."

Michael Sr. looks at Raven and throws his arms in the air. "Welcome to my world!"

After Junior leaves the room, my mum asks if we found out anything new. "Mum, the only thing we have right now, is more questions than answers." I let out a big sigh of frustration. Raven takes my hand like it's a lifeline. "It seems that the kidnappers were after Junior and Raven was only a bonus. The problem is, they now know who Raven really is, which puts everyone around her at risk. Max thinks there is a leak, possibly at the FBI and also at Raiders Inc."

Bella turns to Raven, "I hope you understand that I'm not saying this to be mean, but you can't go back to teaching at my son's school. Until you can get to the bottom of this, you should stay away from my family, including my brother."

"Bella!" I jump up.

Before I can say anything more, Raven grabs my hand and pulls me down. "Jax, please."

"No, Raven. No one will tell me who I can or can't be with, not even my family."

Everyone is yelling until my mum stands up and tells us all to be quiet. "First, my grandson is upstairs and can probably hear everything. Second, son, I understand your need to protect Raven and Bella, I understand your need to protect your family, but this is *my family too*, so please listen.

"Raven, you can't possibly go back to school until all of this is resolved. Too many children would be at risk and I don't think you would ever want that on your conscious. We know that my grandson was the original target, so that means he will still need more protection. Sending him back to school might not be the best thing right now. I think the best thing would be for you to home school Michael until this gets resolved. This house is locked up tighter than the White House. When a message was left here, Vito scared the person off.

I think Raven should stay here. She home schools Michael, and we add tighter security. Everyone will be safe. Michael will continue to get the education that he deserves and Raven will be doing something, rather than nothing. I already spoke with Maxwell, and he thought it was the best idea." she finishes her rant (a logical one, at that) and all we can seem to do is stare at her, speechless.

Bella stands up and takes Ravens hand, "Come, I'll show you to your new room."

Mum goes with them, leaving me and Michael, stunned at what just went down.

Michael looks at me and starts laughing. "What's so fucking funny?"

He's now in hysterics. "Raven's room has a twin bed and it's right next to Junior's. You poor bastard, you're so not getting laid!"

My fucking dick hurts at the revelation—*no cock heaven anytime soon.*

Chapter Thirteen

Jaxson

I CHECK IN WITH Duke, all is quiet at Raiders. So I call Joseph to see if he found out anything new, but nothing has changed. I head to the kitchen for coffee. I find Mum in there, already having her afternoon tea. "Hey, Mum, is Raven all settled in?"

Her breath quickens as her spoon rattles against her cup. It breaks my heart that she is afraid. "Jaxson, I'm worried, very worried."

I try to comfort her, "I know, Mum."

She shakes her head. "No I don't think you really do." She stirs her tea.

"Mum, I understand, but she wasn't even a target. It was Junior, all because of me, and now they're both targets. Unfortunately, I'm the one who started this ugly ball rolling and I'm the one who has to figure out how to stop it. I don't want their lives ruined because of me."

A tear escapes her and she quickly wipes it away. "You're a good man, don't ever forget that."

Raven comes in, I can't help but hug her; she's so brave. "You okay, sweetheart?"

She seems to be trying so hard to keep it together. "I guess. I just called Jackie. She's going to come by with stuff for me so I can homeschool Michael. I still haven't heard from Marco. Have you heard from Joseph?" She leans against the counter, crossing her arms. My mum quietly excuses herself, grabbing her teacup and saucer, nodding towards the living room.

I offer my mum a meek smile and turn my focus back to Raven. "I called him, but he has nothing new to report. I'm going to head back to the office for a little bit, then I'll come back here."

She shrugs her shoulders. "You don't have to do that. I know you have a lot of work to do."

Christ, this is killing me. "Sweetheart, I'm going to be stuck to you like glue, so just get used to it." She starts to cry. *Oh, fuck!* "Stop, *right now*. just stop. I can't take it when you cry. It tears at my soul, so please don't." I plead. She throws herself into my arms and holds on tight, kissing me like I'm her lifeline. "Raven, we need to stop this, like *right now*." She looks at me like a wounded puppy. "Oh fuck, Raven. Michael informed me that your room is next to Junior's, and it has a twin bed, so my dick has been booted out of cock heaven. If you keep doing that, I won't be able to control myself!"

"Follow me," she whispers, grabbing my hand. She leads me to the washroom off the kitchen and locks the door.

"Now, Jax, you'll do as I tell you, because after all, I am the teacher." I nod, "Yes ma'am!"

She rubs her delicate hands under my shirt, and my cock has jumped to attention—he's such a greedy bastard. She brings her hands back out, reaches for and slowly unbuttons her blouse. She lifts each one of her breasts out of her bra. I go to reach for them, and she backs away.

"Did you forget that I'm the teacher? You have to do what I tell you." She rubs each one of her nipples until they are hard. Throwing her head back, she licks her lips. It's taking all I have just to watch. She undoes my pants and my cock springs to attention. "Sit down."

I hit her with my Jaxson smirk, "If I don't, will the teacher punish me?"

She moans, "Jax, is that something you want to find out, right now?"

I sit down and my head is level with her chest. She opens my legs and gets on her knees between them. She takes my cock in her hand, and it takes everything I have to control myself from just ramming my cock in her right now. *Oh, Sweet Jesus.* She takes me in her mouth; it's so warm. She licks up and down and then around. *How the fuck does she go so deep?* She finds that spot, just under my sac, presses, and just like that, I'm losing it.

"Oh fuck, baby, deeper . . . bare your teeth for me." I growl, "Fuck—harder!"

That's it! I'm coming from the depths of my soul. It's endless and she takes it all.

When she finishes, she places my cock between her breasts, rubbing up and down. Oh, fuck all that's holy; I'm hard as stone, again! She takes off her bra, tossing it onto the floor. She gets up, taking her jeans off real slowly, and then she slides her knickers down. She stands before me in nothing but heels. I know I'm growling as I try to reach for her. But she backs away, shaking her head. She takes the clip out of her hair, letting it cascade down, brushing her nipples. She slides her hands down her chest, playing with her nipples. Then she continues sliding her hands down and reaches between her legs. Her head tilts back as she dips her fingers deep into—what I like to refer to as—my cock heaven. She lets out a low moan and I think I could explode just from watching the show—giving herself pleasure the way I do. *What a lucky bastard I am!*

"Oh, Jax, oh, baby. . . so good." I'm fighting with myself not to touch her. She takes her fingers out and slips them into her mouth. Fuck, this is so erotic. I don't know how much more I can take. "Jax, I'm so wet for you." She puts her finger in my mouth and I taste her arousal. Sweet Jesus! She straddles me and slowly, lowers herself onto my cock. I'm back in my happy place. It is the most beautiful place in the world. She starts riding me really slow. "Jax, you're going to make me come really, really hard. Do you feel how wet I am for you? Just for you, baby, and your wonderful cock." Wow, she's picking up my habit of dirty talk, and I've got to say, it's beautiful . . . just fucking beautiful.

"Raven, look into my eyes. Are you there yet?"

She leans in. "Almost, baby. Play with my nipples, please." She doesn't have to ask me twice. I nibble each one and that's all it takes. She's falling, and I'm right behind her. Her forehead rests on mine, and she clenches my cock like an iron fist. I think I will definitely have to thank her Pilates instructor! She kisses me long and slow. "Jax, are you feeling better now that you've been to cock heaven?"

Hmm. "All better, baby, and you?"

She smiles. "I'm good now, but I hope no one missed us." We get

THE UNRAVELING OF *Raven*

cleaned up and sneak out with the hope that no one was looking for us.

Duke

AFTER EVERYONE LEAVES, I call Erica on my cell phone. "Erica, I need to see you. Please call me back!" I don't know how I let myself get *this* deep into this mess. I don't know what I need more, to get out of Michigan or inside Erica's warm cunt. Either way, I'm in way over my head. I sit at my desk, happy that I planted the bugs she gave so I could hear what was being said. Jax is too busy, fucking Raven, to think about anything else. But that guy, Max?—He scares me. Not even Joseph scares me like Max does. Max is not thinking with his dick; he's looking at the big picture, unlike Jax. How the fuck did this guy make so much money anyway, when he can be so easily distracted by the opposite sex. Erica said he is shrewd, but damn if I can see it.

I'm gathering up my stuff to leave for the day when I turn around and find Max, standing there, in the shadows, just staring at me. I nearly jump out of my skin. I'm not set out for this kind of shit! "Oh, I'm sorry. I didn't see you there. Can I help you with anything?"

Maxwell

MY TINGLE SENSE IS firing up. "Actually, Duke, I have some questions for you. Let's step in to Jax's office." I suggest. I can tell he's apprehensive.

"Is this going to be long because I have an appointment I can't miss?"

"I'm sure you do, Duke, but this is important, please follow me. Would you like some water? You seem to be a bit nervous."

He shakes his head. "I'm fine. I just can't be late for my appointment."

I walk right up to him, invading his personal space. I love to do that when I want to throw someone off balance. "I'll get right to the point then. Do you know how the second interoffice envelope was delivered to your desk?"

He shrugs his shoulders "How would I know? I wasn't here."

I take another step closer, and he steps back. "True, but it might have been delivered the night before and only found in the morning. I'm just covering all the bases."

He shakes his head. "I never saw anything. Now, if that's all, I really need to go."

I back up. "Sure, Duke. Sorry to keep you."

THAT GUY IS A little fucking weasel. I need to call Jax, but first, I want to sweep the office. I decide to call Tony, I'm sure he's still here. "Hey, do me a favor. I know Jax sweeps this place weekly, but something is bothering me, so do it again."

Tony never questions my tingle sense. "Sure, Max."

As I wait at Jax's bar for the all clear, I see Tony coming towards me, motioning me to be quiet. He holds up a bug but doesn't give me the all clear. He pulls out a laser and some spray before motioning me out of the room. He walks through the room spraying some stuff.

I've never seen anything like this. He backs out of the room leaving the bug, turns on the laser and the fucking room lights up like a Christmas tree! He closes the door and turns to me, but still motioning me to be quiet. Now, he begins spraying around Duke's area—nothing. "Max, it's fucked up in there,"

I'm in shock. "Tony, this makes no sense. Jax sweeps this place every week. He had special lead put in the walls. The only place to get a cell signal is in front of the window, and since it's all glass, a bug could easily be seen." I throw my hands out, miffed. Tony shows me one of the bugs, and it's the size of a grain of rice.

"Max, the reason there are so many is because of the lead in the walls. They are bouncing off of each other. There has to be a place in the office that doesn't have lead walls, where someone is listening with some hi-tech shit."

It's time I call Jax and get his arse here, now!

JAX GETS TO RAIDERS in record time. "Okay, I'm here now. What is so earth shattering that I had to rush here?"

I motion him towards the office. "We need to show you something, but please, be quiet." I open his office door, and Tony hits the laser. Jax turns to me, and I can tell he is going to lose it. He steps back and closes the door. He motions to Tony if the area we are in has been swept, and he nods yes.

"Max, what the fuck is going on? We sweep that office weekly, plus the added protection of the lead walls. How is this even possible?"

Tony clears his throat, "There has to be a weak spot somewhere in that office, and with the new technology that's out there, they are bouncing from one transmitter to the other. We need to find the 'mother', which is what they are all feeding into."

Max is pacing. "Are the private bathroom walls lined, also?"

I shake my head. "I honestly don't know. I never thought about it. Heck, I didn't even think about any of this until everything went down with Erica."

Tony instructs us to wait while he goes in to sweep the private bathroom. He comes back out, letting us know the device is, in fact, in the restroom.

"It is the size of a capsule. I can deactivate it or we can leave it on. Now that we know it's there, we can monitor what we let them know." He sits on top of Duke's desk, waiting for our thoughts.

"Leave it for now." Jax finally decides. I take a deep breath. "Tony, please go and sweep Max's office."

"Please don't tell me you think I'm involved?" I feel my eyes practically bulge out of their sockets in disbelief.

"Max, don't be ridiculous. I just need a safe place to work and think." He gives me a look as if I'm crazy.

Jaxson

AFTER WE GET THE all clear from Tony, I inform him that I want Max's office swept two times a day. And no one is to know but me and Max. "Max, I don't want anyone to know what we're doing, understood?"

"What about Joseph and Raven?"

I shake my head. "Until we get to the bottom of this, no one."

"Okay, understood," he agrees.

"All right, Max, bring me up to speed."

He starts his pacing and surprisingly, it is calming me. "Jax, you know that second envelope is bothering me, so I questioned Duke today about it."

"But, Max, you know he wasn't even here."

He stops pacing. "I thought of that, but who's to say it wasn't delivered the night before? And why was there no footage like the first one? There are too many questions and not enough answers. I know we did a check on him before you hired him, but I'd like to dig further, if that's okay with you?"

"Sure, but what reason would he have?"

"Try fifty million of them, Jax. Let's not forget the original ransom was fifty million for Junior. Raven was a bonus. The whole truth about Raven's family came out in your office, which we now know was bugged, between the last sweep and today. So who ever was listening, learned about her family when Joseph showed up."

I feel like my fucking head is going to explode. "Okay, Max, we need to find out who bugged the office and stop them before they auction off Raven's information to the highest bidder."

He starts pacing again. "Jax, I've been thinking about that. I think the key lies with the half-brother."

"I agree. I want to see the file on the kid. See if Joseph will play ball. If not, I'm not opposed to calling in favors. I'm going back to my place to pick up a few things and then I'm headed to Bella's. Any sign of that fucker, Marco?"

He shakes his head. "No, but when he shows up, do you want me to keep him there?"

"Yeah, Raven needs to confront him, and I plan on being there." I tap my finger hard on his desk.

I HEAD TO MY place to pick up some stuff. Max put a guard on me, even though I don't think I need one. Right now, I'm so distracted that, it's probably for the best. The doorman informs me that there was a delivery for me which is strange since, I don't advertise where I live. He hands me an envelope that was messengered over. On my way upstairs, I call Max and tell him about the envelope. He tells me not to open it, and he's on his way. I throw the envelope on the bar and pour myself three-fingers of Johnny Walker Platinum and wait for Max. Max shows up with Tony and asks him to sweep my place. "Max, is this necessary? This place is like Fort Knox with security."

Tony waves at us to get our attention and puts his finger to his lips to silence us. When he is done, he tells us all is clear, but do not bring anything from the office into the house.

Max puts on gloves and opens the envelope. Inside is a file, which contains everything about Raven/Cara, her mother, father, and her half-brother. The only thing that is conveniently missing is a picture of the brother.

There is a note:

We know it all. The starting bid fifty million. We'll give you first crack at it. We'll be in touch.

I stare at the folder. Words just aren't coming.

"Jax, there is that number again. I just don't like it."

My heart is driving the bus and not my head, which is never good. "I have to protect her. I can't let this fall into the wrong hands. Did you pull reports on her real parents?"

He pulls out a folder. "Her mother, Gabriella, was an only child. Gabriella's father was a prominent doctor in Virginia and Gabriella's mother was a district attorney. Her parents died in a car accident while she was away at college. A drunk driver hit them. There was a large settlement that was invested for her." He shuffles papers around. "Antonio's family is really bad news. They can be traced back to the early 1900's, to a Sicilian immigrant. Antonio's father, Dion, was the 'Boss of Boss.' Antonio had an older brother, Monti, who died before Antonio did. Monti died in a bar room brawl. There's a younger brother, Vincent, and a sister, Annabelle. Annabelle was a surprise because Joseph never mentioned her. It seems when Dion died, Vincent took over the business, which includes a lucrative, drug business.

"You remember when John Gotti was in power in New York? It seemed none of the charges ever stuck to him, earning him the nickname, 'Teflon Don.' Well the same could be said for Vincent."

"Max what are our options here?"

He pours a scotch, "Well, I think we need to play ball until we can figure out who the moles are."

"You think there is more than one?"

He downs his drink. "Yeah, I do. I think there's one within the FBI, which is obvious by this file, and I really think there is a leak in your office."

"Max, take the file and lock it in your office safe. I already have the money ready, but I need some guarantee that this is the only file. Other than you and me, who else has the combination to the safe?"

He shakes his head. "No one and I plan on keeping it that way." He takes the file and puts it in the safe, locking it up. I can't believe all this is happening. I gather my stuff and head to Bella's. I really need my girl right now.

WHEN I GET TO Bella's, everyone is in the family room watching a movie. I snuggle up to Raven, holding her as close as possible. "What's the matter, Jax?"

I shake my head. "Nothing, I just need this right now." She doesn't press for information, which is good because I'm on overload.

"Jax, did you eat dinner?"

I look into those beautiful eyes, "No."

She takes my hand, "Okay, come in the kitchen."

I know I have a look of shock on my face. "Why, Miss Raven, are you going to cook for me?"

She looks offended. "I may not cook, but I'll have you know that I make the best peanut butter and jelly sandwich this side of the Mississippi!" She swats my arm. Raven pulls out everything she needs to makes me a PB and J and surprises me with a chocolate egg cream.

"Wow, okay, how do you know this is my favorite drink ever?"

"Jax, when you watched the video of Michael and I being held captive, did you wonder what we were laughing about?"

I forgot about that. "Tell you the truth, I barely had time to process everything, but now that you mention it, what were you two laughing at?"

She smiles at me. "You."

I freeze mid bite of my PB and J. "Excuse me?"

She repeats. "You."

"I heard you, but I don't get it. Why were you laughing at me?"

She takes a deep breath to steady her nerves, I think. "Well, I realized that I was the same age as Michael is when I was kidnapped, and I felt I needed to distract him from the situation. First, we talked about his dog and I told him about mine. Then I asked him about television shows, and it was right at that moment he told me that his favorite show is *Doctor Who*. Needless to say, I could not control my laughter. He told me how the two of you have a ritual of watching *the doctor* while you eat PB and J, drinking chocolate egg creams, and all while wearing bow ties."

"Oh." I give her a shy grin.

She leans in and kisses me. "Yeah, *oh*." She puts her head on my shoulder. "So, Jax, are you ready to tell me what's going on?"

I shake my head, "No, and before you jump all over me, I know you need to know, but I really only have bits and pieces. Right now, I want to block everything but you, out of my head, just for tonight, please."

"Okay, but tomorrow we talk," she states, adamantly.

I kiss her, "Okay, it's not like I'm going to cock heaven tonight, right? I'm just making sure." *This is going to kill me I just know it.*

"Well, if everyone goes to sleep early, you might get to visit your happy place."

I swear my cock has ears because he has just sprung to life! "Sweetheart, maybe we can slip sleeping pills in their drinks? Oh relax, I'm joking." Okay, maybe I'm not joking but I would never tell her that.

It's getting late and everyone is getting that end of the day, glazed over, look. Michael carries Junior upstairs. Bella and Mum finally go up, too. Raven curls up into my side, and I realize, there is no way I'm going to the happy place with everyone under the same roof. I want my girl, and I want her screaming. That's just not going to happen tonight. I look down to break it to her and realize she is out cold. It's okay. She's safe in my arms. It's not cock heaven, but it's still my happy place.

Chapter Fourteen

Duke

I WAIT ALL NIGHT for Erica, and she doesn't call or show up. This is so fucked up. Finally, I get a text message, telling me to meet her at the coffee house on 52nd street again. When I show up, she is already there waiting. "Duke, you need to calm down."

I glare at her. "Calm down? You don't have Max breathing down your fucking neck!"

She starts stroking my arm. "What did Max ask you?"

I'm trying to remember everything, but I'm not cut out for this shit. "He was questioning the second envelope and how it got there. I told him, I wouldn't know since I wasn't there. I made sure Jax found it before I got there, just like you said. How did they find the warehouse, Erica? You said they would never find it?" I ramble on. I can't help it, I'm in panic mode.

She looks pissed off. "Raven had a second cell phone that Jax was making her carry. The crazy motherfucker put a tracking app on the phone."

I just want this over with. "So what now? We've got nothing; no kid and no money."

"We have something worth a hell of a lot more."

I swear I'm going to crack soon. "What do we have, because I'm not seeing it?"

She smiles. "We have your sister's true identity that we are going to sell to the highest bidder."

I grit my teeth, "I'm too nervous. I'm not cut out for this shit!"

She grabs my arm. "Nonsense, your father is a cold-blooded killer. That same blood is running through your veins!"

I feel bad for Raven, but I can't let Erica know that. "What about my sister? I read the file. What happens to her through all of this?"

She studies me for a moment. "Up until a couple of days ago, you didn't even know you had a sister, now you're worried? I hope whatever happens to her, torments Jax for the rest of his fucking life!" With that, she gets up and walks out. I just sit here, not knowing what to do next.

Jaxson

I WAKE UP IN The same spot I was in when I fell asleep last night, with Raven still curled up next to me. I'd like to enjoy this for a little bit, but then, my cell phone starts vibrating. There's a text from Max, "Get to my office, stat." I look at the time and it's only 6:30 am. I place soft kisses on Raven's face, when all of a sudden, I feel very hot breath near my head and hear a distinct growl. *Oh shit.* I'm not an idiot. I stop moving. Raven starts to stir, I tell her that Vito is behind her, very upset, and to please not move.

Raven looks back at Vito, "Hey, big guy, everything's good. Down."

He lies down at once. Wow, that dog never listens to me. As a matter of fact the only one he ever listens to is Junior. "I can't believe how he listens to you, it's truly amazing." I sigh.

"Well, I need to jump in the shower and pop over to work for a little bit."

She smiles at me. "Why don't you use the shower in my room? I can meet you in there."

I scoop her up and race up those stairs with only thoughts of the happy place. "Sweetheart, we still need to be really quiet, so no screaming."

She steps into the shower. She is so beautiful, I could just look at her all day, but there are other priorities. However, cock heaven is at the top of the list! I pull her towards me. "Wrap your legs around my waist."

She grabs my hair and pulls my head back. Our eyes lock and I slam into her—hard! She kisses me to stifle both of our screams. "Hold on tight, baby, this is going to be hard. I need it to be hard." I pull back and hit her cervix again and again. I feel myself starting to shake and my cock feels like the head is going to explode! "Oh fuck, oh fuck, oh fuck, Raven! I'm there, are you there?"

I don't have to wait for her answer—she locks on to my eyes, and it's the peak just before the fall, the look into her soul. We fall together. I slide down the shower wall with Raven still latched onto my cock. I thank all that's holy for my girl and cock heaven. It really is a very happy place.

WHEN I GET TO Raiders, I head up the back way to Max's office. "Hey, sorry I took so long."

He's fuming. "Sit down, Jax, I have some video to show you, and you're not going to be happy."

He turns his computer towards me and hits play. I can't believe what I'm seeing. All I can do is stare at the screen in shock. *What the fuck?* Erica and Duke, sitting in a coffee shop together.

"Where are they now, Max?"

He takes a deep breath. "I have someone tailing Duke, but I don't know where Erica went. The security guy thought he should stay on Duke since that was his assignment, however, he e-mailed me the video so I could get a heads up."

Fuck, this can't be happening. "I want to rip him from limb to limb, and forget what I want to do to her!"

I look at Max and admire how he remains so calm. "Jax, you need to calm down."

In one sweep I throw everything off the fucking desk! "Don't fucking tell me to calm down! This fucker has caused so much trouble and danger, and for what? Money! And that *bitch*—I should have sent her to prison when I had the chance! Was this all about revenge?"

"Jax, I don't know, but again, you need to calm down if what I'm suggesting is going to work."

I take a few calming breaths. "Okay, what's your plan? It better involve a lot of pain for these two fuckers."

"We leave Duke in play—let him think we're idiots. Duke is the low man in all of this. We need to find the leak at the FBI and then we need to figure out what to do about Raven's family. Jax, I have a feeling that Duke could possibly be the half-brother."

How the fuck did this get so out of control? "Are you fucking kidding me?"

He shakes his head, "No, I'm not kidding. The background report only said he was adopted and that's not a crime. His adoption records are sealed and he has no police record, no flags at all. I just think it's all too neatly wrapped."

I know he's right. "Okay, I trust you with my life and the lives of my family. I'll go along with the plan. What do you want to do about Joseph? Should we tell him about Duke or should we wait?"

I know the answer before I even ask the question. Max plays all his cards close to the vest, always has. "I'm not in a rush to tell anyone anything, Jax. Let's just sit back. In the meantime, I have my guy following Duke, and I'll put someone on Erica, as soon as we locate her. I really think she is the key to this mess. Has Marco shown up yet?"

"No, which also seems very strange. First, he was up her arse all the time, and now, he's nowhere to be found."

Hmm. "Do you think Joseph might have him stashed away?"

Max begins his ritual of pacing. "Well, Jax, maybe you should meet with Joseph. You don't have to tell him everything—just enough. I don't want to you to meet him in your office."

I stand up to look for my keys in the mess on the floor. "I'll tell him I'm working from the penthouse."

"I'm going to give you a small camera device. I want you to film him. Just humor me, Jax. There are things that I'm trained to look for, plus, I'm not emotionally invested like you are."

Who am I to argue with him? I call Joseph and get back to my place to set everything up.

WHEN JOSEPH GETS TO my place, I pour him a scotch, making sure I keep him in camera range. "Joseph, I'm going to get right to the point, where is Marco?" I spit out.

Joseph stares at me blankly for a moment. "Jax, I have no idea. He hasn't checked in, and he hasn't been to his day job, or back to the apartment. We also haven't heard anything from the kidnappers, have you?"

I watch his every move, trying to read his body language. "Everything has been very quiet, Joseph, almost too quiet.

Have you been able to get the file on the brother from Lansing?"

He looks embarrassed, as he should be. "It seems to be lost."

If I didn't need this man right now, I think I would just kick his arse out. "You're the director of the *fucking* FBI and you can't even find a *fucking* file? I'm really feeling very safe right now!"

He slams his glass down. "Don't be sarcastic, Jax. I'm doing the best I can. I will keep you in the loop, and you do the same." With that, he gets up and leaves.

I upload the video to Max before I go to pick up Raven, we need alone time.

Raven

I'M HAPPY THAT JACKIE is on her way, I need girlfriend time. As she gets here, I notice she has a guard, too, and I feel so guilty about it.

"Hey, Jackie, I'm so sorry you got dragged into this mess."

"Don't worry about it, It's been interesting for me."

Hmm. "Oh really. Okay, chocolate, coffee, pastries, and girl talk!" I saw the sparks flying with her and Max. "So this is about Max?"

"Jump right in, Raven."

"I've been hanging out with Jax and his family; they pull no punches," I giggle. Jackie joins in but then begins to tell me everything that has happened with Max, leading right up to his kiss. "Oh my God, he kissed you, and?"

She throws her hands up, "Nothing. That's just it, he doesn't do relationships."

This man is such a mystery. "Then why kiss you? Maybe he does want a relationship and maybe it's all new to him."

She pops another chocolate in her mouth and I have to laugh. She loves chocolate like I love Nutella. "Raven, he's thirty-eight, I doubt it's new to him."

I roll my eyes at her. "That's not what I meant. Maybe he never had the time for a relationship until now. I can't believe you were ogling him in the mirror!"

We are both laughing now. "I can't believe it either, but let me tell you, he has a wickedly, awesome body."

I put my hand up. "Too much information, girl. I have to look at him every day!"

Jackie gives me a look and I know what's coming. "Have you heard from Marco?"

I'm fighting the tears of betrayal. "No, not a word. I can't believe he was being paid by Joseph to look after me."

I can tell it doesn't surprise Jackie. "I'm sure he will be showing up soon with his tail between his legs. Are you going to continue to room with him?"

I don't even know if I want to live in my apartment anymore, but I'm not ready to share that. "At this point, I'm not sure what I'm going to do."

She pulls me into a big hug. "Well, you can always room with me."

I thank God I have her. "You really are the best friend anyone could ever ask for, Jackie. Thank you so much."

She picks up her stuff and pops another chocolate. "No worries, and on that note, I've got to run. Let's try and get together soon."

Raven

I'M GOING CRAZY JUST sitting around here. I decide to take Vito out for a walk—not that I'm alone, some huge guy that I have nick-named ," Tank", is following me around.

I really need to talk to Marco. I just don't get it. I understand

Joseph wanting to keep me safe and all. Here I thought I did so much on my own yet, I was being monitored the whole time! Add to that, the fact that I have a brother. I just can't believe that somewhere out there, I have a brother. And this information has been kept from him and me. Suddenly, Vito starts crouching down and lets out a low growl. "It's okay, boy, there's nothing there." He's probably just jumpy.

Marco steps out from behind the trees just as I turn around. Tank is on Marco in a second. *Holy shit.* I'm trying to control Vito and stop Tank.

"Vito, heel!" At least he stops. "Tank, it's okay, please let go of him."

Marco looks up at me. "Thank you, baby girl."

I put my hand up, "Please, don't call me that ever again." I just stare at him, not really sure where to begin. "Why?" It's simple, but it's all I can manage at the moment.

"I was young, with great computer skills, when Joseph recruited me. It was supposed to be real simple—just keep an eye on you and report to him over the years. I never expected to become friends with you, let alone, be roommates. I found myself getting in deeper and deeper, until there really was no way out. I was going to back away when you started going out with your ex, but then that relationship went terribly wrong, and I realized, I couldn't leave you. I thought with Jax, you had a chance at a real relationship, but then everything just got so fucked up."

All I can do is cry. "Do you know where my brother is?"

He shakes his head, "No, I never knew anything about that. I was only there to watch over you. Raven, you have to believe me, I would never hurt you. I love you like a sister."

We start walking back towards the house. I see Jax coming towards us and he seems really mad. He grabs Marco by the shirt, "What the fuck do you think you're doing here?"

"Look, Jax, I came here, in good faith, to make a mends with Raven."

"Good faith? Make amends?" Jax yells. "Do you realize how fucked up everything *really* is? Your and Joseph's lies have put Raven and Junior's lives in danger!" He reaches back, and in a flash, Jax takes one swing and Marco goes down.

"Jax! Was that really necessary?" I yelp.

He turns to Tank. "You're fired! You let this man—who is a potential threat—get close to Raven. He could have also gotten to Junior. Get the fuck out of my sight, and take this piece of shit with you!"

Tank picks Marco up and drags him away. "Don't look at me like that. I'm not a crazy man. I did what was necessary to protect you. I understand you wanted to talk to Marco, but I told you, I wanted to be there when you did."

I'm staring at him in disbelief. "I don't understand why you needed to be there. Tank was there and so was Vito. It's not like he was going to kidnap me or hurt me anymore than he already has, so why the need to be there?"

He growls, "Another threat has come through. I'm not saying anything to Joseph or Marco. At this point, the only one I know we can trust is, Max. That's why I wanted to be there."

I put my hands on my hips. "Well, maybe you should have told me, and I would have handled it differently. When you keep me in the dark, this is what happens."

Jaxson

WE WALK BACK TO the house in silence, both of us trying to regroup, I think. "Get your stuff, Raven." I have to calm down I don't want to scare her and have her pull another fucking runner on me.

"Where are we going?"

I pull her into my arms, "I want to spend the night at The Tower. Geez, now you have me calling it that!" I chuckle lightly. "I really need to be alone with you, no interruptions, and no worries. Just you and me."

She pulls me close and I think she gets it, "Oh."

I whisper, "Yeah, *oh*."

Raven

WE HEAD TO THE Tower. Midtown traffic seems to part like the Red Sea whenever Jax is driving. Thankfully, we arrive in one piece. When he pulls out the elevator key for the penthouse, it's just another reminder how removed we are from the outside world. Every time I walk into the penthouse, the view takes my breath away. I turn back around, Jax is right behind me. "Aren't you worried that someone can see in here?"

Jax graces me with that beautiful, crooked smirk. "Do you think I would ever let anyone see you? If it were up to me, I would lock you in here, forever! The windows are mirrored on the outside. We can see out, but no one can see in." He begins caressing my arms and then he lifts both my hands to plant kisses on the inside of my wrists, and there's that jolt—right between my legs! He starts to slowly remove my clothes and I'm left with just my bra, panties, and heels. He growls, "Undress me, sweetheart, real slowly."

I slowly unbutton his shirt, being real careful not to touch his chest. I know if I do, it will be game over before it even starts. I pull his shirt down and let it fall to the floor. Next, I bend down and take his shoes and socks off. *Even his feet are perfect.* I stare up at him. He's so beautiful. "I still have pants on, baby." I snap out of my trance and with shaky hands, undo his pants. He is left with his black, Calvin Klein, boxer briefs, outlining his delicious hard cock. I pull them down to expose my prize and what a wonderful prize it is. I lick the pearl of his arousal off the head. I kiss his cock. It's hard, yet so delicately soft. I take him deep in my mouth, and he growls, "Fuuuuuuuuccccccckkkkkk!" Up and down, then swirl around the head, and back down again. I love that I can give him so much pleasure. He lifts me up before I can finish and kisses me deeply. He slowly removes my bra and panties, but not the heels. He trails kisses down my neck, stopping at each nipple along the way, slowly nipping and sucking.

"Oh, Jax."

"I know, baby, I know."

Kiss, nip, suck, and then lick, over and over again. He hits spots on my body I never knew were so sensitive. He finally makes his way between my legs. He does the kiss, nip, suck, and lick, but then he blows on my clit; I'm shaking and screaming. He guides me down to him and enters me very, very slowly. My legs wrap around his waist and my heels are digging into his ass cheeks. He takes both my wrists into one of his hands and holds them behind my back. He lifts one of my legs and puts it over his shoulder; oh fuck, he's so deep! I arch my back, raising my breast up and closer to his face. I can feel the slight graze of his scruff as he leans down to suck and nibble on my nipples. "Jax, I can't take it, it's too intense!"

"Hold it, baby, you know you can." He starts to slow down, giving me time to get some sort of control.

I need more; I want more, "Damn it, Jax, harder!"

He pulls my leg off of his shoulder, and now both legs are wrapped around his waist, again. I dig my heels into his ass, trying to push him in harder. He looks at me with that crooked grin and twinkling blues, "You want it rough, baby?" His accent so thick now.

"Yes!" I yell. Before I can even think, he has me flipped over.

He growls, "Put your hands against the window and lift that beautiful arse of yours in the air now!" He positions his cock, holding onto my hips and in one swift move, he rams into me.

"Fuuuuuuucccccckkkkkk me!" He's giving it all to me.

"Hard enough for you now, baby?" He backs out and rams in again, this time, smacking my ass over and over again. I'm on fire and at the same time, losing all rhyme and reason. I feel like I'm going to go right through the fucking glass! He gathers my hair into a ponytail in one hand and pulls it back, bringing me into a sitting position; my back to his front. He kisses my neck, nibbling painfully at my ear, and pounds into me, all at the same time.

"You're going to come, baby." He grunts as I clench. I turn my head to find his eyes. Blue to violet and he's done. Bam! His body is convulsing, shaking, quivering, and falling apart.

He turns me around, lifts me up, and carries me into the bed. He takes my shoes off and covers us with the comforter. The cool sheets on my ass feel good and I drift off to sleep in his arms.

I WAKE A FEW hours later and find that I'm alone. I hear some talking.. I put on one of Jax's shirts and head towards the voices. It's Max and Jax, they're talking about me.

"Have you told her yet . . . about Duke?"

"No, Max, I haven't told her that my assistant is actually her brother and that my ex seems to be working with him to sell Raven to the highest bidder," he replies. "I also didn't tell her that we think there is a mole at the FBI. Truthfully, I don't know how much more she can take. I know it's still bothering you that Jackie was supposed to be on the playground that day, not Raven, and that there were two cots in the room where they were held."

"Her father is a powerful man," Max says. "I mean, let's face it, someone who's able to negotiate a peace treaty, is not a lightweight. However, he's very well-liked and respected. Her brother, on the other hand, not so much. He owns a computer software company in Japan. He has had some questionable dealings. Tony is still digging. In the meantime, I am keeping a guard on her. I'll keep you posted."

I hear Max leave. They don't know I was listening, and I am in shock. Duke is my brother? Jax knew and didn't say anything? I'm being auctioned off to the highest bidder, like some prostitute or cattle. I run back to the bedroom. If I try to leave, he will know and then what? I get back into bed just as he comes in.

"Hey, beautiful, you're finally awake. You okay?"

I smile, "Yes, of course." I need some space, but I know that's not going to happen with this man. He is operating on the assumption that I can never be alone.

"What would you like to do?"

I need to distract him and I know just how to do it. "How about a nice, hot bath? Your tub is so much better than mine."

He leans in and kisses me. "Okay, I'll set it up."

He leaves. I throw on his shirt and my yoga pants, grab my bag, phone and shoes. I make a run for the door. I grab the elevator key, jump into the elevator, and finish getting dressed on the ride down. When I jump out, the doorman stops me. "Mr. Phillips asked me to hold you here until he gets down."

"I believe it is still against the law to hold someone captive." I yell in his face. I must look crazy, but I don't care.

He doesn't seem to know what to say and I run out the front door. I know I will never get anywhere with a cab in midtown traffic, so I decide to run through the park. I know it's dark, and I know it's a stupid thing to do, but none of that matters. Right here and now, absolutely nothing matters, but getting as far away as possible. I run through the park, and when I come out the other side, I hear my name. It's not Jax, but another voice I know.

Jaxson

WHAT THE FUCK? SHE'S gone. I get down to the lobby and the fucking doorman didn't keep her there. He said she ran into the park. It's night time and she's running through Central Park?

I do what any crazy man would do—I take off running after her. I'm yelling like a nut, and it's a wonder I don't get arrested. Just as I get out the other side, I see the back of her, getting into a black town car. And just like that, my girl is gone.

I pull out my phone and call Max. "Max, tell me you have someone on Raven?" I'm trying to breathe.

"Jax, are you okay?"

I'm going to lose it, "Do I fucking sound okay! Tell me you have someone on Raven?"

He growls, "Why would I have someone on her? You fired *Tank*, and you said she would be locked away with you."

Christ. "Yeah, well, she just pulled a fucking runner again! She got picked up by a black town car."

"Jesus, Jax, she's going to be the death of both of us! Where are you?"

I look around to figure out which exit I came out. "I ran out of my building and across the park, coming out on the other side, just as she got in the car."

I hear keys clicking. "Hold on, let me pull camera footage from the area." I don't even want to know how he is able to do that.

"I see her exiting the park and running towards the car but the person never gets out. She just gets in. I might be able to get the plate number from other cameras. I'll put Tony on this."

The fear hits me. "Max, she is out there with no idea about the danger to her."

"Do you know why she ran? Did she say anything?"

I start jogging back through the park. "She didn't say anything. The only thing I can think of is, maybe she heard us talking. If that's the case, she knows about Duke and Erica. This is so fucked up. I have to find her." I know Max will move heaven and earth for me. I just hope it's enough.

"Jax, maybe it was Joseph in the car. She's not stupid. She would never get into a car with a total stranger."

I know he's right, but it's hard not to panic. "Where's Marco?"

I hear Max ask Tony about Marco. "He's still at his apartment, never left, but he did have Chinese food delivered."

I need my girl back now! "Have you found Erica, yet?"

"No sign of her, and she hasn't hooked up with Duke anymore." This is so fucked up.

"I'm going back to The Tower. If you find anything out, call me." I hang up and head back into my building, hopping on the elevator. Once inside, I pour myself a rather large glass of scotch and down it in one shot. Definitely not the way scotch was intended to be enjoyed. Then I pour another and just sit on the floor in front of the window with the bottle. I can still see her handprints on the glass where only a couple of hours ago my cock was in his happy place. I down another, and I can smell her. Everything smells of her. I look down at my cock. Even he misses her. Poor, cock, you're never going to see the light of day again. Fuck me, now I'm having conversations with my dick! Oh bloody hell, how could everything have gotten so fucked up? There is so much I need to tell her. It's not just sex with Raven. It's *everything* with her.

Jackie

MY DOORMAN INFORMS ME I have a visitor. Maxwell Fleming is on his way up. I open the door as soon as I hear the knock. "Hey, Max, what's up?"

He comes in slowly, watching me. "Hi, Miss Jackie, have you heard from Raven?"

I shake my head. "Not since I saw her this morning, why?" I can tell he wants to tell me, but he is so used to not saying anything, it's hard for him.

Maxwell

"SHE WAS AT JAX'S. But she pulled a runner, and then got into a black town car" I inform her and quickly take her arm as she gets a wan look about her. "Miss Jackie, maybe we should sit down."

She's shaking. "I know she was very upset about Marco and the lies. Raven bases everything on honesty. I think that is why she likes Jax and his family so much—they are brutally honest and direct."

I have to laugh. "Yes that they are. Sometimes it's a problem."

She cocks her head. "Why is it a problem?"

"People don't always like with they hear," I whisper. I can't help but grow more concerned the worse she looks. Damn, I can't get involved. I decide to make her some tea. That's what Mrs. Phillips always does, and that seems to work for her. "How about I make you a hot cup of tea?" I wait for her answer but am met with tears, instead. "What? It's just tea," I say in a panic over her reaction. Oh fuck, her lip is quivering. *No, no, no.* Her eyes get wide and she looks right at me, almost as if she can see through my walls. This is not good.

"Raven is my best friend. She's the sister I never had." She takes the tissue, I'm offering, out of my hand. But it's no match for her impending sobs. Oh damn it! I scoop her up and cradle her in my arms. "Please find her, I can't lose her."

"Miss Jackie, what do you know about Marco?" I ask as I hold her tighter to me.

She looks up at me, "I know I don't like him, and Raven knows how I feel."

I don't know why I feel this is important, but for some reason, I feel it is. "Why?"

She shrugs, "I don't trust easily, and something about him is off. I can't explain it, but he's the reason Raven and I don't share a place."

I hold her tight because I know this next one might do her in. "Do you think he would hurt her?"

She gasps, "When people are pushed, anyone is capable of anything. He knows I don't like him. So when I'm at Raven's he makes himself scarce. Do you think he is involved in any of this?"

I wipe the tear rolling down her cheek. "Well, I know that he was able to hide the truth from her for a very long time, so that tells me, he is capable of anything. What do you know about Mick?"

She smiles at the mention of his name; seems everyone likes this guy. "Mick is a good guy, Max. He just suffers from the horrible side effects of war. He worships Raven and would never hurt her."

At least there is some good news about the people around these women. "Okay, that's what I thought, but since you've known him longer, I thought I'd ask."

The tears fall and I decide to just hold her for a while, so she can find some comfort.

"Please find her," she whispers.

Chapter Fifteen

Jaxson

I FEEL THE SUN on my face. I try to open my eyes but it feels like they are filled with sand. I need to get a grip and try to find my girl before she gets hurt or—God forbid—killed. I pry my eyes open. Oh fuck and all that's holy, I drank the whole fucking bottle of scotch!

I check my phone for messages; nothing. It's 6:30 in the fucking morning. I decide to head to the shower. I look around the bath and am reminded of my girl everywhere. I don't know if I can ever take another shower in here again. Everywhere I look, I see myself fucking her, every way possible.

I walk out and use the guest bathroom. I call her, but it goes right to voice mail. I decide I'm going to e-mail her. *I need her*. Fuck me, I've never bloody needed anyone! I pull out my laptop and just stare at the blank screen. I don't know what to say or how to start. The elevator door opens and I jump up, thinking its Raven, but it's my mum. Without saying a word to her, she knows I'm hurting bad. "I'll make the tea, lad, and you can spill your guts." I really want to laugh—Raven is right, all the Philips have that direct gene.

"Oh, Mum, I really fucked up royally."

She puts the tea down and takes my hand, "Sit down and tell me what happened."

I spill my guts; my mum has a way of making people do that without even trying. "Well, son, it sounds to me that she is probably more upset that you kept the truth from her than the actual truth."

Now I'm confused. "Mum, why do you think that?"

She takes a deep breath before continuing. "Because no matter what has been thrown at this girl, she still plugs along. She's very strong, but you don't see that. All you see is someone you need to protect. A relationship is: trust, communication, compromise, and forgiveness. It's like a juggler, who is trying to balance all of these balls, and if he drops one it cracks form.

"First order of business is, to find her and make sure she is safe. The second order of business is, to sit down and tell her how you feel," she states and I jerk my head back. "Don't look at me like I have three heads. I told you she would be my daughter-in-law. When you face the fact that you love her, then you'll know what you need to do next. Have you called Maxwell?"

I nod, "Yes, Mum, he's working on finding her, too." Before I can even say another word, she gets up and leaves.

Sitting here, thinking about my situation and how to handle it, I realize there's only one thing I can do; how I can explain what's in my heart. I always write stuff down. From when I was a kid, I found, that if I wrote it all down, then I could make some sort of order out of the chaos around me.

Raven,

My beautiful, violet-eyed girl. I'm so sorry I hurt you. I never set out to do that. I only wanted to protect you from more pain. I realize that I should have told you everything as I learned it, so that we could handle it together. For that, I am so very sorry. Please know that I only wanted you safe. My world has been off kilter since that wonderful morning, when you dumped your coffee on me, and it will never be the same. We can get to the other side of this, but only if we are together. Please come home to me, sweetheart. I need you.
Your Jax xo

I decide to text it to her and see if she answers me. Now, all I can do is wait. Something I've never been good at. I get dressed and decide to go see Marco. If he really cares about her, then he will be concerned that she is out there somewhere.

"MARCO, IT'S JAX. LET me in, we need to talk."

After a lot of pounding, he still doesn't answer, "Marco, I'm not going away, so open the fucking door now!"

Finally, he opens it a crack, "Jax, I'm not alone." *Like I give a fuck.*

"Do you know where Raven is?" I ask. He seems genuinely surprised by my question. "By the look on your face, I gather she hasn't tried to get in touch with you."

He shakes his head, "No, I thought she was with you. What the fuck happened?" He has the audacity to ask me. I swear I just want to punch the fucker.

"She found out some information and she is upset. She pulled a runner through the park and then got into a black town car. I haven't seen or heard from her since. Marco, think. Do you have any idea where she might go?"

He looks down. "No, have you tried Jackie?"

"No, I'll call her next, but if you hear from her, please contact me." He doesn't even answer. He just slams the fucking door!

When I get downstairs, I call Max. "Hey I just left Marco's place, he said he hasn't heard from her. He suggested I call Jackie."

Max is silent, "Um, don't bother. I've been with her all night, and she hasn't heard from Raven."

I've noticed the way Max looks at Jackie but, he doesn't do *relationships.* I've been so preoccupied with everything going on, that I never took the time to talk to him about her. What kind of friend does that make me? "Oh, okay, I think we need to talk to Joseph. I'm going to call him to come to The Tower. I'll meet you there as soon as possible, please."

I know there is something I'm missing. It's just floating around in my brain, but I can't put it together.

Max and I reach The Tower at the same time. "Max, did Tony find out anything on the car that she got into?"

"He got a partial plate, and we're running it now."

Joseph finally shows up. And I ask him in an accusatory tone. "Do you have Raven?" Max is watching Joseph's every move.

"Jax, maybe if you told me everything, we wouldn't be in this position that we are now!" Joseph seethes.

"I'll take that as a yes. I just need to know that she is safe."

He nods, "I have her in a safe house, but she is refusing to tell me anything other than she needs time to think. I disabled the tracking app you put on her phone, and when she is ready to talk to you, she will. For now, just wait. Having her locked away and safe will give us time to figure out what to do next. I know you don't believe me, but I really just want what's best for her. Putting her up for adoption was one of the hardest things I ever had to do, but if I had kept her with me, it would have only put her in danger."

"Max pulled files on her family. They are a nasty bunch, and apparently, there is a sister. Did you know about her?"

He shakes his head, "No, I didn't find out about her until after Antonio died. You need to understand. He disowned his whole family and cut all ties. He never spoke to them, or of them. It was one of the conditions for joining the Feds. His knowledge of the inner workings of the Mafia was beneficial in bringing down key players in the organization, but that also brought enemies."

Max shoots me a look. I understand what he's asking and I nod. He turns to Joseph, "Listen, we found out some interesting stuff that might be beneficial, but you need to understand, this is for your eyes and ears only; trust goes both ways." He pours Joseph a drink.

"Okay, Max, what do you have that requires me needing a drink first?"

"For one, you need to know about Erica."

He nods. "That would be Jax's ex, correct? My understanding is that she was a real piece of work; corporate spy shit. You really know how to pick them."

Max doesn't give me a chance to respond, he knows I'm teetering on the edge.

"You also need to know that we found out who the half-brother is. And he's right here, in Manhattan."

His eyes light up, "Really, who is he?"

Max starts pacing. "He's the same person who bugged Jax's office.

That's how they found out that we knew where they were being held. We left the bugs in place, so that we can feed them what we want them to know."

Joseph puts his drink down, "So, who is he?"

Max takes a steadying breath, "That would be Jax's assistant, Duke. But there's more. He is working with Erica. Oh, and one more thing, there is a mole somewhere in the FBI, and that person is close to you. We need to find this third player."

Joseph stares at us like we have three heads. He's doesn't say anything, and then he gets up and starts pacing. I realize that like Max, this is his way to process the information..

He turns to us, "This is not some Hardy Boys mystery. We are talking kidnapping, extortion, and a slew of other shit. When the fuck did you find this out?!"

Max grabs his arm, "We just found out, and that is what Raven overheard. That's why she ran. I know you think she will be okay in the safe house. Now that you know everything, including the fact that there is someone near you who is a mole, do you still think she is safe?"

The realization on Joseph's face is a horrible. All three of us start running for the elevator.

Max jumps in the Rover's driver's seat and Joseph and I follow; me in the passenger seat, Joseph in the back. "Joseph, tell me where to go."

He shakes his head, "Max, I can drive us there."

I turn back to Joseph, "Trust me when I tell you, no one can get us there faster than Max, not even me."

It seems to register with him to just let Max drive. "Okay," he gives Max the address. Max is flying around the traffic and then decides to cut through the park, where cars are not allowed. Joseph has a death grip on the seat, and he's starting to sweat. "Good God, man, where the fuck did you learn to drive?!"

Max never even breaks a sweat. "I spent my summers in Italy, working for Lamborghini."

Max looks over at me, "Jax, get the light from under your seat and put it out, so the coppers don't bother us." I do so and now we have lights and sirens to clear the way. And Joseph looks to have aged quite a bit.

We get to the house. The door is wide open and Raven is gone. The agent that was guarding her is dead—shot in the head at point-blank range. Now, we have to add murder to the list.

We drive back to the tower in silence, each of us lost in our own thoughts. My girl is gone, and in so much danger. How could this have gotten so out of control?

WE HEAD UPSTAIRS AND try to form some sort of plan. We need to go through all of the events leading up to Raven's most recent disappearance. I just know we are missing something. Max makes coffee and starts with Joseph. "I need you to start with when you picked up Raven last night."

"I was on my way here, to see her. When I saw her run out of the park, I stopped my car and opened the door. I called her name, and she got in. We drove to the safe house, but she didn't want to talk. So, I got her settled in for the night, then this morning, I got the call from you and came here."

Max starts pacing, "Was your driver the dead agent at the house?"

"Yes, when you called, you said to come alone and not to tell anyone where I was going. I left my guy there to guard Raven and came here."

Max takes a deep breath. "Did you tell anyone else that you had Raven at the safe house?"

All the color drains from his face, "Yes, I called Marco when I found her running from the park. I told him I was going to take her to the safe house. I knew he was worried about her. The only other person who knew was the agent who was shot."

Max turns to me, "Okay, Jax, you're up next; what did you do?"

I have to organize my brain. "My mum came by and after she left, I texted Raven. Then I headed to Marco's place to see if he had heard from her."

"What exactly happened at Marco's?"

That fucker. "I kept banging on the door until he opened up a crack, then I told him about Raven."

Max's hands fly up! "Hold up. What do you mean, he opened the door a crack?"

"His exact words were, 'Jax, I'm not alone.' Then I told him about Raven. He was shocked and suggested I call Jackie, and I left." I run through. I'm confused. "Max, what's the problem?"

Max turns to Joseph, "Joseph, Jax had me pull a file on Marco, and he is squeaky clean. However, before Raven, there is nothing on him; what do you know?"

Joseph is now as white as a ghost. I pour him three-fingers of scotch. "Drink this. You look like you need it."

He takes the glass, but he is shaking. "Max, Marco was a street kid who was a wiz with a computer. The Bureau nailed him for hacking, and rather than prosecute him, we decided to go with hiring him."

I run my hand through my hair. "Max, it couldn't have been Raven with Marco. She was still at the safe house with Joseph. He knew Raven was at the safe house when I was there. You said he got a delivery of Chinese food last night. Did anyone see the guy leave?"

"Jax, he would never hurt her." Joseph pipes up.

I growl, "I'm not prepared to take any chances."

"Jax, I can get a warrant, within the hour, to pull footage from the cameras around the building."

Max is already on the phone to Tony, "I'm not waiting around while you get a warrant. Max is getting the footage now."

Joseph starts to protest, "If you get the evidence without the warrant, it will get thrown out of court!"

"Joseph, get your head out of your fucking arse, I'm not waiting on some fucking warrant. I want my girl back *now*, and God help anyone who gets in my fucking way!"

Max grabs me. "Jax, where's your laptop?"

I go get it from the back office. Max opens my MacBook and before I know it, he has all the footage from last night. Max freezes the frame and blows it up.

I just stare at it, in shock. Staring back at me, from the footage, is Erica, dressed as a delivery man. Max and I are frozen, staring at the screen. *It can't be.*

"Who the fuck is that?" Joseph yells.

Max looks at him, "That, my friend, is Jax's worst nightmare come to life, Erica."

I can't move, I can't think, and I'm holding my breath. It's amazing what stupid random shit comes to light in your brain when you're in shock.

"I thought Marco was gay?" Even after it left my mouth, I knew what he was going to say, and personally, I could give a royal fuck who he's shagging. However, my girl's life is in danger by a woman who despises me, and a man whom, by all accounts, she thought was gay.

"Well, not that it has ever come up in conversation, but I believe him to be bisexual. Why do you ask?"

"Well, we all thought he was gay. Marco with Erica changes things. Erica is a predator; she uses sex to get what she wants. Raven trusted Marco. Did he know where the safe house was?"

Joseph grabs the bar, his wan appearance only getting worse as he probably just came to the same realization that I did. Marco had to be the one that shot the agent, point blank—the kill shot.

Neither one of us is paying attention to Max, but then I hear him talking on the phone while he starts to pace. "Hold on, Tony, let me ask him." He pulls the phone away from his ear a bit. "Jax, you know that tracker app you put on Raven's phone?"

"Yeah, but Joseph said he deactivated it."

He grabs me. "Do you remember which version you purchased?"

"Yeah, the deluxe, but it's only because she kept running away and I wanted to find her. I was not being all stalker-like."

Max looks pleased that I was acting like a crazy stalker. "Tony, did you get that? Yeah, thank Christ the crazy fucker got the deluxe package. Can you do it?" He takes a deep breath, "Okay, mate, call me back, as soon as you know."

Before I can say anything, Max hands the phone to Joseph, "Call the clean team you have at the house and make sure they didn't find a cell phone."

He heads over to me, "Jax, the deluxe package comes with a code that enables you to remotely turn on the tracker app from any computer. With the access code, I had Tony hack your account and he is turning it on now. Hopefully, she had the phone on her and didn't leave it in the house."

Joseph hangs up his phone. "No cell phone was found at the house."

All we can do now is wait. Something I've never been very fucking good at doing.

Chapter Sixteen

Raven

JOSEPH HAD TO GO out. And now, suddenly, Marco shows up with a girl. How did he even know where I was? Joseph said no one would know I was here. I see Marco talking to the agent. He puts his arm around him in a loving gesture, puts his gun right between the agent's eyes, and pulls the trigger! I scream. Dear God, no please I can't believe this is happening, again.

"Marco, please no, not you, too! What the fuck are you doing? Why, Marco, why?!" I cry. The smell of blood and gunpowder fills my nostrils, catapulting me back to that one moment in time—the moment that changed my life forever. I scream a silent scream; the shrill sound, only in my mind. I'm seven, frozen with fear. Blood is everywhere. The metallic smell, turning my stomach. I'm trembling. I can't breathe. *Help me, Daddy, please don't die.* Marco slaps me out of my haze. His eyes are dark and he's wiping blood splatters from his face.

"Raven, this is my friend, Erica. She is going to help you deal with everything."

I look at him confused, "What do you mean, help me deal with everything? I don't even know this woman, and at this point, I'm not even sure about you anymore!" And without another minute going by, I suddenly realize—Erica is the same corporate spy that Jax was in love with. My knees give out and I hear the most evil laugh right before I pass out.

When I wake up, I find I'm tied up, in the back of a van. Sitting next to me, is Duke; the other player in this mess. My eyes engage Marco's, and I feel my tears pool again just before they start to fall. I have to look away. I feel beyond betrayed. At this point, I have no idea who to trust or what to do next.

We get to a small house in a quirky town. The sign says, *"Welcome to Woodstock, we're all here 'cause we're not all there."* I almost want to laugh at the truth behind it. Slowly, it's starting to snow. Erica asks Marco if he was able to stock the house with all the needed supplies. He just nods. We get inside the small house and Marco unties me. "Don't think of going anywhere. It's snowing and dark out; you'll get nowhere fast."

Marco comes in with tea. He knows me so well. Stupid me, I thought it was because we were friends, but it was his job. I thought I knew him, but I really don't know him, at all. Duke is glaring at Erica because she is hanging all over Marco. The fog is clearing, and I'm realizing so much that I really don't want to know. "Marco, is Joseph in on this, too?"

He shakes his head, "No, Raven, he is clueless, although he did call me last night to tell me he found you running out of the park, apparently away from Jax. He said he was going to take you to the safe house and he would disable the tracker app on your phone. He practically gave me the keys to the kingdom."

"Oh," I whisper.

He smiles at me. "Yeah, *oh*."

I avoid his eyes. "I don't have my phone. I left it at the safe house." It's really in my pocket, but maybe he won't figure that out.

"It doesn't matter. You couldn't get a call out from here anyway."

I sip my tea while I watch the three of them. Erica keeps eyeing me up and down. Finally, she stops and looks me in the eye. "Raven, you're a smart girl, have you figured out why this is happening yet?"

I'm so overwhelmed, I can't think straight. "I have an idea, but why don't you enlighten me."

She laughs, "That day at school, when we took Michael, you were just collateral damage, and I was prepared to kill you."

My whole body tingles. "So, what stopped you?"

Marco smirks. "I did."

"Why did you stop her?"

He takes a deep breath. "I stopped her because you're worth a lot more money alive than dead to the right people."

I'm shaking. "So, it has nothing to do with friendship or loyalty?"

He throws his head back and laughs, "Oh, baby girl, get your head out of the clouds. You're a high maintenance bitch and I'm tired of being your babysitter. I have been watching your ass, for the past twelve years, and now you're my golden goose; my ticket out."

"I wasn't supposed to be on the playground that day. If it was Jackie, what would you have done?"

"She would be dead right now. Although, her father would have paid big bucks for her safe return," he informs me. I believe him, and I'm happy she switched places with me.

"I don't understand how Duke comes into all of this? I think I deserve to know how my half-brother, that I never knew about, was brought into this plan."

He takes a deep breath. "You're right, you deserve to know the truth. Six months ago, Joseph was diagnosed with advanced stage prostate cancer. He was worried what would happen to you when he died—ironic, I know. So, he sat me down and told me the entire story of your life and your parent's lives."

"I was already with Erica, and she wanted revenge for being blacklisted from every major corporation, thanks to Jax. I had a friend, in the Lansing office, pull the file for Duke. After reading Duke's file, I realized that he would be a perfect mole, just like I was Joseph's perfect mole. Poor Duke didn't know anything about you. He's in it for the money and the sex. We just needed to get him into Raiders Inc."

"Erica still had some contacts, so she reached out to the ones that were burned by Jax. It didn't take long for one of them to help us. Duke was supposed to find out everything he could about Junior, imagine my surprise when I found out that you were his teacher!" He throws his head back and laughs. "After that, all the pieces just fell into place, which started with you dumping your coffee all over Jax."

I'm in shock. I can't believe this man, sitting in front of me, is the same man, that I have been friends with, for the last twelve years.

"But they didn't fall into place. We got away from your kidnappers."

He nods. "Yeah, well, thanks to the bugs that Duke put in Jax's office, we found out that your phone had a tracker app. Believe me, I would much rather have gotten the fifty million wired to my off shore account, then having to abort that mission. Instead of sitting on a warm beach, drinking champagne, and living off the interest, I'm now sitting in a cold house, with snow all around me, and still dealing with your high maintenance ass!" He gets up, kicking the chair as he leaves the room. I look at my tea, betting it's cold. Duke is still glaring at Erica, and she is smirking at me. *Ugh!*

Jaxson

"MAX, WHEN THE FUCK is Tony going to have this done?" Now, I'm the one pacing.

"He's working on it. There are a lot of security walls in place."

I look over at Joseph and he doesn't look good; his skin has almost a grayish tint to it. "Joseph, can I get you some water or something."

He nods, and as I hand him the glass, I notice his hand is shaking. Max turns to him, "Joseph, how long do you have?"

I'm floored. How does Max know anything? *Oh fuck, what am I thinking?* It's Max, for Christ sake. He knows if the wind shifts. "They told me I had a year, that I should get my affairs in order. That was six months ago."

"Is that when you told Marco the whole story?" Max asks.

Joseph laughs, "Max, you amaze me. You really should be working for us."

Max chuckles. "Joseph, I could never work for the Feds. I need things done yesterday, and you guys have too much red tape. Not to mention, in your world, too much information is put on paper. I'm thinking that's when Marco went off the rails, but you can't sit here and blame yourself." Joseph has a grave expression on his face, apparently Max's words don't seem to help him.

The phone rings and Max puts it on speaker; It's Tony. He's narrowed it down to the Catskills Mountain range. Max orders Tony to pull everything he can on Erica, Duke, and Marco, to find their connection to that area and get a better pin point of what their location might be. I grab the phone off the cradle before he can hang up. "Tony, Erica had a quirky uncle that became a recluse. He moved up to Woodstock. He wanted to live the rest of his life with nature and weed. Pull whatever records you can find. She used to joke that Flynn was flying without leaving the yard. We're going to start heading that way now. When you get the information, call me."

"Jax, we need the Rover. It's snowing here, so it will probably be heavy up there."

I toss him my keys, and I see Joseph flinch. "Don't worry, Joseph, Max also drove for the Royal family." I don't think that helps. We race out of the penthouse. The elevator ride down to the garage seems to take forever. We get to the Rover, Joseph gets in the back seat, double checking his seat belt. Max's driving through the blinding snow. All I can do is pray we can get to Raven in time.

"Jax, what did you do to this woman that she would want this type of revenge?"

I don't like to reveal too much of what I do, let alone to a Fed. "Joseph, my business is complex, but I'm good at it. I'm able to see the big picture and all the little pieces at the same time. Erica wanted in to my world, but she used sex, not brains. That was her first mistake. I was young and used to think with my cock, so I was vulnerable. When I realized what she was, I sent her packing."

"Why didn't you prosecute her?"

Right now I'm wondering the same thing. "The justice system here is for the rich and not the poor. She would probably have gotten off with a slap on the wrist, so I opted to blackball her from the only industry she knows. Because of it, her family also blackballed her, and her grandfather took her out of his will. We're talking millions here, Joseph."

He stares out the window for a while, "You said her *first mistake*. What was her second?"

"Crossing me and putting the people I love at risk."

He says nothing more as we speed through the night.

Raven

ERICA SITS ACROSS FROM me, her eyes glued to me. "I can't believe you're the girl that landed my Jax. You're so simple. You fucking teach second grade kids for Christ's sake!"

I just want to bitch slap her! "I think it's safe to say, if he was *your Jax,* we wouldn't be having this conversation."

She bangs her fist on the table and it makes me jump. "I would watch your mouth, bitch. I can fuck you up royally, just remember that."

As she walks out, she kisses Duke's cheek. Duke is being taciturn. My guess is, he doesn't know what to say or do with me.

"Duke, why are you doing this to me? I don't even know you."

He sits down at the table. "I wouldn't say that, Raven. We have the same blood running through our veins."

My eyes instantly fill with tears, and I have to fight to hold them back. "If you really feel like that, then why are you doing this to me?"

He takes a steadying breath. "I got sucked in real quick and deep, first by Erica, and then Marco. I don't see this ending well for any of us." He looks away.

"Duke, look at me, please don't look away. If you really believe that, then do something to end this."

He laughs. "What? Like going to the police? Marco shot that agent right in the head while Erica just stood there, talking to the man!"

I shake my head. "Just call, Jax. He'll know what to do."

I see such pain in his eyes. "You don't get it, Raven. Erica and Marco, they are just the tip of the iceberg. I did some digging, on my own, looking up our family tree. Even if we do get out of this, we are both fucked. They're all ruthless. I mean, Jesus, apparently my father killed your father, his own brother, and then raped our mother. If that's not fucked up, then I don't know what is."

I sit there for a while, thinking about all of this. "Duke, what do you think our family would do to us, when they find out about us?"

He shrugs, "They might embrace me, but for sure, they would kill you. It really doesn't matter, because they already know."

"Oh." I whisper.

We both sit here, watching the snow falling outside. I wrap my arms around my body and I can smell Jax on this shirt. *I wish I had never run.* As I watch the snow, I wonder how something so peaceful could be happening in the mist of such evil.

Jaxson

WE STOP IN KINGSTON for gas, when Max's cell rings. He's pacing. That's never a good sign.

"Okay, Jax, Tony has an address. It's just off of Route 212, past the elementary school. Tony is worried. There's been some chatter and internet hits about the Chicago family, they might know already."

"Fuck! Okay, just keep driving. We will have to take our chances."

Joseph's phone rings. The caller ID says: Marco, and we all freeze. "Put it on speaker."

He takes a deep breath before he answers, "Hello, Marco, where are you? What the fuck is going on?"

Marco laughs, "Joseph, I want seventy-five million wired to my off shore account. You have thirty minutes from when I hang up."

"Hold on, Marco, how do I even know she's still alive? There is a lot of blood at the safe house." Joseph yells.

"Joseph, she is of no use to me dead, but I'll let you say, hello. Raven, say hello to Joseph, I'm sure he has you on speaker and Jax is probably sitting right next to him."

"Hello, Joseph. Jax, I'm okay. Please protect yourselves, I'll be okay," her voice quivers. What I hear next, slays me. He slaps her and she's crying.

"Marco, touch her again and I swear I'll rip you from limb to limb! You'll wish you were never born!" I yell. My adrenaline is so high; I can hear my blood pumping through my veins.

He laughs "Now, now, Jax, you need to play nice with me or I'll mess her up good. I've been babysitting this bitch for the last twelve years. I'm done."

"You listen to me, arsehole, I'm the one with the seventy-five million, so harm a hair on her pretty, little head and you will royally fuck yourself!"

"I just sent you a text with wiring instructions. As soon as the money hits, you'll get her location." He hangs up.

Raven

"MARCO, WHY ARE YOU doing this to me? I thought you loved me?"

He laughs, "Yeah, well you thought wrong, baby girl. I was just waiting for my cash cow to come in, and now it has."

"So, what about Erica, what happens to her?"

"You're so wrapped up in all your own drama, you stupid, little girl. Erica's my wife, what do you think is going to happen to her?"

My mouth falls open. "Wife?! When did this happen? I thought you were gay?"

He glares at me. "So many questions, and of course, you're so behind. I'm bisexual, and Erica is fine with that."

Suddenly, there is yelling between Erica and Duke, and he's shaking. "I loved you! I thought you loved me, and now I find out that you're married to him!" He's waving Marco's gun. Marco keeps his focus solely on the gun and where it's being waved. This is bad . . . real bad. Erica doesn't look as nervous as Marco does. She's laughing lightly and taunting poor Duke.

In the same moment, I see Duke snap. He turns towards Marco. "Duke, just put the gun down, and let's discuss this."

"I'm done talking, Marco." Duke shoots him, "That should, finally, shut you the fuck up."

Duke turns to Erica, "Now you're a widow."

I can't breathe. Duke just shot Marco in the head. Erica is looking at Duke, and then finally, she looks down at Marco's body. There is no grief, no crying—not even shock. Nothing but a blank stare.

"Well, Duke, I guess that leaves just you and me." She smirks. Is she serious? What kind of psycho was Jax and Marco involved with?

Duke glares at her. "Do you really think I want or need you?"

She laughs, "I think you do want me, and I know you need me to get out of this place."

There is some noise from downstairs. That must be the police, here to rescue me, thankfully. However, I notice neither of them panicking at this and I can't shake the sudden feeling that my first assumption could be very off. Duke scoffs, "I don't want Marco's leftovers and I, sure as shit, don't need you to get out of here."

Fear finally registers on Erica's face just as the door opens and in walks a man who could be my father's twin. "You gonna do her, son, or should I?"

Duke glances over to him but he turns back to Erica, "I wish I could stay, but our ride is here, and your number just came up!" He puts the gun right between her eyes and pulls the trigger. Her life is over, just like that. I'm left, looking into the face of a killer, my father's brother, and his murderer. "Raven, let me introduce you to my father and your uncle, Vincent."

My heart switches back and forth between racing and breaking all over again. "We met twenty years ago, when I watched him kill my father."

Jaxson

MAX IS SPEEDING INTO the night. The snow is coming down hard. Joseph is staring out the window, lost in his thoughts until he tells Max that the local police are on their way and should be at the house in twenty minutes. Max looks back to Joseph. "Do you really think I'm waiting for them? We will be there in five."

He takes a shaky breath, "Max, I know that you're a former Special Ops with the Royal Army, I'm sure you can handle yourself. I'm armed. I'm sure you are, but, Jax, you're not, and you need to stay in the car."

Max looks back at me, "Jax, under the seat, pull the panel down."

Joseph's mouth opens as if he's in shock. . "Are these even licensed? Fuck, are they even legal?"

Max just raises his right eyebrow at Joseph. "Jax, load up and get ready. We're here." Max tells Joseph that he will go around back and that he and I should cover the front. Just a few minutes and I'll have my girl back. We all step in at the same time. It's quiet—too quiet. We start searching room by room.

When we go up to the upstairs, the scene that awaits us makes me want to hurl. Two bodies. The first one is Erica, shot right between the eyes. The second body is Marco. He's been shot in the head. Their bodies are still warm. There is no sign of Raven and I can't help but feel paralyzed. I turn to Max, "Who?"

He looks around. "I venture to say she and Duke are together, and the family knows who they both are."

"God, forgive me, what have I done?" Joseph places his face in his hands.

Max grabs Joseph and throws him up against the wall. "Joseph, what the fuck *did* you do?!"

Just when I think things can't possibly get any worse, Max starts pounding on Joseph. I try to pull Max off of him. If he kills him, we'll never know.

"Joseph, before anyone gets her, you need to tell us *everything*."

"When I found out I was dying, I told Marco everything about Raven, and why I felt so protective of her. *Her father died for me!* Antonio jumped in front of me, *just* as Vincent pulled the trigger. Cara saw the whole thing. That's why she stopped talking. He convinced me that he would take care of her, and that for her safety, he needed to know where her half-brother was staying. I was blinded by loyalty, and that will probably get her killed."

My rage is rising to the surface as I hear his words. "So let me get this straight, you hired Marco twelve years ago to work his way into Raven's life? You then told Marco everything you knew about Raven's family, about her half-brother, that she wasn't aware of, and you told him where the brother was located?"

He nods, "Yes."

That's it. I look at Max, and before he can stop me, I punch Joseph in the face. Judging by the amount of blood, I've probably broken his nose. Max and I walk out, leaving Joseph with the mess he helped create.

"Max, where do you think she is?"

"Well, it's safe to say, that she is with Duke and he probably contacted his newfound family."

"So, Chicago?" I stare out the window.

Max is quiet for a bit. "No, Jax. That would be too easy. They don't want you finding her or Duke. With the amount of snow that is falling, it's safe to say, they are driving, not flying. I just don't see them driving back to the city, to get a flight out. It's too risky. Even Logan airport, in Boston, is too close. They'll still have the weather to deal with. I think they'll drive south. If it were me, I would drive to Atlanta. It is the largest international airport in the world. I'll have Tony check all the private airports from here to Florida. I also have him working on Duke's computer." Max puts a call through to Tony. "Hey, Tony, you're on speaker. I need you to check all the private airports from New York to Florida and look for any last-minute flights, heading out of the country. Did you find out anything from Duke's computer?"

Tony sounds excited. "I did find something interesting, but not from Duke's computer. Who's in the car, Max?"

Max gives him the go ahead to talk freely. "Okay, I hacked into Marco's computer. I just felt there might be some clues as to where they were taking Raven. I found out that Marco got married six months ago, but here's the shocker—he was married to Erica. It seems they've been together for almost a year. Oh, and it seems Marco has a very expensive, online gambling habit. That's how he met Erica, in one of the gambling chat rooms."

I can't speak, and I can't think. My entire world has been thrown off kilter so many times, over the past three weeks. I'm glad Max still has his brains, because mine are fried.

"Tony, were you able to access the logs from the chat room?"

He sighs, "Yeah, they are an interesting read. Really shows how twisted they both are."

"Well, Tony, they're both dead." I pipe up, finally finding my voice.

Max tells Tony to get on the airport search and pull the files for the Chicago crime family as we head back to the city. I sit in silence, lost in my thoughts.

Raven

THREE WEEKS AGO, THE biggest thing I was worried about was parent teacher conferences. In that short time span, I have been kidnapped, for the fourth time in my twenty-seven years. I have seen four people murdered, right in front of my eyes. I have been lied to and manipulated, emotionally, by the people I trusted the most. Why is this happening to me, when all I want to do is teach my second graders?

As we are driving through the night, I notice that we are heading south. Where we're going really doesn't matter to me; I'm sure my life is over. Poor Jax, I think about him and feel so sorry. His life was somewhat normal, up until I came into it, although, the crazy ex and the assistant was his. We were both manipulated by people—the trusted ones. I think about Marco and the fact that Joseph put him into my life. How much of the last twelve years, with Marco, was real? How much was staged? I think about Joseph, and I know he blames himself for so much, starting with my father getting shot. He's dying, and I can't be there for him. So much pain and sadness, and for what—money? Is it worth it? I think I really understand, now, why Jax keeps himself tucked away in The Tower. I can't believe that Jax was ever involved with someone like Erica. She was so cold, and she had such a hardness to her, that I would never have expected someone like Jax, to be attracted to the likes of her. How could I not know that Marco was bi-sexual? Marco said that he married Erica six months ago, but when was he seeing her? Every time I saw Marco with someone, it was a guy. Pulling out of my thoughts, I realize we've already passed through Virginia. "Duke, where are we going?"

He doesn't answer. In fact he is just staring out the window, almost in some kind of trance. I know he is a killer. I've seen what he can do, but I don't think he was always like that. I honestly believe he was manipulated and just snapped. In the past twenty-four hours, three people were murdered, and I'm probably next.

As I sit here and reach back into the deepest, darkest parts of my mind, I close my eyes and I'm back to that horrible day, twenty years ago. I was coming home from school when a man picked me up, telling me that my parents were in an accident and I needed to go with him to the hospital. That day changed my life forever. That day changed the lives of so many people, actually, from the grandfather I never knew, to me—a clueless, little seven-year-old girl, just playing with her dolls without a care in the world. That day when Joseph and my father rescued me, I saw the man that shot my father, and now I'm looking at him again, sitting in the front of the car. *Talk about life, coming full circle.* I don't know if Joseph realized that I saw the man pull the trigger. I saw my father jump in front of Joseph, when that shot rang out. I wonder how much Duke really knows. I can't ask him now, not while his father is in the car. We all sit in silence. I finally fall asleep, but it's not peaceful, and it probably never will be again.

Duke nudges me awake. "We're here, you need to wake up."

I look up. "Where's 'here'?"

He points to the plane. "We're at a private airport in Charleston, South Carolina."

Oh God, this is it. "Where are we going?"

He doesn't answer. He just pushes me out of the car. If I get on that plane, I will never be found, but I don't know what I can do. "I need to go to the bathroom."

Vincent gives me a look. "You can go on the plane."

We climb up the steps, and I head into the restroom. I realize I still have my phone in my back pocket. I have very little battery left, plus Duke is right outside the door. I notice I have a message from Jax. He says he needs me. *Oh Jax I need you more, so much more.* What I wouldn't do to turn back the hands of time. I decide to text, rather than call Jax.

Jax

They don't know I have your phone. The battery is low, so I will shut it off, after I send this. Duke killed Marco and Erica. Duke's father, Vincent, showed up and took us out of the house. We are taking off from a private airport in Charleston, SC. I don't know where they are taking us. This madness needs to stop. I have seen three people murdered today, and I need to know that you're safe. Please don't look for me—this needs to end. I'm probably going to die, so I guess I'm not running anymore. You need to know, I only ran because you

made me feel too much and it scared me. For the first time in my life, I've experienced pure love, and I will die, knowing that, for a little span of time, in my life, I was really happy, and it was all because of you.
Yours always
Raven xo

I hit Send. When it's done, I shut off the phone and go back to the cabin.

Vincent is looking at me, and then he smirks. "You look just like my brother, and we all know how that ended."

A chill runs through me. "Cara, I see in your eyes that you remember me. I was not aiming for Antonio. I was aiming for that prick, Joseph. But leave it to my goody-two-shoes brother to jump in front of him."

I glare at him. "Vincent, my name is Raven. Is that little confession supposed to make me forgive you for murdering my father?"

He laughs. "I see you have your mother's fire in you."

My eyes fill with tears. "Where are we going?"

"Some place far away from here." he replies. He looks like pure evil. I close my eyes. I can't look at this man, let alone talk to him. I drift off to sleep as we jet through the night sky.

Jaxson

WE WALK INTO MAX'S office, and my phone beeps. I pull it out, and it's a text message from Raven!

"Jax, what is it?"

I can barely breathe. "A text from Raven," I read them the message. Does she really think I won't look for her?

"Tony, you need to start checking the airports in Charleston for flights that have left tonight. Max, we need to go through the stuff that Tony found."

I see a look on Max's face that scares me. "Jax, if she doesn't want to be found, it will make things much harder."

I mentally count to ten. "Max, I'm going to find her—no matter what."

He starts pacing. "Jax, I didn't say we wouldn't. I'm just telling you, it will be harder."

I take a deep breath. "Then I guess we better get started."

Raven

DUKE NUDGES ME AWAKE, "Buckle up, we're getting ready to land."

I look across at Vincent and he is just smiling at me, making my skin crawl. "Cara, I'm looking forward to getting to know my niece."

I just close my eyes, fighting the bile that is rising in my throat. "Duke, where are we?"

"Italy. Sicily, to be exact."

There is a driver waiting for us when we land. Vincent is speaking to him in Italian. There's no need to let them know I understand what they are saying. When Joseph sent me to boarding school, I was housed with children from all different parts of the world. I learned Italian, Spanish, French, German, and a little Norwegian. I never thought this would be how I would use my language skills. We drive in silence, until we reach a beautiful villa on the coastline. Under different circumstances, this would be breathtaking. The gates open, and we drive up a long driveway that wraps around the cliff, to the top of the hill. The colors are magnificent; so many pastel shades, set against the blue Mediterranean. As we step out of the car, Vincent looks at me. "Welcome to your new home, Cara. You are free to wander around the grounds, but there is no escape. There are armed guards that have been told to shoot you, if you try to leave. All your needs will be taken care of during your stay."

He turns to Duke. "Son, come with me. We have lots to discuss." He takes Duke into the house, and I'm left standing here.

I walk into the villa. A housekeeper introduces herself as Maria and she shows me to my room. I look around the room, and it is beautiful. So much attention was paid to even the smallest of details. I decide on a bath, and then I need to figure out if there is any way out of here. The closet is filled with clothes. They are the right size, but they are dated. The bathroom is also well stocked. As I soak in the huge tub, I try to think of what to do next. I won't turn on the phone. I can't put Jax's life in danger anymore. I don't know when, or how it happened, but I realize, that I not only love him, but I'm *in love* with him. *He is a part of my soul.* I put my head back, trying to block out everything but his touch. His touch rendered me speechless. His kisses on my wrist were like a lightning bolt, jolting me right between my legs and curling my toes. That crooked smirk that could launch ships. When we were ready to fall and he would demand we lock violets to blues—that's the moment I knew I loved him. I found his soul, and he found mine. Before Jax, I thought I made a nice life for myself, just teaching and enjoying life with my friends. Now I know, there could have been so much more. I close my eyes and let the tears fall. I wonder about Jackie. I saw the way she looked at Max. What's not to like in him? Marco was right, he is very Daniel Craig like. My thoughts wander to Marco. The betrayal just blows me away. How stupid and foolish am I? I loved him like the brother I never had, but now I do have a brother—well, a half-brother, and he's a killer; a cold-blooded killer just like his father. How much more does Joseph know that he hasn't told me? Twenty years ago, I stood in that room next to my daddy and Joseph, just watching and listening to Vincent and Daddy yelling. After it was over, I blocked the whole thing out, never wanting to remember. Joseph sent me to therapy, but I never talked about it—what was the point? It wasn't until Marco came into my life and convinced me that telling someone might help me find closure. It was Marco, I told about my darkest days. Those days died with Marco. My skin is pruning. I need to get out of the tub and find something to eat. I find a pair of jeans that fit, but the t-shirt is snug for me. Time to explore my prison and figure a way out of here.

As I head downstairs, I see Vincent and Duke having coffee. It's amazing how Duke just fell right into place with Vincent. As I pour a cup of coffee, I feel their eyes on me.

"Cara, I see you found your mother's clothes." My eyes fill with tears and the bile, that I was fighting to keep down, is back. "Your mother loved it here. I don't know what Joseph told you, but I'm here to set the record straight."

My mother's clothes. That's why the styles are so dated—they're twenty years old. I have nothing that belonged to my mother. How ironic is it, that I'm being held prisoner, in the same clothes that she was?

"Vincent, I was told that you held my mother for two months, after my father died. I was also told that you raped her repeatedly before she was rescued. She was pregnant with Duke. I was sent away to boarding school, and she gave birth. My mother could not look at Duke and hung herself. Joseph put him up for adoption. That about covers it." I ramble through the information like bullet points on a paper.

He looks at me with fury in his eyes. "Well, Cara, I think you'll be surprised by what I will show you." He gets up from the table, leaving Duke and me alone. We have a stare down. The family resemblance is amazing, and I can't believe I didn't notice it before.

"Duke, please tell me you're not buying into all this family crap."

By the look on his face, I know he is. "Raven, this is our family, and you need to understand that. Joseph was not your family—we are."

Oh my God, he really believes all of this. "What about your adopted family, don't you love them?"

He sighs, "They tried, but there was always something missing, and now I know what that something was; my blood and my heritage. I'm where I need to be . . . where I want to be. I hope that will come for you, too."

Vincent returns and hands me a photo album. "This was your mother's, when she was here, and maybe it will help you."

I take it and decide to head outside to look at it alone. As I sit on one of the lounge chairs, I slowly open the book, and it's like going back in time. The book is like a diary with photographs, attached to her deepest, most private thoughts. I feel like an intruder, but I have to read this. No, I *need* to read this.

I arrived here two days ago, after the surgery I performed failed. He was just too far gone for it to work, but I had to try for my Cara and Antonio. After the surgery, Vincent showed me a videotape of Antonio being shot; taking the bullet that was meant for Joseph. All of this, while my Cara looked on. I don't think I will ever forget the look on her scared, little face. It will torment me always. I was told that Antonio died and if I wanted to keep Cara safe, then I needed to remain here, so here, I sit.

Oh my God, my mother watched the video of Daddy being shot,

and she thought I was still being held! Does Vincent think this will somehow make me feel better or makeup for all he took from me? I need to keep reading.

The views here are tranquil; there is a peace that the sea brings with the incoming tide. Vincent is back. I don't want to see him or deal with him, but I must. For the sake of my daughter, I will do whatever he wants.

"Gabriella, you look so well rested today, I'm glad I brought you here."

"How long will I be held here, against my will?"

"You're free to go wherever you want; explore the grounds."

"I just want to go home to my daughter and get on with grieving Antonio."

"I can have Cara brought here. if that would make you feel better."

"I'll do whatever you want. but you must promise me that you'll stay away from Cara."

He smiles and walks away. He is pure evil. How could my Antonio have been cut from the same cloth?

I never knew my mother was an artist. The next few pages are filled with etchings of me. It's like she was doing them to try and remember me. They are beautiful and very detailed.

It's been a week, and I'm realizing I might never get out of here. I miss my Cara. She was just finding her independence, and it was beautiful to watch her. It's funny what little things you remember most. Whenever Cara was deep in thought, she would tug at her ear lobe. When she is angry, her eyes get the deepest violet color, just like my mother's eyes would. Daddy would say my mom's eyes could render him speechless, and I never understood what he meant, until Cara.

The next few pages are filled with violet eyes, all different shades.

Two weeks have passed and Vincent said, he is not waiting for me any longer. I realized I had no choice. I tried fighting him off, but he's much stronger than I am. My life is over, even if I do get rescued from this place. My tender-hearted husband is dead, by the hand of his brother. My husband's brother has repeatedly raped me. Every time he finishes, he looks up to heaven, laughs and says, "That's for you big brother." He thinks Antonio is watching this nightmare. I can only hope that Antonio is too busy watching over Cara.

I've had enough for today. Reading about my mother's abuse is gut wrenching, and I am just too nauseated to continue. As I walk up the steps to my bedroom, I have a moment of clarity. I realize I never got my period and I never took my pills that last week. I'm usually so good with them, but getting kidnapped could render a person a little dense. I'm sure I will be fine, but then I remember how much Jax loved to go to cock heaven, and I smile for the first time in a long time. It figures it's because of Jax and his wonderful, dirty bedroom language.

I decide to take a nap. I enter my room, and Duke is sitting in one of the chairs. "Why are you in my room?"

"Raven, I'm not a monster. Well, maybe to you I am, but I'm really not and I want to know more about you. I mean, after all, you are my half-sister."

I take a calming breath, "So, you choose now to find out about me?" I'm looking into his eyes, trying to understand him.

"Raven, we have the same mother, so I would like to think that some of what I'm seeing in you, is part of her. Vincent said he would tell me all about the family, but he has only told me his side, I want more."

I sit across from him. "Okay, what do you want to know?"

"What was she like? I really want to know all the little things you find out about a person over the years."

The tears fall; I can't stop them. "Duke, she died when I was seven, so I don't know much. My memories are faint, at best."

He takes my hand, "Please, Raven, whatever you can remember would be great."

I wipe away my tears. "Okay, well, she loved to sing and dance. She was very graceful and beautiful."

"Vincent showed me some pictures of her from when she lived here."

My anger is back. "Duke, she didn't live here. She was held prisoner here and raped repeatedly by Vincent." I can tell he doesn't know what to believe, as he picks imaginary lint off of his pants. Maybe if he sees the real Vincent he will understand how evil and vile Vincent really is. "Let me show you something that he gave me today." I pass him the book. "Please read this passage."

He starts to read and his eyes fill with tears. I know he murdered two people, but I also see how tormented he is, and how used he must feel.

"Raven, thank you for sharing this, but I just can't take any more of this." He hands me back the book and walks out.

The rest of the book is filled with all of the torment that my mother went through for the two months she was held captive here. Maybe Vincent gave me this book to show me what I can expect. Except, no one will be rescuing me. I'm so tempted to turn on the phone, but I won't put Jax in danger. I can't put him in danger. *I love him.*

I get up, and am hit with a wave of nausea. I'm very dizzy. I really hope it's not what I think it is, this could be really bad if it is. There's a knock on my door, and it's Maria asking me if I want lunch. Judging by the look on her face, I must look really bad. She helps me to bed and says she will bring tea and dry crackers.

I spend the next two weeks going from my bed to the bathroom, throwing up my guts all day, every day. Vincent calls in a local doctor to look at me, and Maria is translating for him. I won't tell him I understand what they are saying. I just don't know if that will come in handy.

I know I'm pregnant, and I have to fight for my child to get out of here. The doctor confirms what I already know, and says I am dehydrated. I need fluids, and I'm suffering from 'hyperemesis gravidarum,' which is severe morning sickness. He wants to put me in the hospital, but Vincent just sends him away.

I curl up into a ball and cry. I'm crying for my baby, that has to go through this, and for Jax, who will never know that his love created another life. I'm crying for all the time I lost with my parents, but most of all, I'm crying because I can't see a way out.

Maxwell

I'M SEARCHING EVERY LEAD that comes through and calling in all kinds of favors, but they all lead to dead ends. I've never seen Jax like this. He really loves Raven, and now she is gone. I can barely look at him. I keep trying to be positive for him and for Jackie, but they are both lost without Raven. Jackie keeps looking at me like she knows I'm going to save Raven. I don't have her faith that there will be a happy ending. I lost my faith in happy endings years ago. The longer time goes on, the less faith I have that we will find her alive. I can only imagine the kind of torture she is enduring at the hands of a madman. Time just keeps dragging on, and I have no answers for anyone. I know Jax's pain, I've lived it. It's a pain that slowly kills a man, one day at a time. I'm reliving a nightmare, except this time, it's Jax's nightmare, and I can't stop it. I try to distance myself from Jackie, but I just can't do it. I know it is best for both of us, but I'm losing all reason here. Three months since that horrible day, and it's like time has stood still for all of us.

Isabella is getting ready to send Junior back to school, but I know she is scared to let him out of her sight. We are all just going through the motions of life, but not really living.

Mick accepted a job, as a security guard, in the Raiders building. He seems to be getting his life back, one day at a time. Sometimes, I go and have a coffee with him, and his first words are always about Raven. Raven doesn't even realize the impact she has had on so many lives, without even trying.

Jax's mum is all over my arse about Raven and Jackie. I know she likes Jackie and maybe she thinks I should have a relationship with her. I swear, sometimes I think she thinks I'm Superman. I'm trying everything I can to find them, but nothing pans out. They have to be running low on money. There are no hits on any credit cards or at any ATM's. I've contacted a friend that specializes in wire transfers. I have Tony working with him to look for anything that will tie it to the family.

I find myself making all kinds of excuses to spend time with Jackie. Sometimes we silently run through the park. There is such ease with her. I really don't need to talk and yet she understands. I don't know when it happened, but she slowly broke through the barrier around my heart, and for me, this is not good. I decide to head to Raiders and try and go over a hunch I have with Jax. I need to put Jackie out of my mind, unfortunately, that is easier said than done.

Chapter Seventeen

Jaxson

IT'S BEEN THREE MONTHS since I lost my beautiful girl on that horrible winter night. There has been no contact, and all leads have gone dry. I have Tony hacking every computer that I can think of for some sort of potential lead. We know they left the country. They had to, after the murders. Max wants me to prepare myself for the possibility that she might not be alive, but I won't believe that. Every day, I bring Mick a coffee and check to make sure he is doing okay in his new job. He lets me just be miserable. He understands the loss, he loves her too.

"Don't give up on her, Jax. She is a lot stronger than you think."

I find comfort with his words. "I will search forever, Mick."

I head upstairs to try and do some sort of work. I'm barely running my business, and I am seriously thinking of selling it. I have a new assistant, and bless her for being patient with me. I made sure that I hired someone that I felt I could trust. I had Max check her all the way back to her birth hospital. Her name is Mrs. Osla. She's a fifty-five-year-old widow, originally from Edinburgh, Scotland. I think Max and I are the only ones, other than my mum, that understand her when she's talking. I know my mum is happy with her. She feels like Mrs. Osla takes good care of me and my business.

Mrs. Osla buzzes me, letting me know my mum is here. I love my mum, but my family has done nothing but hover over me since the incident. My mum flies through the door announcing it's tea time. *Really?*

"Mum, can I ask you a question?"

She smiles at me. "Of course, you never had to ask before."

"What do you think I do all day long?"

She opens her mouth to speak, and then shuts it. "Well, you don't have to get all snippy just because I'm your mother, and I was only in labor with you for twenty-six hours. I am worried about you and thought I should just pop in and have a spot of tea with you. However, if you're too busy to make time for your mum, then I'll just go see what Maxwell is doing." She clasps her hands in front of her. I knew the guilt trip would come, but what's even funnier, is Max, walking in at the end of her speech and realizing he was next on her list! He tries to quietly back out of the room, and I swear that woman must have eyes in the back of her head. "Maxwell, don't even think of leaving now!"

He is so busted, and I laugh a good laugh, which I haven't had in months. I lean in a kiss my mum. "Thank you."

She points to the sofa "Tea. Both of you, now." Max sits right down, and I'm trying not to laugh at him.

"Now, I have questions for both my boys. Maxwell, how is Jackie doing?" She inquires. He looks surprised that my mum knows about him and Jackie. "Don't look at me like that, Maxwell. I'm a mother, and I know."

He shrugs, "Um…she's doing okay. She misses Raven, and she hasn't heard anything, if that's where you're going with this."

Oh boy she's giving him the eye . . . that's never good. "Don't smart mouth me, young man, I'm just concerned."

He takes a deep breath "I'm sorry, ma'am."

She smiles, "That's better. Isabella sent Junior back to school today. The doctors suggested that he gets back to a normal routine."

I know I need to spend some time with him. "Mum, I will pop over there tonight and see if he is up to a *Doctor Who* night."

"How is Mrs. Osla working out?"

I laugh, "Good, Mum, it's like having another you around the office all day."

As I hit her with my Jax smile, Max laughs until Mum pulls his ear. "Maxwell, will you never learn?"

I love the look of fear on Max, "Sorry, ma'am."

"Hmm, that seems to be the story of your life, lately." With that, she leaves, just like the whirlwind that she blew in with.

"Max, you know she is going to be on you about Jackie. Mark my words, it's only a matter of time."

"Not that I need any more motivation to find Miss Raven, but that would do it."

"Speaking of which, what do you have for me today?"

"Well, I took your advice about the money trail, and now I have Tony working with my contact that deals with wire transfers that are questionable. What about you, Jax, do you have anything to report?"

I take a deep breath, "Yeah I paid off the mortgage on Raven's place."

Max has the grace not to say anything. I know I look like a lovesick puppy, but going into her home every day, I can still smell her, and I feel close to her. Fuck, I really need some help.

"We already went through Marco's stuff that first day, but you know I think I want to pop over there and take my time looking through his stuff again. I just have a hunch that we missed something. I also had all of Duke's stuff sent to Tony so he can double check it all." Max gets up. "Come on, I'll drive."

As we head over to Raven's, Max's phone rings. "Tony, you're on speaker. It's just Jax, you can talk freely."

"Okay. First, Joseph died today. Second, a notice just came that both of you have been requested at the reading of the will, along with Raven. Third, I found a money trail leading to a small town in Italy. Before you ask, I have the plane getting ready for the international flight. You leave in four hours from Teterboro."

Max finishes the call, since I'm just sitting in shock. Could it be that there is some hope to find my girl? Do I even dare hope? We pull up to Raven's, and I can't tell Max how much I come here just to be near her. When we get inside, I just sit on the sofa and think about all of our times together. It was fast and furious. I miss her so much, it hurts. Even my cock—who is usually always on alert—has gone dormant.

"Jax get in here!"

"Max, I don't want to be in this fucker's room."

"Jax, just shut up and get in here."

Okay, Max is pacing. "Jax, when I walk into this room, the hair on my neck tingles. Okay, I know it sounds strange, but something is off. Do you remember the day that Junior was kidnapped and Vito was in your office?"

I'm thinking, "Yeah, he was flipping out as usual. Only Junior and Raven can control that dog."

"He flipped out when Duke and Marco were in the room. He knew something was off with them, just like I feel something now. We need to rip this room apart. There has to be more, especially since Marco was a poker player. They always have an ace up their sleeve." He taps my arm with the back of his hand. We start at one end of the room and rip apart every inch. Nothing. Max turns to me. "Bathroom next."

I just want to get on that plane. "Max, I don't see anything."

"Look, Jax my *tingle* sense has never been wrong, keep looking," he raises his voice.

I pull apart the medicine cabinet and I pull out a box of condoms. I open it, and inside there is a thumb drive. "Max, I think I just found the ace."

He grabs his keys. "Okay, Jax, we need to get this to Tony, and we have to be at the airport.

Where is your passport?"

I have to think a minute. "It's in my office."

We race to the car and, of course, Max drives. "Jax, call Mrs. Osla and have her get your passport and mine. Tell her to give them to Tony and have Tony meet us at the airport."

"Where is your passport?"

"It's in my office safe."

I'm confused "I thought only you and I have the combination?"

He nods. "You can give it to her."

My shocked face registers with him. "Jax, there only two people I fear, your mum and Mrs. Osla."

I almost bust a gut laughing. We just make it to the airport, and Tony is waiting. Max gives him the thumb drive. "As soon as you know something, call me."

"Tony, where in Italy are we going?"

Tony hands me the passports. "Sicily."

I look at Max. "Who knows where we are going?"

He reads me better than anyone. "Only Tony and the pilots, and that's the way it will stay."

We get on the plane. I sit back and put on Raven's iPod. She has such a wide variety of music. I put it on shuffle. The first song that comes on is by Nickelback called "I'd Come for You". Hang on, baby, I'm on my way.

Raven

EVERY DAY, THE SICKNESS gets a little better. So today, I decide to leave my room to get some fresh air. When I go downstairs, I hear Vincent, yelling in Italian. He is talking fast, but I get most of what he is saying. He's telling someone that they should have hid the wire transfer better. The American and European bank system was hacked and no one knows where Phillips and Fleming are.

Oh my God, I hope Max and Jax are not coming here; it's not safe for them. Vincent turns around and hangs up when he sees me. "Cara, do you know what is going on?"

I barely look at him "Vincent, I have been in bed for weeks, I have lost all track of time. I don't speak Italian. What are you talking about?"

He changes the subject. "So, my brother's special baby girl is nothing more than a common whore, getting knocked up by the biggest tycoon in New York. At least your mother was married when I fucked her."

"Don't you mean—when you raped her—you pig?!"

He bangs his fist on the table. "Don't try my patience, little girl, or you will be very sorry."

I know I shouldn't egg him on, but I can't control how much I despise this man. "What has you so riled up, Vincent?"

Duke walks in. "Vincent, stop yelling at her. How she chose to live her life is none of your business." He snaps lightly. Vincent glares at me and walks away.

"Thank you for defending me to Vincent."

"I wasn't defending your choices, I was standing up to Vincent.

He's not your father, and he can't tell you how to live your life. You're looking better. How are you feeling?"

I sigh, "I'm weak, but holding down some light food and more liquids than before." I sip some juice. "How long have I been here? I seem to have lost all track of time."

"You were pretty sick. To answer your question, we've been here for three months."

I'm in shock. I can't believe I've been in and out for so long. I've missed so much, yet life keeps going on, whether we want it to or not. "Duke, do you know why Vincent is so mad?"

He shakes his head. "No, but whatever it is, it must be bad because he went in his office to call the States. When he talks here, it's always in Italian because we don't understand it, but when he calls the States, he has to speak English, so he goes in his office."

My eyes fill with tears. "Is Vincent holding you here against your will, too?"

His mood turns bleak as he looks down at his hands. "Raven, I have nowhere to go, so it really wouldn't matter. If I went back to the States, I would be in jail or executed for murdering a federal agent. I mean, even though Marco went off the rails, he was still an agent."

I still feel like there is more to the story than I know. "Duke, how did you ever get mixed up with them?"

"Erica was the key. She used me. She was like a black widow spider, and I fell for her hard. I didn't know about Marco or you, until later on. It was a fluke that you were Michael's teacher and Marco's roommate. I think if Marco thought he could turn you, he would have, because, let's face it, you would have been the perfect mole. No one would ever suspect the teacher, but you're a good person.

"You weren't supposed to be on the playground that day. I guess Jackie was lucky that you were otherwise, she would be dead right now. Then, when you met Jax and started a relationship with him, the plan had to be escalated. In the end, Erica and I were supposed to take the money and live off the interest on some small island. I never knew she was with Marco. I was told he was gay, and I believed them. It's hard to believe they were not only together, but they were married!"

Vincent steps back into the room and he doesn't look happy. "Cara, I have a question for you. Do you think that it was right that Joseph hid my only son's existence from me?"

I look at him and then Duke. "Duke, is this the garbage he's filling your head with? Joseph gave you the chance at a normal life. If you would have grown up in his world, you would be the same ruthless animal that he is."

Before Vincent can answer, Duke gets up. "Maybe I already am."

"Vincent, I would like to go for a walk. Am I allowed to get some fresh air?"

"Cara, there are guards throughout this place; you can walk around outside."

I decide to walk out back, through the gardens. They stretch to the cliff, and below the cliff, is a white sandy beach and the beautiful Mediterranean Sea. I stand at the edge and let the wind blow through my hair. The warm sun feels so good on my face after being in bed for so long. I walk over to the cluster of chairs and sit for a while.

Before I know it, my eyes close and I let my mind wander to a happier place. I look down at my tummy and smile. " My little one, you're causing quite a ruckus, and you're not even here yet. I wish you could know your daddy; he is such a beautiful man. He has the bluest eyes, almost like the Mediterranean Sea. There isn't a thing about him that isn't beautiful, inside and out. You have a cousin too, Michael Jr., and he is very tender-hearted. He has the coolest dog. His name is Vito. I hope someday if we get out of here, you'll get to meet them all." At least I can still dream that maybe my baby and I will make it out of here alive.

Jaxson

AS WE TOUCHDOWN IN Italy, I have a sense of urgency that I didn't have before. The minute Max turns on his phone, Tony calls.

"Max, are we on speaker and is it safe to talk freely?" That's usually means Tony did something illegal.

"Yes, Tony."

He's excited. "Good, I was able to hack Marco's drive and, considering he was a hacker, that is pretty impressive. Anyway, I have big news."

We both stop dead in our tracks. "Go on, Tony."

He takes a deep breath. "I know what Joseph had in his will, and it's big. Gabriella did not kill herself. She is currently at a clinic in Switzerland, and Joseph pays all her bills using a trust fund from her parents."

Will this ever end? "Hold on, Tony. Joseph said that he used that money to set up a fund for Raven?"

"I know, Jax, but what he did was take the money that was from Gabriella's parents, plus the settlement money from the accident, and he set it up to pay for her care. He then took the money from Antonio's insurance, and putting his own money in with it, he created a fund for Raven. She has no idea that her mother is alive. I also obtained a copy of Joseph's will. It names the two of you co-executors. You are both to take care of Raven and Gabriella. He named you both in the event that one of you dies." Max's jaw becomes tight and he grimaces. He has a white knuckle grip on the phone, probably trying to gain his self control.

"Jax, he left three sealed letters. One is for you, one for Max, and one for Raven. I also pulled Gabriella's medical file. It appears that after she gave birth to Duke, she had a mental break down. Joseph had her sent to the clinic."

I turn to Max, "Why would Joseph hide her?"

He shrugs, "Look, Jax, I venture to say this has to do with Vincent. The first order of business is to rescue Raven then, we go for Gabriella."

Tony informs us that he back traced phone calls going from Sicily to the bank in Chicago. Then he cross-referenced that with holdings that Vincent has, and he was able to find a villa that was under the great grandfather's name. He sent the coordinates to Max's phone.

I thank God that I have Max; he is fluent in Italian and knows his way around this country like the back of his hand. Max being Max, is making some calls; calling in favors and reinforcements, I'm sure.

"All right, Jax, I have everything arranged. The villa is at the top of a cliff. It is surrounded by beach, which will work to our advantage."

"How does that work to our advantage?"

We head to the car. "We'll be coming in by sea, just like regular tourists. Let's go, we have to be at the marina in an hour."

Waiting for us when we get to the marina, is by far the brightest, loudest monstrosity of a speedboat I have ever seen! "Max, first, what the fuck is that? And second, they will see us coming from ten miles away!"

He laughs. "Relax. Jax, your right. It's loud and that is what I'm hoping for. It's the perfect distraction. This boat is called *Phenomenon*. It's the world's fastest speedboat, going up to 250 mph. People will have all eyes on the boat, which gives us the perfect distraction."

It looks like a bright orange submarine that rides on top of the water. "I trust you, Max. So what's the plan?"

"Diving gear and every kind of artillery is already loaded. We head out now and anchor off shore. After sunset, we move in with backup."

Waiting till sunset will kill me, but the thought that my girl is coming home is all that really matters. "Okay, let's go!"

WHEN MAX SAID FAST, he wasn't fucking kidding me! This boat is going so fast, that it glides on top of the water. We get to the anchoring location, and I'm in shock. I know Max said the villa was on a cliff, but it is so high up. I have no fucking clue what he's thinking. Max looks over to me, "Jax, I have some ideas so, just keep an open mind. The cliffs are very high, and with shear rocks. How do you feel about BASE jumping?"

I don't answer him. I'm just looking through the binoculars stunned at the sight before me. *It's Raven!* She is just sitting in a chair looking out to the sea. For a split second, I swear we lock violet to blues. I have to be mistaken. She can't possibly lock eyes with me from here, but then, my dead cock springs to life! What the fuck, now you decide to make a fucking appearance?

"Jax, are you with me?"

"Sorry, Max, but I see Raven." I yell over the sound of the engine.

He grabs the binoculars from me. "Well, at least she is allowed to walk around and is not locked up."

I jump up, "Max, let's go. I need to get to her."

He grabs my arm. "Hold on, buddy. I understand, but we have a plan and we need to stick with it. The goal is to get her out of there alive.

Stop thinking with your cock, mate."

I hate it when he is fucking right! "Okay, what's the plan?"

Raven

THE BREEZE IS SO nice. I love to look out over the sea and wonder what it would feel like to be swimming with Jax. My mind wanders to him always, but today something seems different. I feel him around me. It's probably the baby.

A really ugly looking boat just pulled up. *Who would ever want a bright orange boat?* I try to see the people on board, but I can't. I decide to close my eyes for a little bit, but all I can see are the bluest eyes. God, I miss him. As I drift off, all I can think of is how much I love that beautiful man.

Maxwell

"OKAY, JAX, HERE IS the plan. You and I are going back to shore. We'll glide toward the villa. When we are above it, we parachute in, landing on the roof, in the dark. We rappel down the backside where the bedrooms are located. We get Raven, and then we'll BASE jump out towards the boat."

I'm looking at Max like he has three heads. "Jax, just hear me out. I know you have done BASE jumping before, and I have done it enough that I can tandem Raven with no problem. Once we get to the boat, they won't be able to catch us."

I sit back, trying to think of the different options, and there really aren't any. "My concern is, finding her once she is inside the villa, Max. What if she's not in her room or what if we pick the wrong room?"

"The men on the boat are watching her, and they have determined that her room is on the back, left corner. She has a balcony."

I sit there, stroking my chin. I wish I could come up with something else, but we're out of options. "Okay, but I don't have to tell you I'm not leaving without her. I will lay down my life for her."

He hands me my chute. "Jax, I promised your mum and Mrs. Osla that I would bring you both home, and they scare me a hell of a lot more than Vincent and his goons."

Raven

THE MORE I READ the book, that my mother made, the more upset I get. She believed she would never see me again. Vincent, mentally and physically, tortured her daily, and yet, she found a way to go on. I don't understand why she killed herself. Joseph said she couldn't look at Duke, but she gave him up for adoption. She fought to stay alive through two months of nonstop torture, yet right after she gave birth, she killed herself? Something isn't right, but I guess I'll never know.

Joseph knew about Duke, and yet, his answer was to ship me off to boarding school? Maybe if I was around, my mother might have survived. Joseph did all of this, thinking he was protecting me, but all he did was make this mess even bigger.

I think about Marco, and part of me wants to grieve for him while the other part of me is still in shock by his actions. I still can't believe he did all of this for money, trying to kidnap poor little Michael. If he really needed money, I would have given him all of my trust fund with no questions asked. Now, so many people are dead, and lives have been changed forever.

I skipped dinner tonight, feeling nauseated, but now I'm getting hungry. I get up, but I hear a noise on my balcony. I turn just as the doors swing open. In walks the most beautiful sight; two men, all in black.

My eyes only lock on to one thing, the bluest of blues. I stifle a yell and feel my knees buckle. He is on me in a second. "I've got you, sweetheart; I will always have your back."

I throw my arms around him, flooding him with kisses, and then I realize he put himself in danger when I specifically told him not to. I don't know what gets into me, maybe the fact I'm pregnant and highly emotional. I reach back and smack him across the face! He gets a shocked look on his face, and Max is trying not to laugh.

"You crazy man, I told you not to put yourself in danger, but you just don't listen to anything! Do you think you're Superman or something? Do you realize how dangerous this is?"

He grabs me and kisses me hard. Oh fuck, I'm done! "Sweetheart, as long as there is life left within me, I will always come for you!"

"Jax, Raven, this is all nice and stuff, but we have to go now."

I'm trying to catch my breath. "Just how do you boys plan on getting me out of here?"

"Well, right now, everyone is asleep, including the guard that I hit with the tranquilizer dart. We are going to rappel down to the garden and BASE jump out to sea, where a boat is waiting for us."

I freeze. They both turn and look at me. "I can't do this."

Jax's eyes bug out, but Max is calm. "Miss Raven, I understand your fear of heights, however, I promise, I will get you to that boat safely."

This is not how I would have ever pictured telling someone something this important, but I don't have a choice. "I'm pregnant."

They both stop, and I swear both their chins are on the ground. I instantly see the fear in Jax's eyes and I realize what he is thinking—that Vincent did to me what he did to my mother.

"Jax, it's your baby. I'm a little more than three months along; Vincent never touched me, especially when he found out."

"Miss Raven, do you trust me?" Max asks.

"Yes, without any doubt, I do."

He puts his hand out "Good. Give me your hand. This might be a little bit unconventional, but I need to have you wrap yourself around my front like a monkey hold. Can you do that for me?"

Jax is frozen.

"Okay." I climb on Max.

He heads towards the balcony, "Hey, Jax, snap out of it, we are leaving now! Jax, I need you to go first and guide us down," he calls softly.

Jax doesn't say anything. He just does everything Max tells him. When we get to the bottom, Jax unhooks us, and we head towards the cliff. I think I'm going to puke. No, I know I'm going to puke. Jax is holding my hair back while I empty my stomach.

"Miss Raven, we really need to go. Climb back on me. If you have to puke again, just do it, I won't care, believe me I have seen a lot worse than that."

"Raven, you're jumping with Max. He's trained for tandem jumping." Jax finally finds his voice.

We hear yelling and running. "The party is over, we have to go now!" Max grabs me under my ass and takes off running. I close my eyes. Now I understand the statement 'take a flying leap.' I swear I scream the whole way down. I look up, and Jax is above us, gliding.

Max is gliding us towards the boat, and I realize it's the ugly boat I saw this morning. I hear gunshots, and they are whizzing past us. I feel something hot and wet, but it doesn't register that it's blood. We all land. The men from the boat get us on board, and in seconds, we are off.

Jax unhooks himself and comes running towards us, and I realize Max is shot. "Max, don't you dare die on me!" I yell at him. I don't know what that is supposed to accomplish.

Jax unhooks us, "Raven, you're shot!"

I look towards Max. "It's not me, Jax. Max is shot in the shoulder!"

"Make this fucking boat fly!" Jax yells to the captain.

Jax starts to take off Max's shirt, and they both look at his wound before turning to look towards me. "What, why are you both looking at me?"

They both jump up and grab me, but I don't understand why. I feel that wave of nausea, and the world starts spinning. "Max, it's a fucking through and through and she's hit!" I hear them yelling and my shirt being ripped off.

Then, nothing, but a quiet hum.

Chapter Eighteen

Raven

I'M SLEEPING AND HAVING the most wonderful dream, those beautiful eyes are staring at me, and I see that crooked smirk. I love when I dream of Jax. I go to stretch, and I have a sharp, burning pain in my left shoulder. My eyes fly open, remembering what happened and I'm instantly hit with the bluest, most calming eyes. "Jax," I whisper.

He grabs me. "I'm here, sweetheart, always here."

I try to jump up. "Max!" I'm looking around, but I don't see him.

"He's fine, just rest."

Realization hits me "Oh my God, the baby!"

"Hush, the baby is fine, everyone is good." He's really here smiling at me.

Jaxson

"LOOK, I HAVE SOMETHING for you." I hand her the scan of the baby. "See, the baby is just fine."

She stares at the picture, smiling. "I want to see Max. Where are we? How did you find me?"

I have to keep her calm. "One thing at a time, okay?"

"Okay."

I open the door and call Max and Jackie in her room. "Oh, Miss Raven, you're awake. I'm so sorry."

"Max, what on earth are you sorry for? You risked your life for me and you were shot! If anything, I'm sorry for putting you in that position."

Raven

BEFORE I CAN SAY anything more, the door flies open and Mrs. Phillips comes storming in.

"Maxwell, you should be sorry. I told you to bring her and Jaxson back safely. Jumping out of planes and leaping off of cliffs is *not* bringing them back safely. Plus, you were both shot!"

Max is looking down at his feet. "Yes, Ma'am, I am very sorry."

Oh my God, Max is afraid of Jax's mom. I start laughing and I can't stop. Everyone turns towards me, probably thinking I have totally lost my mind, and I realize I need to say something. I snort, "I can't believe big, bad Max is afraid of you!"

Max turns beet red, and I start laughing again. I really can't help it. Max grumbles, "Miss Raven, you should be too, she's really tough."

Before I can answer, she reaches up and pulls him by the ear! "Maxwell, you'll mind your manners, if you know what's good for you!"

Jackie hugs me, "I'm so happy that they found you, and you're safe."

"I missed you too, Jackie." I have so many questions for everyone. I look around and I realize that I'm not sure where I am. "Jax, where are we?" I ask.

He squeezes my hand. "We're back in New York. Max's wound was a through and through. Yours, however, was not. The doctor got the bullet out, and I had a plane on standby to take us back to the States. The doctor said you could go home tomorrow."

Wow, I can't believe we are already in New York. "Jax, we need to talk."

He's shaking his head. "No we will talk when we get home. Right now, I need you to rest; you've been through too much." He brings my hand up to his lips and plants a kiss on the back. I allow myself to be distracted by his affections for a moment, but I need some answers.

"What about Duke and Vincent, where are they?"

The mention of their names makes Jax grip my hand even harder. "Vincent escaped but Duke was apprehended, however, the Italian government has not decided what they are going to do with him. Now, enough! I said rest, Raven, and I mean it."

I can't even argue, my eyes feel so heavy, and I fall back to sleep, knowing for now, my baby and I are safe. Safe with Jax.

I WAKE AGAIN AND look at the clock; its 3 am. Jax is beside me, asleep. He is so beautiful, and I can't help but stroke his face. I hope the baby has his chiseled cheekbones and his soft lips. He has such long eyelashes, and they are so dark. I take my finger and run it along his cheek, so very beautiful. I let my fingers roam down his chest and slowly make my way down his happy trail.

"Busted, sweetheart," he whispers.

I yelp, "Jesus, Jax, you scared daylights out of me."

I can see him smile at me via the moonlight shining through the window. "You're supposed to be sleeping, and yet, my beautiful girl is copping a feel."

"I was not copping a feel, mister!" I squeal. Then, he opens his eyes and hits me with that crooked smirk and I can't help but giggle. "Yeah, I was, but it's your fault."

He laughs at me "Wait, I'm sleeping, you're copping a feel, and it's my fault?"

I'm never getting out of this one. "Yes."

He takes a breath. "Okay, how is it my fault?"

I stammer, "Well I can't explain it, but trust me, it just is."

He looks in my eyes and growls, "Don't look at me like that. I'm not taking advantage of you in a hospital bed, and besides, you were shot! Curl up next to me and I'll stroke your back so you can go back to sleep."

As I drift off to sleep, I hear him sing in almost a whisper, and it is such a beautiful song, one of my favorites, "Little Things" by One Direction.

MORNING COMES. I OPEN my eyes, and Jax is gone. *Oh no.* Was last night a dream? I start to panic. My body trembles and my breath quickens. Please dear God . . . please don't let it be a dream. I've got to get up. What if Vincent finds me? I'm half out of bed when the door flies open, and Jax comes in. "Where do you think you're going?"

I take a few steadying breaths, "I woke up and you weren't here." My teeth are chattering, "I was going to look for you?"

He's in his 'take charge' mode. "I was just outside, signing you out of this place. The nurse will be in a few minutes to take out the IV."

All I want to do is get clean. "When can I take a shower?"

He laughs. "I know you are in love with my shower, however, when we get home, you can soak in the tub, no shower until the stitches come out."

I am just about to ask him about work, when the nurse comes in. After she leaves, Jax gets me dressed and then the nurse comes back with the wheelchair. Jax ignores her, scoops me up, and walks out with me in his arms and the nurse following behind us, yelling about rules. I just laugh. Jax and rules don't mix well.

When we get outside, Max is there with an SUV. "Hi, Miss Raven, how are you feeling today?"

I smile, "I'm good, but how are you?"

Max is worried about me, but he was shot too. "I'm fine, nothing to worry about, just another chink in the armor."

After we get into the vehicle and drive away, my mind wanders to Marco. I feel so hurt, and tears fill my eyes. I'm trying not to cry in front of Jax because it really makes him crazy. "Aren't we going back to my place, Jax?"

Jax's jaw gets tight "Raven, we're going to The Tower."

"Oh."

"Yeah, *oh*," he whispers.

In the usual record time, we arrive at The Tower. Max comes upstairs with us, so they probably have some business. "Max, has the place been swept?"

Max nods as Jax steers me towards the bedroom. "I'm going to get you set up in the tub, and then I have some stuff to go over with Max. Are you okay?"

I'm searching his eyes "Yes, I'm fine."

He fills the tub and puts in some mandarin spice bath oil. The bath feels wonderful. I think I may have had fallen in love with Jax's bathroom even before I had fallen in love with the man! I open my eyes when I notice the water is starting to get cold, and find Jax, leaning against the counter, watching me.

He smiles, "I'm here to wash your hair for you. Scoot forward a little"

I do as I'm told. He turns on the water, wets my hair, and works in some shampoo. He is so gentle. It's a simple thing, but it is such a turn on! He conditions, then rinses, and then he towels me dry with heated towels. A girl could get very spoiled with all of this attention. He seats me at the vanity and dries my hair. "Jax, are you ever going to talk to me? You haven't said much of anything, since yesterday. Why?" I need him to be his usual bulldozer self.

"You're right. We have a lot to talk about, but I don't want to overload you or pressure you. I'm trying to figure out what you need. You are my *main* focus. As for me, it's simple; all I need is you, sweetheart."

We lock violets to blues. "Jax, what I need is your usual fast and furious self. I need the Jax that asks whatever he wants, whenever he wants, and damn anyone to hell that gets in his way."

"Okay, let's start from the beginning then. Why did you run away that night?"

I let out the breath I was holding. "I heard you and Max talking. I was hurt. You can't keep stuff from me; only telling me what you think I can handle. That's not life, and it's not fair to me."

He nods. "Okay, you're right, but you never gave me a chance. I only just found out that stuff, and I would've told you, but you ran, again," he defends himself then lets out a big sigh. "I thought you were on the pill, so how did you end up pregnant?"

I don't want him to think I got pregnant to trap him. "I was on the pill, but when I was kidnapped, I missed them, but we never abstained. I didn't plan this. I expect nothing from you. Look, maybe I should just go back to my place."

His jaw tightens. "There you go again, deciding for me what I can or can't handle! I didn't say I didn't want the baby, so if that's what you're thinking, just get it out of your head! Those three months you were gone, I died a little every day. And then to find you and find out you're carrying our child; It's overwhelming.

"Raven, so much happened in three months, but I don't want to overload you, so can we take it a little at a time, please?"

"Yes, but you must know I have so many questions, and I need to talk to Joseph," I plead and watch him quickly turns pale. "Jax, what happened?"

$\mathcal{J}axson$

I HAVE TO TELL her. I just don't know how much more she can handle. "Joseph died three weeks ago from prostate cancer. That's part of why everything happened with Marco," I lay it out for her. I take her in my arms and just let her have a good cry. I don't know how the fuck I'm going to tell her that her mother is alive. "Joseph told Marco he was sick, and Marco convinced Joseph to tell him who your half-brother was and where he was living. Marco was heavy into gambling, and he hooked up with Erica in a chat room. They plotted to kidnap Junior, and when Marco found out you were his teacher, it just made things easier for him. It made it easier, that is, until he realized that Junior's uncle was also your Starbucks guy."

Raven

I WIPE MY TEARS. "Jax, if Marco wanted money, all he had to do was ask me. I would have given him my trust fund. When we were in that cabin, Marco said Joseph was sick, but I didn't know the difference between truth and lies with him anymore, when he was trying to justify his actions."

He's takes my hand, "Oh, sweetheart, there is so much more that you don't know."

I need to know it all. "Go on, Jax, just get it all out, so we can get past this and close the book."

He closes his eyes and lifts his head back, seemingly fearful of what he is about to tell me.

"If only it would be that easy." He has a really tight grip on me and I see fear in his eyes.

"Jax, what is it? What is so bad, that you're afraid to tell me?"

*J*axson

I'M SILENTLY PRAYING FOR her to have the strength to deal with this whole mess. "Raven, your mother is not dead. When she gave birth to Duke, she had a breakdown. Joseph had her put in a clinic in Switzerland. He took the money your mother inherited when her parents died and invested it. That money is used for her care. He took the money you received when your father died and put that, plus some of his own, into a trust fund for you."

She suddenly loses color to her face and starts shaking, her bottom lip is quivering while the tears spill out of her eyes.. "My mother is alive?"

"Joseph left Max and me in charge of the estate, and the care of your mum was left to Max."

She wipes away a tear, "Why would he do that?"

"We don't know. He made these changes the week before he died. I do know that he admired Max's tenacity; he called him a 'bull dog' when it came to never giving up. He also left three envelopes, one for each of us."

She clutches my arm, "I want to see my mother, is she safe?"

I nod, "Max flew there the other day and increased her guards. He is in constant touch with her doctors, and he is going to have her moved to a facility here. He is just waiting until he feels it's safe to move her, and he gets the go ahead from her doctors. Raven, we only found out when we landed in Italy. I don't want you to think that I kept this from you."

She takes a steadying breath. "Where are the letters that Joseph left?"

Raven

HE JUST KEEPS STROKING my arm, and I'm not sure if, it is for his benefit or mine. "They're at his attorney's office."

I stand up. "I need to talk to Max. Please, Jax, I need to see him now."

"He's here. He knew you would want to talk to him."

He stops me as I start to head for the living room, "Raven, you need to put on something, other than a towel, or I will lose it."

"HI, MAX, PLEASE TELL me what happened when you went to see my mother."

"Miss Raven, I don't know all the details about why she is in her condition. I'm hoping there is more in the letters that Joseph left. I can tell you, that she is comfortable. She seems to have understood me when I was talking to her. I did not tell her anything about you. I felt it would just be too much, too soon. However, she doesn't speak at all. I gave all of the proper paperwork, that grants me guardianship of your mother, to the Swiss doctors, and as soon as everything is filed with the authorities, she'll be moved to a facility here in New York. I promise you that I will take the upmost care of her."

I smile. "I know you will. Do you know how long it will be before we can move her here?"

He takes a deep breath. "I'm hoping for the end of next week. We do, however, need to get to Joseph's attorney's first. I took the liberty of making an appointment for tomorrow morning at ten."

I'm tired, but I need to know everything and then, process it, so I can move forward. "What about Duke and Vincent? I remember Jax telling me that the Italian authorities have Duke, but Vincent got away. Has there been any more news on either of them?"

"I am in contact with the Italian authorities. They move very slowly, but as far as Vincent is concerned, I was able to track him into Greece and then to Los Angeles. Miss Raven, for now, that is all I have, but be assured, as soon as I know anything, I will advise you and Jax. Is there anything else you need?"

I shake my head, "No, Max, thank you. I could never repay you or Jax for all that you've both gone through for me."

He gets up to leave. "Miss Raven, you are very welcome, and now, I will let you rest. I'll be by tomorrow morning at nine, to pick you both up."

"Jax, there is so much we need to talk about, but right now, can you just hold me?"

"Sweetheart, always. Come here." He pulls me into his lap, and I curl up into a ball in his arms. I don't think I have it in me to shed another tear. I cried so much, when I thought he was gone from my life. I cried for Marco, Joseph, and a mother, whom I thought was dead. I have gone through and witnessed more in my twenty-seven years than most people will ever experience in their lifetime. I know there is so much more to come, but just for tonight, I need to forget the rest of the world.

For tonight, I just need Jax. "Jax, will you please take me to bed and make love to me?"

I feel his cock twitch underneath me. "Raven, you just got home from the hospital. You've been shot and you're exhausted…"

Before he can say any more, I look up and kiss him. I lock violet to blues "Jax, I need you—*now*."

He gives me a slow nod. He lifts me in his arms and carries me to the bedroom. He, slowly and beautifully, makes love to me all night long.

JAX IS STILL BURIED within me when I wake up, his hands are latched on to my ass. I can't help but giggle. I take a peek at him, but his eyes are closed. I like to look at him when he's sleeping; he is just so beautiful. He always has scruffy facial hair, and it's such a contrast to his deep blue eyes. He has such long eyelashes, and his mouth with lips soft as pillows. Thinking of all the things he can do with that mouth, makes me instantly wet. I trail my finger along those lips, down his chest, around his nipples.

"Sweetheart, are you done taking inventory?"

I hum, "I thought you were sleeping."

His eyes are still closed, but he tilts his hips up, and his morning erection has sprung to life.

"Jax, he is always ready for action. Oh my God, now you have *me,* referring to your cock as a *he*!" I can't help but laugh until Jax lifts my hips and then pulls me back down.

"Raven, he is in cock heaven, so, of course he is ready. Feel free to talk to him whenever you want." He gifts me with that crooked smirk, and I start to move up and down, slowly.

"Take the lead, Raven, and ride me however you like."

I love that he doesn't always have to be in control. "Really, Jax? Anything?" I continue up and down, real slow.

I stop, and he watches me like he's waiting to see what I will do next. I lean down and run my tongue along his lips. I follow it with kisses. Traveling to his neck and down to his nipples, taking each one in my mouth—sucking and nibbling—just like he does to me. I lift myself up really slowly and then come down even slower, feeling every inch. I lift myself up again, but this time I climb off of him. I work my kisses down his happy trail. I nip and lick up and down his V. He is so hard. I kiss the top of his cock. I can taste myself on him, and it is so erotic. Nothing like I thought, as I swirl my tongue around the top and down to the base, I take him in my mouth and latch on to him, hollowing out my cheeks. I take him deeper than I ever have before, and I can see by the look on his face he is in shock. I start to slowly move up and down, going deeper with each pass.

He's moving his hips with me now, "Oh, Raven, what you do to me."

As I bare my teeth, his head flies back, and his hips shoot up. He screams and comes the hardest I have ever seen him come. I devour every drop of him that he offers up. I climb up his beautiful body real slow, leaving soft kisses in my path. When I reach his lips, my eyes search his. "I love you, Jax, heart and soul. And I always will."

"Raven, sweetheart, I never thought I would hear those words. The three months without you almost killed me." He lets out the deep breath that he had sucked in.

I kiss him. "Jax, the only thing that gave me any hope was, knowing that your baby was a part of me. I needed to stay strong to keep our baby safe. What were you doing while I was gone?" Once I ask, I see him avert his eyes like he is ashamed or embarrassed. "Jax, you can tell me," I stutter, "Did you try to move on?" I lower my eyes unable to look at him.

"Raven, *Look at me!*" he bites. I return my gaze. "I was dead inside without you. Even my cock didn't want to be bothered with me. I do have a confession for you, though. I purchased your apartment."

"Why?" I widen my eyes.

That glaze of embarrassment washes over his face again. "Well, I needed to keep the place to feel close to you somehow." He admits and I furrow my brows. "Don't look at me like that. I know I wasn't thinking like a normal guy. Hell, normal flew out the window the day you doused me with your coffee. I couldn't take a shower here. I couldn't sleep in my own bed. I wouldn't even let my housekeeper clean the living room because your handprints were on the window. I practically lived at your place for three months so I could be close to you, and while we're at full disclosure, I was seriously considering selling Raiders, Inc."

I just stare at him, in total shock. "Why would you sell your company?—you love it!"

Jaxson

"I LOVE YOU MORE." It was just a whisper, but I know she heard, and I know she understood. I told her once that those words are said too much, that it's a person's actions that speak louder than those words ever could, but I know she needed to hear them. "Raven, what happened for the three months you were held prisoner? Did they hurt you?"

She shakes her head. "You want to know if Vincent raped me like he raped my mother?"

Raven

HIS GRIP TIGHTENS AT the mention of Vincent's name. "I want to know everything you want me to know. I want to help you get all of this behind you, so we can move forward together."

I know he needs to hear this as much as I need to tell him. "On the first day, Vincent gave me a book that was left there by my mother. It was her account of what Vincent did to her while she was held at the villa. Every time he raped my mother, when he was done, he would look up to the heavens and tell my father that he did it for him. It was also her thoughts about my dad and me. There were pictures that she drew. I never knew my mom was an artist. She kept it almost as a diary. Unfortunately, we left it behind when we escaped. But to answer your question, Vincent never touched me."

I see relief in his eyes. "What about Duke, what did he do while you were there?"

I'm sad to think I have a brother and I will never know him. "Duke came in my room one day to talk to me. It was after Vincent gave me the book. He wanted to ask me questions about my mother. He needs to know she is still alive."

He shakes his head. "I'm not sure that's possible, especially if he is in contact with Vincent."

I know he's right, but what does that make me if I withhold that from him? "Jax, I need to talk to him."

"Please explain why, because right now I'm trying not to lose it."

I take a deep breath "When Duke came into my room, he was looking for answers. Jax, he was lied to and manipulated. I'm not excusing what he did. I mean, he did murder two people. I saw him pull the trigger. There was no remorse in his eyes, but he protected me from Vincent."

His grip on me tightens "What do you mean, protected you from Vincent? I thought you said Vincent didn't do anything?"

I stroke his arm to calm him. "He didn't physically attack me, but he did flip out when he found out I was pregnant. Duke stood up to him in my defence. Vincent called me a 'common whore, that was knocked up by the big New York City tycoon,'"

Jax winces. "Jax, please don't."

"Don't what, Raven? Don't get pissed off that you were made to feel like filth, for no reason? Our child was not conceived out of common, everyday lust. Our child was conceived from two halves becoming whole, two souls that are meant to be together. The fact that you had to go through this, makes me sick!" He gets up and heads to the bathroom. "I'm going to jump in the shower before we need to head out. Do you want me to set up the tub for you?"

"How about setting up the tub for us?" I can tell by the way he's stroking his chin that he's thinking. "Jax, what's the problem?"

He's staring at the tub. "Um, well, okay, so here's the thing, I've never had a bath."

I gape at him. "You mean you never used that beautiful claw foot tub?" Oh my God, he is blushing and looking down. "Jax, why did you even have such an elaborate tub installed?"

"For resale purposes."

"Did you design this bathroom?"

"No. Bella did, she loves baths. Even as a child, she was always soaking in the tub."

"Well, I will have to thank her. She did a wonderful job."I don't know what to say, I have ever met anyone who never had a bath. "What about when you were a child?"

He shakes his head, "No. As far as I can remember, my mum always left me to shower on my own. I've always been very independent. Plus it seems such a waste of time to just sit there, doing nothing."

Wow. "Okay. Well, Mr. Phillips, I am going to introduce you to the wonders of a big, beautiful tub. You wait here."

I go about filling the tub with that wonderful vanilla spice that I have come to love so much. I can't believe it. If I had this tub, I'd be soaking in it all the time. I love a good book, some soothing music, and a soak in the tub. I'm so excited that I'm going to give Jax a first.

Jax walks in and smiles at me, "What's that look for?"

I must have the most ridiculous smile on my face right now. "I just realized that I'm going to be giving you a first, and there is not too many firsts that I can give you."

He pulls me towards him "You're giving me another first—my first child."

Realization hits me at that moment, he's right. "Oh."

"Yeah, *oh*." He climbs into the tub, and I watch as he sinks into the water. "Are you getting in too?"

He is so beautiful; I could watch him all day long. "I just wanted a minute to look at you."

He opens his arms for me and I climb in. "Jax, can I ask you a question?"

"You can ask me whatever you want, you know that."

I turn and face him, "I understand that you love *Doctor Who*, but you never said why?"

He strokes his chin then, stops to move my hair from my right shoulder to my left. He places several soft kisses in the crook of my neck.. "I knew you would eventually ask me this, and I don't want to hold anything back with you but I have to say, this may be a little hard for me to share." He takes in a deep breath. "When I was a kid, the only thing I ever shared with my father was sitting down with him once a week to watch the show. I don't have very many memories of my father, but that is one that is so clear. My sharing it with Junior, I guess is, in some way, my sharing his grandfather with him. I hope that he will share it with his children, and I know, I will share it with ours."

I throw my arms around him. There are no words left to say. Oh, how I love this man.

Chapter Nineteen

Raven

MAX IS ALWAYS ON time and today is no different. "Max, where did you learn to drive?" His driving is fast, but not reckless.

"Miss Raven, I spent my summers in Italy working for Lamborghini. Why are you laughing?"

"When Marco first met you, he said you reminded him of Daniel Craig. Then when you and Jax rescued me, I realized, not only do you look like him, but *you are* James Bond. If I had any lingering doubts, your driving proves it." I lightly smack his shoulder. Max gifts me with a very large smile, which is so rare for him.

Jax leans over, "Sweetheart, don't encourage him, his head is big enough."

We arrive at the attorney's office right on time. We're ushered in, and then we have to wait. Finally, a man enters and introduces himself as Joseph's attorney. He looks to me, "Raven, I am sorry for your loss. Joseph left three letters with a codicil which names, Jaxson James Phillips and Maxwell Fleming, as executors of his will. Mr. Fleming has also been given legal guardianship of your mother.

"All of Joseph's assets were put into the trust, which controls both your trust and that of your mother. Your mother's trust is to be used for her care. In the event of her death, everything rolls into your trust. If you should precede your mother in death, then your trust would revert to your mother's trust, unless you have children. In that case, everything would revert to the children. Under no circumstances is anything supposed to go to Duke Jensen. Do you have any questions for me?"

Questions? Probably a million, but I doubt that he will have the answers. "Yes. Why?"

"Pardon me Miss. Anderson why, what?" He asks me in an uncertain tone.

I have tight grip on Jax's hand. "Well, first, why did he name Max and Jax when he really didn't know them? Why did he hide my mother from me? Why did he hide my brother from me? Why didn't he tell me he was ill? I guess the list of questions is really endless."

He nods. "Well, there really isn't much I can tell you, because I really didn't know the man very well. I can tell you, he made the changes in the last weeks of his life. The letter to you has been here for a long time, although he did add to it. The letters to Mr. Phillips and Mr. Fleming are new. Maybe the answers you seek are within these letters." With that, he has us sign some paperwork, hands us the letters, and then asks us if we wanted to use his conference room.

"Jax, I would like to go home," I say. Jax nods his head and excuses us from the meeting and the law office, letters in hand. We drive home in silence, the three of us lost in our thoughts. I really want to ask Max to stay. I want to know what Joseph wrote to him, but it's is personally addressed to him. Jax and I sit in front of the fire, and he pours a scotch for himself and water for me. We put the envelopes on the bar and stare at them. I just can't do this now. "Jax, I'm going to lie down for a while, I'm just not ready yet."

He kisses me. "I'll be here for you when you get up."

Maxwell

WHEN I GET BACK to my place, I check my voicemail. I have a message from Jackie, letting me know she's there for me. She's a sweet girl. Too good for me, but I can't walk away from her. I just don't get why Joseph did this; he hardly knew me. And at our last meeting, Jax smashed his nose and we both left him in a broken heap. I decide to pour myself a hefty scotch and sit down with my letter.

Dear Maxwell,

By now you're wondering . . . why? Well, it's what I saw in you, when we were searching for Raven. I saw a man that would not give up, a man of morals, and principals. When I pulled a check on you, I was impressed with your military record. If the Queen can trust her grandchildren to you, then I feel comfortable trusting Raven and Gabriella with you.

When I rescued Gabriella from Vincent, I had to choose to rescue her, knowing he would escape. I never forgave myself for that. She told me that every time he was done raping her, he would look up to the heavens and tell Antonio that it was for him. The man is a vicious pig. If he knew Gabriella was still alive, I don't doubt that he would come after her. When I got her back to the States, I had the doctors examine her, and that's when she found out she was pregnant. She would never have an abortion, so she opted to give the child up for adoption. If Vincent had found out, he would have come back for her. I had to protect Raven, and the best way to do that was to send her to boarding school. My plan was that I would keep Raven at school until Gabriella gave birth, then she could come back, and I would relocate both of them in the Witness Protection Program. You know what they say about best laid plans. Every day that Gabriella carried that child, she was driven more and more mad. She felt Antonio was looking down at her with disgust. I tried to get her into counseling, but she refused. Doctors really do make the worst patients.

By the time she gave birth, she was withdrawn, and then, she was hit with postpartum depression. She tried to hang herself. It was a fluke that I came by that day to find her. She never fully recovered, and I couldn't trust her to take care of Raven so I sent her away to the Swiss clinic and had Raven adopted. I had to do it this way. I needed everyone to think that Gabriella and Cara were dead. With the help of the former director, we staged a car accident in California and then announced to the world that they both died. If Vincent knew that they were both alive, he would have come after them. If you decide to bring Gabriella back to the States, you must protect her from Vincent. If he finds out she is alive, he will come for her and torture her; all in the name of his brother. He has a sick obsession with her. That night when you left me at the Woodstock house, my biggest fear was Vincent. I saw what he did to Gabriella, and I feared what he would do to Raven.

I know that Jax really loves Raven, but I know what you're capable of doing. I know what happened to your family, and I know you understand. So, please, protect them with all that you have.

I trust you with my family; they are all I ever had.

Joseph

I sit here, staring at the letter, and I decide to pour another scotch. What the fuck was Joseph thinking by making me Gabriella's legal guardian? Why does he think I'm such a stable person? I'm a loner. I have been since my Gram died. My mum was a weak person, and gave her life to drugs. I never really knew my father; my Gram raised me. I've had more heartache than one man should have to bear. He knew what I went through. So, what? He thinks I'm stronger because of it?

I'm not stronger because of it; I'm shattered. My only friend is, Jax, the man I trust with my life. He's the brother I never had, and now we're in this together, past the point of no return. He loves Raven, and she is sweet. She's good for him. She doesn't care who he is and how much money he makes. She loves him for him, and all his craziness. This, though, is a huge responsibility. I don't know that I can do this. I don't know if I have it in me to be this responsible person that Gabriella and Raven need right now.

I consider calling Jackie, but then opt for another scotch. The last thing Jackie needs is me blowing her world apart. I look up at the clock; it's late, and I have finished half the bloody bottle.

Yeah, Joseph, I'm so fucking responsible.

Jaxson

I HAVE NO CLUE what the fuck Joseph was thinking. I'm glad Raven decided to try and lie down for a while. I just don't know what to say to her. I decide to pour another scotch and read the letter.

Jaxson,

I never thought I would have to have this discussion with you, but in light of recent events, I guess I must. I have asked Maxwell to be legal guardian for Gabriella. However, I would like for you to manage the trust fund for Gabriella and Raven. I feel that you would be the best person for this task, since you seem to have a golden touch when it comes to money. I know that you love Raven, and I hope you and Maxwell can get her back safely. I know I should have been more up front with you, but I have always played it pretty close to the vest.

Everything I did was to protect Raven and Gabriella from the horrors of Vincent. I know firsthand how sick and twisted Vincent is, which is why I chose to hide Raven from her mother. I promised Antonio that I would protect her, even if it meant my own life. I put Marco into her life to watch and protect her, I never expected him to turn on her. After her adoptive mother died and her adoptive father did what he did, I felt if I stepped back in to her life, Vincent might find her location. That's why I put Marco with her. I would much rather have kept her with me, but I couldn't take that risk.

Vincent had a jealous streak where Antonio was concerned that is like nothing I have ever seen before. If he found out about Raven, I have no doubt, he would have hunted her down and do to her what he did to Gabriella. When I rescued Gabriella, she told me things . . . things I would not want Raven to know. He did things to her, some very sick and twisted stuff. It was then, that I knew, I had to let the world believe they were both dead. With the help of the former director, we announced that Gabriella and Cara died in a car accident in California, when their car plunged off of the Pacific Coast Highway.

In the eyes of the world, they were dead. I knew Raven told Marco about her adoption and what little she knew about her family. It was not until six months ago, that I revealed to Marco that Raven was the niece of one of the most feared and vicious crime lords in the country. I told him about Duke, but I never told him about Gabriella. I hope you can bring Raven home safely, and that you will protect and love her forever.
Joseph

Wow, I understand the man had all the best intentions, but what a cluster fuck! I don't even know where to begin. I have learned that. no matter what, I have to tell Raven the truth about everything. I will not have her running away, ever again. No one is safe until Vincent is found. I have some thoughts on where Vincent may be, but I need to talk about them with Max. First and foremost, I need to check on Raven and feed her. I walk into the bedroom, and find Raven in the throes of a nightmare. Jesus, when she hurts like this it, slays at my core. I crawl in bed and pull her close, stroking her back.

She wakes and looks up at me, and I use my thumbs to wipe her tears. "Raven, what can I do to help you?" I keep stroking her back, trying to sooth her.

"You're doing it. Just being here with me means so much."

I kiss her soft lips. "I wouldn't be anywhere else, sweetheart."

I take a deep breath, "Did you read your letter from Joseph?"

"Yes I did. What about you, do you want to read yours now?"

She shakes her head. "No, I'm not ready. I'm not sure my heart can take any more."

I pull her tighter. "I will be here with you when you're ready." I need to start going over details with her, but I know I can't overwhelm her. "There is a lot we have to talk about, starting with your security."

"I agree, and I've been thinking, I don't think I can go back to work. It would be too dangerous for the children."

Finally, I feel like we are on the same page. "Agreed. You need to understand that I'm not letting you out of my sight." Fuck, if I could, I would lock her in here with me and throw away the key.

"Jax, that's unrealistic, you have a company to run and a life to live."

"My life is with you. From that day you doused me with your coffee, I knew my life would never be the same. I finally came alive. I agree I have a company to run, but your safety is first on my list. Maybe you should work for me. What do you think about that?"

Oh no. She's looking at me like I'm nuts. "Do you have second graders at your company?"

I thought about this everyday she was gone, and I actually think this might be a great idea.

"Actually, I have an idea that you might find intriguing. I was thinking of creating onsite childcare for the employees, ranging from infancy to elementary. I have been doing some research, and I found out that the cost of daycare is almost as much as a mortgage payment. If I had a school here on the premises, I could keep the cost down, and my workers would be more productive." She's listening, so that's a plus.

"I wouldn't know how to set such a thing up, Jax, I teach."

I know it's all in how I pitch it. "I understand that. I have done all the research, and I have a business plan already done. I got all the specs from the school board. I wouldn't need funding from the City, which means, we could get things done much quicker with no red tape. We can go over it later, but just keep an open mind." At least she didn't say no. It's all about negotiation and me getting my way.

"When can I go back to my place?"

Okay, I need to be calm here before I answer, "Sweetheart, Vincent is a major threat to you and your mother. I don't want to discount your feelings, but . . . never." Okay, maybe that didn't come out the way I intended, because the way she is looking at me I can swear I see fire in her eyes.

"Jax, I have a home and I would like to go back there. I will agree to protection, but I'm not a prisoner."

I need to calm down or I will lose it on her. "Let's talk about this later, okay?"

She shakes her head, "No, not okay."

I'm not good at calm, never one of my finer points. "Are you sure now is the time to do this?"

"Yes, Jax. Now is as good a time as any."

I take a deep breath and try to prepare myself not to come across as a bully. "Okay, Raven, here it is. You have been kidnapped numerous times, you have been shot, you were in the Witness Protection Program, all of this and you're only twenty-seven. Call me crazy, but I think you should be about done with all of this drama now."

She glares at me, "Jax, I was done with it all when I was seven! If I give in to all the drama then, the drama wins. I can't give up, and I won't give up. You can't keep me locked up here forever. I understand I can't go back to the school. I would never put anyone else in danger, but I can, and I will, go home!"

Does this woman think I would actually let her go back there? She doesn't get it. When it comes to winning, I'm a ruthless, fucking bastard. I will win! I pace around the room, no shirt, with my hands in my hair. Yeah, I know I'm good looking and I'm not opposed to using it to my advantage when needed. Her eyes are running up and down my body. Oh yeah, sweetheart, keep looking. I'm making a show of undressing, trying to distract her.

"Jax, don't think that you can flash your good looks and I will bend to whatever you want. Not this time, mister."

Fuck it all to hell! "Well, sweetheart, not only do I own your place, but I purchased the entire fucking building. If I wanted to, I could find a way to keep you out of it for good!" She has no idea how far I would go, and locking her in here is looking better and better.

"You wouldn't!"

We are nose to nose and I growl, "Watch me!"

With that she goes into the bathroom and slams the fucking door. Okay, I'm not a fucking moron. I do realize that I was probably over the top when I purchased the whole building, but in my own defense, I was not thinking clearly at the time. However, now I am thinking with all my pistons firing. There is no fucking way I'm letting her live anywhere but with me. Now, I just need to convince her of that.

I NEED TO GET in touch with Max. "Hey, Max, call me back. I need to go over Raven's detail with you."

I turn around, and I'm hit with her violets. "Where do you think you're going?" I ask.

She smirks at me. "For a run, so if you plan on being stuck to me like glue then, get your ass in gear, bucky."

It's got to be the hormones, it just has to be. I remember Bella was a nut case when she was pregnant. I need to call my sister later.

I change with the upmost speed, and before I know it, we are in the park. She's a runner in more ways than one, but if she thinks for one minute that she will ditch me, she can guess again. Her biggest problem is that she really doesn't know me. Not only am I ruthless when it comes to winning, I'm like a crazy man when it comes to safety. I've watched over my mum and sister my whole life. I'll be damned if this woman thinks she will rule me! Well, at least when I'm not thinking with my cock.

"Will your detail run the entire time with us, Jax, or will you have mercy on them?"

I turn to her and give her the Jaxson smile. I cock my head, "Not only will they run the entire course with us, but I have men stationed throughout the entire park, and at all the various entrances."

She glances over at me, her chin on the ground and eyes as wide as the moon. I reach over with my finger and close her mouth. "I told you, I'm a ruthless bastard, sweetheart. You've just touched the tip of the iceberg." We do the rest of the run in silence, and for once, I'm happy about silence.

Max is waiting for us, and of course he's not happy. Lately he's never happy. I need to talk to him. "Jax, why? Just please tell me why you chose to make my life harder?" He looks at Raven next, "Miss Raven, I understand your need for your independence, but please, can you try to work with me, instead of against me?"

Her eyes fill with tears "Max, what have I done other than go for a run?"

"Well that's just it, Miss Raven. There's a very sick, vicious man on the loose out there, and he is gunning for you. I'd like to get through this without getting anymore kinks in my armor, if that's okay with you!"

I grab his arm. "Cool it, Max. She's not use to this. Dial it down."

Max paces. "Jax, I'm trying! I mean. I'm really trying. However, I can't have unnecessary risks right now. I'm trying to deal with finding Vincent, keeping you and Miss Raven safe, figuring out what to do about Gabriella, and keeping watch on the rest of the family. I just need some sort of cooperation from everyone! Just until, I feel I have gotten a handle on Vincent, is that so much to ask?"

Raven gets up and hugs Max. "Okay, Max, I will do whatever you need me to do."

My head swings around so fast, it's a wonder I don't snap my own fucking neck. "You're listening now?"

"Well, Jax, maybe it's the way Max laid it out rather than bulldozed me." She arches her eyebrow as if to challenge me.

"Miss Raven, I have some things I need to talk to you about; they are personal. However, I know you want no secrets. I have to ask, do you want Jax here?"

"Yes, I have nothing to hide from him." He takes a deep breath. God, what else are we going to have to deal with?

"Okay, when Tony was looking through Marco's thumb drive, he found a letter addressed to you, along with pictures of the two of you. Tony put them all on here for you to decide what you want to do with them." He hands them to her and I can tell by the look on her face, she is in shock.

"Sometimes, good people do bad things. Sometimes they can't help it, but other times they don't think it's bad. Life is complicated, at best, Miss Raven. Have you both read Joseph's letters?"

"I did, but Raven didn't read her letter yet." I sigh. Max paces again. Oh boy, not good.

"Miss Raven, you can read my letter if you want, I have nothing to hide. You need to understand that Vincent hated your father his whole life. What he did to your mother was because of that hatred, and if he knows she is alive, he will go after her.

"After she gave birth to Duke, your mother snapped. She probably had a bad bout of postpartum depression on top of it, plus months of blaming herself for your father's death. It was too much for her. She tried to kill herself. Joseph found her and got her the help that she needed. His plan was to have you both declared dead from a car accident and then move you both within the Witness Protection Program."

"After your mum's attempted suicide, Joseph realized that your mum couldn't take care of herself, let alone you. That is why you were adopted. Joseph wanted to keep you himself, but he knew the danger. He did what he thought was the safest thing. He had you both declared dead, you adopted, and your mum moved to a clinic out of the country. The danger lies in moving your mum to the States. I can't let Vincent know she is alive."

She nods. "Max, I knew how sick and twisted Vincent is my first day as his prisoner, he made me wear my mother's clothes."

My mouth drops open in disbelief. She didn't tell me this, only about the book.

"He also gave me a book that belonged to my mother. Inside of it was a detailed account of what she went through. There were also some beautiful pictures that she drew. Vincent made my mother watch a video of my father getting shot and me being held prisoner. He physically and mentally tortured her for two months. So, what is it that you need from me, Max?"

Max takes her hand, "First, I need to read your letter from Joseph. I need to know if there is anything in there that might help me. Second, never ditch your detail. Don't even think about trying. I'm assigning you two people, whom I vetted personally.

"Dominika is your female guard. She is originally from Russia and she is former KGB. Your male guard is Daniel, and he is former Secret Service. You will also have a dog. His name is Bo. Bo is listed as a service dog. I don't have to list which service he falls under. You just need to remember never leave this house without him, and he must at all times wear his vest. The vest has a tracker and a weapon in it. No one ever checks the dog. Also, I want you to wear this bracelet. It looks like one of those magnetic ones, but it is also a tracker." He puts it on her wrist.

"Okay?"

"Jax, you have your standard detail that you usually have, however, I am giving you a bracelet to wear too. I have increased the coverage on all the family. Everyone is currently wearing a bracelet. I also put the same protection in place for Jackie and Mrs. Osla."

Raven looks at me, "Jax, who's Mrs. Osla?"

"She is my new assistant and Max is afraid of her."

Raven looks between the two of us. "Really, I thought you were only afraid of Jax's mom?"

I'm trying so hard not to laugh at Max right now. "Miss Raven, you will see for yourself, but heed my warning, she is scary. Okay, Miss

Raven, let me introduce you to your new detail."

Raven

I TAKE TO BO right away. He is such a sweet boy. "Max, what type of dog is he?"

He loves getting his ears scratched.

"He is a mix breed, part German Shepherd and part American Pit Bull. He is strong, loyal, and has the best of both breeds."

"Was he bred for security work?"

"No. Bo is a rescue dog. When I was a young lad, my grams told me that the measure of a real man was what he gave of himself, unconditionally. Grams insisted that I volunteer my services to wherever I felt needed. I spent most of my youth at a rescue shelter. It was at the Battersea Dogs and Cats Home that I learned about the loyalty of a rescue dog. I can see that you and Bo will get along fine. Daniel will walk you through the different commands for Bo while I go over some stuff with Jax."

While Raven is working with Bo, Max and I go into my home office. "Jax, what did your letter say?"

"Nothing that you don't already know. He asked me to manage the money, of course, and the standard warning about Vincent. What did your letter say?"

"Just more of the same." Max leans back against my desk.

"I understand the concern about Vincent, but are you being extreme about the security?" I squint, rubbing the back of my neck."

"No, the man is sick and twisted. He repeatedly raped Gabriella, and when he was done he would look up to the heavens and say, 'that's for you, Antonio.' That is not someone to take lightly." He begins pacing again.

To think my girl was alone with this fucker for three months! "Any news on where he might be?"

"I have a lead. I'm leaving in an hour to head down to New Orleans to follow it up."

"What was in the letter from Marco?"

He stops pacing. "Just the ramblings of a tormented person. I think he was sorry for what he was doing, but the gambling and Erica just twisted him. You need to encourage Raven to go for therapy. Have you talked about her place and the baby?"

I stroke my chin before I go into a full frustrated, face rub.. "Max, I can't overload her. We already had a *come to Jesus* about her going back home. I venture to say, that every step will be a challenging one, when it comes to Raven."

"Did you tell her that you now own the entire building?" He raises both eyebrows.

I growl, "I can't hide anything from you. I did, and let's just say, she wasn't happy."

"You know you can't keep her from there forever." Suddenly, he gets a suspicious look on his face. "Jax, what the fuck did you do, mate?"

I can't hide anything, fuck! "I'm having the entire building tented for termites."

"You're dead serious, aren't you?" His mouth opens only to throw his head back and laugh hysterically. "Jax, you really are a crazy fucker. Does she know?" He finally calms down.

"Of course not. You know she'll hit the roof when she finds out."

"Will you ever learn? What about all the other tenets living in the building?"

I take a deep breath, "I put them all up at the W."

He shakes his head. "Before I leave, I need to see that letter."

Max reads the letter and then puts it back in the envelope, a stolid expression on his face.

"Max, anything I need to know?"

He nods, "There is a key in here for a safety deposit box."

I throw the letter on the desk. "Fuck, will this ever end?"

Max exhales loudly through pursed lips, "Not until Vincent is taken care of. I need to get to the airport. I will call you later to let you know what I found out. Monday morning, we go to the bank" Just like that, he's gone.

When I get back into the living room, I see Raven has made coffee for her detail. She needs to stop thinking of them as company and pretend they are not even in the room. They at least look embarrassed that she is serving them coffee. Bo leaps up and starts growling at me when I step closer to Raven. Daniel turns to Raven, "Miss Raven, you need to introduce him to Mr. Phillips. Teach him that he is not a threat to you."

She issues a command "Bo. Down. This is Jax." I don't know what else she's telling him, all I know is, both my hands are covering my crotch, protecting the *Crown Jewels*. He calms down, and then, Raven tells me all about the dog and the different hands signals she can give him in case she is unable to talk.

"Let's go inside and talk, please. We have a lot to go over." I lead her into the bedroom for some privacy. "I know you never had detail before, but you need to pretend they aren't even in the room."

Her violet eyes show a hint of sadness. "Why?"

I kiss her hand. "That's what will help them do their job effectively, by blending in without being noticed." I explain. "I promised you I would tell you everything as I find out about it. Well, Max just left for New Orleans to follow a lead. If you want to go to your place to pick up stuff, I will concede to that, but I will not let you out of my sight, until Vincent is caught."

I brace myself for the fight of my life. I've learned she can be like a pit bull, but so can I.

"Are you telling me that I am living here, or I'm just staying here temporarily?"

I need to dial up the charm here. "I want us together for the rest of our lives. Is that such a bad thing?" I bring her hands up to my chest. Tears fill her eyes. Okay, fuck me, what did I do wrong now?

"Jax." She jumps up and runs into the bathroom crying. For Christ's sake. I decide to call Bella.

"Hey, sis, you busy?"

She takes a deep breath, "Jax, oh my God, I have so many questions, and I need to see you."

Maybe she can make some sense of what I'm doing wrong with Raven. "Can Raven and I come over?"

"Why are you asking? You never ask." She's talking fast, her voice almost a shrill.

I sigh, "It's Raven. I can't seem to do anything right. I keep reducing her to tears."

She laughs, "Jax, she's pregnant. And the hormones will do it, plus all the additional stress. It's a wonder she can even put two words together."

See, I knew she would understand. "Okay, we will be over in a little bit. How's Junior doing?"

"He's quiet, and I'm worried. Maybe seeing Raven will help. Max came by with bracelets and more guards for all of us. Jax, none of us are fighting this. We won't give you a hard time, not even Mrs. Osla!"

I can't help but laugh, "Don't tell me you're afraid of her, too?"

She laughs, "Shit, yeah, aren't you?"

I don't get why Bella and Max are so afraid of her? "No, she's like Mum on steroids."

"She's scary. Even Vito cowers when she's around."

"Well, part of Raven's detail is a dog, and let me tell you, he will scare you."

Bella laughs, "I'll cook something. Come around six. Love you, bro."

God, I love my sister. I can understand how lonely Raven must feel without a sibling to lean on. "Me too, Bella."

I go back inside the bedroom and find Raven, staring at the laptop, crying. "Sweetheart, what's the matter?" *I can't take the tears.*

"I want to look at the flash drive that Tony sent, but your laptop is password protected."

I throw my hands up. "Is that why you're crying?"

She nods, "I realize I don't know anything about you."

She has a point here. Everything has been so fast, and then she was gone. "You know I love you."

Now she's really crying, fuck! "What do you want to know?"

There must be a hundred tissues all over the bed. "Jax, you don't understand, it's not what you can tell me. When you know a person, you know all the little things that make up that person. I sat here looking at this screen, and I realized, I have no idea what you would choose for a password!" She sobs.

"Raven."

"What?" She blows her nose.

I lean in and kiss her, "That's my password—*Raven.*"

"Oh," she whispers.

I kiss her. "Yeah, *oh.* Sweetheart, just know I love you and would do anything for you. I promise you, the rest will follow. Now, I'll leave you alone to read what's on the drive, but we need to leave in two hours to go to Bella's house for dinner. Junior really needs to see both of us. I'm worried."

"Jax, what's going on with Michael?" She straightens up, her focus, seemingly, anew.

I love how much she loves Junior.

"He went back to school, but he's very quiet. Bella is worried, and so am I. I think seeing the two of us will help."

She nods, "Okay, I'll be ready." I offer to bring her coffee, but she's already lost in what's on the computer, so I back out of the room as quiet as possible.

Raven

Raven,

If you're reading this, then I know you must feel really hurt and betrayed. When I was seventeen, I got caught up in a FBI sweep of hackers. I was really good at it, and I used my skills for illegal shit. Joseph saw something in me that, he must have felt, was redeeming. He put me through the Academy, nurtured, and mentored me. My parents threw me out when I was thirteen. They were extreme religious freaks and felt my being bi-sexual was the work of the devil. Joseph had been dealing with a bunch of personal stuff, but he still made time for me. Then one day, he came to me, and told me about you. He said, "Just keep an eye out for her, because I can't." He never told me anything more. That day, I showed up at the shelter, I felt like I found the most precious thing in the world—a friend. I was just supposed to keep an eye on you, but before I knew what was happening, we were roommates. Joseph only gave me one rule, and that was not to sleep with you, no matter what. It was by far the hardest rule to follow, especially after the ex-boyfriend. I just wanted to hold you in my arms forever. I think that's when I started to gamble. I'm not blaming you. I'm just trying to help you understand.

I'm sorry, I never meant for anything to hurt you. I got so caught up in gambling. Oh sure, it starts out simple, but it never ends that way. Before I knew it, I was in really deep. I was going to tell you and ask you for financial help, but then I met Erica. I fell in love for the first time. At least, I thought it was love. She made me believe I was her end all, but I realized too late that I was not and by then, we were married. My gambling was getting worse and I was about to come to you again, but Joseph came to me first, to tell me he was dying. He sat me down and gave me more details about your adoption than you knew. He also revealed everything about Duke. I had a friend in Lansing and had him pull the file on Duke. Erica came up with a plan to get Duke hired on at Raiders, Inc. She told me all about her affair with Jax and why it ended. She told me about her plan to seek revenge against Jax and how I can get out of the mess I was in. It was all supposed to work out, until that fateful day you met Jax. The entire plan became one big cluster fuck, all because fate had to bring you and Jax together.

Baby girl, I was in love with you, no matter what you think. I really did love you. Somewhere along the way, the lines were blurred for us, but I did.

Marco

I am in shock. I can't believe he was in love with me. *How could I not see this?* What fucking planet was I on? Am I that so self-absorbed that I couldn't see what was right in front of my face? There is another file on the drive labeled *pictures*, so I open it, and I am hit with one man's total obsession of me.

I pick up the laptop and fling it across the room, breaking it to a million pieces. Jax comes flying into the room. Bo, and my detail are right behind him. Jax looks to me and then to the computer, but he stays quiet.

"Jax, say something!"

He takes a deep breath. "I have always imagined throwing my computer across the room, but never quite had the nerve to do it."

He opens his arms, and I run into them. He nods to my team and they leave—all except Bo.

I hand Jax the thumb drive, "Here please put this away for now."

"Okay," he whispers. He's not even upset.

"That's it? Okay? I throw your computer across the room and its trash now. I just read something that obviously upset me greatly, and all you can say is *okay*?"

He kisses me. "Yep." *What the hell?*

"Why?"

He takes another deep breath. "Well, when you're ready, you'll tell me what you want me to know. I trust you with my heart and soul, and when you're ready, you'll trust me with yours."

The tears are trailing down my cheeks. Oh, how I love this man. "Oh."

"Yeah, *oh.*," he whispers. "Let's get ready."

Chapter Twenty

Raven

I DECIDE TO WEAR my black pencil skirt, red sweater, and my favorite stilettos. I figure I better enjoy this now, since it won't be long before I can't wear any of this. We head out to Bella's house, and I don't know why I'm nervous—I shouldn't be. "Jax, who knows I'm pregnant?"

"What do you mean, who knows?" He glances over as he lowers the volume on the radio.

For such a smart man sometimes I just want to smack him. "Just what I said, who did you tell?"

"My mum, sister and Michael, why?" He looks at me strange.

Like I wasn't nervous enough. "I'm nervous, and I don't want them to think I got pregnant on purpose. I'm an educated adult and should have been more careful."

Jax presses a button and the privacy glass slides into place, and then he turns to face me. "I won't even dignify that with an answer. I'm very close with my family, and I can only hope with time, you will come to feel close to them, too. We created a new life together out of love, and I will not have you taint it with anything else."

Wow, I hit a nerve. "I'm sorry, Jax, I just don't want anyone to think that I'm after..." Before I can finish, he's on me. He kisses me, our tongues doing a slow tango. He nibbles his way across my chin to my ear. He loves to nibble on it. He kisses my neck, following the trail down with his tongue. My nipples are instantly hard.

He leans me down, and as he does, he sees my thigh high's and garter. "Oh, bloody hell! Oh, fuck me!"

"You okay, Jax, can you breathe?"

He takes a steadying breath. "Barely, sweetheart, I can come just from the sight of you!" His eyes keep roaming up and down my body.

"Jax, you can touch me, I promise, I won't break."

He takes my hand and places it on his heart. "Raven you take my breath away. I just need a minute please. If I don't take one, it will be like a teenager, when he gets his first shag. Do you feel my heart? It beats wildly, just for you. If I died right now, I would die a happy man.

You have taken me to heaven and there is no going back. You gave me a life worth living."

My God this man renders me speechless. "Oh."

"Yeah, *oh,*" he whispers.

He takes a few more steadying breaths, and then he lifts my sweater, nibbling my nipples through my bra. He reaches over and presses the intercom, "Keep driving around Bella's house until I tell you differently." He lifts my breast out of my bra and latches on to my nipple—nibble, lick, suck. Oh wow, they are so sensitive. On to the next one, all the while he's humming, which radiates to my core. He pushes my skirt all the way up to my waist. "Are you wet for me?" he asks as he travels down my body.

I nod, "I'm always wet for you." *Holy, he just snapped my thong!* "I want to taste you now." He's nibbling and licking me, one finger in, and then another. Oh my God! He pulls his fingers out and offers them to me for a taste. It's so erotic, and it's all in the back of a limo. I taste myself on him, mixed with his Vanilla spice and I moan.

"My cock needs to be in the happy place," he breathes. I close my eyes and hear the sound of him working at his zipper. My heart races and my core aches for him. Suddenly, his cock is sliding up and down my wet folds. A moan escapes my throat as he enters one inch at a time. When he is all the way in, he stops. "Look at me!" My eyes shoot up to his. "Do you feel that? We are a perfect fit." He doesn't move but holds us at this intensity; so full . . . so perfect. He leans down and starts kissing me, slowly. He rests his forehead on mine. He's not moving his hips at all, and he's just locked onto my eyes. "Raven, you have unraveled me. Do you feel me? Do you feel how deep I am? I just have to be inside you, locked onto your eyes, and I will explode." Just like that, his cock starts to throb and pulse right before he floods me. "That's what you fucking do to me." Then he pulls back, and he's still rock hard. *How the fuck?* But before I can think, he slams into me with all he's got. "I could go all night in cock heaven. All night." He growls, "Fucking better than anything in the world."

I'm not going to hold it much longer. "Jaxxxxxxxx!"

He yells, "Fuck, baby, I'm falling with you!" Our breathing starts to slow down. He nudges my nose with his. "Never, ever enough. Never." He leans down further, kissing my neck and nibbling my ear.

"Jax, we need to be at Bella's." He gets up and it looks as though he is going to clean us up, but then he takes an ice cube and pops it into his mouth. He leans down and takes a nipple in his mouth with the ice. "Jax, holy hell! Oh my... oh, Jax." Then he takes another ice cube for my other nipple. The sensation is crazy! First hot and then cold, oh how is this even possible? He put one in his mouth and goes right between my legs. And I lose it, screaming, coming, and swearing like I never had before. I'm fisting his hair. It's a wonder I didn't pull it out in chunks.

"You're all clean now." And with that, he tells the driver to go to Bella's!

As we pull up to Bella's house, I am very aware that I have no panties, and that Jax loves it.

"Bella, thank you for having us on such short notice. How's Michael doing?"

She smiles, "Better now that I told him you were home safe."

"How much does he know?" This family has no secrets from each other, which is refreshing, however, he is just seven.

"We told him that you were away for a while. I didn't want him to know you were kidnapped, again. I think his fear is that the men are coming back."

I nod. "Okay, well that makes sense since it was always my greatest fear." When we get to the living room, Michael comes running right to me. I assure Bo it's okay, and then Michael leaps into my arms. This is what family is about—unconditional love; and I can't stop crying.

"Miss Raven, are you okay?"

I nod. "I'm more than okay."

He looks at me confused, "Then why are you crying?"

"I'm very happy to see you." That seems to do the trick. He takes me by the hand and leads me to the dining room for dinner. After dinner, the men go to the living room, and I'm left with Bella and Mrs. Phillips. I know what's coming next. With this family, there is no subtlety.

Mrs. Phillips starts the questions. "So, Raven, have you spoken with the doctor about the baby?"

I shake my head, "No, Mrs. Phillips, only what Jax told me at the hospital. I have a follow-up appointment this week with an OB."

She smiles at me. "Can you please call me An? After all, you're family now." She gets up,

"I'll leave you with Bella," and she heads into the living room.

"Bella, did I do something wrong? She seems upset."

Bella takes my hand, "I was pregnant with Michael before I was married, and now you're pregnant before you are married. It's just Mum is old school in many ways."

Oh what this family must think of me. "I'm not after Jax's money."

She stops me. "Hold up, Raven, no one said you were after his money. We are just concerned about him, that's all. My brother is a very strong and proud man, and I know, in some way, he blames himself for what happened to Junior, and then to you. Anyone just has to look at the two of you to see how much you love each other. I know that none of what happened was your fault, however, you have the ability to bring my brother to his knees."

I'm really confused. "I'm sorry, Bella, but I don't understand."

She takes a deep breath, "Look, Raven, Jax doesn't do anything half-arse, that's why he is so successful in business, when you run, it kills him. When he couldn't find you for three months, it was really bad here. Not even Max could help him. He blocked out his family and his business, he was always distracted, and he bought your building. He would stay in your apartment every day. He doesn't think any of us knew what he was doing, but we did. If you left, there would be no coming back for Jax. For the first time in his life, he loves someone so completely." She lets out a big breath. I don't know what to say to her to assure her I'm not running. "I know you're very emotional now with the pregnancy, but you need to cut him some slack if he is overbearing. It's just coming from the fear of you running or being in danger. As far as Mum is concerned, just know that she is worse than Jax when it comes to family. If you need me for anything, call me. Remember, I've been pregnant. I know all the crazy stuff you're feeling." She gets up and hugs me. "Let's get coffee and dessert." Just like that, she is done.

As we head back to The Tower Jax tells me that he heard from Max and New Orleans was a dead end. "Now what do we do?"

"Well, first, you need to read Joseph's letter. Apparently, there is a key to a safety deposit box in it."

Jaxson

THE REST OF THE ride is in silence. I don't know how much more stress she can take, but we agreed—*no more secrets.*

"Monday, we'll be at the bank when it opens and you can see what's in the safe. You also have a follow-up appointment with the OB at noon, same day. Raven, are you listening?"

She nods. "Yes, Jax. Are you planning out my life for me? Do I get any say, at all?"

I'm trying not to flip out on her, but it's really hard. I decide not to say anything for the rest of the ride home.

"Raven, would you like to be alone when you read the letter or would you like me with you?" I ask as we walk through the door.

"Can I use your office?" She takes the letter and Bo, goes into the office, and locks the door.

I decide to go next door to Max's place and vent to him. When I get there, I realize he's not alone, Jackie's with him. "Hey, sorry to bother you, I just needed to vent, no big deal."

As I turn to leave, Jackie stops me. "Jax, when can I see Raven?"

"You know what, she is next door reading Joseph's letter. I'm sure she will need you after that. Why don't you both come back to my place?" I hope I didn't just ruin Max's night with Jackie, but I need my best friend right now.

"Jax what's up? You're crazier than usual!" Max slaps me on the back.

He's right, I am. I know it. "Look, mate, I know I'm nuts right now, but I don't know any other way. I am operating out of fear and I don't know how to control it. I want, no, I *need* her safe, and I don't know how to stress that to her without scaring her or having her pull a runner."

"Jax, I really understand your fear, but you don't want to push too hard, otherwise it will have the opposite effect. You might want to give her a little breathing room. She's a smart girl, and she saw firsthand how evil Vincent is. Put yourself in her shoes—she's pregnant, she has been kidnapped four bloody times. She found out she has a half-brother who is psycho, and her mother that she thought was dead for the past twenty years is alive. Think about it, how would you feel?"

I pour another scotch. "I guess now is not a good time to demand that she marry me."

He just rolls his eyes and laughs.

Raven

I KNOW I NEED to talk to Jax, but right now I need to read this letter.

My Dearest Cara,

I have so much to say to you, but unfortunately—time is up. We live our lives, thinking we have all the time in the world, only to have it end so quickly. I'm sorry you had to find out about your mother like this. Everything I did was for your safety and for Gabriella's peace of mind. You need to understand that she agreed to your adoption to protect you. She knew how evil Vincent really was (still is); she experienced it firsthand. I can't stress enough, how much danger you and Gabriella are still in.

I made promises to both your parents to keep you safe, no matter what the sacrifice. I brought Marco into your life because I could not be there. I know that you saw what happened that day Vincent shot Antonio. The bullet was meant for me but Antonio pushed me out of the way. There is a reason he did that. Ten years before that night, Antonio and I were working undercover. The perp realized who Antonio was, he had him dead to rights, but at the last second, I stepped in front of him. I was shot, and years later your father did the same for me. In the weeks that he lingered, I asked him. 'Why?' He said, 'If you didn't take that bullet for me, then my greatest gift to the world, my Cara, would never have been born.' In the last few weeks of his life, he made a recording for you and Gabriella. It's in a safety deposit box, along with some precious mementos from your parents and grandparents.

When the time came to move you, I chose your new name because of your silky black hair. I hope in time you can forgive me. I hope someday, it will be safe for you to reunite with Gabriella. Life is short, so make the most of each day. Jax is a good man, he comes from a good family, and I believe, that with him, you will blossom into the woman that your father knew you would be. I have total faith that Jaxson and Maxwell will keep you and Gabriella safe.

God Bless you, I love you always.
Joseph

I decide to go find Jax, and I see that Jackie and Max are here. I throw my arms around Jackie. I really need her now. "Jackie, I'm so glad you're here. Let's go inside."

"Raven, what's the matter, I can tell something is bothering you."

She knows me so well. "I love, Jax, but he is such a take charge type of guy that I don't have a chance to think for myself. It can be very overwhelming, at times."

She hugs me again. God, I need her around more. "You need to just tell him. He can't read your mind. Maybe he thinks he's helping to relieve some of the stress. He was a total basket case when you were gone. No one could get through to him. I think he fears losing you more than pissing you off."

I know she's right. "Let's talk about you. What's going on with you and Max?"

"He doesn't do relationships, yet he is always trying to be with me. For the three months you were gone, he came by to see me every day. I just don't know what to think. Something stops him every time, and it is frustrating."

"Well he is under just as much stress as Jax is, so I think maybe you need to cut him some slack, as well."

Jackie starts laughing. "What's so funny, girl?"

She smiles, "We just gave each other the same advice."

We head back inside, and the guys are having a scotch by the fire. I stand there and enjoy a second of normal. Max and Jackie leave, and I decide to talk to Jax about what's bothering me. "Jax, can we talk?"

He hugs me. "Of course. If I did something to upset you, I need you to tell me."

I have to try and explain his overbearing way, and I'm thinking, *good luck*. "I just feel overwhelmed by everything. I know you're trying to manage everything, but I need to be in on making the decisions. I feel like you're dictating my life." He's looking at me and stroking his chin, so I know he is thinking about what I said. "Maybe I don't want to go to the doctor that you picked. I just want to be part of the decisions."

He takes a deep breath. "Okay, you're right. I tend to just pick up the ball and run with it. That can be over powering, if you're not use to it. If you want to pick another doctor, that's fine, but you need to get the follow-up quickly."

I sigh. "I'm sure you picked the top doctor in New York, and that's fine. I just need you to understand my feelings."

He kisses me, "Come here, I need to hold you, sweetheart." I crawl into his lap and find instant peace.

"What was in Joseph's letter?"

"Well, apparently, there is a video and some mementos in the box."

He's softly rubs my back, and it calms me. "Did he say what's on the video?"

I shake my head. "The video is a recording from my father. Apparently, Joseph took a bullet for him ten years before, and that's why he stepped in front of Joseph when Vincent tried to kill him. When Joseph asked him why he stepped between Vincent and him, he said, If Joseph didn't take the bullet for him then, his greatest gift to the world would have never been born."

Jaxson

CHRIST, HOW MUCH MORE shit is going to be thrown at her. "Wow, that's some heavy stuff. How do you feel about all of this?"

She cuddles into me, "I have so many mixed emotions, but in the end, I love Joseph for all he did to protect us. I'm proud of the parents I had. I need Max to find Vincent so I can get some closure, and maybe have some sort of relationship with my mother. I'm going to try and be the best mother I can be. I want our child to know he or she is loved, and wanted. I knew my adopted parents loved me, and I believe my adopted father was just grieving. To know that my mom has been alive all these years makes me feel sad. We lost so many years that neither of us will get back.

I wipe the tear, trailing down her cheek. "I know you're going to be the best mum ever. You're kind hearted and very loving. Our child will know true love. Maybe having a baby around your mum might help her, especially if she sees you're happy and made a good life, even after all the shit you've gone through."

"Jax, can I ask you something?"

I smile. "Anything, you know that."

"What do you think about Max being with Jackie?"

I see this is bothering her, but why? "Why are you asking me this?"

She starts twirling her fingers, "I just worry about Jackie. You know, she is old fashioned and innocent. I don't want to see her get hurt. Max is older than she is, he's um—more experienced."

"What are you trying to tell me here, Raven?"

I growl, "Jax, why are you being so dense?"

He laughs, "I'm not being dense. I know there is a large age difference, but age is only a number. As far as experience, are you trying to tell me something here? Oh my God, she's a virgin, isn't she? You don't have to answer that. Your face just said it all. Well I can tell you that Max is a man of honor. He would never use her or be abusive. The Royal Army has awarded him numerous medals, and he guarded the Queens grandchildren. As far as financially, he is set for life. I hired him away from the Queen, and I had to make him an offer he could not refuse. He has no mortgage, no car payments. He owns a 20% stake in Raiders Inc. He has unlimited use of the private jet, and has full medical coverage for life. Does that make you feel better?"

Oh God, how I love this man. "Wow, Jax, that's impressive, but I'm more worried about her getting her heart broken. She has never shown an interest in anyone past a couple of dates.

Max told her he doesn't do relationships, why?"

He shrugs. "I honestly don't know. All you can do is just support her in her decisions about Max, and everything else will fall into place. Enough about them, I think I need to be kissing you all over."

Jackie

"MAX DO YOU THINK Raven is safe?"

He takes my hand, "Miss Jackie, as long as she follows protocol, and doesn't try to ditch her detail, she will remain safe."

He's like a dog with a bone! "You're never going to let us forget about that, are you?"

He smirks at me. "Nope. Do you know how worried I was, and how much danger the two of you were in? Vincent is a very dangerous man. Now that I know what I'm dealing with, I have increased security."

I know I should be afraid, but Max has a way of taking away the fear. "I promise I won't ditch my detail, and I will be extra careful."

He pulls me close. "Thank you." He begins to kiss my neck. I want this man, but I'm scared. He is so much older than me and very experienced. I've had a couple of boyfriends, but no one that I ever wanted to give myself to.

"Max I need to get home."

He stops and looks in my eyes, "Are you sure?"

I nod. "Yes, I have to go." I reiterate. He doesn't push me. When we get to my place he, of course, has to come upstairs to make sure I'm safe. As he is leaving, he turns around pulls me close to him.

"I'm a patient man, and I will be here for you when you're ready for me."

He kisses me and is out the door. I'm so confused. I want this man, but I'm scared. God, I really need to talk to Raven, but it's too late now to call her. I decide on chocolate and a glass of wine. This man is going to break my heart, and there is nothing I can do about it. I'm about to go to bed when I receive a text message.

Raven: I need to talk to you alone. I need to get away from Jax. He's too protective. Will you help me, please?—Raven

Me: Raven, you seemed okay earlier. What went wrong?

Raven: Can't talk now, will you meet me in an hour, coffee shop on 52nd street and 3rd?

Me: Okay.

The one thing I'm not, is stupid, and it makes me mad when people think that a woman is stupid. I call Max and he answers on the first ring. "Are you okay?"

I take a deep breath, "No, Max, I'm not. I need you back here now. I just got a text, and I don't think it's real."

His mood changes instantly. "Do not leave your place. Do not answer the door. I'm staying on the phone with you until I get there!"

I hear him running, "Hold on, Max, someone is buzzing me."

"Fuck, Jackie, do not answer!" he yells.

I get back on the phone. "Max, calm down. The door man said there is a package for me."

"Jackie, I swear if you open that door, so help me woman… Go into your bathroom and lock the door, *right now*!" He's scaring me. Maybe I shouldn't have called him.

"Why?" I yell back.

"Why? Why are you fucking trying to put me in an early grave?!"

He sounds nuts. "Okay, please calm down. I'm in my bathroom, the door is locked, but someone keeps buzzing. Max, are you still there?" *Oh my God, there are gunshots*! "Max? Max? Please answer. Please."

"Miss Jackie, I'm outside your front door. I'm alone, look through the peep hole first," he instructs.

I let out the breath I didn't realize I was holding. "I can come out of the bathroom, then?"

He growls, "Yes, please let me in."

I open the door, and I can't help but throw my arms around him. "Did you look through the peep hole?"

Crap. "No. You said to let you in."

"I could have had a gun to my head, you should have looked."

I realize that I'm wrapped around him and holding on for dear life. He walks inside carrying me. "You can put me down now, Max."

But he doesn't. "Maybe I don't want to." He walks over to the kitchen, placing me on the counter.

"Max, what happened? I heard gun shots."

He takes a deep breath. "There was no package. The doorman was knocked out. Someone was waiting to take you. He pulled his gun on me, and I retaliated. Pack your stuff. You're coming home with me now."

"I thought I was safe with my detail?"

He shakes his head. "Your guard is on his way to the hospital. I'm trusting no one, but myself, when it comes to you."

"What about work?"

His jaw is tight. "You tell me. What do you think would happen, if you were at school, and all of this went on?"

Of course, what am I thinking? "I would never put any of the children in danger. I'll pack up. Maybe I should go home. My father has tight security, and right now, he is at our Switzerland compound."

"The only place you're going is home with me, right now." Max has a tight grip on me with a lost look on his face. Wow, I've never seen this side of him before. We head back to his place in silence. When we get upstairs, he shows me to his guest room. "I need to see your phone." As he reads it, he's heading over to Jax's door.

Maxwell

"JAX LET ME IN now!" I don't think this is from Raven.

"This better be fucking good because I was really happy until you banged on my door."

I push past Jax. "I need to see Raven now."

"What's going on, Max?"

I pace. I can't help it. "Jackie got a text from Raven."

"Mate, that's not possible. We've been a little tied up for a while."

"Get me her phone, it might have been cloned."

Raven comes to the door, "Hey, Jackie, what happened?"

Her chin quivers, "Someone pretending to be you, tried to lure me out of my apartment alone."

Jax is looking at the messages, and then hands the phone to Raven. "Jax, I never sent these messages."

He pulls her into his arms. "I know, sweetheart."

I pocket both phones, "Okay I'm taking this phone, and Jax will give you another one. You will have a new number, and so will Miss Jackie. These have been compromised. I'm concerned as to when this happened. Miss Jackie will be staying at my place, and will not be at work."

Raven takes Jackie's hand "Jax, I'm going into Max's with Jackie to help her get settled in."

He nods, "Take Bo with you, sweetheart."

J axson

"MAX, WHAT THE FUCK is going on?"

He paces. He seems to be doing this more and more lately with all that has been going on. "I left Jackie's place, and was almost home, when she called me. She said she got a text that she thought was fake. I stayed on the phone with her while I raced back to her place. While I was on the phone with her, the doorman was buzzing her that she had a package. I made her lock herself in the bathroom until I got there. When I walked into the building, the doorman was out cold and so was her guard. The guy that was there pulled a gun on me, and I shot him. He's not dead, and he is in police custody now."

I'm so tired of this. "Max, this shit has got to stop already."

He nods, "I agree, but it won't stop until we get to Vincent. I just have to figure out a way to draw him out."

"What's going on with you and Jackie?"

"Jump right in, Jax."

"Yep, you know me too well to think I would do anything else."

He takes a deep breath, "She's a sweet girl, Jax, and I'm just too distracted right now. I can't concentrate on anyone. Besides, you know

I don't do relationships. What's bothering you, Jax? I can tell you have something on your mind, so spill it, mate."

Now I'm pacing. "Raven asked me about you today."

He cocks his head. "Really, why?" I hate this. I want to just come out and tell him, but Raven will be pissed at me, and I manage that real well on my own.

"She is worried about Jackie. Jackie is young, and innocent, especially when it comes to any kind of relationship." His stolid expression tells me that he's not "getting" what I'm trying to tell him.

"She's twenty-five, Jax, so what's the problem?"

I give him a look and then all of the sudden, I see it finally hitting him like a fucking brick. "Oh, bloody hell, no fucking way, mate. Are you serious! She's twenty-five. How is that even possible in today's world?"

I finally stop pacing. "Look, Max, I shouldn't even be saying anything to you, but I don't want to see her hurt. She's old fashioned, and she has dated, but no one she would give herself to. Don't you dare say anything, otherwise, I'll be in the fucking doghouse, for sure."

Max gets up. "Jax, I have to go." Oh boy, he's pissed now.

"What about the phones?"

He growls as he's running out the door. "I'm giving them to Tony in the morning. Right now, they are both shut off."

Jackie

"JACKIE, I'M SO SORRY that you have been dragged into this mess."

I hug her. "Raven, it's life, I'm okay. Things are going to be very different for us until they catch this nut."

"What about you and Max? Are you okay staying here? If not, you can stay in Jax's guest room."

I want to be here with him, that much I do know. "I'm okay here, he is the perfect gentleman. My problem is, I usually call my parents every Sunday night, and when I don't check in, they are going to be worried."

Raven

I'M TRYING TO FIGURE out a way around this. "Can you check in via email?"

She shakes her head. "No they will know something is up, we always Skype on Sunday."

I take her hand, "Okay, let's ask Max and Jax what they think we should do."

We head back next door just as the guys are finishing up, but Max looks lost in thought.

"Hey, guys, Jackie needs to check in with her parents. She usually Skype's with them every Sunday night, but the problem is, they will know something is wrong, especially when she doesn't call from her phone."

Jax turns on the fireplace. "Jackie, can you tell them you're on a ski trip with Raven, and we'll sit you and Raven in front of the fireplace?" Max is very quiet, more so than usual.

"Jax, I need chocolate." Jackie announces.

"Excuse me?"

She laughs, "When I'm nervous, I eat chocolate. It calms me. Do you have chocolate?"

"Yes, I do. Bella keeps a stash here," he chuckles.

"Jax, don't laugh. I bet you don't know Raven's vice?" She baits him.

Jax looks at me. "Oh my God, you're blushing! Do tell, sweetheart. What's your vice?"

"Well, aside from coffee, warm Nutella will bring me to my knees."

Jax smiles. I wish I knew what he was thinking right at that moment. "Okay, let's get this phone call done."

Jackie

MY PARENTS ARE VERY happy that I'm on a trip with Raven; they want us to visit soon. We let them know that we will on our next break from work. I miss them and really need to get out there soon.

"I'm glad the call worked out okay, but on that note, Max, Jackie, you need to go home now." And with that, he ushers us out the door.

Raven

I CAN'T BELIEVE HE'S pushing them out the door. What is he up to? "Jax, why did you push them out the door? That was rude."

He doesn't say anything, but he is doing something in the kitchen. "Raven, you can wait for me in the bedroom. I have a present for you." He pushes me along and runs back to the kitchen.

I'm in bed, waiting for him, when he comes in totally naked with his arms behind his back.

He jumps into the bed and he hands me a jar of warm Nutella! "Sweetheart, tonight I'm a canvas just for your pleasure."

I dip a finger in and lick it off, he moans. "Oh, please tell me you're going to slather that all over my cock and slowly lick it off."

I have to laugh at my beautiful crazy man. "Is that what you want me to do?"

His eyes grow wide with anticipation, "Yes, please!"

I dip my finger into the Nutella and spread it all over the head of his cock. I lean down and lick it off, and he's moaning. I do it again, this time making a trail all the way down to the base. I slowly lick up from the base to the tip. When I get to the tip, I nip a little, and he's screaming for more. Okay, I do it again and when I get to the tip again, he holds my head there, begging me to nip him harder. Just as I bare my teeth he loses it. "Oh fuck, fuck. Harder! I'm coming. Fuck!" I think he might pass out! "Jax, you okay?" His eyes are closed, and he's breathing heavy. "Jax?"

His breathing is becoming more normal, and I'm trying not to laugh. "Give me a minute to come back to earth."

"Jax, what happened, you look dazed?"

Oh my God, he's panting! "The warm Nutella, and then when you nibbled on my cock it just sent him to orbit. Why are you laughing at me?"

Oh my crazy man, "It's just the way you constantly refer to your cock as him." He gifts me with that crooked smirk and his twinkling blues.

"Come here, it's time for *the happy place*." With that, I'm gone.

Chapter Twenty-One

Jackie

WE GET BACK TO Max's and he is very quiet. "Max, are you okay?"

He nods, "Yeah, just a lot on my mind. Do you have everything you need?"

Wow I feel like I'm being dismissed. "Yes."

He nods, "Okay, I'll see you in the morning."

Maxwell

SHE HEADS TO HER room and closes the door as I take a bottle of scotch and sink into the couch. Fuck, what am I doing? This girl is too young and too innocent. I don't do relationships. I hate drama, and I won't ever give my heart away again. *Oh, who am I kidding?* I've got it bad for this girl and that's the problem. This is all Jax's fault. He couldn't get involved with someone who had a simple life. If I understand Jax, which I usually do, Jackie is a virgin, and I'm me, a man who is far from innocent. The fear came flooding back tonight when I thought they would kill her. I can't live through it again, not that this is living.

Jackie

I DON'T UNDERSTAND WHAT happened, it's like Max just flipped a switch. What do I say to him? Why did I have to fall for someone like Max? He's out of my league, but who am I kidding? Like Raven, I don't have a league! This is so messed up. Maybe he figured out I'm a virgin. It's not like I can say *hi, my name is Jackie, and I'm a virgin,* but maybe he figured it out. He probably thinks I'm too young, and he doesn't know how to tell me. I'll back away gracefully; giving him an out. I would leave, but I have nowhere to go. Maybe I should go to my parents' place. I'll pack up and have the guard take me to the airport. I'll call my dad to have his plane waiting.

I pack my stuff and head towards the front door when I hear him growl. "Where the fuck do you think you're going?"

I look at him. "Are you drunk?"

He takes a deep breath. "I asked you a question."

I step closer, "I asked you one, too. Are you drunk?"

He shakes his head, "Not drunk enough."

I take a step back, "What's that supposed to mean?"

He takes a step towards me, "Where are you attempting to go?"

I look into his eyes, "Home, to my parents, where I know I'll be safe, and you won't have to worry about me."

"What makes you think I would stop worrying about you?"

I take another step back. "Max, I'm a burden to you." He's searching my eyes, and I don't know for what.

"And you determined this all on your own."

I take a deep breath, "You're trying to take care of Jax, Raven, and now you have to worry about me. I saw the change in you when you had to bring me back to your house. I'm not a charity case, and I'm not a child that you need to watch over. I'm a grown woman who has been put in a bad position. I can have my dad's jet ready by the time I get to the airport. I'll be safe at his compound in Switzerland. I'll be out of your hair, and you can go about doing whatever it is you need to do."

Maxwell

I CAN'T BELIEVE HER. Yet I knew from the first day I met her, that there was a fire buried deep inside, just waiting to explode, and it decides now to rear its head! I walk up to her and pull her up against my body. I'm hard, really fucking hard for this woman. "Kiss me now, Jackie."

Her eyes grow large, "What?"

"You heard me, fucking kiss me now!"

If she does, then I know she feels what I do. If not, she'll slap me and walk away. She grabs a hold of me and kisses me long and hard.

"Just like I thought. Jackie, I want you, but I needed to know that you wanted me. All reasoning tells me to walk away —that you're too young and too innocent, but fuck it all to hell. I can't walk away, I'm in too deep." I lift her up and carry her to my room, kissing her deeply along the way. "If this is going to happen, I need you to be totally honest with me. I won't settle for anything less."

"That's all I ask for, Max, is total honesty. I don't do secrets and I don't play games."

I take a deep breath, "Okay, Jackie, have you ever been with anyone?"

"No." She looks down, so submissive, and very quiet.

I'm searching her face for answers that I already know. "Are you sure you want this to be your first time?"

Again she gazes down, not answering. "It's okay, if you want to say no, I will respect your decision, whatever it is."

She looks up to me, "I want you. Max, I'm just scared."

I need answers. "Are you scared of me?"

She shakes her head, "No, never. I'm scared that I won't be enough for you. You're so experienced, beautiful, and worldly, and I'm just a second grade teacher."

"Look at me, Jackie." As I look into her beautiful golden eyes, I'm lost. "My past is just that—past. I can't change it. There is no one in my life for a reason, but I'm not ready to share that yet. I never had anyone in this bed. I want to be your first and your only. It is a very special gift that can only be given once. I want you to be sure, really sure."

She leans forward and kisses me. "I'm sure, Max."

"Okay, I'm going to undress you very slowly." He takes off my shirt, and I thank God I'm wearing nice undergarments. He slowly starts kissing me, long and slow, nibbling on my bottom lip. Oh, I want this man bad. He gets up and takes off his shirt and I gasp! He smiles, "We're going to take this nice and slow." He lifts me up and places me in the center of the bed. He straddles me, kissing me. His lips are so unbelievably soft, and I swipe my tongue across them. "You're so beautiful. I tried to resist you, but that day in the park, when you massaged my leg, I knew right then that I was done." He's kissing down my neck. His stubble is soft and speckled with gray. His eyes are the palest blue. He takes off my bra and is nibbling my nipples. I'm not big chested, but I'm not small. He pinches and tweaks them and I'm fidgeting while he's humming.

"Max, I don't know how much more of that I can take."

He gets up and starts to take off my jeans. "These legs are so long and so beautiful." He kisses my legs up one and down the other. Before I realize it, he is between my legs kissing and nibbling, working his tongue into me. I never felt anything like this in my life. My skin is burning and my mind is buzzing.

"Max, Max, I can't think."

He looks up at my face. "That's the best part. Just relax and let me take care of you. I'm going to take you to a place you've never been before."

He dives back in, and I think I'm going to explode—No, I know I'm going to explode. " *Oh my God!*" My body is quivering and shaking and I can't put two thoughts together. My nails dig into his shoulders, and I scream!

"That's not God, baby, that's all me."

I watch as he finishes undressing, and he has the most beautiful body. He is very lean and he has the 'Loin of Apollo.' He has no chest hair. Only a little down the happy trail. I get a look at his cock and he's huge. "I'll go slowly, and if it hurts we can stop," he reassures me. He must sense my fear.

I nod. "I'll be okay." I can only hope. He's back between my legs licking and now he is working in a finger, then two, *oh my*...

"I have to open you a little, or it will hurt." He's working his fingers in and out real slowly. Wow, this is unreal. He climbs up my body. "Are you sure you want this?"

I nod my head yes.

"I need to hear the words. Tell me."

I take a breath. "I want you, Max, please don't stop." He slips on a condom and starts rubbing his cock up and down my opening real slow.

"I'll go slowly, but it's going to hurt, there is nothing I can do about that." With that, he starts to enter me, and then he stops to let me acclimate to him. "Breathe slowly. I'm going to move again." He pushes forward. I feel a lot of pressure and then, something pops; he's in.

"Look at me, baby, I'm in. Are you okay?"

I nod yes.

"I need you to answer me!"

My eyes shoot up to his. "Yes, I'm good." He starts to move real slowly in and out.

"You're so tight, it's like you have my cock in a vice grip!" As he pushes in, he tips his hips up and down, hitting all the right places. He's nibbling and sucking my nipples while his fingers are fluttering up and down my ribs. *How can he do all of this at the same time?*

"Max, I'm… I, oh, Max!"

He kisses me, "You're going to come for me, baby, I can feel you quivering. Don't hold back on me, just let it go." His hand reaches down, and he swipes his thumb across my clitoris. That does it! I feel my core tighten and my skin is flushed. It's like a rippling wave taking over my body. I'm screaming my release, and he is right behind me. "Baby, are you okay?"

"You took my breath away."

He laughs, which is so rare. "I'll take that as a good thing." He ditches the condom and pulls me close to him. As he pulls the comforter over us, he barely whispers, "You sleep here in my arms, forever, baby."

Jackie

MORNING COMES, AND AS I stretch out, I realize Max has a grip on me, and he's not letting up. He's so protective, even in his sleep. I get to really look at him since he's not watching me. He has so many scars on his chest; they make me want to cry. Who would do such a terrible thing to such a beautiful man? He keeps his hair very short, and his dark-blond facial hair is specked with gray. There is not an ounce of fat on his body. He is breath taking to look at. His hands are strong and his muscles are rock hard. I run my fingers down the V and I notice he has a scar on his hip. Oh, what this man must have been through. I lean in and kiss one of his nipples and he groans, "Are you having fun, baby?"

I nearly jump out of the bed. "I thought you were asleep."

He sighs, "I figured that. I've been up for about an hour."

"Why didn't you tell me?"

"I wasn't going to deny you your fun."

I kiss one of his scars, "You have so many scars."

He's stroking my back, "Does it bother you?"

"It bothers me that someone would do that to such a beautiful body, I never want to see you hurt." He doesn't say anything more about the scars and so, I just drop it.

"How are you feeling this morning? Are you sore?" He brings his hand to my face, palming my cheek. I look down, sheepishly. "Hey, don't ever hide anything from me, talk to me."

I look back up at him, "This is all new for me, not just the sex, but the intimacy—I've never experienced it before. To answer your question, though, I'm not too sore."

He takes a deep breath, "Did you like last night? Was it what you expected?"

"Okay, I have to tell you, I only know what I have read. I only have one girlfriend, Raven, and it's not something we talk about. She only had one boyfriend, and he was abusive, so there really isn't much to draw on."

He looks at me. "Why do you have no other friends?"

I shrug, "My dad's work, and the constant security was a problem. By the age of sixteen I had already finished high school. We were always moving, so I was home-schooled. I could have skipped a year in college, but I wanted to enjoy the entire experience. Raven was my roommate in college. The other girls where either intimidated by the security or thought I was their personal cash cow. It's a sad way to grow up, but unfortunately, reality. Can I ask you a question?"

He pushes my hair behind my ear and runs his hand down my back. "Always, you might not like the answer, but you can always ask."

"You said you don't do relationships. So what is this?" I ask nervously.

"I honestly don't know. I never expected you to blow into my life and turn it upside down. I just want to get all of this stuff with Vincent behind us, and then let's see where the rest leads us, okay?"

"Yes, thank you for your honesty. It's what I always need. I hate sugar coating the problems."

He smiles, "Okay, well then let me tell you, we have a couple of hours before we *need* to leave, so I think we *need* to stop talking and I *need* to be buried deep inside you."

Just like that, we are done talking. He is all over me, and I love it.

Chapter Twenty-Two

Raven

MAX AND JACKIE ARE waiting in the living room with Jax while I finish getting ready. I'm nervous about what I'll find in the safety deposit box, but I have to do this, not just for me but also for my mother. As I step into the living room, I notice Jackie and Max are holding hands, and he's not letting her go. She looks at me, and I'm seeing something very different today than yesterday, and it hits me. Oh my God, she took the plunge! I wish I had time for us to just have a girl day, but we have to go. As I walk up to her, she blushes, and I have to stifle a laugh. If Jax noticed anything, he would never say. "Okay, everyone, I'm ready. Thanks for coming with us, Jackie, I could use the support."

She hugs me, "Later,." she whispers near my ear. Of course, Max has to drive us. Even Bo is getting used to his driving.

Jax is the banks best customer, so they're opening up early for us. After giving the manager all the proper paperwork, he takes me into a windowless room and puts the box on the table.

"Jax, will you please stay with me?"

He pulls me close, "Of course, sweetheart."

When I open the box, there is a VHS tape, some photos, two letters—one addressed to me, and one to my mother. There is some jewelry that appears to be very old. Maybe the letter will explain whose it was. "Jax, I don't have anything to play this on, do you?"

He takes the tape, "Let's stop by the office, and I can have Tony transfer it to a DVD."

As we head to the office, everyone is quiet and then Jax just starts to laugh. We're all looking at him. As I'm about to ask him what's so funny, Max starts to laugh too.

Jackie and I shrug at each other. "Okay, both of you, what is so funny?"

Jax turns to me, "You're going to finally meet Mrs. Osla."

Jackie's eyes get really wide and fear seeps in. "Jackie, by the look on your face, I take it you met her already?"

She gasps, "Raven, she is unexplainable, and good luck understanding anything she says. I speak six languages, and I don't understand a word of what she calls English."

"Wow, Jackie, I never knew you spoke so many languages." Jax says, sounding intrigued.

She smiles, "My father is Swedish and my mother is Japanese. We had to move around a lot, so it was more for survival purposes that I learned them. Once you master one, it kind of becomes a little easier."

$\mathcal{J}$ axson

RAVEN LOOKS OVER AT me with fire in her eyes. "You see, Jax, this is what I mean, we don't know anything about each other." She crosses her arms. Oh fuck, here come the tears again, I can't wait till she sees the fucking doctor today. "Do you know that I speak other languages?"

All right, she got me on this one. Now, how the fuck am I going to get out of this mess? "I was too busy wrapped up in your beautiful body to even think about anything else, sweetheart."

Then I hit her with the Jaxson smile. That should do it, but she just rolls her eyes.

"Really, Jax, that's all you can say? *Je vous jure que vous pensez que vous pouvez juste me donner ce beau sourire et tout ira bien!*"

He's just looking at me and not saying a word. I wonder if he even knows what I said. "I said, I swear you think you can just give me that beautiful smile and all will be well!"

"*Je suis dur.* I speak some French, sweetheart. Oh, look, we're here. Out you go."

Jackie and I get hysterical, laughing. "This isn't over, Jax, not by a long shot."

Jackie leans over. "Jax, no matter what you say, you're fucked, so just take it like a man."

Max starts laughing. I grab Max's arm, "Keep laughing, Max, I'll get even just wait—Mrs. Osla." That's all I have to say. Everyone shuts up knowing how Max fears her. We head to the elevator in silence.

"Wait, Jax, is that Mick?"

Everyone smiles, "Oh, yeah, something good happened while you were gone. Mick now heads up security for the building, and he moved into his new apartment."

Oh fuck, here come the tears. "Jax, just when I think I couldn't love you more." She runs up to Mick and hugs him. His face lights up.

"Raven, I'm so happy that you're back and safe. We all missed you."

"I'm happy for you, Mick, that you're working and have a warm place to live."

He takes a deep breath, "I owe it to you, Raven. You believed in me, when no one else did."

She shakes her head, "No, Mick, you believed in yourself. I just helped you to see it."

He hugs her as we head to the elevators.

"Max, is the office clear?" I ask.

"Yeah, Tony swept it right before we got here."

As we walk into the office, Mrs. Osla is following behind us, giving Max a hard time about Tony making a mess of things. Boy, he really fears her. I'm about to laugh, and she turns on me. *Oh crap.*

Raven

"JAXSON, HOW DO YOU expect me to keep things in order if you don't check in on a regular basis? I don't mind running things in your absence, but a wee bit of help now and then. Have you called your mother today?"

Tony comes barrelling in, and before he can speak she's on him too. "Young man, have you no manners? I told you that you must learn to knock. Now go back out and try again!"

Oh, my God, he goes out the door and knocks!

"Jaxson, Tony needs to see you. Is that acceptable?" Jax bites his lip to control his laughter, I'm assuming.

"Yes, ma'am, but let me introduce you to Miss Raven Anderson, my beautiful girl."

She smiles. "About time you showed some manners, Jaxson. Pleasure to finally meet you, and I'm glad you're back safe. Maybe now you can get him to cooperate with me. Can I get you some tea, Miss Anderson?"

I nod. "Yes, thank you, and it's Raven, please."

Just like that, she is gone and all heads turn towards me. "Why is everyone looking at me?"

Tony steps up. "Can I get the VHS tape, please? And I don't know how you did it, but you need to work here full-time."

As I hand him the tape, I ask "Did what?"

"Tame the Shrew," he mumbles.

"Give me a half hour and I will have this transferred for you. Welcome back."

"Tony, I want to thank you for everything you did to help find me. I will be forever in your debt."

$\mathcal{J}axson$

RAVEN HUGS HIM AND I swear I want to get all cavemen on the poor guy!

Mrs. Osla comes in with tea. She gives me all the business that I need to address. "Max, any new leads on Vincent's whereabouts?"

"Yeah, Tony is following the money trail. Since the guy only had so much liquid cash, I figure he would have to eventually move something and he has."

"Okay where is he?"

"He just got to a Miami compound that is owned by a top drug lord. He came by way of Cuba. I'll be leaving shortly. I'm taking the plane and a couple of DEA agents with me to pick him up. You stick with the girls, and I added another female guard for Jackie."

"Why am I not going with you to Miami?"

He gives me a look and it hits me, he wants to know that Jackie is safe, and he will only be comfortable with me.

"I get it, Max. Never mind, I'll stay and watch the girls, but you be careful."

$\mathcal{J}ackie$

HE PICKS UP HIS keys. "Jackie, walk with me to the elevator, please."

I'm scared for him. "Max, I'm worried about you. Do you have to go?"

"Yes, but you need to promise me that you will do everything Jax says, and you will not ditch your detail."

I take a deep breath, "I promise."

He takes my hand, "Come here, babe." He pulls me into his arms. He gives me the most sensual kiss, and I almost forget where we are. The elevator opens, and just like that, he's gone. I stare at the doors. My heart aches and I lose it. It hits me that I might never see Max again. I crumble into a ball on the floor, the fear and the angst over the last few months comes to the top and the dam of tears breaks open. Jax lifts me onto the sofa and Raven holds me.

Jax starts pacing. "Raven, what should we do for her?"

She shakes her head, "Nothing."

"What the fuck do you mean, nothing? I can't sit here and watch her cry."

"Sometimes the only thing we can do, is nothing. We're here for her, and we will be no matter what. Max is smart and strong and, by your own omission, very skilled. We need to have faith that he will be okay."

Jax is stroking his chin and pacing. Neither is a good sign. "We need to go, Raven. You have a doctor's appointment, and, Jackie, you're coming with us—no arguments!"

Raven

I DON'T KNOW WHY I'm nervous, but my emotions have been all over the place, lately. I'm sure it's probably pregnancy hormones. As I look around the waiting room, I'm totally embarrassed. There are more security guards than patients.

"Don't. They're doing their job, and I will not make them wait outside. While we are in the exam room, Jackie, you will not leave this room," Jax says, flipping through a magazine.

"Wow Raven, is he always like this?" she asks.

I roll my eyes. "You don't know the half of it."

The nurse comes out to get us, and looks at the scene in the waiting room but says nothing. The doctor finally comes in, and I'm happy that it's a female doctor. Knowing Jax. I'm sure he is happy too. "Hello, Raven, I'm Dr. Leanne and I will be your OB throughout the remainder of your pregnancy. Looking at your chart, I see you had a rough start with morning sickness and then a gunshot. I hope all the drama is now behind us. I'm going to do an exam, and then an ultrasound. We'll get you started on prenatal care. Have you decided on what type of birth you want?" She hits me with all of this information, like it's a race to see how quickly she can freak me out.

By the look on Jax's face, I don't think he was impressed with that presentation, either, and I swear I think he's going to flip out on the doctor. I know he is trying, but he doesn't take orders from anyone, except maybe his mom. "Dr. Leanne, Raven, and I want a healthy child and a calm delivery, so you need to do your job to make that happen."

I'm about to apologize for him, but Dr. Leanne laughs. "Don't worry, Raven. I'm used to first-time fathers, they don't scare me."

The nurse is back with an ultrasound machine and Jax watches without saying a word as she sets everything up. "What type of ultrasound is this?" he asks when the doctor starts and the picture pops up on the screen.

"It's a 2D machine , since Raven has been through so much already, I just want to make sure everything is on track."

I'm holding Jax's hand, and I realize I have a death grip on it. He starts rubbing the inside of my wrist, and I instantly relax.

"Do you want to know the sex?" The doctor asks.

I shake my head. "I don't. What about you, Jax?"

He shakes his head. "No, I just want to know that everyone is healthy. Gender doesn't matter to me."

"I will note on your chart that you want to be surprised."

The sight of this baby just hanging out, all safe and warm, is beautiful. "Okay, everything is great and right on track. You're due the first week of August, and you need to think about what type of birth you want. The nurse will give you all the information when you leave. You need to put on a few pounds. You're a little too lean for my liking. I'm giving you prenatal vitamins, and I suggest you take them with some crackers."

"What about travel, and will my mood swings get any better?"

Her expression when she responds is compassionate. "I don't see a problem with travel and as far as mood swings. Honestly, they won't get better. I'll see you in four weeks for a check-up."

After she leaves, Jax turns to me, "Where exactly do you think you're going?"

"I would like to see my mother," I answer quietly.

"Raven, I'm not going to yell and demand. I told you as soon as it's safe, I'll have your mother brought to a facility in Manhattan." He pinches the bridge of his nose. Seems like he's trying anything to not freak out on me.

My eyes fill up, and I'm trying not to cry. "What if it's never safe, then what? I have been without my mother for twenty years. Don't I deserve to have her in my life again?"

He pulls me into his arms, "You're thinking of a mother that you had twenty years ago. She's not that same person anymore."

I finish getting dressed. "Don't you think I know that, Jax. This is just so fucked up."

"Don't curse, the baby will hear you."

Is he out of his mind? "Jax, let's get Jackie and go home." I know I'm mumbling under my breath how crazy this man is.

We head back to the tower, each of us lost in our own thoughts."Jackie, I moved your stuff into the guest room in my place until Max gets back." Jax finally breaks the silence. Her tears start to fall, and silence is back again. I know Jax is worried about Max. I can see it all over his face. He keeps checking his phone, but it is silent. All we can do now is pray.

Chapter Twenty-Three

Maxwell

I HATE THAT I had to leave Jackie, but I need to do this. I can't leave it to anyone else. Six of my own men and four DEA agents just to bring in one man, but I know how vicious he really is. I'm sure we will be met with resistance and it doesn't matter that we are also working with the local agencies—anyone can be bought. As we approach the compound, I can see it's heavily guarded. I have everyone on the ground in place, and we will be coming in by air. The Coast Guard is also on alert. "I want him alive, if possible."

"Sir, we are over the target, are you ready?"

That's my cue. I jump. The compound is large, but I went over the blue prints, so I know where everything is. There is a lot of gunfire, smoke, and confusion. I keep my target in my head and nothing else—that's how I'll stay alive. I search room by room until I get to the wine cellar. I hear him before I see him. He's yelling in Italian for transport by air, telling them he'll be coming out the other side. I enter the room and he's gone.

Fuck. Think, Max. As I start my usual pace, I realize there has to be a tunnel. I find it behind a wine rack. The race is on. I can hear him running, and I'm pretty sure he hears me closing in. As I round the corner, he's looking right at me—his gun aimed at my head.

"Game over."

We both pull the trigger and everything goes black.

To be continued...

Darkness into Dawn

Chapter One

Jaxson

I T'S A COLD WINTER day in New York City, but the sun is shining. I decide to take the ladies out for a bite to eat while I wait to hear from Max. I'm very distracted, and I know it's because I have to wait for Max's call. I'm not good at waiting, but I have no choice. I just push my food around the plate while Raven and Jackie are talking about our baby. I want to get married before the baby comes, but I haven't broached that subject yet; it seems I can't get anything right lately with Raven. As I look around the restaurant, I realize we must look ridiculous, sitting here with six security guards and a dog, but what the fuck do I care? I would have a hundred security guards if it meant they were safe. As the waiter comes with the dessert menu, my phone chirps with a text from Tony to call him stat.

"Ladies, I need to make a call, I'm stepping out front." They are so engrossed in baby stuff, I don't even think they notice, but it's okay. I'm glad to see Raven having some normal girl time.

"Tony, what's the problem?" He's talking but I can't believe what I'm hearing. I'm in utter shock. Everything he's saying sounds like white noise. "Tony, I know my jet is in Miami, but get a private jet ready for me to leave within the hour—at any cost." I go back inside to collect the ladies, and pay the bill.

Raven only has to take one look at me to know something is terribly wrong. "Jax, what's wrong?" I think she can see the fear, I'm feeling, on my face.

"We need to leave now."

She pulls her hand up to her throat, and her eyes instantly fill with tears. "Jax, you're scaring me, please, what's wrong?"

Before I can say anything Jackie, turns white and starts shaking. *Fuck!* "Jax, its, Maxwell, isn't it? I can feel it." Her tears start falling. I'm trying to hold onto both of them.

"Ladies, I need to leave for the airport, now!"

Raven, puts her hands on her hips ready to stand her ground. "We are going with you, no arguments, Jax!"

I want her with me, close to me. I need my lifeline, my beautiful girl. "I'm not going to argue, let's go."

I get everyone settled in the main cabin, and I head to the office area. I need to make some calls. Raven and Jackie are holding onto each other; comforting each other. I can't. I know I should be strong for them, but right now, I'm best at setting up top doctors, and dealing with the authorities on the ground. All I know is, that Max and Vincent were shot, and it's bad. My phone rings and it's Bella. I don't want to deal with her right now, but I have no choice, I know she won't let up.

"Bella, I'm really busy right now." I try to rush her off the phone.

"Jax, it's all over the news, where are you?" she cries.

I take a deep breath, trying to steady my nerves. "I'm on my way to Miami with Raven and Jackie."

I hear my mum in the background. "Jax, hold on, Mum wants you." I don't want to deal with my mum right now either, but it looks like I have no choice.

"Jaxson, you go get him and bring him home, and you tell him he hasn't seen mad!" Her voice cracks and she starts to cry. When my mum cries it shreds me.

"Okay, Mum, I love you," I whisper. I hang up and just sit in my chair, with my head in my hands. I don't hear her come in, but I can feel her; my skin tingles whenever she's near. She takes me in her arms, and holds me gently. She doesn't need words, she knows what I need and she knows, right now, that she is my lifeline. I need to be strong for everyone else, but with her I can just be.

WE TOUCH DOWN AND there are cars waiting to rush us to Jackson Memorial Hospital. We head towards the ICU where the nurse informs me that only family is admitted. I was prepared for this and give her Max's consent form. We made preparations one night in a drunken state, always hoping they would never be needed.

"Let me go in and assess the situation, then I will be back to let you know what I find out. Please stick with Jackie and your detail." I beg of Raven.

I look over at Jackie, and I realize, she's not said a word since we left the restaurant. I hope Raven can help her, because I don't think I can. As I walk into the room, what I see shocks me. It rocks me to my core. My best friend—the man that I consider my brother—looks pale, weak—almost frail. "Nurse, where is the doctor?"

"I just paged Doctor Scott, and he will be here in a minute. Do you want to see the other man that was shot?"

I growl, trying to rein in my temper. "Vincent, is *here?*" I think I just scared the shit out of the nurse.

"Yes, in the next room. He is under guard."

While I wait for the doctor, I call Tony. "I'm here, and apparently, they have Vincent in the next room. I want extra guards put on his room and around this whole fucking hospital!" I inform the nurse that the man in the next room is a murderer, rapist, and kidnapper. She glances at me, but says nothing as she checks Max's vitals.

Doctor Scott, finally comes in. "What's the prognosis?" I ask.

He is looking over Max's chart. "The next twenty-four hours are critical. As you know, he was shot in the head. I was able to remove the bullet, but his brain is swollen. I have put him into a coma to give his brain a chance to rest. I also have him on a ventilator. His heart stopped during surgery, but I don't think there will be lasting damage from that. My concern, right now, is Mr. Fleming's, brain. As everyone heals differently."

I'm not a betting man. I always need to have all the information. I leave nothing to chance. "What are his odds?"

He begins examining Max. "I can't really say, if I were a betting man, I would say his odds are good. He is in good health, although, from his scars I can tell he has taken many hits. Like I said, the next twenty-four hours are critical."

I'm growling again. I feel my frustration with this man growing by the second. "What about, Vincent? The other man he was brought in with."

He nods, "I gather by the amount of government officials that are watching over him, that he's a very dangerous man."

I want to rip this guy in half; he is so fucking calm. "You have no idea how sick and twisted that evil man is."

None of this seems to matter to him. "Well he was also shot in the head. However, the bullet can't be removed. I won't know what damage he has until he regains consciousness, if he ever will."

"Okay. First, the two women outside need to be in here, and second, when can I move, Max?"

"Sir, do you understand the gravity of this situation?"

Now the guy is really pissing me off. I know I'm getting louder. "Doctor Scott, let me explain a few things to you. First, I do understand the '*gravity*' of the situation. Second, that man in the other room kidnapped one of those women when she was seven. He killed her father in front of her. Raped her mother, and then kidnapped her again, just a few months ago. So, now I ask you, do you understand the '*gravity*' of the *fucking situation*!"

He is trying to calm me down but I still want to smack him! "Sir, I understand your frustration, however, I need to consider the well-being of both my patients."

I'm not a patient person, and right at this point, I'm thinking about just punching this fucker. "I think maybe, just maybe, you should be thinking about the welfare of *all* of your patients. Since the man in the next room poses a major risk to this hospital, and before you tell me he's not conscious, you need to understand that he is a major crime figure with many people that will be gunning for him. So how fucking safe is everyone *now*?"

The fucker concedes my point. "Let's see what happens in the next twenty-four hours, and the two women can stay in here, but the guards need to remain in the hall. Is that understood?"

I nod. "If that's all you can do then, I guess that will have to do. I have ordered more guards in and around this whole place."

He leaves and I'm left alone with Max. "Max, I don't know if you can hear me, but Mum said you're in big trouble so you better get your arse back to us quickly, or she will probably be on the next plane out here. Jackie is here, and I know you probably don't want her to see you like this, but I'm sorry, there was no choice." No movement. Not that I was expecting any. I thought maybe the Mum threat might do something though. Fuck. How am I supposed to be strong for everyone else?

I go get the girls, Jackie still isn't talking, and she looks deathly pale. Raven is hanging onto her, trying to offer comfort and support.

"Doctor Scott, said he has been placed in an induced coma for the next twenty-four hours, to give his brain a chance to rest, come." I put an arm around each of them, and head into the room with Bo, following closely behind us. Jackie moves away from me, and sits on the bed, stroking his cheek. Raven is shaking and crying. Fuck. I don't know what to do for either of them. Raven pulls herself together, and goes to be near to Jackie, offering her silent support. Now we wait—something I am never good at.

Acknowledgements

I must first thank my husband, Rick. You are my rock, always and forever. You keep me grounded when I need it but never hold me back. After 33 years of marriage, you still don't know what to expect when you walk in the door. You have always believed I could, even when I didn't. You're my better half . . . my soul mate. I love you madly.

To my mom, Jean, thank you. You taught me so much about life, things that could never be taught in school. You are always there for me, always believing that I can. I'm proud to call you my mom and my friend.

My beta girls, you rock! Living this crazy journey with me, always listening to my ideas, and yelling at me to write faster. I love you all.

All my friends and family who have supported me and always encouraged me, I love you all.

Tracy, you took the picture of what I thought Raven should look like right out of my head and made her come to life with the most beautiful cover.

Erin, what can I say? This little idea for a book grew from you're encouragement and support. You might be my cousin by marriage, but you're my best friend by choice.

Finally, my son, Leif, for the last 30 years I thought I was teaching you, only to find out, you have been teaching me. You're my everything; you support me and encourage me. You hold me to a higher standard. You have taught me to except nothing but my best. You never made me feel like I couldn't do whatever I wanted to do, no matter how crazy the idea. You really are everyone's wingman.

www.ingramcontent.com/pod-product-compliance
Lightning Source LLC
Chambersburg PA
CBHW070848250626
47159CB00003B/981